GRAV Death by design
Graves, John

DEATH BY DESIGN

JOHN GRAVES

© *2019 John Graves. All rights reserved.*

No part of this book may be reproduced, stored in a retrieval system, or transmitted by any means without the written permission of the author.

Turning and turning in the widening gyre
The falcon cannot hear the falconer;
Things fall apart; the centre cannot hold;
Mere anarchy is loosed upon the world,
The blood-dimmed tide is loosed, and everywhere
The ceremony of innocence is drowned;
The best lack all conviction, while the worst
Are full of passionate intensity.

—W. B. Yeats, "The Second Coming," 1920

PRELUDE

> The rapid death of unusually high numbers of human beings through disease can seriously dent the human population. Carried to an extreme, it is not too hard to imagine it wiping out the human species
>
> —Isaac Asimov

She was a combat-trained field veteran, having led several special ops units' incursions globally. She had done so for the Navy SEALs and for the Mossad. She had emerged from Iran, Palestine, and China unscathed, her team unbeaten. Her failure rate was zero. In her own fashion—restrained, elegant—she never resisted a first-class fight.

She never lost that fight. Her quick motions belied her real skill. She knew the use of her entire body as a weapon, a tool of death. She knew no limits, physical or moral.

Yet her true strength lay hidden. Deep within. She knew you as an animal knows its prey.

She scented an opponent, quite literally.

She could smell degrees of fear, of loathing, and of hatred. She listened to your heartbeat, your breathing rhythm, the cadence of your step. She was perfectly adept at using each of them against you. You had no chance of survival. An animal instinct was woven into the hard frame of a less-than-human body.

In appearance, she was conservatively dressed yet mature, wearing small jewelry bespoke from an old-world designer. Immaculate, composed, and graceful, she never gave the impression of a skilled killer. She took a certain pleasure in the perfect weapon; the ideal thrust of her body with a weapon was her secret.

She was tall, with thin red hair. Her angular face was almost hidden by a red scarf that dropped to her waist. Subtle beauty. Very frank, she ensured there was no way you could ignore her. Her pale green military blouse was double starched. She wore her position with quiet authority. She expected complete command. She exuded complete confidence. You were a fool to disagree, to comment without being spoken to, or to even raise your head up to look into her eyes.

Her decade with the Mossad simply enhanced her Navy SEALs background. When she left to start her own company, those who knew her personally (fewer than four) assumed she would be successful.

None of them knew to what degree they would be correct.

Twenty-five years ago, a hotel in Berlin had been attacked by Islamic jihadists. They had seized an Israeli diplomat and his family, resident there for a few brief days of family summertime. Escaping down a drainpipe into the sewers below, they took their four captives to a "safe house".

Their captives' trials began here. Summary execution was the punishment. Father was beheaded, slowly, before a camera, with a thick rusty blade. His wife and two children were far more brutally executed. The same camera kept rolling. The images were repugnant in the extreme.

The children, a boy and a girl, were skinned alive, slowly. Their screams brought laughter and joy to the voices of the perps. The mother had acid poured on her, slowly, purposefully. Each orifice of her body endured a slow drip of hydrochloric acid. The video lasted for too many days. She survived far too long.

An older child had been left behind in Israel at the kibbutz. Fourteen years old, she received the video before the police. She watched too much of it. She screamed, sobbed, and attacked the video.

Then she went into the desert, for the requisite forty days. She survived on beetles and morning dew and scorpions' blood. She sickened but survived. Hardened. She became less than human. More than animal. She had become one of them, or so they thought. An Azazel is what she sought—and became.

She knew the world differently. She had simply found a core, a solution to the madness. Hers was a brilliant mind.

Her work was just beginning. When Tracker finally turned her focus upon Makkah twenty-six years later, she had forgiven her family's torturers—only because they could kill no more.

They were the first to be eliminated. Her hunt for the Berlin perps was easy. She knew how to search Islamic records. She knew when she found them where to bring them. They had each taught her how to kill each one of them.

The difference was the absence of any recording of the event. Each of the other jihadists saw what she did to his cohort, slowly and with precision, in his own turn. Only they would know how long it could take to die. Only their screams would go unheard.

ACT 1
Scene I

I suspect that eradicating smallpox was wrong. It played an important part in balancing ecosystems.

—John Davis, *Earth First!* journal

IN MEDIA RES

October 2, 11:30 a.m.

Tracker had planned this allegro impeccably.

She was upbeat. Speed had to match precision. These attacks would be deep, penetrating. Without remorse. She was just getting started.

First to go would be the health-care workers. And then, the defenseless masses. She would take down the biodefenses and then penetrate the cells. CDC was the human species' global primary defense. It was formidable.

During the first week of October 2018, the Center for Disease Control and Prevention in Atlanta would be tested far beyond its limits. Stretched thin by the previous four months' global onslaught, the center was facing in too many directions simultaneously. Survival would be terrifying.

The international emergency operations center (EOC) call-in on the iOS began at 8:00 a.m. JIC members—the Joint Information Center—had been up all night communicating with the twenty-four global response teams. No good news was forthcoming. No real abatement of disease incidents had yet occurred for any of the five infections now running rampant across four continents.

Senior World Health Organization (WHO) members were on the call, as well as the twenty-four CDC incident managers who ran each local rapid response team (RRT). CDC epidemiologists and laboratorians were in the field across the globe in each of these different teams.

With the emergence of global pandemic threat events, the CDC had expanded its reach globally—and nationally. Two dozen airports had small CDC facilities with IMs that could be up and running in less than an hour.

The international sites were more extensive. Communications networks, health-care stockpiles, and staff support were in place at several locales in anticipation—particularly where epidemics had begun. These were the swamps and jungles and shantytowns of humanity.

CDC's presence in these locales greatly facilitated rapid response times. Ongoing training events held onsite made each participant familiar with the operations, and systems responded quickly to a disease outbreak, to prevent it from becoming pandemic.

A recurrent case of Ebola in Nigeria a year ago had brought the troops out en mass. It then occurred in DRC, deep in the Congolese jungle. Again, the CDC troops rallied in response. Still, these were "normal" events in the biome world.

These five new irruptions of bacterial and viral pandemics were unexpected—simultaneous, without precedent. They opened the floodgates of response from CDC's RRTs across the globe.

Dr. Mooney, the CDC director, listened to the updates from Europe, Africa, Asia and India. Overnight, a further 28,000 had been infected in Bilbao, Spain, with 323,564 deaths; Bujumbura, Burundi, had 39,000 new infections with 489,190 deaths; Jakarta, Indonesia, listed 182,000 new infections with at least 5 million deaths; India was a rolling disaster, with 624,000 new infections estimated and at least 34 million deaths recorded.

No one was certain of these figures. They were handwritten notes compiled in homes and streets and villages half a world away. Many were stained with the blood and mucus of the dead.

Her teams had been dispatched within two days of each epidemic's outbreak. Each team had been trained to the response. Yet the facts were overcoming their response training.

Pandemic preparation began with the assumption of a dichotomous relationship between transmissibility and clinical severity—the assumption of an incident gradient for a disease. It had a start, a buildup, a plateau, a further increase and an ultimate decline—in incidents and in deaths.

These five simultaneous pandemics were multilocal. Their clinical severity ran the gamut, from seasonal to truly global mortalities. They ran up, dropped off, and ran back up—as if they interreacted with one another.

Infection and death reduced the functional capabilities of drained teams. Both boots on the ground and medicine in tents were in shorter supply now.

There was no previous global event on this scale. This was the influenza epidemic of 1918 factored by ten. Isolation, interviewing, intervention, and treatment were simply impossible. The diseases continued to overrun the populations.

The president had just been on the line with the entire room. Dr. Mooney had said in response to his questions, "We simply don't have the resources to respond to all of these outbreaks. While AMD" (advanced molecular detection) "has allowed us to ident the diseases rapidly, there are too many sick individuals across the crisis arena to track."

The Kenyan CDC office head, Mburu Kenyatta, chimed in, "Our contact tracing is immaterial because there appear to be dozens of 'patient zero' individuals. It is as if these diseases are spreading simultaneously—purposefully. Our efforts are being coordinated through our eleven local offices, but we are no closer to one single patient zero.'

Señora Del Campo from Spain added, "We are overwhelmed. Tens of thousands of dead and dying. The evacuee camps are overrun before we can stock each one. People are afraid and angry. We cannot even help our health care workers. Are 'select agents' at work here—"

A sudden dull thud shook the CDC building, tossing Mooney to the floor, bloodied. Another followed, and then two more—closer, splitting the wall seams. The floor above partially collapsed. Many ran for the exits. Dr. Mooney remained with a dozen others.

She was speaking to the screen monitors as they flashed and, one by one, went dead. "I think we are under attack! Please see to your own safety and that of your crews. We have to evacuate, but we shall be back with you!"

Smoke filled the hallway. Dr. Mooney coughed as she crawled down the emergency stairwell with those who had remained at their stations. Each one was thinking of a cool September morning in 2001.

Not again.

The attack came from just across the CDC headquarters on Clifton Road, to the west of the downtown complex. The newly built fashionable apartment units were the main elements of a new four-story, block-long complex. The maze of warrens below included shops, offices, stores, restaurants, and coffeehouses.

The living quarters, fully leased or sold, were above. The top floor was filled with luxury condominiums that had been the first to sell at more than a million each for a three-bedroom unit.

The massive CDC complex wove its way along the opposite side of Clifton Road. The new buildings followed this weave.

The warp of construction was always ongoing at CDC. The rising interior buildings were soon to be occupied, allowing the older outer structures to be removed within four years. Eight stories of the CDC complex rose above Clifton Hill for an eastern view of the Georgia countryside and downtown Atlanta. To the west stretched the colorful block-long building and the suburban landscape beyond.

Four men had moved into the top-floor apartment a few weeks ago. From this fourth-floor apartment, the serpentine exterior of CDC HQ dominated their view. They had been bringing in their equipment for weeks, in small parcels, in backpacks, and in grocery bags.

They came as if pursuing their own American dream of the future. Their plans were American; the future was distinctly different.

In their flat, four loaded RPGs were lying on the floor, ready to be aimed at the second and third floors of the complex. Two dozen additional rounds lay on the floor, ready for action. Their Yasins were nicknamed Jackals after their progenitor, Carlos the Jackal, who had used them against an El Al airliner in Paris in 1975.

In fact, they were simply Russian-augmented Vampire RPGs. Their ammunition was far more lethal, however, than the typical rounds found across the Middle East and Africa. Each projectile had at its core four hundred grams of uranium. Spent rods from Iran had been the source—far less spent and far more lethal in a collapsed building.

They were designed for explosive force rather than armor penetration. The shooters knew their targeted offices. These men felt their munitions were just retribution for Western medicine's invasion of central Africa.

The shooters had been told that CDC operatives had brought Ebola and Marburg and Lassa to their people. They were certain that these deadly infections were simply an opening to further attacks upon their centuries-old culture.

Their "taught wisdom" had brought these men here. Their actions today would revenge the many deaths of Africans and their enslavement to Western culture, values, and health care.

The MSPs, micro specialized prions, in their system urged them on to a joyful entry into heaven. These MSPs were designed to enhance personal self-worth, while encouraging faithful devotion. Minions in her service, they were the pawns for Tracker's second major offensive. The five ongoing disease incidents were simply the andante to her work.

The shooters rose from their prayer rugs and coordinated their timepieces. Their helmets' GoPros would record the entire event, even the deaths of these religious warriors about to unleash hell. At 11:30 a.m. they cut four openings in the glass windows, just wide enough that four barrels had a clear shot across the busy road. They removed the cut glass pieces, dropping them at their feet.

Prayers had been said. The fighters rolled up their rugs. The first rounds fired simultaneously.

Four explosions rocked the CDC campus's main building, shattering glass onto the road, cars, and pedestrians below. Most people scattered at the explosions. A few stopped and stared. They died.

One fighter was knocked nearly unconscious. The other three were knocked backward. Never had they actually fired the weapon. Never had they understood the slight back thrust would be so strong. They arose bleeding from the glass shards, reaching for their second rounds and then fired.

Their aim was distracted by the shouts and smoke. One round exploded in the roadway itself, shaking the apartment building with a low rumble. Another round exploded in the children's crèche just by the entrance, killing forty-eight infants and caregivers.

The third blast took out the fourth floor just in front of them. Two subsequent rounds found their targets at the center of the building. Three more volleys were fired as the smoke and rapidly spreading fires broadened across the complex.

A rending, tearing, crushing whoosh overcame the screams of the injured, the alarms, and the shouts of the first responders. The center of the complex was crumbling beneath the weight of the upper floors.

In less than six minutes, a third of the structure was in flames and collapsing. The street was chaos. Bodies and body parts lay everywhere. Somehow, the internal security team began returning fire to the top floor of the apartment building. One shooter was struck and staggered back. He arose as if in a dream, stumbling to the broken window. He fell to the street below, brought down by gunfire. The two remaining attackers stepped back from the face of their building; reloaded; and fired again, aimlessly.

One shot went completely over the collapsed building and exploded in the foyer of the internal tower, killing those who were trying to escape. The other shot reentered the first wound on the third floor, exploding with its collapse.

Their final rounds were fired into the rubble as if in frustration at their own success. In fact, the shooters were firing blind. Suddenly their entire apartment was engulfed in smoke and flames as a response chopper fired .50 caliber rounds into their haunt. Silenced, the firing finally ceased.

PHASE TWO

11:40 a.m.
Flight of Fancy

The 11:40 a.m. flight to Johannesburg from Atlanta was on the runway, next in line for takeoff. Dr. Sharon Blake had volunteered for duty upon hearing of the multiple viral incidents. Her time in Africa with the Peace Corps brought her name to the top of the file, and she was chosen quickly to head the Burundi team. She and two others were discussing their preparations for the camp.

"Once we get the mobile unit operating, we can begin diagnoses—"

"They have three running now," Joe Quinn interrupted. "We have to get ahead of prep and discuss diagnoses and treatment potentials."

As SA12 rumbled to the east, the tower received the first word of the attack and was ordered to shut down all flights immediately. At 220 miles per hour, the A380 couldn't stop in mid takeoff. All other inbound flights were redirected. The staggered flights awaiting takeoff were flagged away.

As the massive ship rose over the end of the runway, a delivery van hidden in the shadows of an oak opened its rear door. The marksman had an easy shot.

The port wing fuel tanks ignited with the direct hit from below, dousing the truck with burning aviation fuel, killing the shooter and driver. The skipper fought the right yaw, seeing the port wing overwhelmed in flames. Recalling the Concorde disaster in Paris, he pulled the nose around for an attempted emergency landing on 260W. It would take him precious seconds of flight time. He had to bring her down quickly—without port-side power, the wing and engines engulfed with fire.

The width, the very size of the airport, saved hundreds of lives. Captain

Evans crash-landed on 260W. The tower had waved off landings with the attack alarm. The massive plane stumbled down the runway starboard side first, pushing the flames away from the fuselage.

Passengers had been quick to follow the cabin crew's orders for crash landing. Most of the travelers were experienced globetrotters and had seen too many accidents in and on planes. Yet the explosion frightened everyone.

"Look for the ground pathway lights, everyone. The smoke will be intense, so stay as low as you can. Use the oxygen masks now! First yours and then your children's. Breathe deeply despite your fear. Breathe!" The chief stewardess had gone down once before and survived.

"ID an exit and move to it as the plane slows to a stop. Move quickly out the exit doors. Take nothing with you—nothing! Your speed is essential to survival. Help one another to move. Think the stairwells in the World Trade Center. Those heroes were well disciplined despite their terror."

With the port wing in flames, Evans ordered everyone out via the emergency exits to starboard as he cut the fuel supply. One by one, some in pairs, amid the roar and heat of the flaming fuel, 484 passengers and 12 crew members escaped. Another 36 passengers and Captain Evans died.

Of those who escaped, 8 members of the EIS—CDC's Epidemic Intelligence Service—were safe. Included among them were Dr. Marudas and her staff. With the 36 who died, more than a quarter of the current EIS team was gone. On their way to fight the disease vectors in Bujumbura, they gave their lives so others may live.

Tracker had taken out HQ and several lead teams of the CDC in less than twelve minutes.

She watched one of the killer's GoPro units until it was crushed in his fall from the building. She disabled it with a signal to the microchip inside. She did the same for the other units. When found, these headsets would reveal nothing.

News media showed the recovery efforts—until Homeland Security shut down all communication links thirty-four minutes into the action. She listened to the internet traffic and local single sideband.

Two hours after the attack, the coda was repeated yet again. Increased radiation levels were detected across the field of destruction. By then, hundreds of victims had been removed to eight hospitals. Dozens of emergency crews were on the ground. Georgia state reserves had secured the site, allowing no one to leave. More than 9,200 people received deadly doses of radiation. Hundreds more would sicken from contact with the afflicted.

The killers had done their job. In 12 minutes, the CDC had been crippled—but not destroyed.

If you step on the neck of a stricken tiger, run when you lift your foot—run very fast.

MAJOR SOLIZ

12:18 p.m. Je Suis le Croc!

Lt. Colonel Baird was the third person to enter the apartment opposite the CDC. The first two officers on the scene were from the building's own security detail. Mark Smith was a retired cop from Detroit and had seen many such disturbances in thirty-four years of service. Jorge Soliz was retired from the San Antonio force. He had been a detective for his last fourteen years. Both knew not to touch any evidence and to assume everything in the rooms was evidence.

Baird asked, "When did you arrive?"

"At 11:41. Ran up three flights of stairs hoping to get a shot at the perps, only to be knocked back down a flight by the helo shot." Jorge was still shaking his head as the ringing slowly quieted and his headache got worse.

"For me, 11:43. Helped Jorge here get back on his feet. We approached the door quickly, but it was blown by the explosion. We entered to find the bodies just as you see them."

"Who's on the deceased in the street?"

"Don't know, sir. Let's take a look." As Smith approached the window, the entire wall fell into the street below. Baird grabbed Mark just as he was dropping, holding the back of his jacket and swinging him back up and to his feet in one swift motion.

"Thanks for the lift. You're no slouch. I'm an easy 210 in the shower."

"Live rounds over here." This from Jorge. "I see two remaining RPGs."

"Three corpses. Smells like one shit his pants. One in the street below."

"Permission to enter, sir?" Baird's investigative unit of four was at the remains of the door frame.

"Granted. Get the prints back to USAMRID now. Major Soliz, notice anything unusual?"

Major Rebecca Soliz was forensic. She was also part of CDC's Plans Units that pursued "outside vectors" for the epidemiologists. They sought social, religious, and cultural influences that impacted disease vectors.

Major Soliz was French West African, a polyglot, and a senior member of the EIS security team. Three terms of duty in the Middle East, fluent in Arabic and French, a major pain in the ass for bad guys, she took no prisoners—ever.

"Other than the stink of dead rag heads?" Becky looked around slowly. First glimpses of a crime scene could be telling if you look without reservation.

"That one was the first to go down. Looks either scared or shot, by the expression. Those two died quickly. Too bad. I could have had a quiet interrogation before the good guys get here."

The one by the back wall groaned.

"Just want I wanted. Fresh meat."

Becky knelt by the African, felt for a pulse, checked for eye movement, and then jabbed her fist deep into his groin. With her gloved hand she grabbed his testicles, squeezing and twisting simultaneously. He gasped, but her hand was over his mouth. Her Arabic was as flawless as her French. "If you want to see Allah soon, do as I say. Do you understand?"

He shook his head no. She took a pen from her pocket and forced his eyelid open. The point pierced his eye just enough to cause further agony.

"Je suis le Croc! I eat your children who come to the river for water! I love the taste of fresh young children!

"I can keep you alive in far greater pain. Want to die? Answer my questions. Want to suffer? Ignore me."

The head bobbed up and down.

"Where did you train?"

"Addis."

"Who trained you?"

"Abdul al-Baghdadi."

"Are you lying to me?" She crushed his testicles tighter. His eyes bloodied as the pen point imbedded deeper.

"Mohammed Abu Al-Sadr."

"When did you leave Addis?"

"Eid." Just eleven months ago.

"Are you willing to die for me? Or do you want to die for Allah?"

"Allah."

"Then do exactly as I say. Give me their names. Give me your contacts. Now." She drove the pen deeper into his eye.

In three minutes, she had extracted what she needed. The others had turned their backs to her, working on the remains of the crime scene.

She stood up. "He died trying to help. He died a good Muslim." She removed her gloves and tossed them out the remains of the crumbled wall. They drifted on the fetid breeze.

"Filthy bastard."

THE END OF THE BEGINNING

1:48 p.m.

Chaos reigned on Clifton Drive. Despite the efforts of the police and military. Death ruled. Everywhere. The street was destroyed, impassable. Dozens of police cars and fire engines blocked each street entry. Hoses sprayed the collapsed walls as fires raged within. The streets and sewers ran dark with blood—and the invisible ink of death. Radiation seeped through the city before anyone knew.

Hundreds wanted to evacuate their apartments but were told to stay indoors until they were questioned as witnesses. The area was swept for intruders or their tools. The smoking hulk of the outer CDC building was swarming with health-care and safety workers. Anger was palpable. Many knew the children's care facility had been destroyed for no reason—other than poor aim.

Atlanta, in the best of times a traffic war zone, was now both, equally so. The Hill was far enough away from the I-85 to avoid serious entanglement, but fear was enmeshing the city's residents. Many were trying to flee. Others were trying to get home to their families.

The airport access was closed, with the smoking hulk of a major airline crushed on the runway. The city of dreams had become a nightmare of shadows in just a few short moments.

Military units were moving by air and roadway. Traffic was a secondary disaster. The media shutdown only added to the chaos. Even the mayor had a hard time communicating with her citizens. She finally called the governor, who arranged a call with the president—who took their call immediately.

"I am going on the air in a few minutes to talk to the nation. We think this was a terrorist attack. We need to do some quick idents and go on the offensive. What can I do for the city?"

"We need control. We need access to food and our homes. Most of all, we need a statement from leadership," shouted an angry mayor. "I have ordered our Georgia National Guard to manage the state roadways. I'd like your permission for them to do the same for the interstate."

"Done. Jarrod, get me Homeland Security. Inform him of my decision to allow the governor to control transportation within Georgia via his National Guard. What else?"

"We need a statement from you for our citizens. They are frightened and angry. A few words from you will go a long way right now, sir."

"Patch me into Jeff Zucker's office. Now."

A few seconds passed.

"Mr. President, this media blackout has to—"

"Jeff, all political commentary is officially closed from this end until we get past this new crisis. Ask your people to do the same, across the board. We have to work together for the nation, for Georgia, for Atlanta right now."

"Mr. President, I cannot tell my reporters—"

"You can, and you will. I need an open channel to the citizens of Atlanta in five minutes. Mayor Tommey, ready yourself. This will be entirely off the cuff, so speak freely but with consideration for the dead and suffering."

"Please follow my lead. Governor Michaels, you will follow the mayor, please. Just speak honestly. We have to work this out together."

"Jeff, you are free to join in after we have spoken. No holds barred. Be clear and honest. Be brief. That's all I ask."

2:07 p.m.

The intelligence community was aware of the radiation ninety minutes later, after the end of the four-way television meeting with the president, the mayor, the governor, and the CEO of CNN.

NSA Director Nash spoke to the president immediately upon confirmation. "We have a far greater crisis unraveling in Atlanta. The munitions used were radioactive. They were composed of spent nuclear fuel. We know where the fuel came from, which reactor, and when it was released. The Bushehr light water reactor no. 4 on the Persian Gulf—Iran—thirteen months ago.

"More than ten thousand people have been exposed to serious levels of radiation, many of them health care and first responders. Atlanta citizens injured during the attack are in hospitals now. They will soon begin to experience the effects of radiation overdoses."

The president's only comment was, "Those caring for them will be affected. Radiation is pouring through your sewer systems with the firefighters' work to douse the flames. This is an act of war."

2:43 p.m.

The White House had been evacuated quickly. Primary personnel had fled by vans, but the president and his crisis team simply took the elevator down six hundred feet into the war room.

"Jarrod get me through to Rafsanjani now. Wake him up or drag him out of the mosque. He has thirty minutes to respond. If he does not, his nation will cease to exist.

"Pompeo, I want the NSA group up and running now. Have the congressional leadership escorted in as quickly as they arrive. Have McConnell and Pelosi ready a special session of Congress tonight once we hear from the JCS—and if we hear back from Iranian leadership.'

The Joint Chiefs of Staff (JCS) were ready to pass down to the War Room leading the Atlanta military response. McConnell, Pelosi, and Schumer arrived fifteen minutes later. Their faces told the president everything. They were scared and angry.

The president began, "Let's get this started now while we wait for the Iranians. Time is of the essence. Nancy, Chuck, Mitch, you have to be the first to know. The weapons used in Atlanta this morning were built from spent nuclear rods from the Bushehr nuclear reactor in Iran."

NSA whispered, "We know this because every reactor has a particular signature. Their signature has been confirmed by the NSA. Here are the records."

The president passed out slim binders with the information in detail and summarized. They were marked "top secret."

"I placed a call to Rafsanjani sixteen minutes ago, giving him thirty minutes to return it. Chairman, please brief us on our response capabilities."

JCS chairman Jackson said, "We have contemplated this attack since 1980, under seven administrations of both parties. We will work in conjunction with the Israelis and the Saudis, as each of you know."

The president spoke. "Mr. Schumer and Ms. Pelosi, you have been to this rodeo before. You know how the game is played."

"We have no differences of opinion on the strategic or tactical decisions you make today, Mr. President. You have our full support," interrupted an outraged House majority leader.

"Thank you, ma'am. We are all in this together, then. Chuck?"

"You have my unqualified support."

"Mr. President, your call is coming in now."

"I'd like all of you to listen in. This is for our future. Please allow me to do the talking. Keep your ears open."

"Mr. President. I fear you have awakened a sleeping beast. We have no interest in speaking with—"

"Just listen. We have nothing to discuss. Listen to me now. You know our city of Atlanta was attacked today by Islamic terrorists."

"Freedom fighters."

"One was captured and interrogated. He has told us of his training by a member of the Revolutionary Guards. That is immaterial. The munitions used were composed of spent nuclear fuel from the Bushehr nuclear power plant. You can see the technical details on your screen now.

"This is a direct attack on these United States.

"You have fourteen days from now, 12:38 GUT on October 2, to detail to me how this happened, your response to this information, and what you will tell the world.

"Should you fail to meet each of these requirements within two weeks, you will find yourself in a state of war with these United States. The deaths of your citizens and the complete destruction of your nation will be in your hands alone."

He slammed the phone across the Oval Office. The line went dead. His breathing was heavy. He grasped for the corner of the desk and then sat on the edge. Perspiration dampened his shirt. His eyes flared; the passion gradually receded.

"Admiral Jackson, please outline for us our military response."

Composure quickly returned. Yet anger engulfed the room—the white heat of anger and retribution and fear.

Every person felt the weight of the world on his or her own shoulders, realizing only the president could make this decision.

"There are eighty-four potential nuclear bombing sites in Iran. Sixty-eight are military, and sixteen are civilian-populated major cities with strategic or tactical military components. We have the weapons in place to destroy these sites multiple times. Other than the Russian air defense system, the Iranians are helpless.

"The Russian system is partially operable today. We will attack its nodes first with conventional munitions. We will use an EMP to complete the destruction of the Russian air defense system.

"Within eighteen minutes of your issuing the command, Iran will cease to exist. Casualties will exceed seventy million in a nation of eighty million.

"Neutron bombs will be used in the urban attack. Military facilities will be destroyed with medium megaton weapons of sufficient strength to leave few survivors.

"Surrounding nations will suffer fallout consequences depending upon weather, conditions on the ground at zero hour, and the weaponry deployed.

"Cruise missiles will carry the heavy load, with B-2s, and the navy as standoff delivery systems. All weapons delivery systems will be in place in thirty-four hours.

"Leave has been cancelled for all military personnel worldwide. We are informing the Chinese and the Russians of our new DEFCON status and of our current awareness of their innocence of the events we have experienced. Should their complicity be discovered, we shall find ourselves in a real jam from which there may be no escape."

Silence sheltered the anger for a brief moment.

"I am about to become one of the greatest mass murderers of all time. I hold this decision as my own, subject to the approval of Congress of Articles of War. Upon the completion of this horrendous act, I shall consider resigning as president in favor of Mr. Pence. I leave my fate to Congress.

"I have asked the Supreme Court justices to review this decision before I take it, and to review your decision to vote Articles of War. I have suggested they, and you, consider this decision, particularly in the light of the 25th Amendment. Anyone who feels I am acting irrationally or bizarrely or insanely, speak your peace now."

The lights from the mall cast a glowering red hue to the shaded room. Although it was only 5:00 p.m., everyone in the small room was exhausted. Simultaneously, each person was deeply immersed in the moment. The fear. The anger. Each had his or her own grave thoughts. Each feared for his or her family. Each felt the warmth of deep fellowship with this man who would soon be vilified. Each knew that time would heal these wounds but never heal their hearts.

The silence was stilling. No one had to speak. No one wanted to speak. The president rose from the edge of his desk and walked the few steps to the window, opening the shades and then the door. He stepped through the portico, leaving the door open.

"What shall we do?" someone asked, to the room rather than to any person.

"Ask forgiveness for this enormous sin we are about to commit and then commit it with all resolution," the president said quietly. He stepped through to the portico, alone.

Several minutes passed. The others quickly filed out of the room in silence, in horror.

Nancy stepped outside and stood next to the president. "We have had sharp words in the past. We will have them again. Please know that you have my heart and soul as an American tonight." She took his hand in hers, as if the hand of a child.

He was sobbing.

"We could have done so much more!"

AB INITIO

Call Her Tracker

> Human beings, as a species, have no more value than slugs.
>
> —John Davis, editor, *Earth First!* journal

She was simply known as Tracker.

In the lakes of northern Minnesota of her youth, her grandfather had taught her Amerindian hunting techniques, tools, and technologies. She could read a forest for its animal life, the sky for its bird paths. She could kill silently, with her hands and with her weapons. The Chabad in Edina was centered upon educating children in the ways of the North. She led her classes each year.

Her family decided to move to Israel in the late '60s. She was a firm, healthy ten-year-old who fit in well with the kibbutz near Golan Heights. She quickly applied her tracking skills to hunting trespassers into her new homeland. Seven men died at her hand. No one knew who'd killed them. She was bred to track. Bent twigs and compressed moss were only the first lessons. She knew the sex and health of an animal from its scat. She could smell an attack. She sensed in infrared and ultraviolet. Her hearing was so acute it sometimes pained her, especially in the city—hence her home by the lake.

Some of this helped her on the internet. She had developed new hunting skills. Intuition proved her. Senses were just the testing ground.

She could read an email and judge the emotion—no emojis required. The time of a message was as important as the wording.

Solicitations were of particular interest to her because they came from the "forest" itself. She sought the smell, the sight of a sentence. Every line, even the computer that produced it, had a signature, an animal origin. She taught herself how to feel these and respond. It was not difficult to get a "Nigerian hustler" to send his address. She sent a killer in training to respond. Cossack bride offers became death traps—for the sender.

The Russian premier once received an email regarding a certain website designed for his private account: "Stop now or die." A phone call to his private cell followed exactly twenty-three days later, on his birthday, the twenty-third.

When the heads of his four dogs were staked to his dacha compound walls a day later, he was shaken. The link disappeared.

An email followed: "Good dog."

She trusted everyone because she knew everyone's scent. She could immediately discern people's status, their psyche, their health, their self-awareness. Surrounded by the most dangerous killers, she found solace in their insecurities. She knew each one far better than each knew him or herself.

Her weapon of choice was fear. A voiced scowl was deadly. She rarely met anyone face-to-face, only because she refused to be exposed to others' gaze.

The few who were granted computer access had to do so from one of her "rooms." These were located in dozens of towns across the globe—small towns with one- or two-road access, out-of-the-way towns. They were fortified when necessary.

Once you entered the room, she took her time watching, listening to, and smelling you. She could tell from the color of your urine what you'd had to drink and when. She often waited twenty-four hours simply to listen to your sleep. How you ate and dressed and bathed gave you away every time.

You really had no choice.

MOSSAD TRAINING

... a certain quiet fury ...
—Elmore Leonard

JSM was her badge name. She had joined the US Navy as a volunteer at seventeen. She was approved to the Navy SEALs training at nineteen.

Hardened by the training and six years of "fieldwork," she returned to Israel, where she was invited into the Mossad for training at twenty-five. The Israeli intelligence agency taught her more, including the many ways of killing. She excelled. Languages. Tracking. Killing. Interrogation. They had found the perfect recruit—and she had found the perfect foil for her bloodlust.

The first morning at field training, while still unpacking, one of the inductees walked too close to her while checking her out.

"Find anything you want?" she inquired.

"Yes." He smiled.

"Care to take it?"

"Sure."

As he stepped toward her again, she turned aside. As he turned to her, she kneed him in the groin while simultaneously breaking his left arm and gouging his eyes. He wasn't blinded, but he never recovered enough to rejoin the group.

No one ever approached her again.

She found the training both exhilarating and profoundly boring. She had excelled at these things for seven years. She knew that getting better required going up against your betters—and beating them, one by one. The drill sergeants quickly understood they had little to teach her.

"She should be instructing the class," offered Master Sergeant Hafiz. "She could take me down in a few seconds ... So fast you can't see her move. Wish we had a few dozen more like ISM."

She had insisted upon the name badge. "Who wants to change my name?"

No one had responded.

On patrol in the hills north of Galilee, she lived off the land. She drank from the leaves in the morning and from the insects during the day. She ate what she killed—anything. One late afternoon, hearing a viper, she froze. Her breathing stopped. No part of her moved.

The patrol watched in awe. She waited without turning her head, listening for the snake. The third rattle was its last. She grasped the tail and shook it like a dog shakes a rabbit. Slipping her knife free, she beheaded it and drank the blood as it flowed from the writhing torso. Tossing it aside, she continued on the patrol.

That same evening, she took the hand of Jaime Goldfarb. He jumped at her touch. They stood, and she walked him away from the others. Big Jim was strong and fierce and not shy. No one wanted any part of him. When they returned two hours later, he was shaking. He sat down by the remaining embers.

"No one has ever been so passionate with me. Ever. I—"

She slept ten feet away. They never spoke.

Tracker quickly became renowned across the Mossad training units. Everyone wanted to be on her team. It was not as if she needed protection; they preferred to be close to her, rather than opposed to her.

On assignment in Yemen, she saved the crew from disaster twice. Once, she smelled a campfire twenty klicks away. She silently directed the other six toward the Hothi militia camp. Without a sound, she slit the throats of the two guards. Dragging the bodies a few meters, she then decapitated each one. Reentering the camp, she removed the fire poles supporting their meager kettle, drove them into the sand and impaled the heads, and turned toward the six sleeping survivors. Retreating behind a low rise of sand, she whispered in Arabic three times, "Aiwa"—each time louder.

Two awoke. Seeing the heads, each yelped, like a dog. A silencer pistol quickly killed them. Three others jumped up—and died. Quick knife strokes lacerated each throat silently.

The remaining man, the Al Qaeda leader, opened his eyes to her stare. She cut out his tongue as he tried to speak. She castrated him. As he writhed in pain, she poured their alcohol stove over him and set him on fire.

Her six companions were silent. She walked back to their camp and fell asleep before they arrived.

Two days later, she made a rare error, burping her food. A shot rang out, hitting her in the shoulder. She crumpled, and her patrol thought she was dead. They lay still, awaiting the attack. She had disappeared during the turmoil. Nothing happened. As Big Jim finally crawled over the rise of rock and sand, he watched her cut a man's heart out and then shove it down his throat. She shot the three others before they could react.

Only then did she react to the bloodstained blouse. She cut it open. Jim applied the pack and covered the wound. They never said a word.

After eighteen missions over three years, during which no one was lost, she quietly retired. She had completed the next stage in her preparations—a decade of training. She was still preparing.

DEATH BY DESIGN

> Humans on the Earth behave in some ways like a pathogenic micro-organism, or like the cells of a tumor.
>
> —Sir James Lovelock, *Healing Gaia*

Four Years Ago

Now she was on the biggest hunt of all time.

She had met the five directorate members via secure Skype four years ago. They had offered her $2 billion dollars for the task's design and composite arrangements. Another $2 billion more would follow each year until she was successful. No other choice was offered.

They expected her to show signs of success by the fifth year, with a twenty-year time horizon. Further video meetings would be held only as she demanded.

The private bank account was already established in Zurich—and funded for the first five years. She was the sole beneficiary of the account and the sole signatory. She had carte blanche.

A year into her mission for the council, they had tested her. Gaunt asked if she had a heart. She followed the track of her friend Jaime in Israel. She found him. She caged him and set up a Skype link for the council.

They were men of enormous wealth, with little knowledge of the animal world. Their views were intellectual, not real. They had no idea.

They watched in terror as she entered the cage, threw him a knife, and then attacked him viciously. He was far stronger. She should have had no chance. Instead, she ripped open his belly with a deep stroke of her own blade. He collapsed, looking at her in curious horror. She reached inside his ribcage, ripped out his still beating heart, took a savage bite from it, chewed, and swallowed.

"Yes, I have a heart. Are you not satisfied? Are you not satisfied?!"

They never saw her in the camera lens again. Their fear was palpable. Three vomited where they sat. Two sank to the floor in horror. Only Gaunt stood and watched, shaken. He had seen such in central Europe during the war. But that was a different time, or so he had thought.

She reiterated the council premise to her fellows—the five directors of the five developmental sites she had designed in five quite secret global locales.

She had created five teams of research geniuses. Each team would apply their skills to a particular facet of the challenge. She had devised the five projects as:

bio/viral
agricultural
chimera
thermonuclear
nano

Each team had a core competency. Each team had multidisciplinary members. Her primary cohorts would recruit and train the "point guards" for the initial dispersal operations. These minions would be fully dispatchable under her discretion, emboldened by her MSP. They were fully self-destructive, by design. Each would follow the others to their assigned tasks—to their early graves.

She gave them direction at their first meeting via Skype: "We have been retained to eradicate the species *Homo sapiens* from the face of the Earth.

"This species is directly responsible for overpopulation, ocean acidification, excessive farming, ranching, and deforestation. Storms are of greater intensity and duration. Temperatures continue to rise. Expanding ice melts in the North and South Poles. Toxic fumes kill. Species are dying off at alarming rates.

"Humans are destroying their only home.

"The affairs of man have devastated planet Earth. Despite the highest intentions of the finest minds and best politicians, our base compatriots continue to troll with lies and deceit.

"We must take action. We must move on. We must overcome. Our solution is the final solution.

"We must do this. We have the knowledge, experience, and skills to surmount this impossible challenge.

"We must attempt this assault. Exterminating a species has never been done before—willfully. The problems are daunting. The risks are enormous. The possibility of success diminishes with each effective foray. The fewer victims left, the more difficult it becomes to destroy them.

"Anyone can kill a hundred, a million, a hundred million people. Several maniacs have tried, successfully. No one has ever tried to exterminate seven billion plus.

"Bureaucrats will try to defeat us. Medical professionals and entrepreneurs will do what it takes to find and destroy us. The CDC and WHO will organize our rout.

"Politicians will use us. The media will excoriate us.

"We must be driven by our compulsion. Our success is our only alternative, our ultimate goal. Success here is defined as extermination of a species. Nothing less will do.

"We shall be the last to die because we shall survive. We shall be the new humans, *Eco-Homo sapiens*. As the sole survivors we shall direct the planet in its healing mission. We shall be the New Jerusalem for all.

"We have a unique team from many disciplines. Each of you brings a problem-solving view to the world. Each of you is successful. All of you have worked in teams where synergies create more, where syncretic behavior is the norm.

"These expectations are our beginning. From here, we shall discover the choices and solutions to achieve our impossible goal.

"The challenges we face simply in the bio realm are significant. We must be able to grow the bio-agents in appropriate numbers, formulate each agent to enhance stability and 'shelf life,' process it into a slurry for viral pane deposit, develop and build a delivery system effective for 5- to 10-micron particulate size. Upon delivery, biological weapons are vulnerable to drying, humidity, oxidation, ultraviolet, and time degradation.

"The methods of stabilizing, coating, storing, delivering, and dispersing a bioagent are extremely complex and known by only a very select few. The weaponization process is certainly the most difficult.

"Improved bioweapons must become more violent and resistant to antibodies or vaccines. They must alter antigenic structures to break immunity defenses, be better able to deal with aerosolization, and be able to survive detection.

"The attacker has the tactical and strategic advantage. Tactical implies a wider range of agents, easier large-scale production, ease of chimerical design, and microorganism modification. Strategic involves livestock and food agent attacks that lead to the dread effect—the psychological advantage—and, ultimately, starvation.

"We shall deploy significant amounts of contagious agents on urban targets to instill fear, panic, and death. The resulting disruption of economic activity will be global.

"Bioweapons are force multipliers. We shall choose main and subsequent attack vectors. Like a scorpion, we shall surprise, move, and surprise again.

"This will require an interdisciplinary open architecture team of microbiologists, aerologists, formulators, biochemists, fermentation processors, and materials processing and storage and sustenance and delivery technicians of the highest rank.

"As for the nano team, you have your work to do. You will recruit or steal cutting edge technology from the key research labs you can see on your screen list. JBI will do the recruiting. If they are unsuccessful, you will steal. Our AI northern Asia team members are building into their systems now. You should have direct access to their daily work within a month.

"You will be the final solution to this crisis of humanity. You will design its death.

"As for the thermonuclear team, you have the tools necessary to steal five weapons now. You know their locations, sizes, and containment elements. You should focus on the EMT choices.

"I expect your success very soon. Yours will be a very quiet success.

No one affected by the theft will discuss it in public or private. You will assure me of this.

"Once their detonation sites have been determined, you will deploy. I shall control their use.

Her commentary was not offered for review. It was a standing order. Even as she turned off the video link, her work began immediately.

Recruitment in fields unfamiliar to her was delegated to the global search firm, JBI. Their contact was through one of the five council member's executive search branch in Paris. The member's firm was given employment requirements and they passed these on to JBI. Once hired, the professional was brought to the site.

She planned the acquisition of expertise in creating, storing, delivering, and sustaining a wide variety of dangerous organisms. Professionals in prolonged exposure and handling of these agents would be retained.

Experimental and experiential management cooperatives were to be arranged horizontally, designed to manage skills to move agents through a variety of systems—R & D, production, storage, and weaponization.

Once retained, they acknowledged their nearly complete lack of communication with the real world. They had to be committed to action. Their commitment was measured without their knowledge of the calculation.

All contact with family was monitored. Compensation was richly paid to the families. Any questions were promptly answered with a visit to the family member—and a solution achieved. Few further questions were asked.

The work was to be parceled across five remote areas, with each locale unknown to the others. Each setting had multidisciplinary functions, with research assays pursued by engineers, computer designers, geneticists, chemists, and physicists. Production designers, electricians and electronics workers, line and HR managers, and statisticians and ceramicists provided technical support. Lab technicians, endocrinologists, epidemiologists, and epigenesists each did work in teams of eight, two from each profession.

Agronomists were their own separate team. Joined at the research hip to the bio and chimeric teams, they were to develop global attack strains diffusible via local residents.

Microbiologists were recruited from Asia, Central and South. The

Chinese had made significant advances with CRISPR/cas9, and lower-echelon members of these research teams were approached and recruited.

Nano researchers came in from the hacker world and the intelligence community, joined by bioresearchers and poorly paid bureaucrats.

Nuclear delivery and miniaturization specialists were "kidnapped" from North Korea and Iran. Each potential team member was approached at an international conference in private. If someone refused, he or she disappeared. No trace of contact existed—no email, no voice mail, no phone record.

Each team was independent and knew little or nothing of the other sites. No site worker was aware of the overall objective or of the reason for his or her team's work. Each site did know they were "combating terrorism." Only the five project managers— directors—and Tracker were aware of the complexity of the task.

Field managers collected the massive data and filed them via anonymous encryption. Senior managers analyzed the files, collated them, and forwarded all to their directors. There was one director for each locale, who was unaware of the other sites' physical plants or distinctions. Each site was competing against the others—without knowing how or on what track—while simultaneously working on distinct projects.

Funds flowed according to successful assays into each research frontier. She assumed all tracks would be successful. Her primary problem was the degree of success. Anything less than 100 percent was unacceptable to her—and to her overlords.

The directors of each project knew this. Six Sigma was just the beginning. She wanted more. They had no choice but to deliver.

The main project was not about tracking, her true strength. She would look forward to that endgame. In time. In time.

Tracking, hunting, and killing would come to her in due time. She accepted the delay via her annual sorties into the wilderness. For ten days each year, she would plant herself in a wilderness and have extraction set up at a predetermined recovery point. She was on her own for those ten days. She relished each year's prospect. She measured success on these tracks as an "absolute proximity to my own death."

When the bloodlust overcame her, she flew to her hunting lodge and tracked someone. The terrorist or urban killer thought he knew his way around killing. She never lost a "duel in the forests of Transylvania." Not that the deck was stacked against the perp; she was simply a good assassin. Only then did the madness within subside for a few months—the horror, the horror.

THE DIRECTORATE

> When inconceivably cold-blooded evil is in command, the victims are truly helpless.
>
> —Charles Krauthammer

Two Years Later

Tracker spoke directly with the directorate on one other occasion.

"As we expect, our greatest success will be bio/viral, we are just now deploying six different agents. Their operation remains dependent upon stability and sustainability of product. Delivery across dozens of locations is our downstream challenge. If we are to infect globally, we must have near simultaneous exposure across six continents.

"Planet Earth has 150 cities with more than three million citizens each. These contain nearly half of Earth's seven billion plus population. The world has nearly 1,000 more cities of five hundred thousand plus, containing another three billion.

"In Asia, 14 cities contain three hundred million people, mostly very poor and in small, close association. These are the ideal ground zeros for infection inflection.

"The agrarian societies compose a further 1.5 billion primitive or completely isolated groups, such as islanders; polar and desert dwellers make up the remaining population.

"The latter groups will be the most challenging for our infectious teams because of their remoteness. Infections need bodies to survive, to spread.

"Agrarian communities are often the feeder populations for the newest cities in Asia and Africa. Their infection rates, while lower than the urban groups, will be more constant. Farming lifestyles are both isolated and less connected. Infections prefer connectivity—we shall simply enhance this linkage.

"The initial sequences are designed as an attack against health-care professionals first, populations second, political forces third, and society fourth.

"After four years, we have found significant synergies between the pathogens, the chimera, the agricultural, and the nano teams. Simultaneously with our planning, the biogenetics world has discovered extraordinary new approaches utilizing CRISPR. Whether CAS9, Cpf1, or Cas13d, these designer tools will enhance the productivity of the bioweapons.

"This is an ingenious coupling of the millennium-old bacteriophages' defense against viral attack with genetic transcription. A small set of scientists in disparate parts of the world has simultaneously initiated the simplest of designs.

"They can cut and paste DNA molecules. They can put these where they wish. They can eliminate a genetic disease or add a genetic enhancement. They think they have found both the fountain of youth and the cure for all diseases.

"In fact, they have given my laboratories the insight to design and create ultimate biological beasts at the molecular level. These creatures, miniature Frankenstein monsters, have impenetrable surfaces, enhanced RNA tools, and significant reproductive abilities. They have no natural enemies, can use any natural host, and employ infinite infective enhancement skills.

"These 'empty quarter designs' will be egregious. Distinguishing. Conspicuous. Flagrant.

"We rely upon the chimeras to attack the primaries, the developed world. Their 'covers' will allow a broadening diffusion and prevent serious infection-fighting efforts.

"Time will tell. Change can be only anticipated, never built into the delivery process.

"Most outcomes, whether disease or death, are caused by a web of multiple components. Conditions are necessary, sufficient, or probabilistic.

Necessary conditions are of a priori importance. Urban living is a necessary condition for our initial success.

"If a necessary condition can be identified and controlled, then the outcome can be rationalized.

"Control the release and destroy the defenses. These are the sufficient conditions for virulence.

"Probable conditions demand upon our sufficiency of attack. We shall destroy the CDC defenses in four weeks. Then our sufficiency will arise."

A voice came over the line. "We must ensure the probability of each type of condition for ultimate success. Urban releases and defense destruction vastly improve our probabilities. We have margins for error simply because we are working a chaos field. We cannot control all variables. We cannot even ident most of them ab initio and the 'fog of war' obscures more."

The voice was Gaunt's, she knew, the primary leader of the group. His final words were unusual. He enforced her vision. "You know the acceptable success rate. Have the laboratories continue to ident the necessary conditions for success. Then they have only luck to worry about."

"Luck will win this battle, too. If you want to live in the city, you had better bring plenty of luck." Soros was glib, as always. His distaste for humanity was palpable.

"You will succeed where all others have failed," mimed Gore.

She had left the website. The others signed off, wondering who this woman really was.

Tracker's initiation sequencing was less than twenty months away.

WITHIN YOU AND WITHOUT YOU

> The extinction of *Homo sapiens* would mean survival for millions, if not billions, of Earth-dwelling species. Phasing out the human race will solve every problem on Earth—social and environmental.
>
> —Ingrid Newkirk, president of PETA

She had work to do. Clearly individual attacks would be effective, even culturally disruptive—but they had small impact on the greater goal.

She listened as the heads of her five labs spoke, remotely.

First to speak was the bioresearch leader. No one knew anyone else's actual name—simply his or her title. "The creation of a 'superbug' entails a buildup of gene complexes that would enable it to infect human hosts, causing illness and death in significant numbers to be effective at species suppression."

"It would also have to be contagious and capable of spreading across biomes to human hosts. It would have to be able to block human immunological defense mechanisms acquired over millions of years by natural pathogenesis," acknowledged his site science coordinator.

HR spoke up. "Converting a biological specimen into a bioweapon requires a wide variety of disciplinary approaches. Technology results from a complexity of actions between varied professionals with a wide degree of knowledge, experience, and skills."

The senior laboratorian weighed in. "Laboratory success does not imply field success. Organizational and managerial skills are necessary to engender knowledge development and sustainability. These should include absorptive skills, organizational design skills, and managerial design sets.

"Challenges included growing the bioagent in appropriate numbers, formulating the agent to enhance stability and 'shelf life,' and processing the bioagent into a slurry or dry paste for insertion via the viral pane, and then developing and building this nearly invisible delivery system effective for 5- to 10-micron particulate size."

The bio leader added, "These challenges require an interdisciplinary open architecture team of microbiologists, aerologists, formulators, biochemists, fermentation processors, materials processing and storage and sustenance and delivery technicians of the highest rank."

Logistics came in. "The methods of stabilizing, coating, storing, delivering, and dispersing a bioagent are extremely complex and known by only a very select few. The weaponization process is certainly the most difficult."

HR was next. "Good pathologists need a fundamental humility—to be able to challenge any diagnosis, including your own. You need an inner stillness, the moral discipline to observe without jumping to irrelevant conclusion."

Senior Lab inserted, "Bioweapons do not scale up easily, and this is not a linear process. It requires interdisciplinary teams with wide skill set variations that are carefully and continuously integrated and acted upon in deep coordination."

HR added, "It requires explicit, tacit, and communal knowledge. Explicit means protocols, formulae, designs, and so on are in place and respected. Tacit means personal, local, tricks of trade, subconscious clue seeking and usage, unarticulated skills, contextually specific from each team member. Communal implies shared by a group, while unknown to any one member in a collaborative involvement.

"It means complex information exchange mediums, mismatched language salience in a noncompartmentalized, open architecture work sphere. Of these, tacit decays with time, as it is experientially based. The other two grow over time.

"Our new pathogen designs were completed last year. They have now been built into their viral glass surroundings. We are nearly ready for in situ testing."

Sooner than they realize, thought Tracker.

She knew CDC, WHO, and several national governments would unite to find and destroy her. Her clock was ticking.

The ultimate onslaught would begin soon—very soon. This was perhaps a personal trial, a turning of the screw, a turn once received long ago. She had been left for dead once. It proved her mettle. She could survive anything after Berlin.

Could the species *Homo sapiens* survive her onslaught?

She doubted it.

She was the storm.

On-site testing would commence in a few months.

SULEIMAN

Giving society cheap, abundant energy would be the equivalent of giving an idiot child a machine gun.

—Professor Paul Ehrlich, Stanford University

April 4

The crisp morning air was still. The mountain shade cast a gloom into the small adobe room.

He and his brother were wool sorters. They worked in the room with light from three windows, which were never opened. His father had died two years ago, and his mother had been urged to remarry one of his father's brothers. His new little brother played in the dirt beside him on the floor. Abdul, nine years old, had had a cough as long as he could remember. His older brother Suleiman was ten and often sick but worked near him in the enclosed shed.

They had to remove the dirt and feces and bugs from the sheep's wool. This was brought into the room in hundred-kilo sacks after the cutting was complete. On a "good day," they could clean three sacks. Today was such a day.

"You move better when you don't face the light."

"Inshallah."

"It's true. You can see better with the light behind you."

"We see better because Allah wishes it so. Only he can help us. Try to remember that. You have been punished before for your ideas."

"Inshallah," he intoned. He knew Suleiman was right.

They worked through the heat of the afternoon. Soon the rains would begin, and the cooling air from beyond the Tian Shan mountains would ease their workload, if only by a few degrees.

The work was long and tedious. Cries to Allah notwithstanding, Abdul was already sickened. He would die in a month, a day after his brother Suleiman. The infant on the floor lying in the muck and filth and feces would die sooner.

The wool was sent to the packers for shipment to Dushanbe. The road out of the valley was a long treacherous track, deep in mud during the rains, covered with snow during the winter. Steep vertical cliffs pummeled it with house-sized boulders. The comfortable village survived via the snow-cold river running through it. Here was peace amidst a rocky horror.

More children were always available. Parents sold them as slave workers for a few weeks' food. They had no choice. The mullahs dictated who worked, where, and when.

The wool was made into cheap hats for the Russian trade and packed off to the north. Drivers would carry a few hundred wool bundles from Tajikistan to Russia every week.

A few weeks later, Ivan, a trucker by trade, caught a cold—nothing new in this small city of Khorugh. Yet the cold persisted. He told his stepson to wear the hat while he was "resting." Ivan Yerolenko was a broad man, a smuggler by design. He kept his family comfortable and wore clothing from the crates he transported from Central Asia. A few items missing were of no concern. He paid his fees; he was accepted as a good worker.

Ivan died twenty-two days after he wore the woolen hat, just two days after his son died. They were buried with a small funeral—all the wife could afford. The hat remained in the closet for the fall and then was sold to a neighbor for some bread and borscht. The wife moved to her own smaller village with all of her belongings from the closet in November.

The entire city of Khorog was dead before the Tajiks could respond effectively, or at all.

Tracker relied on her own private intranet. She had a singular, secretive access to her own GPS satellites. No one followed her progress because no one was aware.

She used the satellites for tracking, data incursion, and real-time information access around the globe. Her scan and read program—Stinger—noted the significant number of deaths in a small oblast village. It was prompted to trigger certain data sets to her as they were written. While the numbers were low—less than twenty-eight thousand—she assumed the wool link was her tag. They confirmed her test had the expected results.

A test compiled and completed—a small success.

"Inshallah."

ABU

Mankind is the most dangerous, destructive, selfish, and unethical animal on the earth.

—Michael Fox, vice president of the Humane Society

April 17

The boy in the marketplace cannot find his way home.

A man offers his hand, as a guide, an aide.

The man's aspect was ancient. His leathery face broods over a hunched, squat body, a barrel-chested torso with long arms that seem to reach to the ground. He is simian. He is an engineering genius. He also knows how to seduce children.

A wrestling champion in school, he never lost a bout. He knew the arena and won by the rules. More powerful than ruthless, he overcame each opponent by force of will and of body.

"Come with me. I can help."

He leads the boy down darkened steps. The steps are shallow. Wet and cold. The boy begins to shiver, in fear. The room is dark.

Soon the training begins.

He must do exactly as he is told. He must do nothing but what he is told. The pain is the tool of this trade, the only tool ever used.

The boy knows he is no longer alone, yet soon will be utterly alone. The guide is exact. There are no choices other than his choices. Eat. Sleep.

Eliminate. Prayer. Listen. Everything is guided to him. Choice disappears from his mind. He must only do as he is told. Never anything but this.

The boy will never become a man. He knows this. He fears for his mother. He might reveal where she lives if he isn't respectful, if he doesn't obey.

The guide has but one thought in mind. Train the boy to be the man he can never become.

A killer.

It's not as if he doesn't enjoy inflicting the pain, the punishment, the horror. Watching how the boy responds is his greatest joy. It has always been his greatest joy. Their pain releases him from his own. Their suffering gives him great pleasure.

How can these children accept such treatment? How do they continue after all the suffering? How can they remain human? His only task is to ensure their quick access to heaven.

He certainly has failed as a human. He knows this. He revels in this. He is the animal that all fear. He is the serpent, the wolf, the scorpion. He writhes in their pain. He embellishes their suffering simply to extend his own pleasure.

But this is not his task today. Today he must simply train the boy to his task—walk into a hotel filled with infidels and destroy them.

The boy must be ready within the week. He must accept his fate with abandon, with prayer. With humility. The outcome is too important for any other behavior. He must do this right the first time. There will be no practice, no play, no experimenting. And so the indoctrination begins.

To his shock, the boy's mother is brought in. She is weeping. No, she is sobbing. She fears for her family. She doesn't know her son is on the other side of the glass.

He knows. The boy from the marketplace knows.

She rests on the floor. Suddenly she screams. The snake is moving towards her, seeking warmth more than to attack, to defend itself. She moves along the wall, away. It senses her with its tongue. It stops, as if listening.

The snake strikes at her feet, piercing her ankle. She screams. The boy cries.

"Anything! Please, just let me help my mother!"

Abu waits. The venom will take an hour to kill. He knows there is no remedy, yet he waits. Small pleasures in slight suffering.

At last he whispers to the boy, "Will you help her?"

"Yes, please let me help mother!"

"Will you do as I say, in faithful humility, in prayer, in abandonment to Allah?"

"Yes, Allah be praised!"

"Only then can you help her. Only when you are on the other side can you beckon to her to join you, in paradise."

"I will do as you demand."

"Would you like some dates? Some water?"

"No. I will have all I need in paradise."

"Then let us go. She doesn't have much time. You must get there before her, or she will never find you again."

The vest is heavy, almost his own weight. He drags his feet across the road.

"No, no. You must walk upright into heaven!"

He tries again, pulling his back straight despite the weight. He climbs the steps into the hotel, pauses, and intones the name of God.

He stands next to the appointed column and explodes. The vest is filled with steel pellets, nails, and razor blades. He is instantly decapitated. Some say they watch themselves die from above the carnage. No one really knows.

The lobby is filled with journalists awaiting the signing of the treaty—a small peace between warring clans, warring for hundreds of years. Most of the foreigners are killed outright. Some survive, only to bleed to death in the hot morning. The boy had stopped by the pillar, as instructed. The pellets brought the pillar down—and, with it, the center of the hotel. The weight of the third-floor pool crushed two floors, destroying all beneath it. Other columns fell inward. As in slow motion, the entire building collapsed upon itself. No finer explosion had happened since the King David Hotel in 1943.

Hundreds died. More suffered and then died. The peace was broken. Yet others died. As for the boy and his mother …

The trainer, Abu al-Sadr, watched it with binoculars from two blocks away.

He had to move quickly as the smoke and rubble filled the air, as death and fear mixed with blood and bones.

He had seen the explosion, the death. He was overcome with the passion of the belief. He was enraptured by the suffering, the pain, and the blood and body parts.

He had seen into heaven. He had sent them to their just deaths. Allah be praised.

Yet he too had been watched. He too had passed the test.

Tracker had been watching in anticipation. She needed a trainer in the camps, in the desert. She pondered how to incorporate this creature's horrific skill into the process. The choices rapidly raced across her mind.

Atlanta is best.

ACT 2

The Killing Season

> Current lifestyles and consumption patterns of the affluent middle class—involving high meat intake, use of fossil fuels, appliances, air-conditioning, and suburban housing—are *not sustainable.*
>
> —Maurice Strong, Rio Earth Summit, 1972

IDRUS

A pathogen that begins in a remote town can reach major cities on all six continents in 36 hours.

—Olga B. Jonas

June 2

In virtually all commercial aircraft, the cabin air filtration system recirculates half of the cabin air with an equal amount of nonfiltered outside air from the engine "bleed air." Toxic fumes may seep into this system—from hydraulic oil fumes, kerosene fumes, pesticide spray mist, flame retardant's fumes, even de-icing fluids.

Some of these compounds are like Agent Orange and are listed as among the most dangerous in the world. The airlines have the option of a VOC removal filter.

The mixing chamber combines both air sources. VOCs (volatile organic substances), and other micron-sized pollutants do enter the aircraft. This engine bleed air can contain fuel-sourced particulates.

Only the cabin air itself is HEPA filtered. Thus, half of the air we breathe on a flight is unfiltered. When oil or fuel mix with cabin air, the VOCs become part of the air system. Several incidents of illness and death have been reported. The airlines remain mum on the issue. Only the Boeing 787 is safe.

Idrus Mohammed had been with Emirates since its formation nearly two decades ago. He was honored to be an important part of the flight maintenance ground crew. Today his task was to check and replace the air filters on the Airbus 380 prior to its flight from Abu Dhabi. He dropped the small packet into the filter casing, as instructed by his supervisor. He was told this would reduce the organophosphate pollution potential.

Fourteen other maintenance technicians from around the world had attended the class in Germany. Ostensibly put on by Airbus, the facility was actually an outsourced firm.

Each was now trained to perform the same function—upgrade the air filters. They would kill as many people as possible with the inhalation of pulmonary anthrax bacillus.

During the course of the next month, twenty-eight aircraft would be serviced with the new packets. More than four hundred passengers would be on each of these aircraft, each time they flew.

Each aircraft would fly as many as ten flights weekly. Before they were shut down twelve days later, more than one million passengers had been exposed to pulmonary anthrax. Virtually all had inhaled the bacillus, the spores.

As the spores are inhaled, they are transported through the air passages into the lungs. The spores are then picked up by scavenger cells and transported through small vessels to the lymph nodes in the central chest cavity.

Damage caused by the anthrax spores in the central chest cavity causes chest pain and difficulty in breathing. Once in the lymph nodes, the spores germinate, multiply, and eventually burst the macrophages, releasing many more bacilli into the bloodstream to be transferred to the entire body.

In the bloodstream, these bacilli release three proteins—lethal factor, edema factor, and protective antigen. The three are not toxic by themselves, but the combination is incredibly lethal to humans. Protective antigen combines with these other two factors to form lethal toxin and edema toxin, respectively. These toxins are the primary agents of tissue destruction, bleeding, and an 84 percent chance of death of the host.

If antibiotics are administered too late, even if the antibiotics eradicate the bacteria, some hosts will still die of toxemia because the toxins produced by the bacilli remain in their system at lethal dose levels.

By mid-September, the infection rates were plateauing. Over the next month 904,000 travelers would die. Before their painful deaths, they would infect at a factor of one-to-seven. Eight generations of bacillus would flow around the world.

In all, 56.2 million would die.

And this was simply a test run—just as Calicut and the other smaller sites would be test runs. The tests were her key. Tracker had to prove to herself that absolute deaths were far higher than a normal infective rate would produce.

To come close to stabilizing the global population at 7.8 billion, 75 million would have to die each year. Much design had yet to be built into an exceedingly complex system of delivery.

Design by death was still in its testing phases.

FATIMA

> We must make this an insecure and inhospitable place for capitalists and their projects. We must reclaim the roads and plowed land, halt dam construction, tear down existing dams, free shackled rivers and return to wilderness millions of acres of presently settled land.
>
> —David Foreman, cofounder of *Earth First!*

June 3, 2018

Fatima was playing in the garbage dumps of the enormous city. A slight girl of ten, she had inherited the lithe body and muddy skin from her mother. The sky accentuated her warm tones in the early morning heat.

She had been sent there each day for work, not play. But sometimes, out of sight of "the boss," she played in the trash and mud and dirt. They were all rag pickers by birth. Few would live to age thirty.

The little plane she picked up was curious. She knew she must bring it to him. Perhaps he would reward her today. But for now, she just waved it in the air as if flying. It whirred one last time, emitting its insignificant white fog, an invisible powder.

Its slight warmth made her drop it in fear. Picking it up carefully, she brought it down the refuse heap, found the boss, and gave it to him.

"Stupid child. Playing with toys again?"

"When I lifted it to the sky, it became warm. I brought it to you now."

He gave her naan from his packet and cuffed her on her way. "Bring me more!" Neither of the children saw nor felt the powder.

The boy, Fatima's boss, earned a good bonus from the find. He showed his workers before passing it along. They laughed at her foolishness as they played with the flyer themselves. His leader was surprised to see such a modern tool in the rubbish of Calicut.

The boy was rewarded with fresh goat meat and *kush*. He shared the meager meal with his gang as he retold the girl's story.

Sixteen days later, she was ill, as was the boss. Everyone who he had given it to was ill. Everyone died.

Except Fatima.

The drone's flight over the city had been a partial success, with its emissions of fifty grams per hour in the acceptable range. The height was rather excessive, and the afternoon breeze dissipated much of the weaponized pathogen over the kill zone. Its ability to maim and kill was not disrupted—only slightly distracted.

No one understood the little flyer was a smallpox drone. No one knew the nature of the experiment it embodied.

The small success was recorded via video link in the drone. It sent information on all who touched it, all who played with it. The sensors could detect skin type, temperature, locale, and time. The video recorded its own three-day life.

By the time its battery ran down, the infection had spread to several areas of the city. These were, by design, the most densely populated areas. Soon, 48,000 people were sickened. Within six days, 400,000 were infected. The transmittal rate was one-to-ten. By the time the boss had passed, the daily stream of souls departing the city exceeded 120,000. Their remains were burned, as was the custom, to the incredible luck of the community.

A few thousand infected many others outside of the city. Those who traveled on the trains were the most efficient contributors to Tracker's dissemination study. Within three weeks more than 5 million had become infected nationwide. The infection rate exceeded expectations, at one-to-twelve. With an incubation period of nine to seventeen days, the pox spread exponentially over a month.

By mid-July, five weeks after the first case was reported, more than 60 million people were infected, resulting in nearly 40 million deaths across the region.

These illnesses and deaths were diagnosed. Alarms were triggered to the ranks of the CDC. Response teams mobilized globally and with speed as the transmission rate became apparent. By the end of the first week, Atlanta had four teams in place in Calicut and Delhi.

The process was difficult at best in the urban environment—identify, isolate, trace, disinfect, quarantine, and immunize.

Closure was certain, Tracker knew. By the beginning of the monsoon, the experiment would be a qualified success—nearly 40 million deaths from a small drone. She noted the data and returned to her study. It wasn't nearly enough to make a difference, not nearly enough.

The challenge was in the numbers. Killing 40 million was a horrific yet impressive number. But the species-wide impact was negligible. Even the success of each of these test runs would have no appreciable impact upon her goal. Even the tiny figure of 10 percent of the world population was a staggering 760 million. It wasn't enough to ripple the genetic waters.

So much more had to be done. These horrors were just the coming attraction for the main event.

KURTZ

June 28

He was an insignificant man. Brown hair, hazel eyes, medium height, with no distinguishing marks. He blended. No one noticed him. He was everyman. He was the heart of darkness.

Watching something die was his primary, yet very private pleasure. Accentuating the death, lengthening it, prolonging it was his greatest desire. He was her ideal candidate, by design.

During their sole secret conference call, Tracker had said, "You have the leadership qualities needed—emotionless, faithless, fearless. You lack that which is in overabundance today—human compassion. And your final grace? You have none. You are despicable in every respect."

He was an insignificant man.

Two years previous, the O & M contract for Changi Airport had been awarded to Ashram Ltd., a local firm from the Clementi District. He was the lead HEPA technician for Ashram.

The AC system had been upgraded at no cost to the government, as per contract. This system was now HEPA rated, the first airport in the world to achieve such a distinction. No one had to worry about illness spreading through the public thoroughfare of one of the busiest airports, with seventy-eight million passengers annually.

The Emerging Infectious Diseases Conference was set for next week in Singapore. Scientists, physicians, clinicians, and administrators from WHO, NGOs, and the CDCs of the world held their biannual meeting to discuss and learn. They always seemed just ahead of the game.

Until this meeting.

SINGAPORE

> If I were reincarnated, I would wish to be returned to Earth as a killer virus to lower human population levels.
>
> —Prince Philip, Duke of Edinburgh, patron of the World Wildlife Fund

July 1

The thirty-sixth annual Infectious Diseases Conference was scheduled for Singapore in October. Many of the most distinguished researchers—and politicians—in their fields had planned on attending. Given the recent attacks in Delhi and on the Emirates airline routes, many refused or were prohibited from attending. The US CDC sent a minor contingent of associates and physicians. No EIS (Epidemic Intelligence Service) personnel could be spared, even though their tales were the most valuable to everyone. Most were already in the field assessing and trying to stabilize the current hot zones.

Security was tight, even for the friendly police state of Singapore.

Blood samples were required for every attendee from two weeks prior to departure and again on the day of departure. Inoculations for the six class A pathogens were required. No foreign press was allowed.

A subdued crowd of eight hundred sat nervously awaiting opening remarks. Panjachouri was the consummate political beast, reveling in the attention, demanding respect while praising the group for their courage to attend.

Every cough triggered an auto response from virtually every person seated. They looked around. They asked the cougher if he or she was okay, what his or her symptoms were. Nervous smokers tried ginseng to reduce their decades-long hacking.

Tracker watched the paunchy middle-aged Indian physician approach the podium as the scientists' gathering hushed. He cleared his throat and started speaking: "We have seen the worst …"

Tracker stifled a laugh. This guy was trying to calm everyone by overstating the case. They had no idea.

"We have seen the worst onset of a series of pathogenic illnesses ever." He overstated the case for a hoped-for calming effect.

"While we feel we have controlled the Delhi incident, Jakarta is still in flames, quite literally. The Muslim community has taken upon itself the unjust view that they are the subjects of a Western attack.

"Christians have been eliminated in Aceh, and thousands flee Java and Sulawesi. Oil prices continue to spike as Indonesian production has essentially stopped. Offshore rigs are in flames, as are refineries and storage depots across the archipelago.

"Our resources are stretched thin. We are fortunate to have sequestered the Emirates incident when we did—and to have learned from it. The basic approaches of sequester and census are working once more."

Several in the crowd looked at their neighbor, knowing this was only partially true. Sequestering only worked when the local populace participated and supported. India was difficult. Indonesia remained impossible. The Red Crescent workers had been attacked and several already killed. No Westerner had emerged unscathed from the brutal responses to the first waves of attack.

"We know we have accomplished much with these incidents. Our successes prove our approach works.

"The breakout sessions will be available to all attendees. We have three days to learn from one another and contribute to each other. Our professionalism leads us forth.

"We must ensure further, increased funding for our efforts to control disease. Where millions worked last year, now we must have access to billions. The health of the planet depends upon us."

Tracker frowned. *You have no idea.*

Professor Ramanathan's turn was next. He had used the talk many times previously—in educational settings with no real-world application. Now it was real and applicable and severely dangerous. Only Tracker knew what he would say was nonsense.

"Gram-negative bacteria in Indian hospitals demonstrate how hard outer casks—let's call them what they are, caskets—are, making them fairly invulnerable to antibiotics.

"Over 50 percent of bacterial infections in Indian hospitals are resistant to commonly used antibiotics. Many widespread bacterial pathogens in India are also resistant to powerful, broad-spectrum antibiotics. We now have a simple cure. Human excrement. In tiny doses. Used to clean surfaces, instruments, and hands."

With a stodgy walk, Ramanathan was fat and gawky, looking like the proverbial college professor. He had looked this way for forty years. Shy and internal, he could be obdurate and abrasive when making his case. He had been a final recruit, a diffident holdout who valued his honor over his prestige. His honor would be the death of him yet. Tracker listened to his talk.

"In 2010, a team of South Asian and British scientists analyzed bacterial infections in a hospital around New Delhi and found that these infections could resist hospitals' last-resort intravenous antibiotics, called carbapenems.

"They were endowed with a super-resistant gene, dubbed New

Delhi metallo-beta-lactamase 1, or NDM-1, which confers resistance to carbapenems, along with at least fourteen other antibiotics.

"Since then, NDM-1 bacteria have been found in drinking water supplies and in puddles around New Delhi. More important, it has been found in patients in over thirty-five countries. Many of these patients are "medical tourists" who have traveled from Europe, the Middle East, and the Americas to India or Pakistan for inexpensive medical care.

"International travel and patients' use of multiple countries' healthcare systems leads to the rapid spread of NDM-1, with potentially serious consequences. In May 2010, a case of infection with *E. coli* expressing NDM-1 was reported. It was soon to be found all over the globe.

The lecturer continued. "Let's look at how it works.

"NDM-1 is an enzyme that makes bacteria resistant to a broad range of beta-lactam antibiotics. These include the antibiotics of the carbapenem family. You know these are a mainstay for the treatment of antibiotic-resistant bacterial infections. The gene for NDM-1 is one member of a large gene family that encodes beta lactamase enzymes called carbapenems. These bacteria are now known as superbugs because infections caused by them are difficult to treat. Such bacteria are usually susceptible only to polymyxins and tigecycline.

"These play an important role in disease development. The chimera thus created further reduces health-care professionals' ability to fight the vector."

Tracker had retained him for this concept alone. All the rest was fabrication, but the chimera was key to her rapid success in evolving pathogenic attacks.

"The resistance conferred by this gene aids the expansion of bacteria that carry it as a host. By stimulating genetic adaptation, these encourage the proliferation of antibiotic resistance. We simply and purposefully urge these mutations.

"In fact, they allow us to reduce the 'time value' of our vector significantly. We are less dependent upon the disease's reproduction facility. Why? Because we have implanted a TE, a treatment efficiency.

"We have transferred genes that are responsible for antibiotic resistance in one species of bacteria to another species, thus encouraging the genes' antibiotics reception. Our malaria pathogen acquired genetic material from humans that might help facilitate its extended settlement in the body.

"This work now has been applied successfully to our bacillus. The transit vehicle is a tiny portion of human excrement. Encapsulated into a pill, it is easily ingested and absorbed."

He concluded with his usual salubrious comments about long lives for the hard-working scientists and medical professionals.

They had no idea how short their famous lives were. He had no idea that he was talking rubbish—that he was simply saying what he was told to say. That this entire conference was a ruse.

> A reality about our species seems to be we breed a certain percentage of our population that wants to do a lot of harm to others.
>
> —Craig Venter

As the conference ended and the delegates began to return home, they all had to transport through the Singapore International Airport. More than 120,000 moved through Changi this day, along with the conference attendees.

Incredibly, Kurtz had trained the local sanitation engineers to perform the identical filters replacement that had recently destroyed so many on the Emirates flights.

Virtually everyone passing through or working at Changi became infected. Nearly thirty million died within six weeks. By early November, the pale had finished its global attack.

Blood tests and inoculations proved worthless to the conference goers. By their departure date three days hence, the first illnesses were being reported.

Tracker had begun her second large-scale attack on health infrastructure. Within the month, 70 percent of the attendees were dead.

The magnificent experiment in Chinese capitalism, the city-state of Singapore, was tested. It would fail despite intense sequestration and census taking. In fact, it would fail because of these defenses. Of her 5.4 million population, 3.8 million would die.

The sequestration forced infected and healthy together in close quarters. Shared beds and utensils, urinals, and air spread the pathogens more rapidly than Tracker's models had anticipated. The healthy died just as easily—they simply died last.

As Jakarta fell, a few weeks later so did the rest of the nation. A few hundred thousand were infected. Tens of millions died.

And the first to die were the health-care professionals. Their unswerving efforts to help the sick had dedicated their lives to one simple proposition—death.

HENRY

This is a terrible thing to say. In order to stabilize world population, we must eliminate 350,000 people per day. It is a horrible thing to say, but it's just as bad not to say it.

—Jacques Cousteau, *The UNESCO Courier*

June 30

The streets of Bali are crowded, even during the hot winter months. International flights into Denpasar were busy. Some travelers simply ignored the hot tropical winter weather in favor of the cost. Escape from the pathogens igniting the world drove many to seek solace in a friendlier, simpler world.

Henry came for the climate. He had been given the ticket and the cash a few days prior. The flight was long. Must have been the guy in the seat ahead of him—coughing all night.

Henry was a small man, insignificant to his neighbors. Of normal height and stature, slightly stooped and graying around the temples, he was simple. He wore his clothes loosely, a good thing in the tropics. He enjoyed feeling "free" when it was warm and humid. The cold winter in Cumberland, Kentucky, was not missed.

He rested a full day before his meeting at the designated bar. He had no idea he was followed. Tracked actually. She had the packet equipped with GPS, along with the cargo.

The instructions were clear: Leave the packet on the last seat by the exit away from the bar, The Bambu Bar. The sandy entrance was hot, the breeze slight. Sweat dripped from his brow as he ordered a Bali Hai beer. The 10 rupiah it cost was less than a dollar and less than he paid in his local taproom. The boys would stand him one for that!

As he stood to leave, he felt he weighed two hundred pounds. Sitting back down, he asked the boy waiter to call a Blue Bird taxi for him. By the time he was in his Nusa Dua room, he was feverish and had a headache. Thinking it was just the long flight, he lay down.

Just outside, Monkey Hill was thick with tourists and hawkers. Hats or monkey feet, massage or miso—you could have anything you want for a price. Balinese were friendly people. Clearly. Every face had a smile. Every comment was, "Hello," "Thank you," "Are you having a nice visit to Bali?" If you said no to a vendor, she said, "Thank you," and walked away. If you wanted a meal, the menu was clean, and the food was healthy.

The streets were crowded, even in winter. They were either broken up and repaved with cement or simply lumpy by its absence. You watched your steps carefully. Travelers came from Europe and Asia and Australia for the inexpensive fare and friendly attitude toward visitors. The island of one thousand temples was its own minor Garden of Eden.

The stench in Henry's room was palpable. The maid had run to her supervisor, who called the manager. When she saw the mess, she vomited. Henry had passed out in his own filth. Feces darkened his pants, as did urine. Blood seeped from his ears and eyeballs. Dead for a day in a room with little air and no AC, the body was bloated and covered with flies.

The young Ubud fellow opened the packet and assembled the small drone flyer. Twi had practiced with the previous one and knew he would have fun with this equipment. The commentary was simple—track the streets of Ubud for Google.

The young pilot-flyer was the next to be exposed as the little drone took off. He navigated the main street for two kilometers and then each of the three major side streets. The "video" was that, and more. Its GPS did indeed send images of the streets. Its small neighboring motor whirred as it deployed the viral pathogen evenly throughout the thirty-seven-minute flight.

Smallpox had been eradicated more than a decade ago. Only two depositories held any of the spores, and each maintained them in a Level

4 room. Each had a chemical signature for identification purposes. A variation of the Spanish Prisoner routine, this was to ensure that, if any escaped or was removed, its source could be deduced readily.

Now it was infecting an entire town and all of its visitors. Ubud's signature would prove to be from the Russian site, not the most secure prison in the world. Billions would be spent on trying to determine the how and the who for this horrific gambit—wasted resources spent for political gain.

Tracker's first use of CRISPR/Cas9 was just getting under way.

There were fewer than five hundred thousand smallpox vaccinations in the world today. Ubud would soon awaken the kraken. It would consume 110 million people over the following five months.

Again, the CDC would cash in on the beast's slow infection rate and slower death haul. They were still ahead of her game, even without knowing the rules or the players.

The attacks were growing in number, frequency, and effect.

CDC now knew the field—the entire planet.

The first to be overcome by the attacks were the health-care professionals. Few in number and quickly outnumbered by the pathogens, they fell where they worked within the massive influx of sick and dying. They themselves quickly became ill and died before the attacks could be vectored and controlled.

What beast, with the head of a lion, was treading through the desert to be born?

> To unleash something deadly, that could really happen any day now. The pragmatic people would just engineer drug-resistant anthrax or highly transmissible influenza. Some recipes are online.
>
> —Dr. George Church, synthetic biologist, Harvard

Something disturbed her. Somewhere she heard a cry. Was it a child? Was it her sister? Was it an animal?

Was she the hunted once again?

She had been tracked once by a wolf—for days. The wolf never gave up, dedicated to her death. The human had killed her pups, mercilessly. She had simply shot them one by one. She had the opportunity and took it. No regrets, no compunction, simply another set of kills.

Now the she-wolf was tracking her through the deep snows of Kazakhstan's Alma Alta range. She had been left to forage on her own—at her own request. This was as close as she could get to "real life." Despising cities and humanity, she sought design in the deep forests and the tundra of Central Asia. She had few provisions. That was part of the challenge. Survive on your own wits, your own knowledge. Deal or die.

The wolf tracked her for a week. It never relented, never gave up. It didn't stop to kill or rest or drink. It simply tracked her. She was forced into a dead-end canyon at fourteen thousand feet. No way out. The wolf was wiser, by far. It had her. The fight was vicious. Her knife against the wolf's fangs and claws. Both lost.

The human survived. The wolf died. But at what a price? She was maimed. Her left leg was mauled. Her face was nearly ripped off by a vicious, tearing tug that left her bleeding, almost blind from the hot liquid. Only a fatal stroke of the blade to the wolf's throat finished the fight.

She drank of the wolf's blood—in ritual as much as in feast. She splinted the leg, sewing the gash together and adding her own feces as a coagulant, knowing it could not poison in the intense cold. Her face had stopped bleeding in the extreme of -14 degrees Celsius. She sewed it in place, roughly. As she trudged through the snow, she knew the skin would rot upon defrosting, but it was a bandage for now.

It would be at least three days to the escarpment, two more days once she was down. The wolf would be her only food source, so she quickly gutted it and quartered out the meat. Two flanks, a small tenderloin, and the offal. Snow melted for water. Hard snow was for wounds. Two pieces of Siberian pine made a splint.

Dropping through the escarpment was the most painful experience in her life. It never stopped; the pain only got worse. The pain.

The drops were treacherous and steep, ending in hard painful thumps as she catapulted down the hardscape. She thought she broke her leg, three times. Only broken flesh and new blood. What animal was tracking her now, she wondered.

When they pulled her out, she was comatose, or nearly so. She grasped a chunk of the wolf's heart and sank her teeth into it—more out of triumph than hunger.

Six months later she had recovered—to a degree. Her face would never seem human again despite the best surgeons. It wasn't about vanity. It was about power. She was always the most powerful animal in her world. Never question that.

> The only way to get our society to truly change is to frighten people with the possibility of a catastrophe.
>
> —Daniel Botkin

She watched the diseases spread with growing interest. This "indoctrination" could prove far more successful than each of the others. It could also prove just as fruitless, despite the expense.

The Ubud release would result in its first illnesses twelve days later. Some 500 million had died from this monster over the centuries, 50 million during fall and winter 1918.

Once unleashed, a global epidemic could ensue in less than six weeks. Or inoculations could be rushed into manufacture. Perimeters could contain the spreading pox. Money and political power had great influence.

Tracker was convinced she had more money, more control, and deeper political pockets than all of the governments of the world. She was correct, again.

"We shall soon let loose the dogs of war."

This next round of attacks was more widespread. Several diseases were unleashed simultaneously in smaller countries:

smallpox
Crimean–Congo
Ebola
anthrax
Lassa

> The extinction of the human species may not only be inevitable but a good thing.
>
> —Christopher Manes, *Earth First!*

The recruits were lining up now. She had more than two hundred in place, and the dispersals were growing. The "enlistment" was straightforward—earn good money as an international courier. She paid them a comfortable retainer, enough to engage their greed without encouraging their mouthing off to friends and family.

She orchestrated the next releases—Lassa in southern Europe; Crimean–Congo fever across the African continent, the new Ebola strains in both continents. Coupled with the black pox and anthrax releases, these attacks blanketed the globe with death.

By the middle of July, Tracker had a team that was able to create a scalable and dispatchable aerosol of Zaire Ebola. This same laboratory team had genetically altered the Lassa virus for the European release experiment. The test cities were outside of Africa, just to tease the CDC veterans. London, Berlin, and Paris were infected.

Couriers dropped their shaped silicon Lassa/Ebola platelets, their silver bullets. Small rectangular shards of nearly invisible glass, these viral panes were stepped on across the Metros and sidewalks of the great cities by tens of thousands of commuter minions.

The MSP enhancements made the couriers' task readily acceptable. MSP enhanced their self-perception. It made them feel strong and willing to do as told. They had no fear, only joy. MSP was the ultimate drug of choice. Only these druggies would die very quickly indeed.

They were the indigent poor who were more than willing to walk a few kilometers for food for their families, dropping small sheets of glass as they walked.

Over two days, of an ambient population of these three cities of 28 million, 45 percent were infected. Of these, 15 million suffered and 8 million died. Density gradients, isolation, and strict adherence to CDC protocol reduced the regenerational factor to six over the infectious episode. By the end of winter, of the 520 million who suffered excruciatingly from the infection of black pox, anthrax, Marburg, C–C fever, Zaire Ebola, and the attenuated Lassa across the globe, 386 million had died. Much of England, Germany, and France were decimated. Most of central Africa simply ceased to exist as functioning political entities.

Airlines, ferries, trucks, trains, and cars spread the disease across several continents. These illnesses and deaths were diagnosed, and alarms were triggered to the CDCs of the world. Response teams mobilized globally, slowly at first and then with speed as the transmission rate became apparent.

Her membership seed companies also began sending subscribers regular supplies of tainted seed. The minions spread these across the fields of plenty, around the world. The death and destruction would follow during the summer months. When harvests would fail. Worldwide.

She helped the dispersal travelers get their new passports. She provided their tickets through one of the dozens of small companies she had formed around the world. Their instructions were clear. Travel to another country to deliver a package and then return home.

Each also dropped packages at post offices for later delivery to local residents. Twelve countries, agriculturally based, on five continents held deadly dietary pathogens that could remain stable for a century or more and then reemerge into the environment for yet another disaster.

These viruses had but one mission. Survive. Each accomplished this mission by propagation. Fewer than one in a billion of the biomes survived. Yet this survival rate was enormously successful.

Crimean–Congo hemorrhagic fever is an RNA-based, tick-born viral disease endemic across central Africa, the Middle East and Central Europe. The mortality rate can vary between 10 percent and 75 percent, dependent entirely upon timely diagnosis and treatment.

Like rabies, it can be handled easily—or it can be viciously fatal. A one- to three-day incubation period follows a tick bite. Flulike symptoms appear, which may resolve after one week. In up to 75 percent of cases, however, signs of hemorrhage appear within three to five days of the onset of illness.

First symptoms include mood instability, agitation, mental confusion, and throat petechiae. Soon thereafter, nosebleeds, vomiting, and black stools attack. Liver, kidneys and lungs soon become diseased. By the end of the second week, death results.

Vaccines are at best problematic. Deticking the body is the best solution. Once bitten, the host has a one chance in four of survival, at best.

The virus had been silated into viral glass for sustenance and transport. Her couriers continued to present these small irregular patches of clear sand to the corridors and paramours of small nation powers. As long as the population density was sufficient and the health-care facilities were nominal, the diseases spread easily. Their R factor was 8 in most cases. In some it exceeded 30. The release of infected ticks complimented her strategy and showed attention to detail.

Santiago del Compostela and Bilbao were the primary distribution cities in southern Europe. Population densities and absence of health care were each high. Susceptibility was significant. Before CDC could respond to yet another global health crisis, eight thousand were infected. With an average city R factor of 11 and four generations of diffusion, 115 million were infected. Of these, 35 million died.

Lassa is a viral hemorrhagic fever. It is spread via contact with rat feces and urine, usually from the common African rat, a food source across Africa. While only 20 percent of those infected die, if present in conjunction with Ebola, the kill rate climbs dramatically. And 80 percent rates can be verified during epidemics and pandemics.

Bats and bush meat are natural food sources and viral reservoirs for dissemination within the human populations of smaller midcontinental African nations.

African cultural funeral actions involve washing, touching, and kissing the corpse. These cultural artifacts lead to superspreaders. A witch doctor, a chief, or an important wife can spread the disease faster than the microbes can breed. In the tropical rain forests, these become vectors for transmission. Throwing a tubular cast becomes common—shitting out your entire rectum or intestinal lining. Death is gruesome, at best, for these "casters."

Procedures for viral hems include double gloves, surgical caps, and gowns; waterproof aprons; shoe covers; and protective eyewear. In addition, protocols call for containment of infected body parts and clothing in doubled airtight bags, disinfectant sponging, incineration, and minimal corpse contact.

These concepts are entirely alien to primitive cultures. Their introduction by the harried CDC teams was often viewed with suspicion. Fear worked its magic.

Ribavirin, fluid replacement, blood transfusion, and fighting hypotension are usually required to stem the disease onslaught. Absent these drugs, survival is difficult, at best. Perhaps two hundred out of a thousand survive, perhaps fewer.

Ebola kills within sixteen days. Death is painfully excruciating. Bodily fluid loss is a prime means of viral infusion to the ruminant population of humans and primates.

The terminal phase of Ebola is the "cytokine storm." The immune system begins attacking every organ in the body, bursting blood vessels and making the infected person bleed both internally and externally, through the eyes, vomit, and diarrhea. At the peak of infectiousness, Ebola virions pour out of the body. Death rates can exceed 90 percent. Health-care professionals are particularly at risk via direct contact with bodily fluids. Protective clothing and behavior are de rigueur. There is no vaccine. Oral rehydration is the best jungle solution. Outbreaks have decimated entire primate populations and human environs.

While the virus has never been shown to spread via aerosol means, bodily fluids—mucus, blood, semen, milk, and spittle are significant vectors of transmission. Cultural habits of death preparation can be fatal—washing, touching, fondling, and kissing a corpse are clear pathways to death.

Symptoms include physical exhaustion, weakness, decreased appetite, sore throat, and headache. High fever follows, with abdominal pain and diarrhea. External and internal bleeding occur within five to seven days. Bleeding can flow from the eyes or any bodily orifice. Of those infected, 25 to 90 percent die within sixteen days. Survivors will have antibodies for a decade, along with poor hearing, liver inflammation, joint pain, and weight loss.

Four of the five Ebola virus strains cause human infection, with the Zaire strain the most dangerous.

Tracker's labs had perfected the isolation of Zaire Ebola. CRISPR/Cas9 allowed the laboratorians to assemble crRNA into a functional genome. Their work made a particularly challenging task amenable to success.

RNA ligation and expression of viral proteins are no easy tasks, even for the most experienced laboratory technician. The science and art of constructing and expressing viruses in the laboratory is complex, at best.

This "science and art" are, nevertheless, quite widespread in today's laboratory tactician world, and so are no longer found in journals or publications today. They are "for hire."

Viral "helper proteins" are required. They have to be synthesized and introduced into a cell in the correct proportion. Few have the skill to build these proteins, but many in today's advanced biology departments can do so rather easily. The variola virus and most bacterial strains are withheld for obvious reasons.

The Ventor Institute first recreated the entire genome sequence of a bacterial genome in 2010. The process and its cost have become more accessible. The practice has become globalized, available via several internet-based firms with a shipping label and small postage.

Difficulties of retaining and transporting natural viruses have led to their in situ replication by skilled technicians. Tracker's labs had the capital and expertise to rapidly develop CRISPR strains more virulent than those found in the field.

By the middle of July, Tracker had a team that was able to create a scalable and dispatchable aerosol of Zaire Ebola. This same laboratory team had genetically altered the Lassa virus for the European release experiment.

Death By Design

> Isn't the only hope for the planet that the industrialized civilizations collapse? Isn't it our responsibility to bring that about?
>
> —Maurice Strong, founder IPCC

The storm was coming on faster now. Her intranet access to global communications networks in silencio gave her the perch from which to watch the horror, the horror.

Tracker now had control of the entire planet. She was directly responsible for entire nations failing, for the slowdown of most international transportation, for hundreds of millions of deaths.

Bujumbura, Khartoum, Johannesburg, and Ouagadougou were test sites, primarily because of local, clearly causative agents that could mask the true, original sourcing. While CDC sent teams to each location, and their procedures were followed as closely as possible, the diseases were rampant. Literally. They ramped up, dropped off, and then cascaded across the expected sine curve.

As many as twelve thousand infections were recorded by local and CDC authorities in each city, typically a smaller figure than actual infection rates. Given the lower densities of the cities, the R was less than 7. Nearly 1 million of the 1.5 million ultimately infected died.

Johannesburg was a surprising disappointment to Tracker. The KSA authorities responded rapidly, their CDC contacting the American CDC just as the first cases were observed. The center's new field devices allowed for diagnosis within four hours, beating the virus round the track and stopping it in its tracks. Fewer than 100,000 died.

Time was but one of Tracker's tools.

Greed was another. Money worked for her for a pittance. She staggered the releases of each disease as if she were a conductor leading the world's last orchestra. Her work was ethereal. Deadly beyond belief.

In Southeast Asia, 140 million more would die over the following four months.

She knew she was but one player in her greater design. Perhaps more than small; yet she had deeper expectations. She had been retained to complete a specific task. Anything less would mean failure—in her eyes. The instruments at her command were simple, ingenious, and deadly.

Hatred was her finest tool. Its sharp edge pointed her and kept her cold and razor-sharp. Rage was the engine. Rage kept her straight backed and focused. Rage offered her solace and strength. She had been savaged once by brutes in Berlin. She had savaged wild beasts with her own rage. Now she would savage the world.

These "plagues" were simply test runs of infectious diseases, carpeting a few cities to examine the consequences of their successes—and their failures.

The Black Plague followed closely in the footsteps of Lassa and Congo. Its 100 percent fatality rate was the criteria against which all other attacks were measured.

And she had not finished the opening sequence. Much was yet to come.

October was the time for hajj.

But first, the Marburg gambit.

ECDYSIS AND DISPERSAL

> We are on the verge of a global transformation. All we need is the right major crisis.
>
> —David Rockefeller, Club of Rome

August 30

Ubud had been ground zero for her smallpox attack. And now Aceh.

The fatality rate of Marburg, a rare form of filovirus, can reach 90 percent.

It is typically introduced via the African green monkey, a favorite meal for many in the Central African Highlands. Incubating for five to ten days, Marburg's symptom onset is sudden and includes fever, chills, headache, and myalgia. By the end of the first week, a maculopapular rash appears on the chest, back, and stomach.

Nausea, vomiting, chest pain, a sore throat, abdominal pain, and diarrhea may then occur. Symptoms become increasingly severe and can include jaundice, inflammation of the pancreas, severe weight loss, delirium, shock, liver failure, massive hemorrhaging, and multiorgan dysfunction.

Because many of the signs and symptoms of Marburg hemorrhagic fever are similar to those of other infectious diseases, such as malaria or typhoid fever, diagnosis of the disease can be difficult, particularly in areas with nominal diagnosis and treatment facilities.

Jim Spade had arrived in Balogun on the last Thursday of August on the direct flight from Jakarta. He was to work at the refinery as fireman, first class. His hotel room seemed humid, even though it was comfortable outside. He had felt odd on the flight. His throat was tight, and he coughed several times. He had contracted the virus on the previous flight from Houston. It was a turnaround from the Middle East. He would be dead in eight days, but not before infecting the entire Balogun refinery complex.

Andira was a father of four girls. His oldest, Yenni, had become a physician at the regional hospital in Indramayu, a pediatrician by training. When she was called in to the ward, her specialty was less important than the fact that she knew English.

"How do you feel, Mr. Spade?"

He coughed. The ward was warm but not hot, typical for a June afternoon. The rains would keep the area partially closed for days at a time. Flight delays and road washouts were common.

"Cold." He had two blankets over the sheet, which was wet with perspiration.

"When did you begin feeling poorly, Mr. Spade?"

The coughing was violent as he tried to speak. Yenni and the nurse were immediately exposed, even though they were wearing simple masks. Their hands and wrists were uncovered.

Spade couldn't get the words out. He wanted to tell them about the flight from Houston. He passed out with the paroxysms.

"Let's have an EKG to determine the health of his heart."

Four attendees to his care were exposed. Each returned home at the end of her shift.

Within a week, the entire refinery and parts of the city were showing symptoms of influenza. The deaths began a few days after Jim Spade passed away.

To Yenni's sorrow, the children were the first to go and then the grandparents. She was among these, as was the entire staff of the regional center.

The Pertamina refinery was closed by the Indonesian government, too late to prevent further diffusion of the virus. Nearby villages and towns quickly fell as lorry drivers and petro workers acted out the desires of the contagion. By mid-July, nearly half a million were infected. Fewer than 15 percent would survive.

Dhien returned to Jakarta. As head of the government mining ministry, she was proud of her work. Thousands of new jobs had been created in West Java under her sponsorship. She had recently been to the refinery to open the newest expansion and shake hands with several employees and their families.

Her lovely residence in the capital was clean and modern. The soft afternoon light aged her wrinkled skin. Her face appeared both full of light and marked by age. Her hands had a lovely brown texture, with fading gray spots. She wondered where the years had gone.

When she began the cough, she immediately went to her physician for help—and also to her *santet*. Her grandmother had clout in the "other world," and Dhien wanted to be protected from all evil powers. Sunya made the potion strong. Her physician gave her an antibiotic, which was worthless against a viral pathogen.

All three women died, as did the entire group of people whose work Sunya was protecting. This black magic proved too strong—this crow was death—even for her willful skills. Le'ak came out from the graveyard yet again. Fire, earth, and water were reversed. Jakarta became another locus of death.

The deaths were sporadic at first, following the transport systems of the great city. Small boats were the great culprits this time. They plied the waterways without interruption or examination. The humidity, the closeness, and the population density were all aggregators for the virus. It spread very quickly.

A new locus was forming. Marburg had just been presented to the world. In its infancy, it killed without discretion. Its emergence was simply the forbearer of the next progeny.

Tracker's teams had far worse in store for the world. This was yet another experiment—designed to prove a particular distribution method. Which one worked most efficiently was less important than that each one worked in unison.

Her infectious disease team watched and reported to her every day and then every twelve hours. She was as excited as she allowed herself to become. The disease had no cure. It has taken 80 percent of its few isolated victims in the past, under sparse distribution conditions. Now it was upon the denizens of an overcrowded urban jungle.

Perfect.

"We shall begin sending hourly reports as soon as we know they have some degree of accuracy."

"Get the bird over the equator by tomorrow."

"Its route is already programmed. We are executing now."

The calls to Astana, Kansas, and Belo Horizante were brief and to the point. Lombok and Marseilles were not involved—yet.

> Childbearing should be a punishable crime against society, unless the parents hold a government license. All potential parents should be required to use contraceptive chemicals, the government issuing antidotes to citizens chosen for childbearing.
>
> —David Brower, executive director Sierra Club

October 12

Dr. Sharon Blake, epidemiologist, geneticist, and pediatric oncologist stood in the anteroom. She had been raised in Seattle, where her blond hair and blue eyes were an anomaly; she was an oddity in the rain forests of northern Washington. Her interest in science was promoted when she met a friend of her mother's who was a research lab technician. "I want to be like her."

She had been recruited, after several refusals, to at least listen to an offer that could open her career to significant advancement. She didn't yet know that it would also allow her to research her deadliest nightmare—or to research the world's most deadly viral and bacterial attacks.

Her daughter, Sally, had a rare form of leukemia. Diseases of the bone marrow were infamously difficult to track, treat, or heal. Childhood onset was nearly certain death. Many sufferers simply endured a slow, agonizing life. Most suffered horribly. Fewer than 40 percent survived. Those who did waited in the dark for the return of their deadly companion.

Dr. Blake was being offered much more than a new position. She was to become the managing director of an entirely new firm with an annual nine-figure budget. It would have direct ties to the FDA fast-track authority—without a single purposeful solution on hand.

She only had to run the operation. She, however, only wished to seek and destroy her nemesis, leukemia.

T-cell-prolymphocytic leukemia (T-PLL) is the most deadly form of the disease. It almost always affects adults. Almost. Sally began showing signs of it at six. She was nearly seven now and had a prognosis of less than a year to live. T-PLL was the evil horror of Dr. Blake's life. She had no interest in anything that distracted her from her mission. Her mission was simple: Keep her child alive until she could find a solution.

The door opened. The executive director watched as Dr. Blake stepped across the dark wooden threshold.

"Welcome. Please have a seat wherever you'd like."

Several comfortable chairs surrounded the deep view of the bay through tinted windows.

"I prefer to stand. I doubt I shall be here long." Her answer was direct without being rude. She quickly established control of the meeting. "What you propose is intriguing, certainly. I cannot accept. Thank you."

Her gaze swept across the water long enough to show a telltale of curiosity. A new building partially obscured the view to the south.

"Perhaps you are correct. I have been wrong before. If so, I offer my apologies for taking valuable time from your research." He paused. "Perhaps, however, you would like to consider my deeper proposal …"

"Which is?"

"T-PLL research."

"Are you being rude by tempting me or simply ignorant?" She maintained control, despite her rising blood pressure. She suspected he could sense the slight flush to her face.

"Please forgive me, but I am neither rude nor ignorant."

"My turn to apologize." Her words were clipped, without emotion.

He had to match her to his strength; that he knew. She had too powerful an intellect and personality. She was not to be outwitted or indulged. He had already lost the opening gambit and was down a pawn after four moves.

"I—we—propose the directorship as an autonomous position. You will research what you chose. You will determine who works with you, what assays they move down, and how they progress. You alone will dictate every aspect of the firm's executive decisions. All other decisions will be delegated by you to whom you choose. Your contacts in the FDA already await your discretion.

"My role is to provide you with an infinite supply of something to which you have, at best, limited access—capital."

"Which always comes with a thicket of legal constraints. I doubt you can or should cut through such a morass." Her comment was the first sign that he had advanced a piece across the board. She had asked him a question—in her own manner.

"I—we—have established a charity in Switzerland, a stiftung. Its sole purpose it to discover a cure for leukemia, with a particular emphasis on T-PLL. It currently has more than $1 billion Swiss francs on deposit. The Swiss franc currently trades near par with the US dollar.

'You are to be nominated as 'participating director.' You will have all voting rights, excepting funding discovery. The other five members, while discreet, have asked my firm to suggest you as the best candidate for the position.

"Do you have any reason why I should not make such a suggestion?' He paused and gazed at the bridges crossing the Bay.

Her pause was conjunctive. "My passport has less than six months to expiration."

"I have a new Swiss passport for you here. Here is a packet already prepared for your US renewal, along with a GOES approval of course.

"Also, you will find the keys to your US-based research building—look, it's just there." He pointed to the south. "Obscurans" was titled across its leading arch.

"You will also find a directory of names you may find worthy of consideration for your lead teams. Of course, you have full discretion in building such a team, within the confines of the labor regulatory world.

"You will also discover a wide variety of communications and transportation devices at your immediate disposal. If I may suggest, my personal executive manager whom you just met outside has offered to interview with you as head of HR.

"If you decide to accept, your first trip to Geneva can occur at your best convenient time.

"By the way, Sally can be involved, should be involved, as quickly as she is psychologically prepared to do so. Her proximity is of both family and research value."

"What do you mean by 'funding discovery'?"

"Discovery of the other members as to their wealth and its sources."

"No other funding discoveries? No constraints upon funding discernments, dispersals, or deposits?"

"None."

"Keep your list. I know exactly who to invite."

"Of course."

"Mary Blakslee, isn't it? Your executive secretary?"

"Yes. She has been involved with our recruitment of you. She has a significant interest in your field. She prefers medical research to … human engineering."

He slipped it past her. She missed the cue. She was in; he knew.

"How much time do I have to decide?"

"None. If you are to move forward, you have no time. You are already late. T-PLL is far ahead of you, and you are losing ground. Unless you have something better—"

"Count me in."

"I did before you walked in the door."

Checkmate.

EARLY NOVEMBER; GENEVA, SWITZERLAND

Dr. Blake was in a hurry. She had been late dropping Sally off at school after the early morning visit to the physician. Traffic in Geneva was busy for a Thursday morning. The rain had continued throughout the night.

Her pace into the building was direct. People in the lobby knew to move aside. She was not actually unfriendly, just "absent from the present," as her sister had said.

The meeting opened just as she walked in to the comfortable conference room. Staggered seating ramped down a luxurious carpet to her lectern and board. Attendees included her entire staff and their assistants.

Dr. Blake began, "Alex Green developed the first freeze-dried RNA sensors for the Zika virus about five years ago. His work was well received, and he became known as the 'toehold switch pioneer.' We are attempting to do the same with a wider variety of viruses. Please share your progress today." Brief and to the point. The others knew how to respond.

Team leader Jefferson began, "The translation of the *lacZ* gene cleaves a yellow-colored chemical, chlorophenol red-β-D-galactopyranoside, to generate a purple-colored result, chlorophenol red. This technique allows for easy visualization of β-galactosidase expression and activity."

Jennifer Simmons, geneticist, took the lead. "Our team has immobilized and freeze-dried these toehold switches and the cell-free expression system that translates the toehold-encoded gene on paper. Freeze-drying the paper stabilizes the system, allowing it to be taken out of the lab and used in the field."

Jefferson added, "The toehold only allows expression of the reporter protein if there is a specific binding between the trigger and the toehold, making the test highly accurate.

"Amplification is the next step. Human RNA is amplified from a blood sample through a process called NASBA (nucleic acid sequence-based amplification). This method reverse transcribes DNA from the chosen virus RNA genome. RNA genomes from this DNA are built by in vitro transcription to generate enough virion RNA to trigger the toehold switch."

Dr. Holden, biochemist, held, "We have a simplified viral search tool that is easy to use in the field, can be read and understood by the least trained of health-care workers, and has a very high detection rate—in excess of 85 percent."

Dr. Blake asked the most difficult question. "When will we have enough to begin strategic stockpiling at CDC and WHO warehouses globally?"

"In six months, we shall have somewhat more than 100,000 units. That translates into more than 2,500 test units for each of the thirty-nine advance stockpiling locales around the world," said Jefferson in anticipation of the next question.

Jennifer and Jefferson each replied to her further questions.

"Shelf life?"

"Six to eight years if they are properly stored. While these are simply 'pieces of paper,' they do have to be held under temperature-controlled, well-ventilated conditions."

"They can also be held at more secure locales and shipped readily."

"No help to those suffering if the shipment is delayed by a fourteen-hour flight, Jennifer."

"Of course."

"Do we approval from the board to move forward?"

"Yes, certainly."

"Is CDC and WHO preparing to accept their samples? Do they have storage facilities being readied now?"

"CDC is ready. Our friends at WHO across the street are awaiting further review by the EC."

"Which has the best forward site locations for storage?"

"CDC."

"How will the delivery take place?"

"We ship to Atlanta, and they distribute."

"Are we both agreed upon protocol? Has delivery been arranged to CDC HQ?"

"Yes, to both questions."

The help they had designed for the CDC operations worldwide was incredible. They had done it in less than four months. She was very proud of her team's accomplishment, so far. This was her test case.

She wanted to observe their laboratory interactions, their cross functional scientific ties, and how they ate and dressed and talked and belched. She was very pleased. This was a team that could work together well. They weren't afraid to question one another, fully prepared to accept a challenge.

More needed to be done. Leukemia was in her sights.

Fifteen minutes later, they were in the laboratory central complex.

As usual, Blake began the discussion. "Let's move on to the interferon inhibitor issues. Frank, can you come in to the panel please?"

A well-kept, strongly masculine face appeared on the fifty-five-inch screen. "Yes, I'm here, Sharon." Frank Demeter was her lead investigator.

Simmons spoke. "Agents that interfere with cell wall synthesis, the b-lactams, are the most widely used class of antibiotics. The most important of these drugs have seen an expansion of their therapeutic utility by the addition of b-lactamase inhibitors to overcome hydrolysis, the major b-lactam-resistance mechanism in gram-negative bacteria. Interference with peptide synthesis on a molecular level has allowed us to develop b-lactam resistance in both gram-positive and gram-negative pathogenic bacteria."

Jennifer added, "The emergence of resistance over several decades as a result of both chromosomal and plasmid-encoded mechanisms imposes a severe limitation to health-care procedures. The simple acts of hand washing and instrument preparation have resulted in infectious contagions spreading through health-care facilities in the top hospitals in the world. Gly-resistance is at the heart of the problem.

Frank said, "We think b-lactams can suppress these peptides."

Dr. Blake asked, "What do b-lactams have to do with our interferon research?"

Jennifer replied, "Suppression is a two-way street. The opposite direction is infection, of course. If we develop the b-lactams to infect and if their infection rate is severe, then we can reduce the infectious rate in health-care units with the same tool that we are developing for blood work."

Dr. Blake raised her eyebrows. "You want us to infect patients with b-lactams? Not the best verb to use."

Jefferson answered, "We use human fecal matter to restore bacterial count in certain disease environments today. It is simply encapsulated and swallowed with a cup of water. The same concept may apply."

Dr. Blake jumped in, "Then let's change the phrase to 'support patients through a healthy infusion of b-lactams.'"

"I should have thought of that," Jefferson said. "Thank you."

"To continue," said Frank, "bacterial protein synthesis provides an attractive target for antibacterial drugs. New amino glycosides are microbiologically active against multidrug-resistant gram-negative bacteria. Developing agents that display activity against a single organism can follow the lead of the new *C. difficile*—the specific RNA polymerase inhibitor fidaxomicin.

"In short, recent developments in germ-resistant issues in health-care facilities are leading our research into tools for suppression of leukemia as well as serious bacteriologic infections in difficult field arenas."

Blake was pleased. They were approaching the problem from many different angles. "Let's review our new CRISPR/Cas9 work.

"As for our research into CRISPR, gene editing, we now know of several pathways—genetic engineering—that are multiplex. Rapid injection of edited cells back into the bloodstreams of research mice show which editions enhance acute leukemia infection.

"Activation of leukemia suppression genes follows in a reverse engineered cellular factory. These genes are then reinserted into the subject's bloodstream. The tracers for the disease are quickly eradicated. We have to assume that the gene receptors in the blood were changed radically. This change becomes hereditary."

Blake's heart was racing "How can we apply these results to our line of research?" Against her fear of failure, this novel approach offered her hope for her daughter.

"Cellectis, a French firm not far from Geneva, has had success with T cell editing using TALENs. The receptor gene was redesigned to discover leukemia cells, avoid bodily defense mechanisms, and survive long enough for new cells free from leukemia to replicate in the bone marrow."

"We have a contact at Novartis. Ask her for an introduction.

"The meeting is adjourned. Thomas, would you wait here please?"

CRISPR/CAS9

Thomas had her attention now and knew it. He was laconic yet focused.

As the others left, she closed the door and turned to her senior laboratorian. "And what about side effects? This gene editing can often result in unknown side effects."

He was prepared for her challenge. He enjoyed rising to her questions. As a postdoctoral member of the lab, he was the junior ranked scientist. He was also the most readily accessible and friendly.

With short red hair, a lanky frame, and the rare terse smile, he was also the brains behind much of what they were trying to accomplish. He had come highly recommended. His doctoral thesis at Oxford had been interrogated by two Nobel Prize winners. He'd responded with more questions for them then they'd had for him.

Gifted with the ability to listen, Thomas was the bright light in the lab. No one was there later or arrived before he did in the morning. He seemed to have no need for sleep. "Let's build the gene first. Anyone can start in this new field. CRISPR research is growing very rapidly. It is quickly becoming nearly 'off the shelf' in its availability of tools, technology, and base supplies. I know that four of our team members have previous CRISPR experience; they simple haven't been asked to bring it forward."

"We have computational predictive power—"

"Allow me to interrupt you. CPP is not what we need. Let's assume that every CRISPR event of gene editing will have some degree of negative effect. You used the phrase 'side effect,' but that is too limiting.

"Let's simply say that every event has several results. We simply wish to find the most useful ones relative to our search. We can examine tens of thousands of DNA sequences that have been edited with CRISPR and discard every one that does not meet our criteria. Or we can look only for the tiny few that actually survive.

"We know that even a 99.96 percent event results in some genetic modification at odds with predictions. We simply look for that oddity in the cultured cells. We assume ignorance until intelligence is proven."

"I appreciate your candor. Yes, if we can do the lab work based upon gleanings from our French colleagues, we may be able to find the low coefficient-engineered cells without actually seeking them out via CPP. Get started with your lab friends now. Have a report for me as to timeline, functional capabilities, and team IDs by tomorrow morning."

The tiny device in the ceiling was smaller than the head of a pencil yet recorded and broadcast everything in the room—each person's words, health, current condition, pulse, and consumption. The board member was in attendance from afar—actually just a few streets away. Gaunt had chosen him for his vicious anger, coupled with an uncanny ability to be brief in his words. He prepared the report and submitted it via the encrypted network. Tracker would see the details before the board. Her access intranet was universal.

There were no secrets at Obscurans.

MATTHEW

November 2

Delivery of the b-lactams to CDC was expected by the end of March. While insufficient to attack a real biological threat, they could defend and maintain core health-care personnel and systems for a few weeks. Dr. Blake's work depended upon these deliveries. Tracker's effectiveness at infiltration also depended upon them.

By November, CDC had received and stored its new weapons in the calculus of its viral war, this time against the CREs that infected hospitals from within. Apparently clean shelves, sinks, and clothing remained susceptible to the ever-evolving viral world.

Pathogens had had four billion years to perfect the process of change. They were good at it because this was their game. Change was what they did to succeed. At CDC, cool storage was at a premium. The cases of paper were sent down and logged in. When an outbreak occurred, they would now be ready ... or so they have been led to believe.

Another lab technician, Matthew, was struggling to make ends meet. He had a habit and had to subscribe to it. His monkey was their problem. Small in stature yet with a full voice, he had never been easy to ignore.

Yet he held himself in check, as instructed. He had developed a mousy exterior persona as the guise they'd indicated for him. He was to be quiet and unassuming, doing all he was told without question.

He also did what he was told by his handler, a short squat man from Syria. Matthew never disputed him, always did as told.

Now he had volunteered for the final preparation and packing of the new CDC shipment. Within the folds of each box, he had secured four small flexible panels. These were designed to break open when the boxes were opened.

The MERS (Middle East respiratory syndrome) would be unleashed on unsuspecting, very vulnerable CDC technicians in each of the sites where the shipments were destined. They in turn would share their viral attack sequence with associates as they prepared their new field ID process.

The field ID would work perfectly, of course.

So would the MERS.

THOMAS

November 14

Thomas worked until 2:00 a.m. He returned at ten after six, surprised to find Dr. Blake just going into the building. She acknowledged him, and he approached.

"Some further developments for the CRISPR/Cas9. Shall I go on?" he asked.

"When we get into the office, yes."

They emerged from the elevator together. He was too excited, he knew.

"Calm down. It can wait a few more minutes."

"Ma'am."

Once she had logged into her desktop and secured the offices, she said, "Go ahead."

"Last night I recalled that sarcomere transport is based upon microtubule kinesin behavior. The typical ATP/ADP function of cellular motility. If we were to key the phosphate ejection to blue light, we could conceivably control this motion. We could order the Golgi apparatus to eject comparable dynein mutations."

"Yes."

"Leukemia is driven by errant Golgi instructions. If we override these with light-emitted instructions, we can force the Golgi to evict the mutations. Like a library that sells off old books that are torn."

"Of course! Once these were removed, the cellular replication mechanism would no longer have these mutations built in to the units. But what about the genetic sequencing? Unless these are encoded at the molecular level with CRISPR/Cas9, we're right back where we started—a faulty cell."

"Not if we also clip the 'GA' sequence and insert a new construct."

"And how are we going to build this new construct?" She was forcing him to the wall, she knew.

"Actually, I built one last night. Well, I really built forty-five, one for each of the forty-five kinesins in the blood cell."

"Will the actin pathways also accept transcription?"

"I don't know why not …" He stumbled. He hadn't thought of this.

"Then we can rebuild both the roadway and the trucks."

"Yes, I see. We can design them to optimize performance beyond what evolution has done for us."

"Can we eliminate other dynein-based mutation sequencing? Respiratory? Heart? Nerve?"

How much time do I have?"

"A month."

Dr. Blake leaned back in her chair, her hands steepled carefully in her lap. The implications were huge. The cure would be within sight, and her daughter, who had been given a year to live, would make it through her childhood.

Her heart was racing. This young man may have just opened the door to the rest of her daughter's soon-to-be very long life.

The conversation was also recorded and forwarded to Tracker. She knew a genius when she heard one. She sent the record to her Brazilian factory.

CRISPR/Cas9 would be the foundation for the agricultural work. She had already seen it applied to the design of MII and the success of the viral panes. Could the nanos be so designed too?

LA RECONQUISTA

> A massive campaign must be launched to de-develop the United States. De-development means bringing our economic system into line with the realities of ecology and the world resource situation.
>
> —Paul Ehrlich, Stanford

October 4

Tracker had initiated the final testing sequence—in California, via an errant lab worker missing his family in Carmel on the Monterey Peninsula. He is about to infect the nation via the least of portals—Big Sur.

Shades of gray and brown covered the California desert landscape. The midmorning sun illuminated the eastern slopes covered in natural desert grasses. They slowly reclaimed the human wasteland. Shards of broken dreams littered the neglected, fallow fields.

Where water had once irrigated this desert into bloom, most farms were bankrupt. Water was the lifeblood of the California farmer. He pumped it from his deep aquifers. He drew it from his canal allocation. No longer. Mandates had been written. Regulators had reneged. Agreed upon leases, some more than a century old, had been withdrawn. The desert returned.

Reconquista.

Tumbleweeds desiccated the riverbanks. Deep-rooted mesquite drew from its own silent taps. The others survived upon the night's moisture alone. The lizards and snakes and weeds survived.

The horizon was tinged in dirt. The sky's blue was rusted and aged. No birds flew. Dust towers rose from the few tractors plowing their allotted acreage. Scattered plots of brownish green vines and almonds were watered by permit only. They stained the dirty desert with a last promise of food. These small acres appeared as cankers upon the semiarid landscape, soon to be wiped clean.

Signs ran down the freeway like tattered old Tom Waits Buicks. A child raised his palms upward in a shrug.

"Growing food is wasting water?"

"No water means higher food prices."

"Dams or trains—save our farmers."

"There are 1.5 million California workers in agriculture."

"Help us."

Their simple pleas highlighted their urgency. The clapboard signs decayed in the dry heat. Did their message, too, fall on fallow ground? Priuses raced up the road from LA to SF, drivers doing their makeup, earbuds in place.

The run over the dividing hills between the Central Valley and the coastal valley passed San Juan Reservoir. Half empty, its drawing towers rose from the dry bed like *Star Wars* toys ensnared in the sand.

Avenging angels, a few dozen wind turbines littered the crests with broken blades. A few spun aimlessly, uncounted, unconnected. The gearing of one had burst as it faced away from the wind, spinning haphazardly. In the pass, a few farms and cattle ranches survived. Their barns and sheds leaned away from the prevailing wind, decayed and drooping, dropping planks in slow, death throes. This once-thriving community clung to its last water allocations as supplicants begging for a few drops more. Ancient tractors driven by shriveled men worked dying fields.

Fence posts lay broken and tumbled. Their wire coils flung barbs at the sun. California's cold morning light desiccated the bone-dry farms. Pale blue skies chased the rain away beneath the brittle cold of this morning sun. All had turned to brown as the sun ruined the farms.

No relief.

No relief.

Crossing the dried western hills, Louise Edwards drove over the final, coastal range, Carmel her destination. A verdant green now brightened the sky. Here, pale blue was tinged aquamarine.

Equipment sprinkled the hills. Houses and barns stood tall, newly painted and fresh. Eucalyptus trees and palms guarded well kept-homesteads, oases in a sea of green crops. The last of the stately "tree stallions" were being put down, axed by time and disease.

Just plowed fields exhaled rich red soil, altering with luscious fields yet to ripen. Even fallow fields shared their water with all, as robins and hawks and acacia and peppers enjoyed the human bounty of water, pumped from deep below.

The differences between the two valleys was offensive. The Central Valley, for a century one of the major breadbaskets of the world, was now dry and dying. The western coastal valley was fecund.

While you couldn't deny the draught's power, you could fault the city folk for their water wasteful ways. Forty percent of the Sierra runoff is diverted for the environment. No desalination plants are planned for Northern California. Only one in San Diego makes a stab at the water crisis, after too many years and millions deferring to environmental defense lawyers.

Do not doubt the drought. It was taking its toll. It wrapped around the West like a dragon, sucking the life, the minerals, and the water from the land. Vineyards were dry brown. Oaks were cloaked in dust, a dirty, soiled shroud. Much of their leafy cover was dry, dead. Each tree withdrew support from the farthest leaves, retaining only enough moisture to survive. Would any survive? Or would they simply leave it to the seeds to carry on?

Louise had crossed the final line of hills, driving toward the Esalen Institute along the coastal highway. The afternoon sun threw long shadow tails from the ridgeline trees. Black tar repairs spread like rattan over a rough stretch of road convulsed in slo-mo chthonic exhalations of the living Earth.

The sea eroded the shore, leaving a dull drapery of rock and sandstone. The coastal corrugations repeated accordion-like along the entire coastline. Each town could be any other town up or down the line. She was almost home. Louise worked as a massage therapist at the institute. She would be greeted by friends, family. Her heart began to sing again.

Far out on the horizon, a yacht broad reached across the Western Sea, seeking her berth before sunset. An avid sailor all of her life, Louise breathed deeply in the joy of remembering the lift of the swell, the pull of the sail, the gentle urge of the hull toward home.

Sundowner breezes helped the vessel find her way through the wind lines. No one knew her real cargo. Her voyage nearly complete, the dark transit for her passengers had just begun.

Louise braked suddenly. An obstacle partially blocked the curve on Route 1, clearly a body. An arm reached out from the torn shirt as if begging—for death. She had no cell reception here but would in a few miles, once she arrived at the institute.

She got out of the car—and was overcome by the stench of death. Local condors were circling, eyeing the dead meat. A few brave raptors had already landed. Two danced away from her car. They eyed her as a threat. Of course. All humans were a threat.

Carrion was their banquet. They cleared the land for others. Giant raptors, they were the garbage haulers of the skies. She got as close as she could and pulled on the extended arm.

She nearly pulled it away from the body entirely. Louise wiped her hands in the road dust and then wiped the dust on her skirt and got back into the car.

The drive was just a few more minutes down the darkening road. Exhausted from the extended drive out of LA, she slowly maneuvered up the long entrance just as a group was leaving.

When she tumbled out of her vehicle, two men rushed forward to help her up. They walked across the grassy knoll entrance, holding her up by her bloused arms.

"Drunk?"

"Don't think so. She looks like someone I know … Of course. It's Louise Brady from LA. She's worked here for a decade."

"Good heavens, Louise. What happened?" The man wiped his soiled hand across his forehead and brow. The sweat ran down across his lips.

"I saw a man on the road ahead. He's dead. We must call the sheriff's office right away. I think he was very sick …" She collapsed again in shock.

They picked her up and carried her inside. Three women helped her to lie down on the comfortable sofa just inside the entrance of the institute. One woman retrieved a glass of water, another a pillow. They lifted her up slightly and nudged it beneath her.

"Jonas, call the sheriff."

"Already got him on 9-1-1. He's coming over now."

Louise rested her head on the pillow. Her eyes were open and focused. She knew these people, this place. She was safe. Her friend Karen sat on the sofa next to her and was washing her face with a cloth she had dipped in hot water.

"Can I have another warm water towel for her? She is shivering."

"It's the shock. Keep her covered until the sheriff arrives."

"Exhausted ... tired. Saw a man on the road, dead. Tried to move him; his arm kept getting longer. Thirsty."

"Why don't the rest of you go on your travels? We can take care of Louise now. Thank you."

Nine couples had just enjoyed a week of open consciousness amid new friends. Each couple was now traveling home, to their families, to their imminent deaths.

Three couples were from the Bay Area. The other six pairs were from Germany, Chile, India, Canada, New York, and Chicago. They were all planning to have dinner in the city. The long-distance travelers would spend one final day on Mt. Tam and then depart the following evening for their deadly destinations.

They had less than six weeks to live—they would become contagious in just seventy-two hours. Their clothing, shoes, underwear, and hats were even now becoming dangerous—very quickly. The risk was not in their breath. It was in their very touch.

Tracker knew the dead man. He had worked for the chimera team for three years. He'd recently expressed doubts as to the mission.

Several had expressed similar doubts over the past four years. Each had been given their final pay wired to their family's bank and enough time to gather belongings. Each had departed quietly, without excitement. Their MSPs worked well.

He was escorted to the perimeter, the entrance to the Gili caves—where he was hooded, as he'd expected. A ride to the main island would follow and then a short flight to Denpasar and a much longer one home.

What he didn't know was the hood was infected with inhalation anthrax. His flight home was the incubation period for the bacillus.

For him, it was time to prepare for reentering society. He had been away for more than three years. No contact had been permitted with the outside world.

For his pathogen guests, it was enough time to infect his lungs. When he arrived in San Francisco International Airport, he had been away for just twenty-two hours—away from the hood. He had another two days for the incubation time. He had suggested Carmel for his weeklong "adjustment period," as per contract. He had been dropped off at the Big Sur River Inn.

The room was reserved for a week. It had a kitchenette stocked with food. He had been instructed not to leave the room and to allow no one to enter. The inn had been well rewarded for its lack of service.

On his third day, he had cold symptoms, a sore throat and fever with aching muscles. The late morning found him with a slight cough. By evening, he was suffering from shortness of breath and severe fatigue. He awoke several times during the night with violent shaking chills. He vomited and nearly drowned in it.

He had to get out, take a walk, refresh himself. He knew the rules. No contact with others for ten days. He was sure the door was monitored. He had to get outside.

The evening passed quietly for everything on the road—except him. He coughed, vomited, collapsed, walked a few hundred feet farther, and then repeated his suffering.

He had walked along the quiet road for hours. A few passing cars slowed, but he waved them on, knowing the restrictions. By dawn he had collapsed down an arroyo. The cold ground and colder air were a relief from the turmoil inside his rapidly deteriorating body.

An hour of struggle brought him back to the darkened road. He had died just as he recovered the road. Her car was the last contact he would know.

RUNNING DOWN THE SWELL

> Complex technology of any sort is an assault on human dignity. It would be little short of disastrous for us to discover a source of clean, cheap, abundant energy, because of what we might do with it.
>
> —Amory Lovins, Rocky Mountain Institute

October 5th

The yacht had made Monterey Bay by 3:00 p.m. A good twelve to fifteen knots of following wind helped her into the small harbor during the late afternoon. The crew furrowed sail and found their assigned slip just before dusk. After they had cleaned the hull and cabins thoroughly, as per contract, a round of tequila made its way through the crew of four, happy to have found the coast, relieved to be at rest for the first time in three days. The going had been tough. Wind, fog, and rain had reduced visibility and lengthened sailing time—from six hours to three days.

Her instructions to the three-man crew were clear. She had them juiced up on MSP, so they were receptive and congenial to her absurd request.

Upon departure from the Monterey marina, they were to return to the city with the small box they would find in the reefer unit. They were to open it and dust the two trays with the small whisk broom. They were to drop the broom into the nearest trash bin.

They were free to go where they chose once they had checked in to the Holiday Inn at Fisherman's Warf and spent the night in their double suite.

The vessel would be picked up by its owner in a few days in perfect condition.

JAKE

The real enemy is humanity itself.
—Club of Rome, 1997

Community Hospital of Monterey Peninsula was the first to receive patients with severe respiratory problems. Louise was admitted and then a few Monterey citizens. The maid from the motel was too ill to work, so her daughter Yolanda covered for her. She cleaned the rooms, including room 204. Three days later, she and her mother were dropped off at the hospital. But the driver was as ill as they were. The admissions area was overcrowded with people with "the Asian flu." More than forty cars packed the small parking lot.

The small hospital had insufficient resources for such an outbreak. The head physician notified the Monterey County Public Health Service. They alerted the CDC in Atlanta.

Protocols were immediately informed, and two EIS teams flew to Monterey.

The Epidemic Intelligence Service, EIS, was a postgrad program established for and by health-care professionals, physicians, and veterinarians with an abiding interest in epidemiology. Every member was honored to be able to participate. Most went on to significant medical care roles in government, health care, or both.

"Got to get on the plane now, honey." Jackson—known affectionately to friends as Jake—took a final sip of her amazing black coffee that he never tired of and kissed her affectionately, passionately today.

He stepped out the door and was gone. Colonel Soliz showered and dressed in her fatigues. She was meeting with her commanding officer today. The CDC attack would be their only topic of discussion. Her interview of the surviving attacker had been brief but revealing. In a few minutes, they had developed their modus operandi and perp controller.

Jake and his OPSEC (Operational Security) agents made it to the airfield in twenty minutes. CDC's security personnel such as Jake's team had access to the air national guard base just outside of Atlanta. He and four teammates walked across the tarmac, made their way up the steps of the Learjet, and settled down for the five-hour flight.

"What's the prognosis now?" Dr. Matthews was small and quiet, but very much in control. She had boarded before the others. She hung up from the call with Dr. Mooney, CDC director, asking the question of the others.

"You tell us," Jake suggested. A tall broad-shouldered man with reddish hair and a military air, he was calm, methodical, and professional, the kind of person you wanted during a crisis.

"We have an outbreak in San Francisco, with another in Monterey, just a few hours away. Could be related or contiguous. We don't know."

Sam Potter was quiet, taciturn. With an angular walk, he was lean and gawky, looking like the proverbial science geek in high school. He had looked this way for forty years. Shy and internal, he could be obdurate and abrasive when making his case.

A good pathologist needs a fundamental humility, to be able to challenge any diagnosis, including his own. Sam had an inner stillness and the moral discipline to observe without jumping to irrelevant conclusion.

He spoke rarely, usually only when spoken to.

As they settled in for the long flight, they all knew the protocol. They knew their tasks. They knew one another's strengths and weaknesses. They were a team like any other.

Dr. Matthews continued. "The public assumes bioweapons development and transfer are easy and cheap, that expertise is easily acquired, and that new technologies reduce barriers to success.

"The fact is weapons cannot be simply a sum of their parts. Bioweapons do not scale up easily. This is not a linear process. It requires interdisciplinary teams with a wide skill set, variations that are carefully and continuingly integrated and acted upon in coordination."

"The perps always leave trails," offered Jake. "They have no intention of keeping a secret. They want to be known. The media is their thrill."

Dr. Matthews said, "Even the best bioteams need to have explicit, tacit, and communal knowledge. Of these, tacit decays with time. It is experientially based. It must be constantly renewed, like a library book. Converting a biological specimen into a bioweapon also requires the other two disciplinary approaches—communal knowledge, explicit knowledge. Laboratory success does not imply field success."

"We always find markers," said Jake.

"You refer to pathogenic markers." Sam actually was participating in the conversation, a first.

Dr. Matthews resumed her dialogue. "Yes, certainly. But I also mean personnel markers. The way something is performed, the skill or absence of it in the cultivation and release of pathogens. These are their explicit markers, their own knowledge sets.

"Virtually every threat event we have worked on has had the imprint of an individual with known skills—and a pathological hatred of humans. Our challenge has been to ID an emergent phenomenon, out of the darkness. Find the agent, and you find the perp."

Dr. Matthews was well ahead of this pack of dogs now. "If these attacks are consequential, we have a significant level of scientific, organizational, and experiential skills. These deep organizational and managerial skills need interactions that engender knowledge development and sustainability—absorptive, organizational, and managerial design." She was confident but always ready to question her own assumptions.

"The simple change in water pH or change in suppliers can affect outcomes. Scientific knowledge is local, specific, private, and does not have to be cumulative. There is no 'perfect scientific language.'"

"What do we know now?" Jake said, ever the bloodhound. The science was interesting, but he needed facts to fight. He knew when they landed it would be too late for discussions.

"Seventeen admissions to Monterey health-care facilities with flulike symptoms. A dead man on the Carmel coast near Esalen. New admissions every hour in San Francisco hospitals."

"If we find the bug, we can ident it. Then we find the perp."

"Could be anything."

Sam shook his head. "Inhalation anthrax."

"Sam, how do you know this?"

"Just sense it."

Dr. Matthews was shocked into saying, "Get me through to Dr. Mooney."

> Bacteria have a memory. They're carrying about pieces of their evolutionary history in unexpected forms, waiting to be expressed".
>
> Joshua Lederberg, <u>Emerging Epidemics</u>

Outbreak

October 6

Upon arrival, the NCEZID team was driven to San Francisco General Hospital. The entrance was awash in lights and people, the ill and the media. Most were struggling to get in. A few were lying on the pavement, ill or comatose. Inhalation anthrax was emerging like an alien beast upon a foreign shore.

The CDC crew's gear took twenty minutes to put on and the help of at least one other team member. The zippers were military grade; they peeled outward, preventing any contact with inner surfaces. The HEPA internal cooling system channels aired to the headgear, allowing the brain to work reasonably well even in dangerous environments—like in infected villages or on bodies oozing with virions.

The team was surprised by the chaos. This was unlike a typical outbreak event in the industrial world. It more resembled events in the Congo or Guatemala. No one seemed to be in charge. The head count was extreme and growing.

"This doesn't feel right," This from Sam.

They both knew chaos was coming to these bloody streets. Soon. Very soon.

They moved forward in their space suits, as people grudgingly moved aside, pleading for help as they fell over one another. Shouts of fear and hysteria plagued the hallways as the team tried to find someone in authority. The ER was a disaster zone. Dead and dying lay everywhere. Nurses were stepping over the ill and dead.

"This is bad. Very bad," Sam Potter said.

The team knew he was understating the situation. Enormously.

DAY TWO

Six hundred and seventy cases at SF General, forced the CDC to respond with a second Epidemic Intelligence Service team, en route to SFO by daybreak, arriving just before 11:00 a.m. on day two.

NCEZID had the local team analyzing early that afternoon. AMD (advanced molecular detection) tools were quickly deployed. There were 154 of these teams in place around the country. Their bioinformatics approach can lead to rapid identification of disease. Nanopore sequencers were in the field with Jake and his team. Genomics research expanded CDC's capabilities with advanced sequencing technologies unknown just a decade ago. But could these tools keep pace with the attacks?

The second team was sent to Community Hospital on the Monterey Peninsula. This was the first of many tactical errors made by the CDC director. She correctly assumed patient zero was in Carmel. This threw her off the track just long enough—the track that lead to Monterey Bay, to a small yacht, to the infected crew burdening San Francisco. The body count at SFG was a false positive that divided her teams too quickly. Both teams missed the chimera attack. Tracker had led them to inhalation anthrax purposefully. She had drawn them away from the real killer.

The Monterey team found chaos on the hospital grounds even before they entered. Cars were parked across the entrance. People were shouting, some were sobbing, and many more were just coughing. Without hesitation and without donning protective gear, the team leader entered the hospital building, leaving the remaining seven team members outside to suit up. He never came out alive. Nor would any of the thirty occupants or any of the health-care staff of fifty-four.

There were more cases than beds or health-care professionals. Monterey County had asked for volunteers the night before. A dozen arrived once their own shifts were over in Salinas. Another six were assigned from the administration as working nurses. The assumption was a new strain in influenza, and, thus, antiviral treatment was prescribed.

The treatment had no impact on the bacillus. This was another tactical error. Penicillin would have worked wonders at this stage of the outbreak. No effort was made to restrict contact between infected and family.

Everyone who would accept the antiviral shot was inoculated. More than a few refused. By the evening of day two, there were more than three hundred cases of "Monterey flu," as it was named by the media.

Yet more arrived. Yolanda's family had been to church for Assumption Day Mass. More than sixty worshippers were in attendance. Forty-two sickened.

In the city, conditions were initially better. By the time the EIS team arrived about noon, 1,712 cases of the Monterey flu had been admitted. They began their sampling and ident. By the evening, they had 3,243 more cases.

Previous protocol indicating a derived algorithm with three predictor variables (a chest radiograph finding of mediastinal widening, altered mental status, and an elevated hematocrit) was 98 percent predictive. It would have taken two days of testing.

By one that afternoon, AMD had its ID—inhalation anthrax. In both cities. Now in seven hospitals. Within twenty-four hours, 7,500 cases were reported across the Bay Area. Jake's team was down before the end of the first quarter—by a thousand TDs.

By then, Medusa was just rearing its second horrible head.

The EIS team missed the second delivery system and its effects for eight more days. Tracker's team had enabled the bacillus with a virus of its own design.

The events of late fall 2001 defined the actions of the EIS teams. That anthrax attack took five lives and caused billions in capital lost on preventive measures that detected no other bacteria. No one had attacked with anthrax since that date.

Until last week. September 27.

A chimeric attack was spreading the diseases rapidly.

No one yet knew of the Esalen fliers.

No one yet knew of the whisk broom and the small box at Union Square.

There were more patients in Monterey than there were beds—or attendants or physicians or nurses. The overload was being handled by surrounding care centers, which only spread the disease. The vector was contact—contact with clothing, bandages, shoes, bags, and purses. Each of these was a transmitter of the tiny pathogen, a mere 5 microns in diameter. Inhalation anthrax was the deadliest form of the bacillus—and it was spreading quickly.

In the city, cases spread far more quickly with urban density. Marin County had just reported its first cases from Tamalpais Valley. Three hikers had come down with flulike symptoms; they'd been given antibiotics and sent home to rest. Bad case response.

Jake was working on an autopsy. He was speaking with the nurse assisting him and the PA. "The 'secret sauce' in the basic mathematical formula for modeling infectious disease epidemics is population density. Density multiplies the effects of the disease exponentially as it increases. The greater the density of urban life, the higher the infectious rate increases. This is not a one for one increase; it is a multiple of this. Above three to one, and the disease begins to find significant tissue culture for feeding. At eight to one or ten to one, the disease becomes epidemic in proportion. Every sick person infects eight or ten others, who repeat the process."

They nodded behind their suits, sweating in the circulating air within their own private containment zones. Each was frightened but remained professional.

"What shall we do with these specimens, doctor?" The nurse was slight, Asian and very efficient. She had isolated a tiny portion of each body's remains and isolated it into small tubes. She'd then encapsulated these plastic vials into another larger glass vial and placed them into the cryo containers.

"Do you have zero storage?"

"Yes."

"Send them there with instruction for delivery to your AMD team ASAP."

"Jake."

"Sam, we have to move these out to the AMD labs. Ident someone here as an escort."

"They are treating this with flu shots. Ridiculous."

"Agreed. The anthrax is ignoring the response and eating its way through the local population. More quickly with each passing hour. Time has become our newest enemy."

"Sam, get this out to the teams now and to Atlanta. We need serum. Now."

"Done."

Yet another head was lifting into the chaos—CRE (carbapenem-resistant Enterobacteriaceae). In the ensuing chaos, it was completely ignored. Although the disease was increasingly prevalent in hospitals, today it got a pass, as the bacillus became the focal point.

Dr. Blake's team development would have its first trial by fire—except the team's pallets were already infected and the new disease would attack upon release of the solution. One small step for Tracker.

Urban San Francisco was a good locale for epidemic multiplicity, although far from the best. While not as thickly populated as many other cities, it would do for Tracker.

Four hours later, the CDC labs had confirmed the field diagnosis. Inhalation anthrax had been let loose upon the world.

One America burdens the earth much more than twenty Bangladeshis".
The spirit of our planet is stirring!
The Consciousness of Goddess Earth
is now rising against all odds,
in spite of millennia of suppression,
repression and oppression inflicted on Her
by a hubristic and misguided humanity.

- Envision Earth

Call to Arms

November 12

Tracker was orchestrating the entire process. Her intranet followed each outbreak, listening to media and government channels. She heard in real time the emergency responders, the hospitals, and every government agency. Tracker had set in motion the first steps of an international campaign.

Death by design.

More was on the way—much more. They had no idea.

The CDC lead investigator, Dr. Matthews, spoke to the assembled emergency response group for the City of San Francisco. A tall, thin, and angular athlete, she was precise, almost cold in her description. Her blue eyes were hard, merciless. She had thinning red hair and a Scandinavian face, and she was very straightforward. You could not ignore her—or her opinion.

Her pale green military blouse had silver oak leaves. She wore her position with quiet authority. The conference room in San Francisco was bright, with color-striated walls. In the tightly packed room were the major, police chief, and city supervisors, as well as the National Guard commander.

"We have a serious outbreak of inhalation anthrax—several outbreaks actually. Our secondary team was dispatched to Monterey upon arrival from Atlanta on the twenty-eighth. This is our only break to date, as the CDC attack was yesterday, as ya'll know."

They all nodded their heads in sympathy. The news from the CDC headquarters in Atlanta was sickening. Those killed in the initial attacks were being joined by hundreds of others dying of radiation poisoning. Now the West Coast was under attack. By what? Whom? Why? There was no telltale commentary from the mad instigator. No master of evil to tell them why. Just a silent dog.

Matthews continued, "My mistake was in assuming it was the primary locus. Now we see that the city is primary, or so we think.

"We have protocol to follow and must do so immediately. Time is our enemy now. Setting up a perimeter is the first defense. No one within the boundary will be allowed to leave until inoculated. A second perimeter will be set up, a second defensive ring with the same guidelines.

"Once these cordons sanitaires are in place, the virus should run its course and die out.

"Given the time the disease has had to spread, we are very far off the mark. We doubt isolation will work before societal breakdowns threaten the entire state. We do know we must act very quickly."

She paused for the effect to work into everyone, but the silence prompted her to move on. The audience seemed stillborn in terror. No one knew how to respond to the attack. So she continued, "All contact surfaces should be decontaminated with soap and water. Boiling any clothing for thirty minutes is an effective decontaminate. It's not a difficult task, but it's time consuming. We shall need the cooperation of every citizen, every family member, and every neighbor.

"That will be difficult if we do not clearly communicate the danger to everyone of any lack of cooperation. We are past choices. We must act decisively and rapidly. Freedoms will be curtailed very soon, or death is a guarantee.

"Anthrax is not transmittable once patients are decontaminated. The time between ident and decontamination is critical. Those with it would be given a quinolone such as ciprofloxacin, erythromycin or penicillin, and a meropenem plus linezolid for two to three weeks. Treatment timing is critical to success. If delayed, fatality is as high as 85 percent."

"Where are the inoculations?"

"Who is trained to give them?"

"Do we need special equipment to handle the surge in patients?"

The questions were fast and furious.

"Two hundred thousand inoculations have been requisitioned from the federal stockpile. They are at the National Guard armory here in the city now. Each of you will be among the first to be inoculated.

"Using a needle for inoculation is part of every health-care professional's training. Care for the infected is simpler, but requires complete destruction of all clothing, accessories, etcetera of the patient and a thorough washing of the body with disinfectant.

"Chief Sullivan, your forces need to begin the quarantine process immediately. Close down all access to the city. No one enters or leaves San Francisco. Monterey has already been locked down, as I am told."

"That's impossible."

"Shut down BART now. Blockade every road and freeway. Close SFO. Close the bridges. The longer we discuss this, the greater the locus of attack. This bacillus is a week ahead of us. Our only choice now is to act fast, with authority."

"That's the problem. I have no authority to do any of these stoppages. The people at work have to go home; the unions will object. What about the health-care workers' time off?"

"They will have plenty of time off in hell," deadpanned Matthews.

A supervisor spoke up. "We have our Gay Pride parade this weekend. It is one of the biggest events in the city. Thousands are coming in even now. What do we do about the parade?"

"Cancel it immediately. Shut down the airport, roads, and bridges now."

"You can't tell us how to run the city," said another council member. "We are the elected representatives of a free people—"

"Who will all die within three weeks if you do not respond now."

"Ma'am." The guard commandant handed her the phone speaker box.

"Can everyone hear me?"

Each person knew the voice. Most hated him, wary of his threats, his tweets.

"Dr. Mooney has my unqualified support. You will do as she instructs. Please do so in as efficient a manner as possible and as best you can muster from each of your professionals.

"I have ordered martial law for the counties of San Francisco, Marin, and Contra Costa. This will be expanded as necessary. The governor has come on board as of a few minutes ago. He and I are prepared to shut down the state tomorrow if necessary.

"You have no time to lose. You are a week off the mark now. I have spoken with the CEOs of sixteen corporations in the Bay Area, and each has offered unqualified support for your actions. We have six pharmaceuticals committed to rebuilding our stockpile of vaccinations. They will begin delivering within five weeks, but we will run out well before then.

"Your actions now will determine the outcome of this attack. Make no mistake; this was an attack. We do know some of the perpetrators and are responding. We continue to seek out those who would destroy us.

'You should be leaving the room as soon as I hang up. Commander Nelson has orders for each of you. He also has vaccinations for you and your support staff. You will take these before you exit the building. His troops are being inoculated now.

"This is not about politics. This is above politics. We have to rise to this challenge to save your city and our nation. I ask that you refrain from political commentary of any sort until this crisis is behind us. You can then blame me for everything. But for now, everyone involved must present a united front. Please. I ask you as citizens of a great land.

"Thank you for your willing support. The nation depends upon your work today and over the next several weeks. This attack will get much worse before we stem the tide. Many of you will die. Many of your family members, neighbors, and friends will die. You are our new martyrs. You will not die in infamy. We will seek out and destroy this enemy."

The line went dead. The air left the room as if it had been exhaled. No one said a word.

The guard commander finally spoke. "Ladies and gentlemen, the staff outside will inoculate you as you leave. The entire building is under quarantine until everyone here is inoculated. This will take at least two hours. In the meantime, please get on the horn to your people and begin the lockdown. Inoculations are readied for all police and community leaders.

"The media is waiting for a call from this room. Dr. Mooney is ready to speak with them via their conference call. When I open the line, each of you has to be on board. Dissent is no longer an option. You have five minutes to discuss and agree."

The room was silent. No one had the courage to agree or to say no. Each was fearful for family and friends. Each looked down, lost in a frightened rictus.

Finally, the eldest woman in the room said, "I'm ready. Are you?" She looked at each of the fourteen others.

They silently nodded their heads in slow, almost imperceptible agreement.

"Let's make the call, Commander," said Dr. Mooney. "We have already lost a week of time."

No one yet understood that eighteen individuals had departed Esalen on the day patient zero died. No one had yet found the small box in Union Square.

Protocol was established and followed. The first interviews were with the local health-care workers, allowing the bacteria yet more hours of lead time. Inoculations took more than three hours for the urban leadership.

Quarantines were established at each bridge and highway by inoculated police officers. All port facilities were closed down. All military personnel at surrounding bases were put on alert and given inoculations.

CONTAGION

A virus like a river, with strains as rapids, across rocks of natural selection; it flows while it changes and adapts.

—Richard Preston

Six travelers from the Bay Area and twelve others from Germany, Chile, India, Canada, New York, and Chicago were spreading disease as they sat on their porches, on airline seats, in cabs, and in subways. Coats were put on and taken off. Purses were opened and put aside. Clothing was changed and cleaned. Doorknobs were turned. Elevator buttons were pushed. Children were hugged and kissed, as were mothers, fathers, sons, and daughters.

Inhalation anthrax spread across three continents in less than seventy-two hours. Symptoms began to appear in four days; severe illnesses began in six days. Deaths came in ten days.

The worst was yet to come. Hydra was lifting her many heads.

The city police, county sheriffs, and highway patrol closed down the roads and freeways without much difficulty. SFO was quick to shut down. BART was a problem. The union leadership wanted to know why, they wanted to know more, and they wanted to be part of the decision making. When the guard commander spoke to the union leadership, the anger was palpable. Colonel Nelson was polite but firm.

"Either you stop the trains now, or we arrest each of you. Then we will inoculate each of you and hold you in quarantine for two weeks. If you stop the trains, we will still inoculate you and all of the workers who have been on duty over the past week. You will not be arrested or quarantined. Your call. Now, people. You have exactly one minute."

They shut down BART.

"WE DON'T HAVE THE LUXURY OF MERCY"

Day Nine

The fighting was fierce. The initial bacillus attack had a significant lead time. Hospitals across the Bay Area had thousands of calls on the Monterey flu symptoms. Emergency rooms were full. Coopting health-care workers and EMT workers in a surge-capacity strategy was helpful, to a degree. All medical personnel gave of their time and skill—and blood. Most died during the first weeks of the twin onslaught. Few knew how to fight the dual viral/bacterial assault.

Cars lined the streets to the hospitals. Fights broke out. Training had been very good for health-care workers, and they responded in spades. Their efforts saved thousands of lives. Yet their efforts were inequitable against the unleashed Hydra. Many would die in their efforts to protect.

Six thousand were now infected, just in the city. Stopping the loci from expanding was the primary duty of the health-care workers. Monterey was shut down easily. It had only one major road in and out, with four secondary roads, a small airport, and an even smaller harbor. This was also the worst of the attack sites, with every health-care worker now infected.

Treatments were rushed down by helo to the small hospitals and dispensed as quickly as received. Marin County incidents were growing slowly. It was a difficult county to shut down, as it had so many travel interstices. Fortunately, the spread of the disease across the Bay Area was hampered by the lower density and higher responsiveness of the population.

Inoculations for the uninfected were slower to arrive to every suburban location, as the city had a far greater need.

"We don't have the luxury of mercy." Jake was clear and without emotion.

The slogan began appearing surreptitiously and then spread as quickly as the disease. Parents and friends and family members who refused inoculation were quarantined as quickly as their refusal was noted. All were barricaded. Virtually all died.

"We don't have the luxury of mercy."

The isolation work of quarantining a million or more people was difficult and dangerous. There is always someone who thinks they can outwit a bacillus—or the cops. Four cases appeared in Salinas on the ninth day. By then, the quarantine process was better understood—by the police who were imposing and enforcing it and by the populace. Just as with plane crashes, the vast majority of the population cooperated. This, in itself, was a dagger blow to the disease.

"Sam, how many more anthrax inoculations do we have remaining?" asked Jake in the Oakland General Hospital about 2:00 a.m. They had been on duty for four days, sleeping when and where they could. The halls were crowding with more of the sick. The dead.

"We will have less than four hundred after this round. We have six hundred double tips left. There are more than two hundred people already inside. I have no idea how many more are in the street."

Sam was as exhausted as Jake. Yet they both carried on without a concern for their own health. They were inoculated, certainly; but their stamina and coffee would carry them only so far.

Contra Costa County had 475 cases on the ninth day. By day ten, 3,000 were ill in Marin County, and more than a thousand across the Bay in Contra Costa—and every one of the health-care workers was exposed. The bacillus was far in front of the defenders and moving quickly.

Vaccines for California were depleted by the eleventh day. More than half of the federal supply had been set aside for the military, safety officers, and political leaders and families. The vaccine was useless once you contracted the disease, so it had to be used sparingly, ahead of the threat vector. This was nearly impossible, as the disease jumped cordons, showed up far from the locus, and grew exponentially in urban areas.

FEAR AND LOATHING

The gutted CDC headquarters in Atlanta began to get calls from New York and Chicago at the same time the president was speaking with the gathering in San Francisco. Desperately, remaining EIS teams were quickly dispatched.

The president was prepared to speak to each city's government groups within the hour. He hoped they had a better lead time with these cities. Quarantine could be far more effective with efficient local leadership. Members of Congress from both states were in his office as he prepared to speak.

"You have a decision to make. You can politicize this. Thousands, perhaps millions, will die as you do. Or you can work with the CDC and the administration to close this thing down in your two cities now. New York and Chicago are in the first stages of a bacterial attack. We need to respond yesterday. It is your choice as to whether this is politicized—or not."

They had seen the hasty press conference from San Francisco. Governor Brown of California urged complete support for the local and federal response teams. Images from Monterey had been on the screen for an hour.

He had no expertise in health care. He was a builder. He knew concrete and plaster and framing and steel. He could cajole and discuss and dispute. Pathogens were beyond him, completely beyond any of them. Out of his depth, he had to bluster his way through much of this—as did the other politicians. No one had prepared for disasters of this dimension.

If only they knew.

"You have our support during the crisis. We shall see about where we go once this is over. I think we are all in agreement today. Mr. President." The minority leader of the Senate was no friend.

"My people in San Francisco are dying. My family is dying. We are one people during this crisis, Mr. President." The House majority leader was from the city. She knew her staff there was dying, now. They were trustworthy Americans.

"Thank you. Are you all in agreement today and for the duration of this struggle that we work as one team?"

The group nodded as one. Everyone was scared today.

The first international calls came in from Canada and then Germany. Chile and India never reported an incident—their deadly error. The president took the Canadian and German prime ministers' calls directly, as he had been told to expect more outbreaks with time.

"Shut down your borders, your transportation, all roads. Isolation is your first best response. You have to try to get ahead of this monster. We are still far behind here in America. We are currently losing the battle."

"Please. Please." The voice on the other end of the line was clearly desperate.

But it was desperate for him too.

"We cannot release them. We cannot release all vaccines, as we only have a few hundred thousand. But the United Kingdom and the Russian Republic have significant stockpiles. I have spoken to the prime ministers already, and they stand ready to ship half of their units to you today. They will maintain the other half for their own needs." The Canadian PM was desperate. He had never had to face such a national emergency. No one had.

"You must speak with your pharmaceutical suppliers as soon as we are finished. We have health-care professionals ready to administer these within the cordon sanitaires as quickly as they arrive. We also need a significant supply of two-prong needles.

"Contact your local suppliers now. Have them ready to ship within a day. Distribution should be by your military and public safety officials. They must be inoculated first. Backup will need to be resupplied immediately. Set up conference calls with your own pharmaceuticals. Urge them to initiate massive production.

"Remove regulatory constraints. You have already lost time and will lose more as you move forward. This is jumping our quarantines and your borders."

"But we have so many suffering—"

"As do we all. Take a breath, step back, walk with your advisors, and find your own solutions. We will help as we can, but our national priority is our own safety—our survival as a nation.

"You must quarantine, disinfect, and inoculate quickly. You must set up two quarantine sectors, one just beyond the first. If you have the manpower, interviews of everyone in contact with each infected person should run as soon as possible. Each of these people must be contacted, interviewed, and quarantined as necessary.

"We should each go on the media at precisely the same time and say precisely the same words. I suggest in one hour. We are sending you over my script now."

Concurrence was quick. A conference call was set up by his office before the end of this call, and he suggested, "Let's get back on the line with Prime Ministers May and Putin now. They are waiting for us."

"We have loaded one million vaccines at Heathrow and the planes are cleared for takeoff. I suggest we send it to Canada."

"We have two million doses on four Aeroflot flights ready to take off for Berlin now."

"ETA for Montreal is 0612."

"It is 2215 for Berlin."

"Berlin, Montreal, you have your work cut out for you. Contact your pharmas now for production runs. I suggest we hang up and get on with it."

Twelve minutes later

The call from the California governor was desperate. "We are losing the Bay Area. We have infections reported now across the state. Arizona, Nevada, and Oregon have reported the first infections. What are we going to do?"

"Follow our lead. Shut down your borders as best you can. I know it is virtually impossible, but you can stem much of the expected exodus. I am imposing martial law, with your support, in California now."

"Yes, of course."

"We need you to show confidence. The people will break and run at the first indication of chaos. We must instill confidence, even if it is a ruse. We have to have the full cooperation of the public.

"I have ordered the emergency broadcasting system to take effect. No commercial broadcasts for ten days. The internet has been closeted by the military. Don't ask me how. You and I must have a joint session with select reporters from a few media sources.

"We can do this entirely by conference call, but we must have their full participation. I have the individuals in the small Jefferson room now. Can you be ready in an hour?"

"Yes, of course."

"We have six stockpiles of emergency medical equipment around the country. One is in the Bay Area. The local EIS coordinator will be on the line once we are done. Do what he says without question. Time is not on our side. Do you understand?"

"Yes, of course."

"I am empowering the Secretary of Homeland Security to coordinate protection activities for each of the following critical infrastructure sectors—information technology; telecommunications; chemical; transportation systems, including mass transit, aviation, maritime, ground/surface, and rail and pipeline systems; emergency services; and postal and shipping.

"DHS will coordinate with appropriate departments and agencies to ensure the protection of other key resources, including dams, government facilities, and commercial facilities. In addition, in its role as overall cross sector coordinator, the department shall also evaluate the need for and coordinate the coverage of all critical infrastructure and key resources.

"I have asked the secretaries of Agriculture, HHS, Education, Energy, Interior and Defense to coordinate their activities to support the national defense against this attack and to identify the perpetrators.

"These steps are not to be construed as martial law, except in California. We shall avoid such further steps unless absolutely necessary. We are acting to protect our citizens, our transportation web, our infrastructure elements, and our economy from further attack."

The president turned the line over to Jake as the California governor tried to listen to too many speaking to him at one time.

"Will all of you just be quiet for ten minutes? Please!

"Go ahead. Who am I speaking to now?"

"This is Dr. Jake Levy of the EIS. We are the lead teams for CDC ops when a disaster strikes. We have been to this rodeo before. You need to follow my lead and instruct each of your political and administrative subordinates to do the same.

"There are more than fifty tons of supplies on 130 pallets on the grounds of our RSS (receipt, stage, and store) warehouse in Berkeley. I am here now. You need to have five convoys of five semis each, arranged in staggered intervals of two hours each over the next twenty-four hours. Each will load 5 pallets and deliver them to every hospital in the area. We will have the hospital teams ready for unloading upon arrival.

"Any questions?"

"No, thanks. You … are a godsend." The governor was losing control of his state, and he was frightened.

> Rough men stand guard at night so we may sleep tight.
>
> —Rudyard Kipling, 1880

Jake next spoke via secure link to the twenty-five hospital directors in conference. Each was surrounded by administrative personnel and senior physicians. "As you know the situation has been elevated from crisis to critical yesterday. CDC is directly involved with every one of your facilities through the ops center in Atlanta—or what is left of it.

"You will be receiving significant deliveries of medical countermeasures (MCMs) over the next twenty-four hours. We are loading trucks in two hours for delivery of more than fifty tons of supplies to each of twenty-nine hospitals in the Bay Area. Please note the list accompanying this call.

"These tools emphasize antimicrobial and vaccine postexposure prophylaxis (PEP). CDC recommends the use of three intravenous antimicrobials plus antitoxin for patients in whom anthrax has been diagnosed or cannot be excluded.

"You must inoculate yourselves as health-care workers first—all of you. Have those off duty report according to the delivery time list you can now see on your scenes. These stockpiles will arrive along with CDC-trained personnel, whose first job is to ensure the coordinated access and use of the medical supplies.

"You must cordon the entire property of each facility of which you are the director—the entire contiguous property. Your local police are being instructed now to assist by my cohort, Major Soliz of the EIS. She is also a Navy SEAL. Her instructions are to be followed explicitly. You do not want her as your opponent, I can assure you.

"California National Guard units have been dispatched to each of your facilities as well. You should begin to see them arriving as we speak. They have primary orders to assist local officers in isolating your facilities and then to create cordon sanitaires for citizen access for diagnostics and therapeutics. They will also establish strict quarantine zones.

"Their medical teams will triage every citizen prior to his or her access to your facility. Many will not be allowed to enter. They will give the highest priority to those persons most likely to benefit from treatment and to use resources in a manner expected to provide the greatest overall population benefit. These guidelines are right from the manual, folks. You know how this game is played.

"Those who are sickest will be quarantined to their own hospice arenas, where they will receive hydration and comfort. Many will die.

"The rest will be subject to showers and issued new clothes. Tracing questions will be asked as they go through the access lines to your hospitals.

"You will have the resources to slow this attack for at least a week. Manufacturing surge functions will have kicked in by then. This has already been directed to all pharmacological firms."

"What then?" asked the medical director of SF General.

"We will know when we get there. We will have new shipments ready for delivery as soon as they are manufactured. Planes and flight paths are standing ready now.

"For now, you must do your best. Any questions?"

A tall thin man stood and nervously adjusted his tie. "What about the media? They can be quite supportive, or not."

"Agreed. Very good point. Sam, my EIS partner, will address the media next."

"I am Sam Brady from the CDC. I am an EIS member, a physician, and an epidemiologist. For the next fifteen minutes, I will share with you everything we know about the current attack—"

The Oakland hospital director exploded with, "Why do you say 'attack'? Are we under attack? By whom? Or is this just another of the current illegal administration's efforts to collude and confuse?"

Sam tried to diffuse the raw current surging across the lines. "The CDC was attacked several days ago by foreign nationals. We know their tools were designed and built in Iran. We have suffered grievous harm."

He added in his laconic, even pace, "The events on the West Coast over the past two weeks may or may not be related to that attack. They are, therefore, viewed as an attack. It was formulated as a dual-prong, dual-weapon attack that was staged over ten days.

"The Monterey Peninsula suffered the first attack. Health-care facilities were rapidly overrun with the sick. Most HCWs (health-care workers) are dying. The virus then spread to San Francisco via the travels of several

US citizens. These people then boarded flights to six US cities and four international destinations. They infected their fellow travelers, families, and neighbors.

"We at CDC were informed by the local HCWs within hours of the first case. We ID'd the disease within fifteen minutes. Inhalation anthrax is virulent. It is deadly. You can see on your screens the symptoms and their duration.

"It is contagious after the seven- to fourteen-day incubation period. Once the rashes begin to appear, it becomes very contagious. We are in the midst of this stage as we speak. Most of those who have been infected are spreading it as they try to get to HCWs for treatment.

"We need the media to fully engage in knowing about the disease and how to fight it. The gloves are off, people. If you support the communication efforts to make citizens aware, we will be able to get ahead of this attack. If you do not, the deaths of fifty million to a hundred million US citizens will be on your hands."

He paused to allow the tension to diffuse. He took a visible deep breath and continued.

"CDC has stockpiled 'twelve-hour push packages.' These are fifty tons of medical supplies shaped to deal with an amorphous disease-prevention scenario. They have been located in six warehouses across the nation.

"Fortunately, we have one in Berkeley. Trucks are loading these 250 pallets and delivering them to twenty-five of the twenty-nine hospitals in the Bay Area as we speak. Each hospital should be preparing now to receive and store these vital tools.

"The local police and California National Guard are now stationing at every one of your twenty-nine health-care facilities. Their duties are to segregate the facility, to ensure inoculation of all police and military personnel, to triage the population, and to create cordon sanitaires.

"These are semi segregated arenas—lines for people to move through. In these lines, they will be triaged. The sickest will be placed in full segregation and given the best care possible—hydration and rest. The others will be 'traced.' They will be questioned about every contact they have had since these events began.

"Then they will be showered and given clean clothing and inoculated if not infected. If they are infected, they will be quarantined and cared for as efficiently as possible.

"We are currently losing the battle. We need to quarantine the entire state of California and six major cities across the country. We need to produce more vaccine and distribute it as quickly as possible. We need to care for the sick and dispose of the dead.

"There are hundreds of dead now, as you know. There will be more. Probably tens of thousands more. Perhaps millions. The future is up to every one of us to ensure.

"You have a responsibility to report the news. The CDC is asking each of you to refrain from any and all political references for the duration of this battle. We rely upon your discretion and your ethics.

"I will now take questions. We have eight minutes. Then you will be inoculated against smallpox, if you have not already been so."

The Oakland MD interrupted again, nervously, "What do you mean segregated? Will people be interned like the Japanese were during World War II?"

"Every citizen who shows up at the hospitals seeking treatment will be triaged. Recall that it is a crime not to report your illness. Self-quarantine seems to be working for now, as most people are responding to our calls to do so."

The director from the Santa Rosa Medical Center asked, "Will the families of the deceased be notified? Do they have a choice of cremation or burial?"

"Yes, we shall try to notify family. No, cremation is the only choice. Deceased bodies remain hosts for the disease. They need to be destroyed quickly as one of the primary defenses against further dissemination of the pox."

"Who will be monitoring our press, our reporting, our work as journalists?" SF General was trying to get onboard now.

"You will. We rely upon each of you to self-discipline. We need the work of every citizen in this fight. The chance of a complete destruction of these United States is real and growing. We are already ten days behind in our fight and losing the battle as we speak. We—you and us—have no time to lose.

"Thank you. Do the right thing, please."

Communication between DC and Sacramento had been delicate. Now it was precarious. The governor was incommunicado.

The president was on a roll. He had more energy than the rest of his tribe surrounding him, and all of them knew it. He was exhausting everyone in the room. "The bastard in California is wetting his pants now. Worthless. Worse than worthless. A coward.

"Get me the governors of Arizona and Nevada. And the assistant secretary for preparedness and response. I want those push packages on planes now. I want those in state to be immediately deployed. We don't have time for delays of any sort.

"Then I want to see the cabinet members we just discussed. Then the media folks must be ready. When my wife is on the line, let me know."

Her call came back in less than a minute. Struggling with words, he urged her to return to Washington with their son immediately. "The helo will be at the Towers in forty-five minutes. Please get there and get on it. I want you two out of the city and here with the rest of the family, please."

"The call is ready with Arizona and Nevada." Clare had been executive secretary for four presidents. They were all basically similar—forceful children playing with fire, playing in immense sandboxes. She patched the two governors in to his line.

"Folks, I want to be honest with you. This is crushing us right now. It will get far worse. We have no idea how long it will take to beat these bugs. They are too far ahead of us to even see the taillights through the dust."

"That's a start, sir." The governor of Arizona was a true cowboy. No fear.

"We have a shit-scared governor next door to you, a rabid nutcase north of you. I am going into a press conference in twenty minutes with this weakling who runs California. We have an outbreak of inhalation anthrax that is out of control. We have declared martial law across the state as of fifteen minutes ago. So he is at least on board—for now.

"I need you to shut your borders now with the Golden State. I am asking. In an hour, I will have written authorization from the Supreme Court. You should be aware that we have virtually no vaccine for your citizens. Won't have more for almost a month. By then, the whole country could be gone.

"Right now, I need you to show strength—to your people, to your safety officers, to your staff. We need a line of defense, in mind if not in fact."

"You have our support, Mr. President," said the Nevada governor.

"Right behind you," said the Arizona leader. "Do you want us in on the press conference?"

"Not a bad idea, yes. I'll give you guys the lead-ins. Take authority. We need to scare the shit out of the bastard next door, or he will scare the shit out of the nation."

"Agreed."

The press conference was unscripted but recorded. The president wanted to see how they would respond to a true crisis before arresting them—if he had to.

"Citizens," Sarah began, "we have been attacked. The CDC (the Center for Disease Control) which was brutally attacked just a few days ago, has informed me that inhalation anthrax was released in California. The cities of Monterey and San Francisco are under quarantine. Other cities are being closed off.

"The EAS (Emergency Alert System) is now active nationwide. All communications will flow through it until we have solved this crisis."

The president interrupted her. "The state of California has been shut down from any contact with the rest of the nation. Martial law has been declared for the entire state. All roads, railway, and airports have been closed. The neighboring states of Nevada and Arizona have closed their borders with California—and with their neighbors to the east and north. The National Guard has been called up in each of these states to enforce order, ensure available vaccines are distributed, and prevent civil disorder.

"I have asked the governors of these states to join me in this teleconference. Governor McDonald, how is Arizona holding up?"

"We are under state-mandated martial law. Citizens are urged to stay at home. The protocol is clear: Stay away from anyone who you think may be infected. Wash everything you own with simple soap and water. Stay within the cordon of your area. Listen to the emergency broadcast for updates."

"Governor Matthews, what are you doing in Nevada?"

"We have the borders closed with every other state. Quarantines are in effect. Any incident of infection should be reported immediately to the authorities."

"Vaccines will be delivered as soon as possible. As I have said before, as the CDC is telling everyone today, every day, wash everything you own with a simple solution of soap and water. Boil clothing for thirty minutes. This disease can be transmitted by contact with infected articles of clothing and through the air. Be watchful. If you see someone who seems ill, report to the local police on 9-1-1. We have hundreds of workers on staff now for your calls. We have had several reports of infection, and these are under quarantine.

"At the federal level, we have six stockpiles of medicinal goods around the country. While I cannot tell you where they are, four are in position now to dispense critical help to the infected areas.

"We are working closely with several pharmaceutical companies to produce as much vaccine as possible in as short a time as possible. All FDA limitations have been waived. Just-in-time, large-scale production of immunity response vaccines is more helpful today than all the stockpiling we have done in the past.

"We are tracking the progress of the disease. This is not easy, as it leaps boundaries with each new contact. This is why you should remain indoors and have no direct contact with anyone, including family, neighbors, friends, or associates for the next few weeks. Do not go to work, to church, or even to a family dinner for two weeks.

"The protocol is simple. Do not go outside. Do not gather in groups. Do not try to go to a health-care facility unless you have symptoms of the disease, which you see displayed on the screen below me.

"The EAS will broadcast these symptoms hourly at the top of the hour. If you find you have any of these symptoms, call your local 9-1-1. They will arrange your delivery to a hospital equipped to help you. Do not try to go there on your own.

"We are establishing 'double quarantine' cordons. We will disinfect every infected area and inoculate every citizen in the country. We have stockpiled these inoculations for many years. Now we will access them as quickly as possible.

"But we need your cooperation. You are our first line of defense against this killer. The disease spreads by personal contact. If you have minimal contact with anyone, we can stop in before it consumes the nation.

"This is a war, people. We, each of us, you and me and your neighbor and all the health-care workers, are on the frontlines. Each of us is vital to everyone's survival.

"Please. I urge you to do nothing. Go nowhere. See no one for the next two weeks. We must deny these attackers. We can only do so by isolating ourselves for the next two weeks.

"If you have contact with someone who is infected, call 9-1-1. The sooner you do so, the better your chances.

"People, we are a great nation. We are great citizens. I am speaking from my heart now. Nothing has been prepared. Just listen for now.

"We can fight these monsters in our midst. We can win. If each one of us devotes the next two weeks to doing something as soldiers in this war against anthrax, we all have a chance.

"Teachers and students, you cannot go to school, but you can continue to learn. Learn about these diseases. Learn their symptoms so you can recognize them in yourself and others. This will help immensely. Whether you are in kindergarten or writing your doctoral thesis, devote your efforts to helping others.

"This is not just about disease prevention. This is about food and water use. No one can go to the stores because they are all closed. There will be no mail or deliveries. But the internet still works. Share your ideas on how to best use the food and water you have. Share these with others so they can learn from your example.

"Google, Facebook, Twitter, and all the rest work from your homes to keep the channels of commerce and communication open and free. Open architecture has new meaning now. We need to Linux the hell out of our thousands of solutions—open-source funding, with ideas rather than money.

"If you live in a high-rise or condo or apartment complex, your movement will be very limited. Discuss how to use the stairs and elevators safely for all. The military will try to get masks to each building as quickly as possible. In the meantime, make your own masks. Be smart about water. If its yellow, let it settle; if it's brown—well, figure out how to use it.

"Throw nothing away. Recall how our grandparents saved and recycled during the Second World War. Use everything you touch; use it at least three times and then figure out how to use it again. Environmentalists and conservationists teach us again how to make better use of the useless things in our lives—plastic wrappers, paper bags, metal containers, and food products of all kinds.

"Pastors, rabbis, priests, and imams, you cannot congregate, but you can still pray and meditate and submit to God. Work with your fellow believers in prayerful sustenance. Use the internet and the phone systems to support those in need without actually being in the same room. Show your faiths to be the honored tool of the faithful.

"Billionaires, we are a cozy lot. We are 574 here in America. We have extraordinary power. Use this power for good. Follow Google's motto" 'Don't be evil.'

"The monsters who are attacking us with these microbes are doing evil. Destroy them! Keep your workers safe, yes; but keep them employed. Urge them to this battle. Use your strengths in technology, medicine, transportation, energy, and real estate to build a thousand barriers for disease prevention. A thousand tools for survival. Ten thousand ways to reuse and recycle.

"If you are in a hospital or under health care, the nurses and caregivers are needed elsewhere—desperately. Ask what you can do to help yourselves, so they can help others. Take your own temperature, monitor your own heart rate, clean your own bedpans. Free up the health-care workers for their desperate work. They will be the hardest hit.

"To our military and safety personnel, you are the front lines. Teach each one of us how to do some small feature of your work so that you are slightly freer to protect us all. Reach into your deep bag of knowledge. Share with us all so we can do more for ourselves. You are needed in battle!

"Seniors, baby boomers, you can teach us all how to save, how to be wise women and men, how to survive. You and your parents were the finest. Be so today. Guide us with your experience. No more golfing. We need to engulf these microbial monsters with your skills.

"To those who are in perpetual disagreement with me, I offer a truce. My Twitter account will only be used in support of others. I ask for the same from all. If you disagree with these approaches, please do so constructively. We can all learn from mistakes. We make them every day. Let's focus on the things we do wisely.

"I am not going to fool you. This is very dangerous to you—to each one of you.

"It is even more dangerous to the nation. Your cooperation is central to our success in eradicating this pestilence.

"We are at risk of extermination. Today, 318 million souls are at risk—every one of us. If we do nothing, 50 million will be dead in six weeks. By Christmas, 100 million will be dead. There may be no future Christmas if we simply wait for others to act. We must act together, as one.

"We are a nation of caregivers. We help one another in time of need. That time is now. You can help by enforcing a personal curfew, by calling for transportation to a health-care facility if you are infected, by watching and reporting anyone who appears sick, and by staying home.

"By being good citizens.

"We have fought together as a nation before. At Yorktown. At Gettysburg. At Pearl Harbor. At 9/11. We, united as a nation, have put aside our differences and joined hands to destroy the enemy. We must do so again. It is our destiny to survive!

"God Bless America."

He closed the mike.

Gesturing to the reporters on screen, he instructed them, "Be good citizens."

DAY TEN

By the time of the president's nationwide call, worse news was emerging from San Francisco. It was nearly two weeks into the crisis, and the first of a new infection was being observed and reported.

Smallpox.

The disease had been eradicated thirty years ago. The only known viruses extant were in the Atlanta vault of CDC and in their cousin's vault in Russia. Something had escaped from somewhere. Diagnostics would eventually determine the source, but now the challenge was appropriate response.

Cases were showing up at three of the twenty-nine beleaguered city hospitals in the Bay Area.

Jake was the first to report back to Atlanta. "We have twelve new cases of headaches, painful muscle aches, vomiting, and rosy red body rashes. Some rashes have begun to develop purplish subcutaneous spots as they hemorrhage internally."

No one had seen this before—except the EIS people. The diagnosis was as quick as the AMD diagnostics. Both Jake and Sam know what they were facing now.

This was a dual attack. It was a duel between humans and an ancient tag team—anthrax/smallpox.

Most in the ready room were still in shock from their own recent attack. Yet, all responded as professionals. Each knew his or her task and how to work together in a fighting team.

They had done this many times in the past. It was just so far away. In Africa or India. Not in their own homeland. Not against a purposeful dual attack.

Each knew what their responsibilities were; all knew their family's lives were now at stake.

Sam spoke. "We have a new threat. We suspect hemorrhagic smallpox, to be exact—spread by inhalation or direct contact with bodily fluids, bedding, or clothing. As you all know, it is slightly less infectious than other diseases, as transmission occurs after onset of the rash, lasting until the last skin lesion is clear."

"In typical smallpox, light rashes progress to blisters and then to knobby pustules, hard to the touch. Survivors are scarred for life; 70 percent survive.

"In hemorrhagic smallpox—black pox—the skin remains initially unscarred, while the eyes become reddened with blood and the GI tract suffers from a deficiency of coagulants. Black pox is extremely contagious. Five to ten virions are sufficient for infection.

"It is easily spread person to person by respiratory droplets, contact with bodily fluids, lesions, or scabs, and contaminated clothing or bedding. On rare occasions, in enclosed spaces, it has been transmitted in the air. Patients are most contagious from three to seventeen days after contamination.

"The absence of scabs and the pulmonary and gastrointestinal attacks often preclude certain evaluation until it is too late.

"The incubation period lasts from three to seventeen days, during which time the vector is not identifiable. Black pox scabs do not display the typical umbilicated papules—the pustules do not scab.

"Death occurs a week after first signs appear in most cases.

"Mortality rates approach 100 percent, and vaccines are unhelpful.

"Protocol expands to include a census of all victims and anyone in contact with a smallpox victim. Find out who they spent time with, when, how long, and what they did. It also expands to include a two-week isolation for anyone contacting the disease or anyone in physical contact with such an infected person.

"We need to work with each of the hospitals across the infected cities. This crisis may spread very quickly."

The silence was palpable across the screens, in the conference room, and over the video. Fear was the dominant emotion. Soon, every hospital in the state would be aware.

"With quarantines in place for much of the Bay Area, the hemorrhagic smallpox virus has a much smaller pool of cells in which to propagate. Twenty-nine hospitals in the area are overwhelmed with anthrax patients. Now they will have to ID and ISO smallpox victims.

"We are delivering our stockpiles of medical supplies to each of the hospitals as we speak. These supplies include oral and intravenous antibiotics for a wide range of infections and medical and surgical supplies for respiratory and pediatric needs. These are for all hospitals and staff. More is on the way.

"There are no black pox vaccines in our national inventory. Our compatriots in Chicago and New York may face the same issues.

"Staff is beginning to disappear, slowly, a few each day, as the anthrax exposures multiply. Some move away. Some stay at home. Most simply die.

"Fewer people have the black pox, and many are self-identified and isolated—as much as possible—by overworked health-care staff."

He was speaking the truth—to a morgue. Most in Atlanta knew they would be at high risk of contamination. Each thought he or she had but a small chance of survival. The fear moved over the airwaves, as tumescent as the virions.

By the tenth day, more than 5,000 are ID'd and in some form of isolation, ISO. Many simply stayed home, as instructed by the emergency broadcast system.

Smallpox vaccine was stockpiled across the CDC depositories. It is enough for the entire nation. It was useless against "the black pox."

DAY ELEVEN

You Can Rest When You Die.

A small box was retrieved from a city homeless shelter after everyone in the shelter became infected with the black pox. EIS secured it in its recently delivered portable Level 4 containment unit. The box was covered with the thin white powder, the residue from an open drawer. No one knew how long it had been open. No one knew where the box had been found or how long it had been exposed. If the drawer was full when it was opened, it could have held several hundred grams—of pure white death.

Genomic sequencing identifies the strain of the disease—hemorrhagic, the most virulent form of *variola major* and the most severe. Confirmation of the first cases was at SFH.

Fingerprints ID'ed patient zero quickly—one of the three sailors from the yacht in Monterey harbor.

The yacht's owner was found in the city at the SF Yacht Club and questioned by the primary EIS team via Skype.

Jake asked, "Who did you hire to bring your yacht to Monterey?"

"Three guys who were very good sailors. I hired them to bring the boat down to Monterey for the summer for us. Theo was a friend of my brother. He had two others, Fred and Mike, who I met at the club. I checked their backgrounds in yachting circles, and they seemed like good sailors."

"What else did you find out about them? Where were they from? Who could give references for them?"

"Theo's name was on the club roster as a 'six-pack skipper.' He was licensed by the Coast Guard. He came to the boat on the third with his friends, stayed the night, and took off with the ebb tide. Four hours to

Monterey with the wind he had that day. He checked in with me as they tied up about 3:00 p.m.

"A few other owners had used him for races and spoke well of his abilities."

Jake spoke to Eli, his EIS contact in Atlanta. "Get the USCG commandant on the phone and dig into this fellow."

He then asked, "Contact info for your brother?"

"I'm sending his info to you now. Here are all three numbers and his two emails. You can see his address now. What else can I do to help? Jesus, this thing has us all scared. I just want to help—"

"Obviously, stay at home now. Keep this number and get back to me with anything you feel is important. Anything. Thank you."

Jake spun through the screens on his laptop. His eyes flicked to Eli's screen. "Have the FBI get this info on Theo now, and CIA and IRS. Check DHS for his passport."

"Already done. He was in Indonesia on June 23 for a regatta at the Jakarta Offshore Sailing Club. It lasted two days. He returned on the second."

"One travel day back. He had nearly a week in Indonesia. What did he do?"

The USCG commandant said, "We are contacting Jakarta now. They are nine hours behind, so it's midnight there."

FBI and DHS records showed up three minutes later on screen. "Good work, Eli."

Jake looked over to Sam via a screenshot. "Amazing what we can do when we work together.

Sam quickly read the report on his computer. "This guy Theo was licensed as a pleasure craft skipper for eight years. No problems reported. Traveled for work and pleasure to yachting capitals of the world. Well-heeled or well-traveled or both."

"IRS shows his home address in Marin. Rents a slip at the local marina there for his thirty-six-foot sloop *Gili*. Short for Gilligan's Island?"

Dr. Mooney had just Skyped into the call. "Indonesian for small island. Knows enough about the archipelago to name his boat in the language. Interesting. Can you get their MSB on Skype?"

A few minutes later, Sam interjected, "I have a watch officer who speaks pretty good English."

"Good morning. Sorry to disturb you so late. This is Dr. Mooney from the Center for Disease Control in San Francisco." She was strong and tall. Her step was sure. Her vision was clear, her diction precise. She expected response—you gave it. She looked where each footfall would drop, concerned about tripping, about dropping to her knees. She hated falling.

"Lt. Chaijinda here. I am honored to speak with someone who knows our land so well. I believe you were here just last year. I attended your session on infectious tropical diseases as an EMT. We are well known for our fight to rid the nation of dengue fever."

"Thank you for participating, Lt. Chaijinda. I recall your intelligent questions and your infectious laugh— Sorry.'

His laughter eased the weight of the conference call for a moment—to everyone's relief.

She continued, shuffling papers off screen as she spoke. "Now we have a major incident, as I'm sure you know. It has recently been compounded by a *variola major* strain, hemorrhagic smallpox. We are tracing the steps of an individual who may be involved in its transmission. Theo Walker visited Indonesia on June 23 and stayed for six days. He spent two days at your Offshore Sailing Club participating in a regatta."

"He is well known here as an avid sailor and tactician. My uncle is the club manager. Shall I get him on the line?"

"If you would. I know it is past midnight there, but this is of the highest health importance—to the United States and to the Republic of Indonesia. We are at least ten days behind the anthrax infection tsunami, and now we have this new attack."

"Can you wait for just one minute? I will call him at home."

During the minutes she waited, two other calls came in, and she shuddered. Fifteen hundred cases of "HS" (hemorrhagic smallpox) were now reported across the United States. Her fears were met head-on. This was now a two-headed snake, with dual venom. She had never thought this possible in all their previous training. The four attacks overseas were now coming into focus. She knew they were unprepared for the slaughter coming. The horror. The horror.

While they waited for the distant club manager to wake and come to the lieutenant's office, she realized that the disease had escaped protocol because they hadn't been looking for it. Thousands of tourists had been in the city on July 4. It was crowded with people celebrating and sightseeing. Somehow, they had contacted the disease. Now they were transmitters in Kansas City, Omaha, Chicago, Seattle, Miami, and Philadelphia.

She spoke to everyone on the call. "A chimera has been uncovered, a beast inside of a monster. Hydra is lifting another head. The unleashing will be horrible. Not one of us has had any experience in fighting a creature of such magnitude."

The second call was from the White House. The president was direct. "Dr. Mooney, we are losing this battle, and a new front has just opened, actually six new fronts. I am speaking with the city leaders in eight minutes. We know the pox protocol and will impose it immediately. Any further suggestions before I go live with these data?"

"Chicago should be somewhat easier since they already are trying to impose quarantine. Tell the others to do exactly as we are doing here. We are dispatching EIS teams to the other cities now. Can you clear the airways for their flights? I also suggest border closings under Directive 7, as you have done for California. If we can catch this before it explodes, we may still win this fight.

She continued, "Speak with the big pharma CEOs as soon as you can get them together on a call. Their efforts have to be doubled."

"I have already done so. They are replacing the inventories in our six national stockpiles and shipping them as quickly as they are produced and palleted. Masks and needles are the easiest to produce and disseminate. The military is tasked with these basic essentials and their distribution now.

"The pharmas have scaled their production facilities here in the United States to mass immunization tools and expect deliveries within two weeks. They will have five million vaccines for anthrax in a month, twenty million in two months. As for the smallpox—"

She interrupted him. "Call if you need anything else. Good bye."

The remaining participants focused on the new screen shot from Jakarta. A man in silky pajama-like garb and the uniformed lieutenant were standing as if at attention.

"Dr. Mooney? This is Lt. Chaijinda. My uncle is here with me now."

"Sir, we don't have much time. We need to know everything you know about Theo Walker while he was in Indonesia—where he went, who he spoke with, what he did, and when he took a piss."

A few moments of silence followed. "Dr. Mooney, my apologies but I had to request a translation from my nephew. Yes, I can help with much of your request. Theo was a very good sailor and well known here. How much time do we have to get answers for you?"

"None. We now have 1,500 cases of smallpox and more than 8,000 of inhalation anthrax. Condors sanitaire are only partially working. Our borders are as open as your islands."

"Theo was known to participate in local activities. He liked the Hindu women and often dropped down to Bali for a few days. I have the Balinese infectious disease officer on another line now.

"But more important, Theo spent time in Lombok. This was unusual, since it was a Muslim island. He was too carefree for our more rigorous social demands.

"I shall speak with the island police when we are finished here."

"Please call me as soon as you have something useful for us. We need to track his connections now, if only to prevent the spread of the pox to your people. Time is critical. We have so little."

"Given the time, I should be able to get through to everyone I know by waking them. Give us a few hours."

"We don't even have a few minutes. Do what you can, please."

She hadn't slept for three days. She was tough, but even she knew she needed rest. *You can rest when you die*, she told herself. Her hands shook as she took a long draft of the cold coffee. She could feel fear rising in her bones. There was nowhere to turn, no one to help. She was adrift on a virion sea.

JOKO

The call from "Joko," the president of Indonesia, was relayed to the US command center below the White House. The group had been expanded to include six House members and Senators from the opposing party. Intelligence, military, health, transportation, and Homeland Security were all there. Most were in various states of shock; everyone was trying to maintain a strong front. Dr. Mooney and Jake were the outliers in the Bay Area, her image on-screen in the darkened room.

The US president spoke first, "Mr. President, what do you have for me?"

"We have quarantined the port and brought in for questioning everyone who may have been in contact with this Theo Walker. Most are very cooperative. Two did try to escape, and one was shot. The other is undergoing intensive questioning now.

"Theo appears to have traveled within our nation once the regatta was complete. We have records of his flight to Denpasar, and then he traveled to Lombok. We have nothing on him there yet.

"Do you think he was infected?"

"We can only assume so. Act in your national interest. Protect your people first and foremost. Quarantine. Double cordons. Interviews, isolation, and inoculations.

"You know our joint contacts in the intelligence community are working together as we speak. Let's hope they can track this patient zero to his local contacts. Please keep me informed. Thank you."

Patient zero was the first known case of a disease—the source of the outbreak. Find the source, and you can, perhaps, cap it.

"Of course. We have protocols in place for dengue fever, and our people can alter these quickly for both smallpox and anthrax. We do not have any current infections noted."

"Mr. President, what does the word *gili* mean?" added Dr. Mooney.

"Island. We have more than fourteen thousand in the archipelago. Gilis are small islands, usually uninhabited. Why do you ask?"

"Theo named his boat in California *Gili*. We had no idea what it meant."

"This is very useful information. Can you send an image of the boat—specifically the name to us?"

"Yes, coming over now. Why?"

"The script, the spacing, the font can tell us quite a bit about which of our languages he is referencing. The color and size of the letters can be very revealing as to the area, helping us narrow down the search."

Joko, another uniformed officer, and Chaijinda examined the image of the sailboat from Marin for nearly a minute and then spoke to one another briefly in confirmation.

"We see the image now. My intelligence chief is here with me, as well as Lt. Chaijinda, who knows the local seafarers very well. Any immediate thoughts gentlemen?"

"I can see that these are Hindu script in style, rather than Islamic. The color is dark green. That tells me where to look, which islands. We have greatly narrowed our search with your simple question." Lt. Chaijinda was clear and unmoved by the power in the room.

"Keep me updated please, Joko."

"Yes, of course, Mr. President."

"Doug, do you have personnel in place in Jakarta? Someone remaining after my visit last month?"

The NSA director was calm and direct. He had assets globally that he had already called upon. He found it odd that nothing was coming in from the usual threat sources. Where was the threat vector? No one had claimed responsibility for the attacks. Nothing from the Middle East.

The silence was deafening. Inside he was wound up tight. The play never went this way—so long without a culprit, no megalomaniacal heroes claiming the moral low ground.

"Yes, Peter Dingell and his team are still down there. He can move quickly on whatever it takes to source this Theo Walker."

"On the line with him now. Excuse me."

"President Joko is back on the line, Mr. President."

"What do you have for us?

"Theo spent two days in Lombok. The local police and the island governor have nothing on his visit. No records, no transactions. No money spent. No calls. Have you read Conan Doyle, Mr. President?"

"*Silver Blaze*. The absence of the hound's bark was the clue to the case."

"Yes. We have nothing on this Theo, which is something quite profound."

"We don't have time for profound, Joko. We are dying by the thousands as we speak."

"My point is, nothing can happen on such a small, slightly inhabited island without *someone* knowing about it." Few were so direct with the president.

He leaned into the screen. "Go ahead."

Joko continued, rapidly speaking on line and with his subordinates in three languages. "We do have a taxi driver who claims to have taken an American to the far south, virtually uninhabited." He nodded, listened for a moment, and then went on. "He left his fare by the side of the road at an arrack stand. Our local alcohol. The driver thought nothing more than this was yet another American seeking oblivion. We have people at the site now, and you have people coming in by helo as we speak."

"Doug, get a satellite over this arrack stand as soon as you can. Have us patched in to Dingell when he lands. I want this all in real time for everyone here. Anyone disagree?"

Heads twisted in nervous negatives across the room. Tension was splitting the room with knife flashes of fear. Silence dominated a room full of nonstop talkers. Politicians and senior military officers. Presidential advisors. Humans with no understanding of the depth of horror to which Tracker was just now exposing them.

The CDC screen was above the seven other screens for participants from across the globe now. The upper screen was expanding with dual graphs of infections and deaths for each disease—just in the United States—in one hour increments. Red was staining the map very rapidly.

The exponential increases from the six infected areas were chilling. This was hell, and it was getting far worse each hour. At this point, twenty-eight thousand infections had been reported, more than fourteen thousand deaths—in less than two weeks. Everyone in the room had family and friends dying as they sat. Watching.

"Satellite in position in twenty-five minutes, sir."

"Joko, can you get in touch with the local governor? We have a translator on hand. If you don't mind, just go into this with him, and we'll listen in. Please."

"Of course. I'll be on line with him in a few moments."

The pause allowed a few people to share thoughts with neighbors in the room, on the monitors. Voices were subdued.

The president leaned over to a separate line and said quietly, "Thank God you two are safely returned."

Joko came back online. "Governor Wadi, who owns this land?"

"We are pulling the land records now. Of course, they are handwritten here in our small world of Lombok … Perhaps we have too much Le'ak from Bali. They have always wanted to take us back into their kingdom.

"I suspect Le'ak has come out from the graveyard yet again. Fire, earth and water are reversed."

"Get someone down there to help him, now." This from Joko.

"Sir, the records department is closed for Eid—"

"Open the doors now."

"Yes, sir, as you command."

"Records for the land in Batunampar show three foreign business owners on title."

"Can he hold the title up to the screen?"

"No need. Dingell is imaging it now, sir."

"Translator, tell us what you can read now."

"The businesses are from Bermuda, Majuro and Panama."

"Mr. Presidents, Peter Dingell here. I have the images captured and sent to NSA now."

"Joko, thank you. We'll let you continue with your investigation. Please keep us informed."

"I will have our best people working with Mr. Dingell in a few minutes. I'll make you aware."

The call with the CEOs was in forty-five minutes.

DEEP STRIKE

> Unfortunately, the nature of the bioterrorism threat makes determining the risk difficult. The presence of an intelligent adversary who can adapt to successful countermeasures complicates standard assessment techniques.
>
> —Congressional Research Service, 2011

The Panamanian offices were the first to be entered, with the director of security on the line to his NSA connection. The entire office was emptied of everything. Dust was collected and saved for analysis.

The Bermuda offices were forced open at 2:00 p.m. on a Sunday afternoon, unheard of in the tiny island. PM May had issued the order herself. Again, the office was swept clean.

Majuro was six hours from Guam, which was sixteen hours from DC via commercial jet. The helo from Guam was in Majuro in five hours flat. A team of Marines entered the offices at the address listed—to find nothing. Not even dust. It had been a front for years, just an address, nothing more.

Panama and Bermuda came up flat too. It would take a few weeks of deep investigative digging to determine who owned what in the thick pile of dossiers embalmed with the ownership files for the Lombok land.

PRELIMINARY DEFENSE:

Bulwarks and Roustabouts

The extinction of the human species may not only be inevitable but a good thing.

—Christopher Manes, *Earth First!*

"We need the resources of each of your industries to attack these beasts. Tell me how you plan to respond."

"Mr. President, this is Joe Bastardi from Glaxo. I have John Steinem with Amgen, Ms. Crowthy from Bayer, and several others. How can we help?"

"We need a hundred million inhalation anthrax and a hundred million black pox vaccine units yesterday. In addition, we need the 'sticks' and knowledgeable health-care workers to apply the vaccines.

"The United Kingdom and the Russian Republic are sending in five million units to Canada and to Berlin to help with their infections. I need each of you and your cohorts to build millions of units as quickly as you are able. California is quarantined under Directive 7, as are Chicago, New York, and four other cities. Nevada and Arizona will be soon.

"You will have immediate access to the national airways for transport. Your teams have no time to lose. We have thousands of dead now, and the twin diseases are spreading faster than I can talk. There will be millions of dead by the time you distribute your first production units."

"Sir, we have been working on this prior to our call. We can build the inoculations fairly quickly, but not nearly as quickly as the pathogens can spread. We can have five million anthrax doses ready in two weeks, with a million doses daily thereafter."

"In a month we may have ten million deaths in the United States alone; someone here just suggested a hundred million deaths. Your best isn't nearly good enough."

"We have no source for the smallpox. Anthrax we can manufacture quickly, perhaps one million doses daily within two weeks—perhaps."

"All of you have to do better than this. The FDA has moved this from accelerated to emergency use authorization as of an hour ago. I have signed off on the EUA. I expect a call from you in two days."

He was harsh. The diseases were harsher. Humanity had no choice. It had to survive. Harsh was only the beginning.

"Get me Sundar at Google. Now."

Sundar Pichai, CEO of Google, was on the line in less than a minute. "How can we help, sir?"

"I have an idea. How do you catch a tiger?"

"With a dog."

"Mind being my dog for a few weeks?"

"If it means we snuff out this disease, no I don't mind. We would be honored to be the bait. We have lost 14 percent of our workers already. Other firms have lost more. Apple has the worst of it."

"I need you to build an alternate universe for me."

"How much time do we have?"

"None. I want it done before sunset tomorrow."

"East coast or West coast?"

"I'll give you the three hours. Your time tomorrow.

"This is what I have in mind. The bastard who is running this operation is very sophisticated. Very intelligent. Quite like you, actually. I want you to be his doppelgänger. I have no idea if this person even exists, although Premier Zi and I agree that she does."

"She?"

"Doesn't matter for your game. I need your folks to invent a world where she is winning. I mean the whole show—newscasts, media, computer data, stats, piles of dead bodies, people screaming and fighting."

"Should be pretty easy. That's what happening all around me right now, sir." The sarcasm was clear.

"What you don't know is we are going to beat these twin beasts, very soon."

"Twin? I thought—"

"What you thought and what I know are immaterial. What I want is a continuum of what you are seeing right now. Expand it over time. You have three weeks for the scenario to run its course."

"You think you are going to win. You want her to think you are losing. You hope she will show her hand."

"Now we are on the same page. To prevent chaos from interfering beyond what I expect, I will tell you no more. You have no need to know right now. You simply have to build an alternate reality for her that shows her exactly what she expects to see. You are the bait. I want her to devour you. Can you do this?"

"If anyone can, we can. May I ask, why me?"

"Because you like dogs.

"Call me when you are ready to make the switch to your 'programming.' It has to be nanosecond fast and smooth—black ops to the twelfth power."

"How did you know—"

"Never mind. In the big top, we are both showmen—the best at what we do. Show me you are better than she can imagine."

"I love an impossible challenge."

"I know."

FIRST RESULTS

The first principle is that you must not fool yourself—and you are the easiest person to fool.

—Richard Feynman

Oddly, Tracker had no access to these conversations. She was good, but not that good. So, she assumed the politicians and bureaucrats would dither. She knew the coupled diseases were now rampant. Several cities around the world were under attack. Entire nations were crumbling.

Health-care responses had been severely hindered by the CDC attack. Yet Dr. Mooney's forces were regrouping despite their depleted numbers—despite their destroyed headquarters.

This was what CDC's EIS groups were trained for; this was their area of expertise. They would not back down.

Tracker's tests had proved conclusive. Eighty million were infected in the first months—in the most advanced areas of the world. More than 60 percent of the health-care worker populations of North America, Europe, and Asia died in their valiant efforts to control this Hydra, this raging beast.

She learned and waited.

The concurrent phases were just in their opening sequencing. She had staggered the attacks over the late summer and early fall. The virulence was just beginning. Four attacks. Simultaneously. It required incredible planning, far more difficult execution. Then had come the North American attacks, which expanded globally across two fronts.

Timing was everything. The phases were the precedents for a more perfect hajj.

Tracker turned to the next phase of her attack, while still planning the final two phases of humanity's extermination. She had the momentum, she had the trump card, and she knew she was going to win.

Time was her only enemy—as usual.

She was working against a clock over which she had no control. Eventually, the EIS people would stumble upon her labs, learn of a leak, discover a capital funding source. Hajj was coming soon.

SURVIVING

> Global sustainability requires the deliberate quest of poverty, reduced resource consumption and set levels of mortality control.
>
> —Professor Maurice King

October 12 brought thick fog and overcast skies to the city, reflecting the dour mood of the inhabitants. Food was becoming a problem, and several fights had broken out at state dispensaries. Many were trying to get home to other parts of the state.

"I'm going out for a break. I have to get away from this, even if only for a few minutes." Getting in the car, she backed out of the driveway, leaving her husband and children alone. She just had to be alone for a while.

Doris tried to ignore the sores on her hands and under her armpits. She had to save the children.

Doris followed the lights. The roadway was dark except for the taillights ahead. She had no idea where she was or where she was going. She was just getting away from the dead, the dying. The stench. It was overpowering. She had no way to cover it. It nauseated her. Then it became a perfume, an attractor.

She died in the car. No one knew. No one knew her. She was alone. She had been left by the side of the road and had taken a car left by someone else. She was infected. She knew it. She just wanted to get away from home. She just wanted to save her children.

Jimmy had watched her walk to the car, take it easily, and drive away. He followed. Two hours later, she simply slowed and then stopped. The door opened, and she fell out. He knew it was over for her. But not for him. He had a chance. He was not infected. He just had to get past the roadblocks. He just had to get back.

"I know where I am. I know where I can go. I just have to get back to the ranch in the hills. No one will have been infected there, yet. My folks will help. They have always helped."

It was 2:00 a.m. The clock had to be correct, didn't it? Something had to be correct. He looked in his rearview mirror, seeing himself for a moment. What a sight you are! Scrabble beard and dirty teeth. You stink.

The light was far behind him, but closing. He watched in envy and fear. Was it the cops or just another bandito trying to run the gauntlet? He didn't really care. He just wanted to stop running. Once he got to his folks' ranch he would be fine. Safe. He was less than an hour away, if the road was clear. Probably three hours if he took the dirt tracks.

He turned off the two-lane road onto the patchwork of broken pavement and dead-end paths. The dust rose and obscured his vision. He had no idea where he was, only where he wanted to go—south and then east. He knew the sun had to be on his left; it was still morning. The fog was thick on the peninsula this morning. The track fell off to the right and then descended a steep drop. No clearance. No fear. No hope.

The car was crushed on the rubble of the steep cliff. He had rolled too many times. He had been ripped out of the window. He died, uninfected.

By the twentieth day, the entire state of California was red. Red was beginning to grow from the six major cities infected by the Big Sur travelers. The onslaught was ramping up the epi curve, the measure of growth of a disease in a population. It had achieved its first peak. Two more were typical, each greater than the previous.

Yet, the slide down from the previous height was accelerating, or so it seemed. The nation had self-isolated to an extraordinary degree. This was the greatest threat to the microbes—absence of fresh flesh. Contaminated bodies were quickly destroyed by incineration. California was burning bodies by the thousands.

Isolation was having a profound effect upon disease transmission—even in the cities, especially in the cities. The entire nation had responded to the call to arms.

Virtually every citizen had an idea to share or show. Internet traffic hit new highs daily. Kids in Tallahassee had shown how they recycled plastic food wrappers as insulation for blood samples they were taking of themselves.

Pinpricks by children were being sent via websites to the CDC labs in the thousands daily. The nation had created a virology lab in real time across the continent.

Adults in Seattle were sharing best fish recipes, to be cooked in sardine and tuna cans with halogen lights.

A grandmother in Oshkosh taught thousands the basics of knitting in fifteen minutes.

In Harlem, four teenagers had devised a simple means for four hundred tenants to use the elevator safely, wiping it down before exiting each time with disinfectant.

Austin was the current leader in the online "AS battle"—AS short for anthrax/smallpox. With whole genome sequencing (WGS) one of CDC's favorite diagnostic tools, they had cracked the viral structure of the smallpox in fourteen hours and had seventeen ways to destroy it in less than a week. Six of these were in production two weeks later.

The challenge was met by MIT grad students. Whole genomic sequencing the anthrax bacteria, they had reverse engineered the bacteria's RNA to sterility in two hours. Their tools were in production across the

Back Bay campus research facilities—in absentia—by robots in less than eighteen hours.

Getting these prophylactics to the medical consumers quickly was the real challenge. Army and marine helos were dispatched for collection. They deposited these newly designed biometric responses at local military airbases. From these loci, they were flown to the infected cities. Slowly, isolation and the efforts of tens of thousands had turned the tide. Fewer case incidents were reported each day. The spine of the epi curve had been broken.

WINTER IS THE CRUELEST SEASON

> We can no longer pay the ecological price of human mercy.
>
> —Club of Rome, 1977

𝔉all had begun. Temperatures were dropping slowly across the northern hemisphere. The fifth year of solar minimums continued to reduce solar flare activity. The resulting reduction in magnetic storms on the solar surface allowed more gamma rays from the galactic center to penetrate deeper into the solar system. The rare intersecting of these gamma rays with hydrogen and oxygen atoms increased in frequency. This encouraged formation of water vapor throughout the planet's atmosphere. The resulting cloud cover further educed global temperatures, particularly in the temperate latitudes of 30 to 50 degrees north and south of the equator.

Tracker was watching the carnage silently. The media was rabid. Despite the control by the US military, CNN and Bloomberg and MSNBC were virulent. They attacked the president; they attacked his methods. They attacked each other.

Eighty million were infected with inhalation anthrax, thirty million with black pox. Almost forty-eight million died across four continents. The black pox and anthrax together took another sixty-two million over three weeks just in the United States.

The brilliant efforts of every pharmaceutical company in the free world were to little effect. The diseases ramparted and then exploded across the infection zones. Each of the cities was decimated; some simply dissolved under the weight of infection.

Monterey, San Francisco, Chicago, New York—20,000; 500,000; 1.2 million; 4.5 million. Another twenty million on the burbs of the central states and the northeast corridor. The other cities fared far worse. Quarantines and a few million inoculations were as dust in the wind.

Borders were closing. Electronic communications were still vibrant. Food and water had become major concerns for many smaller cities and nations. Stockpiles of grain would carry them through for a few months. But winter was coming to the northern hemisphere.

Or so Tracker thought. In the real world, deaths had peaked at 4,198,452 in the United States for inhalation anthrax and 2,169,814 for the black pox. Global figures were higher: In all, 29.4 million had died of anthrax, while 10.5 million had died of black pox. The deaths were serious. The effects were worldwide.

Yet Google was able to hide this information for three weeks. Every internet search performed showed the horrors of death, the civil disruption, and the political bickering. Tracker was pleased.

Jake and Sam were exhausted. Dr. Mooney had collapsed three days ago. She had literally worked herself to death. She was cremated with the thousands of disease carriers as a precaution.

"I don't believe this. The epi curve continues to drop. When can we expect the next uptake?"

"Maybe, just maybe, we have found the head of the snake." Sam was taciturn again. It was the best news they'd had in weeks.

Google lifted its cloaking device. Actually, it self-destructed with the weight of information demand. The brilliant minds there were pleased that the device had lasted so long.

Tracker was shocked to learn so suddenly that America had fared far less poorly than expected from her attacks. The United States had fared far better than she had been led to believe by the ruse.

She was now on notice. What she had really lost was the cloak of secrecy. They now had a trail. The faintest of wisps, like a curl of smoke in the distant air. A signal. But of what?

SUCCESS IS NOT ENOUGH

> A reasonable estimate for an industrialized world society at the present North American material standard of living would be 1 billion.
>
> —United Nations Global Biodiversity Assessment

She spoke to her senior Indonesian staff.

"You have all volunteered for this mission. You are very well compensated. Your families will be strong as a result of you. None of you have any interest in money, now that they are comfortable. You will remain in your comfortable surroundings, work with your teammates, and achieve our goal.

"We are purposefully remote. This island, this gili, is well off travelers' paths. The waters are swift and deep. The undersea cliffs and caves are inhabited by sharks, rays, and poisonous sea snakes. You each have a GPS implant. We will know who and where you are at all times. Should you try to remove the implant, it will infect you. You have each been told this prior to your arrival. You have accepted the conditions of employment.

"Now is the time to move forward. You have much to do."

Each listener had no doubt about his feral skills. He could rip your heart out at the dinner table and ask you to pass the wine before you collapsed on the bloodied tablecloth.

"We have initial sequences begun now in sixteen cities. These will show rapidly growing infection rates." The biogenetics director was reporting to her via Zoom. He had never actually seen her. He wondered why she wore the scarf that hid most of her face. It was probably just a disguise. He had been in special ops for four years, as a major—the boss who led men into battle. He expected casualties, but only after much enemy blood had been spilled. He knew fear, horror, and death—intimately. His heart was as black as night.

The conversation was direct, military style, as if over a battlefield—which it was in her clear mind. Just as it was clear in his mind. Follow orders. Excel at your task. Eat. Sleep. Kill.

Tracker continued. "The Americans are fully occupied with the West Coast attacks and the CDC bombing. They are just learning of the hidden chimera, our first incident of such consequence.

"Hajj will erupt soon. Very soon.

"We are prepared for this event to commence in two weeks. The operatives have been released. The date is rapidly approaching. The world will be enmeshed in the diseases we have just released. Their distraction will be our opening to a far greater kill ratio.

"Let us move forward."

By mid-October, CDC resources were stretched far beyond capacity. The process of epidemiology was always difficult at best—identify, isolate, disinfect, quarantine and immunize.

She had broken their backs. She had overwhelmed their defenses—blitzkrieg in the best tradition of Rommel. There is no defense against an overpowering offense.

With the significant attacks on health-care workers stripping the field of thousands of experienced nurses and physicians, care was nearly impossible. Treatment and cures were nonexistent for much of her work.

Nevertheless, closure was certain, she knew. The response teams were far better at prevention than her spore teams were at diffusion. The experiments had been a qualified success.

Nearly 40 million deaths had resulted from a small drone.

Another 29 million deaths were spawned by the Emirates attack.

With the first chimera attack, another 40 million fell.

The Ubud scenario took 110 million.

A further 386 million were gone after the filovirus' attacks across five continents.

Only 6 million were dead in America—a huge disappointment, surely.

She noted the data and returned to her study. It wasn't nearly enough to make a difference, not nearly enough. In the end, 600 million was less than 10 percent of the global population.

Yet, seventy-eight days of horror had evolved into those 600 million deaths across five continents—in the three months of summer.

Little did the CDCs of the world know that this was simply a series of test runs. Much worse was planned.

The diseases ran their course. CRE added to the death knoll. The Black Plague was just raising its own head—showing yet another of Hydra's thousand faces.

Density played out its horrific role. Diseases were ultimately slowed in their spread by the simple but effective tools of time and dispersal. Double isolation, census taking, massive rehydration—and mass graves. The latter was the most effective, by far.

As population densities were reduced, so the infections declined. They dropped more by the passage of time than by CDC interventions. Teams were dispersed, protocol was observed, and interventions were upheld by enforced isolation.

Yet whole teams died too, infected from two, sometimes three directions. Well-designed systems are never impregnable. Simply attack the weakest point. Go around. Or under. Or over.

The absence of beds, supplies, and medicine was quickly apparent. Local health-care authorities were soon overwhelmed—in the tropics as well as the temperate climes—simply by force of infection from several pathogens. Simultaneous vectors leading to one unified goal. Reproduction. Or death. Which was it?

Global capacity for response was foreshadowed by internecine political turf warfare. Response teams from the national CDCs and WHO collapsed under the weight of officialdom. Who became more important than which disease. Which became more important than how many died … Data suppression became a means to an end—the end of cooperation between nations, polities, and peoples.

Decision making became noticeable by its absence.

February would see the last of the initial infections. Deaths would decline as isolation and density demographics took their toll. Few cures were in place.

Too few inoculations were a fault, as was an excess of the wrong ones. The diseases themselves simply consumed, reproduced, and then repeated the process. Once the genies were released from their bottles, many had no antidote. After three billion years, their borg didn't really care. It knew only success.

It had caused six hundred million deaths during the initial attack sequences. Unknown millions would die during the winter, perhaps another hundred million. The world was shutting down in response to the dying.

The pallor of death filled the skies.

Some were free from attack. Tribal, island, and northern clans were least impacted because of their remoteness and their insignificant numbers. If one of their groups came in contact with infected humans, or it the pathogens came to their locales, they were wiped out—just as Amerindians had been eliminated in the sixteenth and seventeenth centuries.

But many survived—for now. Tracker would deal with them later.

Commerce, travel, and trade had disappeared in a matter of weeks. Capital was frozen. Work was nonexistent for tens of millions, exacerbating the horror. Starvation would loom if transport routes did not open before the harshness of the following winter. Global stockpiled food supplies would last for a year—for many locations near to the depots. If transportation was available. If the rats allowed entrance. If the winter didn't rot the food.

The sun was approaching new centennial lows in solar activity, allowing cosmic radiation to penetrate the solar system. These gamma rays encouraged the occasional interaction of hydrogen and oxygen. This interaction created more than normal water droplets in the stratosphere. Water vapor became cloud cover, which became rain and fog. Soon it would become snow and sleet and hail.

The weakest and the poorest would suffer the most. The wealthy had isolation capabilities. They could retreat and survive until another day. The rest would suffer and die. Perhaps another forty million would die without a name, without a grave, without a memory. No one would really know.

Yet this was all in the future. In the early fall, the worst of the attacks would begin.

Never underestimate an adversary with a 3.5-billion-year head start.

—Abigail Salyers, microbiologist

ACT TWO

SUBMISSION

> You can sway a thousand men by appeal to their prejudices quicker than by convincing one man by logic.
>
> —Robert Heinlein

October 10–13

Hajj is one of the five pillars of Islam. It is the source of all comfort for the True Believers.

It is also the largest annual gathering of humanity in one place on the planet. Three million pilgrims were expected in 1440 of the Umm al-Qura calendar. Makkah was the location. The center of the Islamic world. One of the origins of their faith along with Medina. The challenges of international travel bans were simply ignored by the Islamic world. If you were going to Makkah, you were invited on board the only flights in the air.

Tracker had decided more than two years ago. Hajj was the best place and the best time to expand the next stage of her operation—multiple, simultaneous, broad-spectrum attacks; concentration of population over a short time frame; universal travel across the globe. It would be panspermia writ large for the species—in reverso.

MII: Son of Frankenstein

Marburg II was far worse than its now distant hereditary cousin Marburg. Quicker to infect, it took longer to kill while allowing more virions to erupt and attack.

Her team had perfected its delivery system. Simple glass wafers. Encased, the virus would break out upon the cracking of the thin glass sheath. Simply step on it.

Hajj would have three million pairs of feet. It was such a simple solution to such a global problem. Destroy the epidemic of humanity with a pandemic of virals—not yet life. Strands of death.

The Kingdom of Saudi Arabia's security was always tight during hajj. After the Iranian attempt to take over the Holy City, the Saudis were prepared. CCTVs closely monitored the pilgrims as they performed the five days of ritual cleansing and purification.

Use of drones would be suspect. Viral glass would be the disseminator of choice. The stoning of the devil on the eleventh of Dhu al-Hijjah would be the place. Seven stones would be thrown at the three pillars of Mina. Everyone would walk around the pillars before emerging to cross the bridge to heaven.

Seventy-two assailants were required. She chose this from the crowd density figures. The difficulty was arranging these many conspirators without knowledge of each other or of the mission.

She had to waste more than a dozen of her couriers for the task. Of the 448 she had recruited, she had made sure that a few hundred were Muslim. Some refused—and died. Those who accepted their task rejoiced.

"Reflect on the words of Mohammed. The infidel must be converted or crushed. Now is your time."

In her conversation with each, her voice made over into that of a strong male with a bedouin-accented Arabic, she told of the deaths to come. She spoke of the Great Satan and urged their willingness to work to destroy it.

Those who agreed were trained—under al-Sadr.

Their mission was simple. Strengthen all true believers for the destruction of Satan. Do so at the holy site of Makkah during hajj. Silently offer the gift of life to all believers who participate. Speak with no one of this gift. Mohammed be praised.

The agent of dispersal would enhance the entire hajj group's ability to fight the infidel. Their fervor would grow one hundredfold as they returned home to destroy all infidels. The ensuing wars would encourage Muslim military forces to come to the aid of the beleaguered holy warriors. These strikes would enable the masses to rise against their satanic masters and destroy them, finally. A new caliphate would emerge from the ruins of the sick and dying capitalist beasts.

EARLY MORNING

Software had created the tracts for the messengers to hear online at special websites blocked from Agency view—all agencies. Each reading was personalized to the recruit, as if he alone would be responsible for the uprising. When their packets were given to them, each unwrapped the gauze with care. They were all told that they were holding the 7th *juz'* of the original Koran:

> We send the Messengers only to give good news and to warn. So those who believe and mend their ways, upon them shall be no fear, nor shall they grieve. But those who reject Our signs, them the punishment will touch, because they did not cease from transgressing.

She gave good news. The gauze they touched was MSP soaked—designed to their body's DNA. They thought they were offering the same enhancement across the entire hajj host. They knew they had become "the Messengers." They would know no fear; nor would they grieve. They would touch the transgressors with pain and death. The pathway to heaven was assured by the strong bedouin voice.

Each flew from his country of origin—Algeria, Egypt, Syria, Mali, Ethiopia, Nigeria, Indonesia, China, Pakistan, Afghanistan, India, Iraq, France, Kyrgyzstan. Each carried his small packets in a fold of the *ihram* draping his shoulders, the symbol of purity and equality. Surely their efforts during this week would purify and make equal all believers! Surely the Great Satan would be brought to its knees by the force of Allah's messengers.

Their tents in Mina were far better than most of their homes. Each was air-conditioned and comfortably carpeted. Hammams were dispersed for every hundred pilgrims. Signs and colors directed them, each to his national tent grouping. For five days they engaged in that most ritualistic and faithful of Islamic duties, the pilgrimage to Makkah—hajj. When they returned, they would be ranked as among the most gifted in their villages.

They partook of the waters of Zamzam. Two of them dropped their healthy additive into the spring, ensuring future pilgrims of the strengths they were bestowing upon this year's contingent.

They chanted as they circumscribe the *Kaaba* seven times, dropping their viral glass along the way. Their strength was increasing with each round as they felt the full fury of their mission unfold. Their MSP was pumping now. MSP (transcranial magnetic stimulation) erased the memory of each operative while enhancing his motor skills.

The induced high would soon be overcome by one of the deadliest viral agents on the planet—Marburg II.

HELL ON EARTH

Marburg is one of five of the genera, filovirus. Ebola is a close nucleotide cousin. Filoviruses infected cells by various uptake mechanisms.

Following fusion of the intersticing membranes, the cell walls, the nucleocapsid is released into the receptor cell's cytoplasm. This primary transcription instructs the cellular translation machinery to produce more viral proteins, the Cas9 sequencing. These are to be the templates for the production of millions of new viral genomes. Secondary transcription produces crRNA for synthesis of virion progeny. Assembly of new nucleocapsids occurs at the budding site—where the virus first entered the cell—and erupts into the host's bloodstream. The cells have been recruited as "transformers" to recreate billions of virions. The host will die within ten days of infection. The virions will spread via bodily secretions of saliva, vomitus, feces, blood, tears, and semen. The process repeats millions of times—for each infection, each death.

As each believer prepared for his departure home, he began to feel weary. Marburg II symptoms include fever, chills, and muscle aches, much like the common cold. These were easy to ignore—and impossible to medicate. Surely, this was the emotion draining from them after such a glorious hajj. Surely, they would soon see the consequences of their pilgrimage. Surely, their impact upon the world of Satan was imminent.

Of course, they were right. Just in exactly the opposite manner.

Siddiqi coughed all night on the flight back to Damascus. He thought the wind must have given him the trouble, but he wondered.

Why do I have blood in my stool? Why is my head pounding? The blessings of Allah are hard to understand.

The incubation period could be very short. Each messenger's illness came on during his flight home, sickening many other passengers. Three of the flights were quarantined upon arrival as the Marburg beast emerged quickly from the sands.

These efforts were futile. Quarantine stations in Sudan, Mali, and Tajikistan simply meant waiting inside the terminal for a doctor. When no one came, the cordinaires simply walked home.

Marburg II began abruptly, with high fever, severe headache and malaise. Muscle aches and pains were common. Watery diarrhea, abdominal pain and cramping, and nausea and vomiting could begin on the third day. Diarrhea could persist for a week. Patients appeared ghostly, with drawn features, deep-set eyes, expressionless faces, and extreme lethargy. A nonitchy rash appeared in most patients between two and seven days after onset of symptoms.

Many patients developed severe hemorrhagic manifestations between five and seven days, usually with some form of bleeding, often from multiple areas. Fresh blood in the vomit and feces was often accompanied by bleeding from the nose, gums, anus, and vagina. Spontaneous bleeding occurs at venipuncture sites, where intravenous access was obtained to give fluids or obtain blood samples. This could be particularly troublesome to health-care workers.

During the severe phase of illness, patients sustained high fever. Breakdowns within the central nervous system could result in confusion, irritability, and aggression.

Death occurred between eight and nine days after symptom onset, usually preceded by severe blood loss and shock. Fatality could be as high as 85 percent. This was entirely dependent upon timely diagnosis, health-care skills, and supplies in each infected area; social and cultural abilities / restrictions of each human vector; and age, sex, physicality of each. Even the time of year was important.

AIRPORT DETENTION

My, my, my! Such a lot of guns around town and so few brains.

—Philip Marlowe

October 27th

The US President is informed of a Minneapolis airport detention just prior to his call from Rafsanjani. His military advisors assume it is part of the Atlanta attack. Intelligence demurs.

'Mr. President, I doubt their ability to act in such a globally coordinated manner,' responds the NSA Director. The question had been asked by HSA; the response was directed to the man in charge.

'This is a quarantine, effected by CDC protocol. It happens infrequently, but CDC has prepared for it. The plane is held in full lockdown for 72 hours while the crew and passengers are fed and watered but restrained onboard the vessel. EIS personnel are on board now.'

'Get us a link to Dr. Mooney now. I know she is struggling with the disasters in Atlanta and the West, but we need to know what she knows in real time.'

The video line to the CDC Director was live in four minutes. She acknowledged, then returned to her personnel on the ground. even from the remote tarmac at MIN, Dr. Mooney was direct.

'We suspect one or more passengers is infected with a filovirus of unknown origin and nature. The passenger is vomiting, has diarrhea and is bleeding from several orifices. The crew have attempted to confine him in the lower galley, but he struggled for quite some time. Several passengers and crew are assumed to be infected. These personnel are also isolated, in a far more friendly manner. The remainder of the people on board are anxious, terrified. The ventilation has been secured and fresh air is now fully confined and filtered.

'Food is being brought to the vessel, but how we get it inside is a problem we have yet to solve. The doors are now secured from the outside. We are in communication directly with the skipper, his crew and indirectly with the passengers.'

'I'd like to speak with the skipper now… Give me his name and some background.'

'Get me ground control…'

'Already on board with your request sir. The channel is open.'

'Captain Bentley, this is the President.'

'Sir, we have an incredibly dangerous situation here that is deteriorating very quickly…'

'Yes, I know. It is going to get far worse. We suspect you have a passenger who has a viral infection purposefully planted on him. We understand he is down below but has infected others. No one can leave this plane until we get a full BSL-4 there. This will take a few hours, at best. You will be provided with food and water as soon as we can.'

'The latrines have to be serviced quickly sir.'

'Flight control, get a sanitation truck then now. General Smithers, have that truck quarantined along with the driver.'

'Captain Bentley, you have to hold your court there for at least four hours while we deal with ground support. Once we can get everyone off the plane and into quarantine, we shall do so. You have to manage expectations in the meantime. If a fight erupts or people go crazy, this entire rescue will be in jeopardy. Do you understand? You were a Marine pilot. I have great respect for the Marines. Now you have to command people once again.'

'Agreed. Understood.'

Bentley responded immediately to his co-captain, 'Put me through to the cabin.'

'Ladies and gentlemen this is the captain of flight 814. We are working diligently to get you safely off the aircraft. This will take a few hours. We are replenishing your food and water and emptying your waste tanks now.

'I am asking you for your patience. This ship has been infected. The

CDC staff are working on identifying the source and type of infection as we speak. We have to do our best to protect each of you as well as everyone on the ground. As soon as we can do so, we shall get you to safety.

'In the meantime, please support one another. If someone is frightened - and I know you all are - try to comfort them. This will comfort you too. If there are military personnel onboard, please ident yourselves to the chief purser and organize as a unit for support and protection.

If there are medical personnel on board, identify yourselves and organize support for anyone who may become infected or ill disposed. If there are religious personnel on board, please offer your care to each who request or require it. If another passenger falls ill, immediately notify the crew who are isolating them in the galley below you.'

MIDNIGHT

October 27th

By midnight, Marburg was ID'ed via NCEZID's innovative online tool, Microbnet. A quarantine hanger was settled at the far right of the main runway. The plane shuttled over, settling inside. The doors were closed, the building was quietly darkened as tarps covered all external walls. The 'Level Four' was brought into the hanger, followed by an EIS troupe of sixteen physicians and laboratorians.

Finally, the cabin doors were opened and passengers and crew filed down the gangway. One by one, each was quickly tested for presence of Marburg. Virtually everyone was positive. 400+ infections. An already overworked and decimated CDC staff began the task of assisting survival for the few who would.

Every passenger and crewmember aboard died. Sixteen CDC workers were infected and seven died. No one had any idea of the disease. MII was unleased.

As the word of the infection spread, the confrontation between Iran and the United States grew tense—and then simply dissipated. Iranian leadership was completely occupied with survival—of their nation and of themselves.

The attacks in Makkah occurred three months after the attacks in Asia, Europe, and Africa. Their news was just beginning to come in to DC and the regulated media. Little information was released to the world on these newest attacks in Makkah. Enough suffering was happening as it was.

But the political leadership teams in Tehran and in DC were confused by the noise of illnesses rapidly spreading. The confluence of events had overcome their ability to comprehend, to respond.

Conditions were deteriorating around the world. Even as the United States was "surviving" the dual attacks upon her soil, much of the remainder of the world was sinking beneath the biome flood.

The call came in to the Oval Office from Tehran. It was ignored, purposefully. Let them worry. With no conclusive proof of a link between the Atlanta attack and the global infections, the administration allowed time to work to its advantage.

Iran's leaders were all aware of the American demands and the timeline. They were also becoming acutely aware of the infection rate within their country. Four days ago, planeloads of hajjis had disembarked and were now infecting the populace. Too late did they quarantine the remaining flights from Makkah.

Despite the deaths and carnage in Atlanta, California, Chicago, New York, and overseas, no attacks were initiated by the US military. Something greater was afoot. More and more administrative and congressional advisors knew this was far greater than a small irascible nation in the desert could organize. There was still no barking dog.

No Articles of War were presented to the Congress. The president ordered a stand-down of the military and a reduction of the DEFCON status. China and Russia were informed first. Weapons returned to their warrens yet again. A brief conversation between the two presidents did happen, finally—initiated by the United States.

"Mr. President, we are withholding our demands upon you for now. We stand ready to offer what support you will accept from your sworn enemy. Mercy exceeds justice in our hearts."

"We shall take care of our own. We suspect your involvement in this horror. This has the markings yet again of the Great Satan. You have more to learn from us."

In two weeks, the Iranian leadership was dead or in hiding.

So close the world came to such horrific blows. So little did the world know of the blows yet to come.

> Slouching towards Bethlehem to be born.
> —T. S. Eliot, 1927

The next five months were hell on Earth. Until the new MII virus ran its course, all of humanity was at risk. The Great Satan had indeed risen from the desert sands, "slouching towards Bethlehem to be born."

In all, 3 million were exposed during the hajj. Of those, 2.7 million became infected. At a global transmittal rate of one-to-nine the infective viral generation drove slightly more than 1.4 billion people to an early grave—in less than three months.

Health-care facilities in a hundred countries were quickly overcome with victims. Most were Muslim—more than 90 percent. Many came from poor communities. Returning to their crowded warrens, they infected at exponential rates. One-to-thirty was common.

There was no cure, no vaccine for Marburg, much less Marburg II. No one at CDC even knew it existed. Some were still quarreling over whether this filoviral strain was new or simply a recombinant.

Diagnosis was difficult, requiring a knowledgeable practitioner, Biosafety Level 4 equipment and either ELISA or PCR testing. Results were available within four days. A Marburg viral generation could replicate itself in just over four hours—twenty-four generations evolving in real time while the diagnosis awaited verification.

The strongest of the remaining CDC teams were dispatched, only to be recalled. The host nations became infected just as rapidly across the Muslim world. Jake and Sam flew to Karachi but were refused access on the tarmac. Their plane flew to Jeddah, only to be refused airspace entry.

They returned home via Spain. The country was in ruins. Between the previous Ebola attack and this new Marburg II, more than 70 percent of the population had died—all in less than four months.

Many teams were attacked and killed as satanic messengers of death. The Islamic Crescent tried desperately to bring aid to the afflicted. Many were themselves infected. Many were killed outright as suspicious carriers of the disease.

Treatment was cursory, at best. Liquids and oxygen replacement were suggested. Barrier nursing techniques were strongly urged upon health-care workers. Watching the patient die in quarantine was the best solution arrived at by field clinicians.

A few exploratory drugs for the first Marburg were in testing stages, but the cost was high. There was no known cure for this new beast. It ravaged entire continents, tearing at the very flesh of humanity. Few escaped the scourge of MII.

Many infections take place in the most inhospitable reaches of central Africa and central Asia, where a health clinic was at best a day's walk away. Brought to these relatively safe havens of underpopulation, MII spread easily across villages and towns. Help arrived. People kissed their diseased family members goodbye—and became infected themselves. They moved on to their homes or their fields. Their entire villages disappeared in a few weeks. The process continued unabated because no CDC doctors were allowed in to stem the tide—as if anyone could.

Now the whole world was exposed. Within ten days of Eid al-Adha in early November, all international commercial flights had been canceled. Riots broke out in dozens of cities. As word of cures and palliatives spread, people gave life savings for worthless water and sand. Health-care workers, clinics, and hospitals were overwhelmed. Soon, many refused to show up for work, fearful of contamination while watching cohorts die on global TV screens.

Tens of thousands of sick or concerned people rushed to government agencies, mosques, and treatment centers for help, for guidance, for mercy.

None was at hand—neither help nor guidance nor mercy. All would die. As images of sick and dying children crisscrossed the internet world, hucksters made millions. Sporting events and all public gatherings were forbidden.

Food shortages quickly raised the specter of starvation. Small villages and towns remained relatively safer than urban areas. With millions in a small geographic area, cities were hot zones for the virions. Roads out of cities quickly clogged with desperate émigrés seeking safety and solace. Fields were stripped of food, ripe and unripe. Pets were killed for food, as were cattle and chickens. Looters shot farmers—who shoot back.

Rats remained in many cities, fattened on the bodies of millions of unburied victims. Bubonic plague surfaced. The fleas of rats infested the human survivors. Rats and their fleas had a habit of surviving and of thriving. The worst environment for human survival was the best for these creatures. More than 140 million were thought to have died from the plague. Unknown millions simply disappeared.

As with the previous attacks, rabies returned. The absence of vaccines ensured a 100 percent fatality rate for tens of millions. Dogs and humans died in their own horror.

Borders were closed. Muslims in non-Muslim countries were interred, imprisoned, or simply shot on sight. Religious battles were fought across four continents. Many of these battles were fought in the streets, many between Sunni and Shia.

With few exceptions, the military of most Muslim nations refrained from combat. Many went to the aid of their dying citizens, even as their commanders ordered them from their barracks to war.

Fifty-four million deaths within two weeks devastated the Republic of Iran. They died there just as quickly as they did in every other nation of Islam. By January, there were a few hundred thousand left in the Iranian desert. The cities were deserted, save for the vultures, the rats, and the dogs.

China fared the best, as did Japan. Monocultural constraints reduced the numbers of hajjis to far western China. The Uighur society died as a cultural entity. The Han viewed this as heavenly justice—more lands for their thriving race.

Western nations suffered deeply. Contamination from the hajj flights began early and spread spontaneously across the globe. Western health facilities were better trained and able to function, but only for isolation and disinfection. No one could do anything to stop the virions from their appointed task.

Isolation was least painful, thus most effective. Political rights groups protested and then fell quiet as they too acquired the deadly virus. Entire groups of peoples set themselves aside from the world and waited for the storm to pass. Survival.

WINTER

> Ceux qui peuvent vous faire croire des absurdités,
> peut vous faire commettre des atrocités.
>
> —Voltaire

The winter accelerated the death rate for Marburg II survivors. Many of the remaining elderly and very young simply died in their homes and hovels. Their apartments become abattoirs. No one knows how many died.

No one was counting any longer.

The dead were left to freeze, only to thaw and rot in the spring. The crows and the buzzards and the rats had an exponential population explosion. The bubonic plague struck the Northern Hemisphere with a ferocity unknown since the fifteenth century. Perhaps three hundred million died.

Other forms of survival emerged. Death became a lust—to strive after, to achieve as a prize. Those who had the strength—or the genes—to survive were confronted by the insanity of the maddened cities.

City people, millennials, and the urban elite died by the tens of millions. Many did so at their own hands. Struggling to suffer, they ignored all warnings.

"*Rue Morgue* parties" opened in the gutters of metropolitan New York, Philadelphia, Boston, London, Berlin, Madrid, and Paris. The ghoulish became the newest normal. People vied to see who could die next. There was nothing to live for; death was welcomed. No one wanted to survive; everyone tried to die.

The more macabre, the better. Clubs opened and closed overnight. A dance of death attracted thousands to penalty pits, where the most sadistic were the most successful. Rewards were offered for the most killed in an evening, the most blood spilled, the most fashionable way to die. Scenes from the Inquisition were reenacted. Torture became a way of "death giving meaning to life."

In Barcelona, a table was set upon the promenade seating five thousand. It was lit by ten thousand human torches. Infected were dragged into the street, tied or nailed to crosses, soaked in organic cooking oil, and set alight. The sickened survivors danced to the screams of the dying. The eating and dancing went on all night, until the dying became ashes in the morning light.

Guillotines spring up across Paris. Thousands flocked to the beheadings, first as observers and then as participants, as sans-culottes. Private homes built their own guillotines and breaking wheels.

Strappado becomes a title of renown for those who inflicted the pain. Skills unused for centuries became renewed by these roué, denizens of depravity. The longer the execution, the more the compensation paid. *Allez à morte* became the new anthem children sang as they played with corpses and body parts.

Oddly, much of deep equatorial Africa was spared once the initial attacks had subsided. This was the birthplace of many of the dreaded diseases. While much of urban sub-Saharan Africa was devoid of humanity within a few months, the deeper jungles survived. Only caravan infections took their toll. As these quickly ceased, the spreading virions were stopped by the desert sands.

An entire religious population was nearly wiped out by the messengers—extermination at the hand of Allah, by his own.

WEB OF UNCERTAINTY

The diseases were given a world map upon which to evolve. The rat-based plague had once again proved its worth, too well. Tracker was pleased—as pleased as she could be.

Three hundred million deaths resulted from an ancillary attack of the Black Plague. And counting. She was beginning to see her vision become reality. A billion and a half more had fallen before her trekking "horsemen" of Marburg. Three billion or more had died over ten months. The bodies littered the streets and buildings and paths and hovels of a disintegrating world. Soon the nightmare from which they came would engulf the planet.

Now she had to make decisions. She had real figures, real deaths. She was on track for the ultimate hunt. She had wiped out 50 percent of humanity in less than a year.

A complex spiderweb of commerce, industry, culture, transportation, food, energy, and capital united Earth's people. A computer image of global airline pathways showed a deep rich red connectivity across six continents and every blue sea. Some were more thinly veiled; others were dense with traffic. This profound, beautiful web of arachno-human endeavor was itself the reflection of a deeper composite of intricate sophistication.

Underlying this mesh wove the skein of kinship, of culture, of society, of music, theatre, the arts, and humane compassion. Deeper still lay the electronic webs of communication. Free flowing electrons had opened humankind to the subterranean, extraterrestrial world of instant, inexpensive global communication—for essentially every man, woman, and child on the planet.

One had to consciously refrain from participating—or be prevented by totalitarian regimes. Capital flowed like water to seek its own level. Wealth ensued as capital eroded rocks of old conduct, rushing the dissolving silt to be reborn as new accomplishments.

Deep, intense, intertwined, and multifaceted, the web ways were emergent as chaos, finding their own organization independent of will. Humankind's geometric increase in complexity drove wealth and health and knowledge ever higher—a rising helix of humanity.

Now, these same web ways of humanity were shredding before the onslaught. Like a match held close to a spider's web, her frisson was melting through five millennia of human communication. And the larger the connected group, the faster the fragmentation.

Air travel had improved her insight. Islam had proven Tracker's devastating point. Humanity was losing control. We were losing touch with one another—with the web lines down, communication was dissolving. Society was disintegrating.

Humankind was disappearing.

COMMUNICATION

How did the bankruptcy happen? Two ways. Gradually and then very suddenly.

—Earnest Hemingway, *The Sun Also Rises*

Tracker's challenge now was communication. She had to wait until these first major waves of attacks subsided, until the world began an attempt to open up again. Global communications systems were under control of a few governments now. The days of a wide-open internet were over. She had to continue to communicate with her agents on her own secure network while avoiding discovery. Her agents were simple people. Their simple tool was the cell phone.

Death rates were highest during the first wave of a new disease. If a disease fatality rate was too high, the host might die before the microbe could be passed along to another host. Higher infectiousness in transmissions linked to virulence could overcome short-term survival rates for the pathogen.

For virions and bacteriophages, survival was the key. Transmission was simply the lock. Both had to function in a binary fashion for successful genetic progression, for species survival.

Tracker had been working on several "new diseases" and their delivery for most of four years. In each of her remote labs, her hired hands had developed death by design—viral, bacterial/fungal. Nuclear, and nano attacks were coming on line next.

Time was now working against her. The defenses of humanity were gaining power, despite her best efforts at crippling them. These defenses were not designed by humankind. They were the result of genetic survival structures deeply embedded in every creature's DNA membrane. As populations diminished, growth was encouraged. The pressure to survive was often far greater than the exogenous pressure of destruction. For most.

Tracker had to pull her genies out of the test tube—so to speak.

Recombinant DNA was her choice of methods. Marburg was her first choice of species. Airborne was her best choice of delivery—always had been. Easiest to use, infiltrate, propagate, and dissipate, it was also most effective for infectious rates.

Her MII was very effective. MERS and the chimeras worked well. Yet she needed more. She needed a stronger shell; a more viable cellular membrane intrusion tool; and an adaptability that allowed for multigenerational, moderately low infection rates. This would prevent the disease from "overspilling" its mutation sequencing. It would survive by fewer mutational events rather than more. The application?

Food.

Global agricultural production. The attack would be simultaneous with the biome attacks. It just wouldn't observed until it was too late—far too late.

UNIVERSAL FORENSICS

> The enemy will never attack your strong position, only where you are weakest. If you do not know your weak link, assuredly he will.
>
> —Lao Tse, *The Art of War*

Randy Murch of the FBI had developed the forensics concept several years ago. CDC's Security chief, Jake Russell was now using it. Murch called his tool ReachDeep. He used it in exploring a crime within the limits of experience and intelligence of all members of an investigative group.

Jake and his partner, Major Soliz, as well as fourteen team members coordinated their actions. Each had a different specialty—blood, psi warfare, drugs, gangs, terrorists, homeland, black ops, hackers (two), bioweapons, political, and chemistry. Each had subdisciplines they developed, as well as sidebars they shared with others.

"The task is absurdly difficult, of course," began Jake. "We shall follow the lead from the FBI's Murch of a few years ago. We are an open book. We all have access to the same info. We each have our specialties. We each have our own agendas and experiences. Everything we say or do for the next few months bends the wills of each of us in this room."

"We know of eight bioweapons attacks in the past eight weeks. We are now learning of five new agricultural attacks around the world. How is this connectivity still happening when most of humanity is shut off from one another?

"These attacks have disrupted lives, families, communications, industry, entire markets, and the flow of people. Societies are falling apart around the world. Entire nations are disappearing before the eyes of the world.

"Who is responsible?

"The issue is less important than how do we stop them?"

"Question."

"Please ID yourself as you ask, so we can quickly get to know one another and our specialties."

"Jewel Banks, psychological warfare." PW. "You said 'them.' Why?"

"Rob Coulter, bioweapons." BW. "The information we have indicates a broad spectrum of distribution networks and tangents of attack. You can see the vector analyses on screen now. Asia. Africa. Southern Europe. The United States. Highly concentrated urban population centers. Aviation. Naval. Ground-based delivery devices.

"Discriminant decisions made purposefully. Delivery tools of advanced yet simple design. The agents in use were specifically developed for the attacks. These attacks must be coordinated. Thus, there must be more than one individual or group. The agents were either hardened, dual-purpose, genetically engineered—or all of the above."

"They call me Ismail, terrorism. We have several links to Islamic influence, but no known group has taken responsibility or claimed ownership. This is very unusual. With the attacks on Makkah, most of Islam has now died, so we can doubt the severity of the links we do have."

"We don't know if the perps had any idea of the force vector they were unleashing. They were pups on a leash. Mary Anne Fitzgerald, political ops."

"Joe Black, gangs. Group ethics forces them to go along with the acts of horror. We see it all the time. Think MS-13."

"We have no way to know if they even knew one another—or had any links. Karen Bell, drug enforcement."

"Actually, we do know something. Major Becky Soliz, CDC SecOps. We know, or I know, the leader of the first attack in Atlanta—Mohammed Abu-Sidr."

Ishmael looked at her closely. "How do you know this? He has been dead for more than a decade. I killed him myself in Riyadh in 2009."

"Interrogation at the scene. He died telling me who sent him. If not MAS, then who?"

"Abu-Sidr had a grown son, Moamet Abu-Sidr. Did you mistake their names?"

She was silent for a very long time and then said, "Yes, clearly I must have done just that. My bad." Major Soliz was not one to admit an error. She didn't commit many. Her truthful acknowledgment set the tone. Her simple admission of fault opened the group immediately. Social and cultural bounds were loosed. Thoughts and experiences flowed like water.

Suddenly everyone had ideas to share. Comments flew fast. Most took electronic notes or recorded the session.

"We have clear evidence of Islamic influence in the Minneapolis airport attack."

"Joko's Indonesian security folks stated the Lombok area was strongly Islamic."

"Did you get an autopsy report on the Atlanta perps?"

"Yes. Significant levels of elevated neurotransmitters serotonin and endorphin throughout the nervous system. Amie Smithfield, blood pathology. We also have elevated levels of CRF and CKK, peptide bioregulators among the surviving population."

"Refugee camps across the country report surprising levels of aid and support from virtually all camps. Optimism is the natural response from the vast majority of refugees—even after the destruction of so much of America. Peggy Klein, Homeland Security."

"We have pathologies on a wide range of victims. The isos from BL-4 show molecular redesign. The new MII is a case in point. Not only is it a new virion, but it was also embedded in a pane of glass. That's highly sophisticated biogenetic engineering, to say the least. These attacks were of the highest caliper. The Magister Ludi is neither a political agent nor a religious zealot. Dr. Joyce Fields, biochemistry and epigenetics."

"The absence of proof can be a proof of absence. Or not."

"Colonel?"

"Yes, Major."

"When the US and Indonesian presidents began speaking during their first contact, they made a reference to a Sherlock Holmes story. They both seemed to know it well—"

"*Silver Blaze*, Conan Doyle. They were talking about the significant clue in the case. While the estate was well protected by hunting dogs, there was no barking when the murder took place. The conclusion? The Master was the killer."

"Jimmy and I (Sol Canter, AI, and Jimmy Jones, AI as well)"—he nodded toward his colleague—"disagree on virtually everything in the hacking world. We are usually both right, which we haven't figured out yet. My point here is this: No hounds barked on the net either. Anywhere. The silence was and remains deafening. This is too eerie for us—and we are eerie … What about a separate global intranet? That would explain the utter silence. We are using a telegraph while they are using smoke signals—totally different signaling properties, totally different methods of communication. We would never know because we aren't even listening."

"Wow, dude. That's the most I have ever heard you speak in a coherent statement since you got married!"

"Shut up. I didn't get married."

"Did too," Sol shot back.

"Did not."

"Straighten it up right now, boys, or I'll shoot you both." Jake opened his holster.

The room went silent. For a very long minute.

"Sorry," they both yelped.

"As usual, the squeaky wheel gets the oil. The hackers have a valid point."

"Sir, you have spoken twice now without ID'ing yourself," said Jake.

"Shen Hai. Deep Sea is the proper English translation. I am black ops. The less you know about me, the safer for all of us. JimSol—may I call you that?—know more about this than they are saying. Even I know of secret intranets. They are extensive across Asia. Governments and Tang use them, discreetly. I'm sure our government has a few."

"And which is your government?"

"USA. I am an American of Chinese Indonesian descent. I have been told that my mother was a great opera singer!"

"Okay, okay, we are all in this room together. We must rely on one another to stop the carnage and to find the perps," Jake demurred. "We know quite a bit more than each of us is sharing. Understood. We have to know we can trust one another. When we can, we will move forward.

For now, let's keep the facts flow moving quickly. A cascade would be preferable."

For the next three days, the group shared knowledge, experiences, and fears. Every one of them had lost most or all of their families to the pathogen cyclone. Each was more lucky than smart to be alive. Each knew it.

On the fourth morning, Becky asked the group, "What will be the next attack? Where?"

"Anyone ever heard of transcranial magnetic stimulation?"

"As a matter of fact, yes. Why?"

"PsyOps found two bodies in Makkah. Brain tissue biopsies revealed a very unusual poling of virtually all cells to one magnetic direction." Ms. Banks was taciturn, brief, and accurate.

"You mean pooling?"

"No, poling—as in north/south poles of a magnet. No cell can survive such a trauma for more than a few hours. These brain cells endured it for at least five days, perhaps a week. The only way these people could have survived is with massive doses of endorphin—high levels of which levels are also present," added Black. "The rue morgues were using these to stimulate their victims across Europe. Every one of them died in ecstasy, or so they were told."

"The effect can be exhilarating," Dr. Bell answered. "Also, deadly. They must have thought they were entering heaven."

"Allah would never allow such a thing. These beasts, these donkeys, carried the Marburg into the holiest of cities to kill fellow believers."

"What if they had no idea what they were doing? What if they thought they were helping others approach the gates of heaven?"

"Through the gates of hell?"

"Yes. Death by design."

"What if the agents were recruited for an act of religious mercy while executing the ultimate in religious intolerance? Force multipliers in the deadliest game on Earth."

"Sounds like a movie."

"This story is too real for the cinema."

"Exactly. Too real. Whoever is behind this is enforcing a form of reality upon willing agents. These vectors think they are doing well by their faith, by their actions."

"Metronome gangs," said Black and Banks simultaneously.

"Explain." Jake was deadly serious now. "QPH offices around the world are beginning to report outbreaks—not in humans but in soy, corn, pigs, cattle. We have to catch up with this monster."

"She is just that—a monster." Ms. Klein was sitting down, looking at her notes, nearly exhausted. "I have no idea why I just said that, but it seems to be perfectly true. Maybe it's because I am so exhausted; maybe I'm just wrung out. The camp where my children are staying was attacked last night … There were no survivors." She never looked up.

Food attacks were common now. As the dwindling reserve supplies were parceled out in the organized refugee camps, outsiders had begun attacking, killing everyone, and commandeering the remaining supplies. Savagery had become the norm of the new world order.

"If it is a woman, that reduces our gene pool considerably," pointed out Coulter. "There are fewer female bioengineers, geneticists, and chemists in the global arena. There are also far fewer black ops women—"

"My mother."

"What?" They all looked at Shen Hai.

"My grandmother disappeared more than forty years ago. My mother told me she was gone from the world. She would never return. Before she left, she had trained my mother in her ways. She was done. She had been hunting and killing for a decade prior."

"Hunting what?"

"The beasts that destroyed her village when she was a child. Japanese troops. Special units trained in torture. Somehow, she survived the destruction of our entire village—a rather large village.

"My mother told me what she did and how. She then urged me to excel in 'the killing arts.' She trained me … to do terrible things. No government would sanction such action, so Grandmother did it all herself. She killed each one in the same manner they had killed our villagers.

"Something happened to her. We say she 'lost her qi,' her breath of life. Dr. Fields, you might suggest she had become addicted to murder."

"Yes. I would think that."

"Mother showed me how to kill. I helped her. Four times. I should today be ashamed of my actions. Perhaps I am. At the time, I relished their slow deaths. For the crimes they had committed, their death was the only punishment allowable under the heavens. Each too had committed horrible acts of violence—against women, against children. We were proud of our work. We stopped their rampages. We broadcast our work to their compatriots. We stopped much killing. Much torture. I too lost my qi …

"Four Star was her stage name. Ma Lianliang. My grandmama." He closed his eyes.

"Why did you say her name?"

"To honor her."

"Why did you think a woman is behind these millions of deaths, Ms. Klein?"

"Just came to me in my fear and horror and exhaustion. No other reason."

"People, listen up. We have all suffered mightily from this global scourge. All are punished. We have work to do if we want to stop the killing. Put away your emotions for now and put on your brain apparatus. More people will die quickly. Soon. Millions more. Food stocks are already low in the survivors' camps across the Earth. If these reports are true, we are now under attack. We have been for some time. This perp is one sick mofo."

"My grandmother would not do these things. My mother would not do these things. They each killed for a specific purpose—retribution. Not annihilation. We each gave up our qi to stop the horror. The horror. The leader is someone else."

Sol had been quiet for too long. Jimmy looked at him and cried out, "Sol? What's up, dude? You cryin'? Baby back! Just ribbin' ya … Sol? What's going down Sol? I've known you since we were street shits in Tel Aviv. You ain't never gone down like this. Hey, Sol!"

"I know."

"What do you know?"

"My *dodah*—my mother's sister-in-law. She was in Israeli intelligence. Had been to America. Joined the Navy. Became a SEAL. First woman to do so. Then she disappeared. She was twenty-six. I was twelve. I think I had a crush on her. She had a piercing eye. She had a sense about anyone. She could read anyone, instantly. She looked at me once when I was ogling her from across the room. She came over and slapped me and then spat on me. Walked out. The shame has never left me."

"Why are we discussing women perps as if they are ghosts, imaginary people? Folks, women kill as easily and as gruesomely as men." Major Soliz was walking, pacing the room. "I have killed. Many people. Most with a clear intent. Never with the slightest inkling of remorse. Most of them deserved my knife or bullet or hand. I bathed in their blood in front of their loved ones. Mercy is a luxury I could never afford."

Jake was silent. He knew these things. He never mentioned them to another, particularly a commanding officer. Killing was a necessity in the military—never a joy.

Jimmy was speaking softly to Sol. "Why did you mention your dodah? I don't remember her."

Sol was just as quiet. The others hushed so they could hear. Energy was flowing through the room like carnal current. None of these people had ever spoken like this before. Not even Becky and Jake had gone this deep.

"She had a bad time as a teen." Sol was crying now, without fear or remorse. "Her family had been killed in Berlin. Killed is too soft a word." He sobbed in Jimmy's arms.

Jimmy had no idea what to do. Peggy Klein came over and put an arm around both young men. Tall, older, Rubenesque, she knew her strengths well.

"Her parents were tortured. Her siblings too. They sent her a video of them dying. She went off on her own into the Negev for weeks. We thought she had died. When she returned … she was … like your mother, Shen Hai. Her qi was absent. She had turned to ice in the desert." He smiled. "Funny … ice in the desert."

"Why did you think of her today, Sol?"

"I don't know. She just came to me. Hard. Cold. Faceless.

"She had gone to Europe, eastern Europe somewhere. We didn't hear of her for years. Then suddenly, my mother sees a huge deposit of shekels into her bank account. Actually, the authorities saw it first and questioned her about it. She had no idea. Then a note came: Keep the money. No need for it now."

Jake spoke up, "People, I suppose this is what Murch was designing for with ReachDeep. We may not have a suspect, but we certainly have a person of interest. Let's get NSA on the horn. I know the ground chief for the Indonesian operation the two presidents ran so effectively.

"While we wait for them, let's go over a plan of discovery for these two women. Let's focus on— Sol, what was your dodah's name?"

"Ruth. Ruth Emmanuel."

"Who has a link to Israeli intelligence?"

"On it now," replied Becky.

ATTACK SEQUENCING

The CIA had been observing the site—the Lake Geneva compound that Tracker had lived in for years. It was still her ops HQ for capital flow, nothing more. It had been under surveillance for ten days—ever since the ReachDeep conclusions had led them to her corporate headquarters. The cash transfer trail to her sister had unmasked Tracker's operations HQ—her public operational unit.

Naval ops had been preparing the attack. Now the Swiss Army was evacuating every home in the surrounding hills under the pretense of activation of its entire force of resident reservists—military readiness exercises during the global panic.

Appearing to their neighbors as reservists, Army XXI were actually the 5 percent careerists who ran the army—in particular, this operation. Going from home to home, they escorted the males—and more than a few female recruits—to their "staging areas." No indication of the coming event was apparent.

In three days, the entire mountainous canton area had been emptied. No one was aware of the "quarantine," except those participating. No one in the compound keyed in to the game. Life went on as usual, as the guise worked.

The property lay between Chemin de L'Etraz and Route de la Chapelle in forested country, purposefully obscure, distant, forgettable. It was just outside of Divonne-les-Bains—the baths.

They had no idea if she was present. Her presence would be a bonus. They simply wanted her to know they had been there. The bunker buster eradicated the entire grounds. Nothing was left—nothing but dust. The hole was 140 meters deep.

Tracker watched the new video stream and listened. The satellite image of the destruction of her headquarters was broadcast globally.

It was another signal—another ruse. The illusion of power from a simple explosion—an explosion that had reduced any potential leads to microscopic dust.

She had been discovered and partially thwarted. Her opening gambit had been interrupted by two guys with their own personal 747s. She knew they had no idea what was next. She sensed it. Whomever "they" were, they had no link to her mission.

They were closing in. But on what? On who?

She suspected that her nemeses had yet to ID her, to learn of her whereabouts, or to understand her capabilities. They had destroyed her operations center for her public business. They could not yet have linked that facility to her five developmental centers. No one was that good. Or?

Tracker had doubts, not for the first time. This operation had impossible written into its program. No one could achieve what had been demanded of her. Even she was less of a storm than she imagined.

She had to get to Istanbul. She had to put into play the sequencing there for the springtime attacks and the nuclear device. The nanos could wait another year. She had that much time.

OPERATION DARK WINTER: AGRONOMIA

> Maybe it is time that instead of controlling the environment for the benefit of the population, we should control the population to ensure the survival of the environment.
>
> —Sir David Attenborough

The agricultural dispersal units had been deployed over the past year. These small discreet devices were invisible and undetectable. Dispersed by minions, these millions of food microphages did their work with amazing simplicity.

Agricultural attack vectors were far easier and yet often more difficult. The workers had to act in unison without organization. It was chaos made simple by the mail.

This second round of blows was meant to disrupt the "power grid" of food supplies. The agriculture attacks were against a defenseless foe. Three firms processed 50 percent of US meat supply. Descend upon these vector sources and they would disperse death for her.

Soybean rust effectively deployed could destroy 80 percent of global production in a single season. Similar tools could quickly disrupt and destroy global cereals production. Security was nonexistent.

Primary distribution channels were normalized by the industries themselves. Global food production had become a universal phenomenon, interlinked and interchained. It was its own best efficiency and its own best demise. Within its strength lay its weakest link—universality. Patience was her strong suit.

The agriculture attack would be the Medusa to her previous kraken. She could not infect all the fields of the world. She just had to seduce a few with myriad small attacks. She assumed that a "mirrored shield" was not to be found.

Corn, wheat, maize, rice, sorghum, and millet were grown in essentially limitless quantities across six continents.

Dr. Borlaug's work over fifty years had dramatically increased yields for several flora and reduced starvation for all of humankind. It had also reduced species variety and biodiversity. This was the point of entry for Tracker.

Just a few global seed manufacturers dictated the supply and price for 80 percent of all seed stock on the planet. She could infiltrate these four firms' stockpiles. She had the chimeric stock ready, in storage. They were added to the reserves over the previous year through normal distribution channels. As spring plantings began, so too did summer harvests—of death.

Beef, poultry, chicken, and swine production was even easier to infiltrate and destroy. In the industrialized world, these bio-industrial plants were enormous. Hundreds of thousands of animals were raised under similar conditions of sanitation, food supply, reproduction, and waste removal.

More efficiently, she had delivery services supplied inadvertently by the anti-GMO crowd. The challenge was one of delivery. Thousands of fields across the globe prohibited complete saturation.

To enhance her results, she had infected bird droppings and tongue scrapings widely distributed by her feckless cohorts. Across Europe and the Americas, animal pastures, fields, feed lots, and abattoirs were still accessible.

Her "agents of change" were unaware distribution vectors for sufficient fields and plants to cause worldwide fear and panic. Human fear—and the media—would do the heavy lifting. In so many ways, agricultural infestation was more effective and less complex than human infection.

She knew from past experience that the media were her strongest tools of dispersal. Generate a fear of food, and hysteria would be spread by the gob smacks in the newsrooms. Her task was not diminished; the required intensity was simply reduced.

Fear would become the medium of mien. Expressing food-based fear would create panic. Panic would destroy livestock populations through massive culling operations dictated by fearful governments and NGOs. Starvation would ensue. Fait accompli.

Her agents had the advantage of systemic cloaking. Time from infection to destruction was a function of mobility. Mobility was its own secrecy. Infection would occur long after the agents were dispersed. Incubation time was the cloaking device.

She simply had to coordinate these activities into one intense storm of disease. The "seedlings" were CRISPR designed. Her researchers in the Brazilian rain forest facility on the outskirts of Porto Velho had designed immunity strengthened Karnal bunt, soy rust, rice blast, and fruit tree virus.

The insight provided by Tracker's contact in Genève had opened new doors for their work. Now they understood the actin versus microtubule transport distinction as applied to flora. This discovery opened the door to enhanced viral transport mechanisms. They could stimulate or suppress dynein phosphate extraction.

They had hardened the casings and expanded the cell wall intrusion chemical sword. With an easily opened cell wall, greater survival rates ensued for the virions. The simple addition of a zinc molecule to their molecular structure added significant survival capabilities.

Wheat fields infected with bunt would be quickly subject to global export bans. Soy rust fungi—*Phakopsora pachyrhizi*—was able to quickly attack and destroy soy fields and reduce production by as much as half in one growing season.

Rice blast—*Magnaporthe grisea*—was strongest in waterless rice fields but was infectious in all rice fields under the right environmental conditions. More than half of rice and cereal crops would be destroyed in a season.

Fruit tree virus, PPV, uses an aphid as its vector. Insects were particularly easy to manipulate with CASPR technology. Tens of thousands of acres of fruit-bearing trees would be uprooted in a vain effort to eliminate the disease.

These four vectors—bacterial, viral, fungal, and insectivore—had been genetically modified to greater immunity and higher survival rates by lowering genetic infectious rates.

The feedstock for this design work had been freely subscribed for within the United States. Stock of each of these diseases had been maintained by the US government for generations. The same government maintained that it had destroyed all stockpiles of these agents in 1973.

The identical US government that maintained the CDC also ran the eFORS (electronic Food-borne Outbreak Reporting System) and Foodnet to track all such occurrences—just in case of an outbreak of these diseases. This was the same CDC that maintained a small stockpile of anthrax—the stockpile that was blamed for the Indonesian outbreak.

CDC would be blamed for the distribution. CDC would be banned from what was left of most countries. It was perfect Trojan horse.

HANDMAIDENS OF DESPAIR

> This planet is on course for a catastrophe. The existence of life itself is at stake.
>
> —Dr. Tim Flannery, research scientist

Six Months Later

Sunitha had worked for children's rights for decades. She was now turning her attention to food rights for the poor. She had joined a neighborhood group advocating for local sustenance farming for all. Her allies were Lakshmi and Kailash. Together they felt industrialized farming was bad for their country, their people.

They received packets by mail once a month from their website subscription. The rice packets were "substitute grains." They stopped along the roads bordering the rice fields in South India, stepped into the fields as if on a walk, and planted hundreds of thousands of these infected rice blast seedlings.

They had joined forces with Obi and Hiroko in Japan, Lenore and Jean in France, Stephan in Australia, Juan and Benita in Argentina, and dozens of others in the United States and Europe. Each was making a small contribution to a changing world.

Small-scale farming was better for farmers. It was better for consumers. It was better for the planet. Healthy locavore organic agronomics was their solution to a dying world. How much their contribution would mean to the coming "dying season" would never be revealed to their communities. They would all die in the vanguard of the attacks.

In Japan, the elderly couple Obi and Hiroko, took long drives across the countryside each weekend. They simply opened the windows of their car. An open canister in the back seat distributed the rice blast as an aerosol. It scattered across the fields.

No one stopped them. No one knew them. Their source was an anonymous delivery they had requested online. Every week they received a shipment. Every week they took a drive. They returned home, cleaned out their car, and washed their clothing and then took a hot bath, as was their custom.

Lenore and Jean were from Rheims. They bicycled every Saturday. Each had a basket over the rear tire. The basket had an open weave that allowed the free flow of air. The wheat smut was distributed across the farmlands of central France without notice. They enjoyed *une petit déjeuner* before they left and *une dejeuner de matin* at a small village café when they were ready for a stop.

Each afternoon was special. Each lunch was in a different village. They enjoyed their rides, knowing they were helping others improve their life in a secret, meaningful manner.

Stephan enjoyed riding across the fields of southern Australia on his BMW bike. He could cover three hundred kilometers in a day. Each ride was different. Each ride spread wheat smut across the farmland. Each ride was responsible for the destruction of thousands of hectares of crop. He was a kind and gentle man who loved his country. He loved it so much he was killing it from within on each weekend ride.

Dispersal methods varied according to the driver, the rider, or the pedestrian. Each anticrop agent was designed to the food basket of delivery. Every participant was convinced that these dispersals were the right thing to do in a global capitalist system gone mad.

Their intentions were just. Their reasoning was sound. Their methods were the lifeblood of Tracker's expertise. She had created a global herd and was driving them to market. They were to be slaughtered for the cause in which they had enlisted. Each was certain his or her own cause was just; each was just as certain of his or her own death.

Food for Life was their link to one another. They had learned from the site. Several distribution methods could encourage local and state authorities to return to sustenance farming. These distribution methods were harmless and effective. They would simply disrupt the free flow of feed and grain within the global food network, nothing more.

Each of these hardy citizens felt very strongly about GMO-based food and protested against its introduction and use. Some were more successful than others. Some entities and NGOs supported this work, such as the European Union and the Union for Concerned Scientists. Some actually provided capital for their ever-expanding network.

WE MUST KILL THEM TO PROTECT THEM

> In the conflict between good and evil, the light and the dark, the light doesn't always win.
>
> —unknown

Jennifer hated the thought of animals suffering. She was a strong woman of twenty-eight with an animal husbandry background. She worked as a vet in the city of Lyme in northern England. Her husband Jonathan was of a similar mind. He worked as a laboratory technician in the local animal hospital. They both knew that they had the responsibility to help all animals. They were born with the gift of care. They would have no children because it was sinful to do so. The planet could no longer support their race.

She had worked for PETA and the RSPCA in the past but felt they were becoming cogs in the wheel of industrialized death. She knew she had to do more to stop this senseless slaughter of helpless animals—her true friends.

She had found the internet site Fight for Life and was an ardent follower. She had paid her subscription, which entitled her to download the ELF-type pamphlet, Animals First. From this, she learned which feedlots near her home were easily accessible by local road. She designed a drive-by for thirteen lots and five abattoirs that she could cover in ten hours. The ingredients for release were shipped to her through an ancillary site of FFL. She had been instructed as to their storage and release in the same pamphlet.

Jonathan had designed his own route through the neighboring district.

He had four feedlots, three abattoirs, and four swineherds. His tools were similar to Jenny's.

FMD would be spread by tongue scrapings. Newcastle disease would be spread by infected bird droppings into feed troughs. African swine flu would travel a similar route. All to save the animals.

Compatriots in Brazil, Argentina, Canada, the US Midwest, Germany, and France had already begun their liberations over the past few days. The infections would take place slowly at first and then rise with increased penetration of the herds. Chinese agents had attacked swine holds and chicken ranches over the past weeks. Russian and Kazak adventurers were attempting the same.

During the spring, Tracker had used the sophistry of the young to spread insect- and animal-borne disease across five continents. The results would begin to tally in another few months.

CDC releases its weekly disease threats reports via the internet. Traces of food diseases began to come in slowly, a few hints every day during April. By the end of the month, a beleaguered center was awash with reports of FMD, swine flu, and avian influenza, as well as initial stories of wheat rust and rice blast. Karnal blunt and soy rust were reported during the first week of May.

The reports came through in greater frequency each day. By the middle of May, the CDC was overwhelmed. The world was about to be pulled under yet again. The billions of deaths of the previous two years still blotted the skies; now new scourges were reported.

The government-controlled media instantly urged termination of all global food shipments for animals and grain. Governments still reeling under the previous year's destruction were unprepared for this new attack. No one knew what to do except more quarantine, isolation, and reporting of contacts. Fields lay unharvested. Tens of millions of animals were slaughtered around the world. Still the diseases spread.

By fall, the toll of death was rising yet again. Crop failures were taking millions of tons of production out of global circulation, just as food shipments were beginning to open up. Food stockpiles were elastic enough to last for the winter—if distributions were permitted.

Twelve of Tracker's formerly public websites began spreading the "peer-reviewed literature" of infestation of silos and storage facilities. Some of this was broadcast.

Inspections were encouraged, delaying distribution. Despite the obvious, several nations and the remains of the European Union forbade importation of foods from any country.

Japan essentially isolated itself from the rest of the world. Its population had been decimated by more than 60 percent from the plagues. Old age and very low birthrates coupled with these deaths to reduce her population irreversibly. Now it chose to attempt to survive unto itself.

Russia demanded Ukraine supply it with grain from storage and invaded in September. Empty silos and cities greeted starving soldiers. The rat population was greater than the human population. Rats became common food for survivors.

In Latin America, *narcotraficantes* who had become adept at global distribution methods for cocaine and marijuana over four decades of literally cutthroat competition were approached by several governments. Could they bring food into their starving nations? Yes, for a price.

Their expertise was quickly shaken down by the lack of bulk shipment expertise. They had no operational capabilities for such huge transshipment demands. No fleet of speedboats and submarines and planes and small cargo vessels could carry millions of tons of grain.

The continent starved while Argentine wheat rotted in the fields. Brazilian cattle died by the tens of millions. The populations of Buenos Aires, Sao Paulo, Brasilia, Santiago, Lima, and dozens of others cities devolved into criminal barbarism. The horrors of last winter's macabre in the northern hemisphere were repeated tenfold. Death stalked the magnificent lands.

India and Africa survived the onslaught, but only outside of the megacities. Joburg, Cape Town, Lagos, Dar, Nairobi, Mumbai, Calicut, Deli, and Colombo had suffered under the plagues. Now these cities simply ceased to exist.

Small villages survived. Lack of proximity to the cities helped. Poor transportation was made worse by the rapid failure of the rails. Northern India had succumbed, along with Karachi and Dhaka, to the Makkah attack.

The urban centers of Southeast Asia and central Asia were crushed. Smaller nations survived, along with small villages, as outposts of self-sustenance. The GMO gangs had been proved right. Their righteousness proved deadly.

China suffered, but again, only in the twenty massive urban complexes. Six hundred million died over the fall and winter of starvation. Smaller cities and villages survived despite their own devastation. Half of China's population died, most of them the dominant Han people.

Of the fifty-four cultural entities that made up China, all but those in the far west—the absent Muslims—survived. The demographics of this carnage raked the coals of Han nationalism, and pogroms began to rebalance the population. During these purges, 150 million more died, echoing the 1960s in human misery.

One year into her "food redistribution program," Tracker had accomplished the destruction of one-half of the remaining human population of the planet. She meant of course that humans had become the food for her virions and bacteriophages and rats and rabid dogs.

Now, for North America. The attack on Clifton Road and the airport had simply been a forward strike action. She had wanted to reduce response rates by taking out the first responders.

CDC's buildings were being rebuilt. Volunteers had replaced the dead quickly. Teams had been rebuilt and multiplied. The director had been promoted to a cabinet seat as head of the new Department of Disease Control.

BEACH TOWN

We Shall Begin at the End.
—T. S. Eliot

The new winters in the northern hemisphere were early, cold and wet. They lasted for six months or longer. Snow covered the fields. Ice and snow and bitter cold broke down urban communications. The harsh winter had reduced the Russian and European populations to a few millions. There were simply too few left to infect.

Only China and the United States were "stable"—a relative term.

Lines formed every day outside of the CDC kitchens. Organized as an afterthought, these food facilities had quickly become the nexus of survival for most of the world. As pots boiled, people waited, talked, and stood for hours.

The squalid little city on the Pacific shore had been a quiet beach community in the middle of the twentieth century, before the gifted classes had gentrified it. Slowly at first and then with a rush, dirty sidewalks left piles of filth at the doors of closed storefronts. Slovenly patrons of sleazy hotels and bars trod their happy streets and fed at their strange food joints. Vegan Korasian and Thai vegetarian demonstrated willful ignorance of true Asian hospitality. No steak or eggs or pancakes for these hangers-on.

The beach was covered with rotting bodies. Dogs ate their decomposing masters, and rats gnawed at the remains. Pyres of burning flesh blackened the skies. Too few were left to dig graves here. The same was a sad fact in most cities and communities across the globe.

A walk into the hills above the city had once been joyful. The western views opened the Pacific Sea to unknown voyages. In time past, the pier had hosted the most significant visitors on the coast, while the carriage road brought lesser folk up from the Valley of Angels.

Before the dying times, people enjoyed a hike to the top and some respite under Two Trees, before they were cut down in fear of some malignant local beetle that might harm the imported grasses and palms. A slight network of trails saw hikers and bikers and walkers and strollers seek solace in the hillside beauty.

Now the blighted hills had been denuded of trees. Even acacias were stripped for fuel for small fires. Survivors reverted to prehistoric remedies for life. Boats went out for fish each day. Hunters brought in deer, rabbit, and squirrel. Water was trapped in river weirs.

As always, some helped others. Even in this rotting borough of warped minds and unintentional consequences, the great force of nature that was humanity perpetually arose. From the ashes of these horrible fires, new life and old survivors united to give sustenance to the remaining, the stragglers.

Phoenix Man was the new term. We could not be crushed. We would aid ourselves and our brethren. What seemed impossible alone became less so in groups. A preternatural instinct for crowds had been so recently exploited by the internet, with Facebook and its minions becoming playgrounds for every conceivable form of gathering. Now it was simple. Grouping meant survival. Neanderthal or Cro-Magnon, each local tribe supported those who gave something of their own.

KATRINA

By the end of this century climate change will reduce the human population to a few breeding pairs surviving near the Arctic.

—Sir James Lovelock, *Revenge of Gaia*

She was tired. Her child had died a few days ago. She'd tried to carry him for a day, but another woman had gently taken him from her and laid the body to rest by the roadway. She walked on, struggling to stay in file with dozens of others. Another man helped her when she drooped to the ground. He gave her some liquid from his plastic bottle, colored water that had been sold as electrolyte replacement a few weeks ago. This simple act of kindness with this simple life-enriching water moved her to stand, to walk on.

When the camp appeared at the bottom of the rise, the file of people simply walked forward. No one rushed; no one could. The die-offs had taken many; those who still walked were emaciated from lack of food, water, and health. A few dozen entered the camp. Women welcomed each with clean water and a few morsels. Dust was used to clean the bodies of caked filth, human waste, and road kill. A bowl of soapy water washed each person's hair, sparingly, slightly, enough to offer hope.

Food was simple, in small amounts to prevent immediate regurgitation. They couldn't afford the loss. Each survivor was helped by a previous arrival who had surmounted his or her own struggle against death. These were the hardy ones. Many died despite these efforts. Work crews dug the graves and buried the bodies with courtesy and ceremony.

Katrina Ustinov sat quietly. She had once had a child. She had lost it along the way. She didn't remember when, or how, or why.

"He will rest easier now that he knows you are safe. I know these things. I can listen to the dead." The speaker was another very slight woman, vaguely familiar. "Yes, I put him by the side of the road. The birds enjoyed what was left of him. It was good."

Somehow, Katrina was comforted—less by what was said than by the simple act of caring, for her child and now for her. She closed her eyes and laid on the bench for a rest that would last. She slept.

"Keep the arrivals quiet for the remainder of the day," said another woman, a leader. "They have to wash their hearts and souls of this wasting. They can begin work when they are rested."

A garden had been started. Rows of seeds were sprouting in the rich deep soil—long rows in the afternoon sun. These would replenish the camp in a few months. For now, they had dog and wheat and rainwater. As the dogs died, or went mad, they were killed and washed and skinned and boiled. The meat was nutritious. Men hunted in the forest and fished in the river. Few had such skills, so they taught the others. Some farmed the garden, extending its raised rows for the newcomers. They always came. More. Fewer now that the die-off had deepened.

"Sally feels we should be better hunters by now. Winter is coming. We have to cut wood, mud the huts, and stockpile what we harvest. We only have a few months of summer and fall, and then it will become more difficult to survive." Joe said more today than any time since he arrived at the camp a month ago.

"We can work harder now that we have good rations and we know the water is safe," observed Jake, another farmer. New to the task, he took it up with passion. He was stronger than most, he had survived longer than many. Now he was eager to offer his strength, play his best hand.

They finished their new rows of raised beds. Sally, Keith, and Marta were planting new seeds as four children brought water in liter containers up from the river, pouring each carefully over the seeded soil.

Ivan and Shlomo walked to the barn, picking up newly sharpened axes. Moving to the trees a few hundred meters away, they began cutting for their wedges. In an hour, they had felled four trees. Trimming went quickly. A group of eight teens arrived to help with the branching. They reduced the branches to kindling with smaller hatchets and bundled these into large piles. They worked as sawyers, reducing the trunk to more manageable sizes for the firepits and lodges. The work was hard. Long hours in the mottled shade made the day move on quickly.

By dusk, the crew had five more cords ready. They had estimated they would need at least a cord each day during the summer and fall for cooking and water boiling. By late fall, they would need to have put aside three hundred cords for the winter—if no one else arrived. Each new group of a dozen meant another two cords for the cold to come.

Svetlana had killed two deer in the traps. After cleaning, she packed the carcasses onto her "branch sled" as she called it and trundled them back to camp. The hides would provide warmth. The offal would be cleaned for casings for sausage. The hooves would be candle-making material, once softened in boiling water.

"Hey," she shouted. "Look what the chef brought for dinner!"

With 348 people, the deer would be sparingly shared, perhaps two ounces meted out for each camp survivor. They were overjoyed.

"Tonight, I will play."

"And we will dance for you."

"The children will sing!"

Hardy pioneers of mid-twenty-first-century Russia.

RESERVATIONS

> Great things can be done with the power of technology; and there are things you would not want done. Most of the public does not appreciate what is coming.
>
> —Dr. Jennifer Doudna, UCB

Dr. Blake had been suspicious for weeks.

The b-lactam was a good response from her team's six months of work. It was well received by WHO and CDC. But the CRISPR/Cas9 work had been slow, far slower than she expected. It didn't help that she was not a laboratory biochemist and had no expertise in genetic engineering.

Some of her staff had experience, true; a few had read extensively on the subject; many were eager to begin work. But few had the knowledge, so it was very slow. They had to teach one another the basics of biochemistry; of gene editing and gene drives and counterediting; of the hard work of building specimen, centrifuging it for hours, and distilling the .0001 percent of resultant RNA that would be of any value.

It was a slow plod.

Then news hit—of the MERS impregnation of the b-lactam pallets. The CDC HQ had her lab quarantined immediately. Jake had all employees in sterilization and lockdown for fourteen days. Only then was the perpetrator found.

He readily confessed, in expectation of leniency. He was shot. His desperate pleas to his handler were noted as routed via Threema and Zello. Once discovered in Aqaba, the handler directed his captors to their "force multiplier" in Iraq. Four days later, the home was destroyed by a flyover drone.

Too late, they were tracking in on Tracker. She knew but remained unimpressed. By the time they might have succeeded, she will have destroyed them all.

THE KRAKEN

The better angels of our nature.
—Abraham Lincoln

Under quarantine, Dr. Blake and her entire crew were subjected to intense questioning. The military authorities clearly believed this team was directly responsible for the contagion diaspora of the past twenty-four months.

Her quiet, dignified responses eventually led Jake and his team to relax some of the controls.

"Do you think you can succeed?" he asked Sharon. "No one has been able to break through the Marburg defense yet."

"Yes, if we can use the genetic pathway already defined by the mutation. She has directed us where we need to go. We just have to discover the correct pathway." Her smile was spontaneous, unaffected.

By the end of December, she and her cohorts were back at work—under military guard. They continued their sequencing process in search of the CRISPR key, now aided by other teams with greater access to faster tools.

They wanted five years for their research; they had five months. The diseases had ramped down with reduced body counts in all the major cities of the world. They had not disappeared. Any group of humans held together by the bonds of family, kinship, belief, or custom became easy entry points for reinfection. Each of the worst diseases—Ebola, MII, "black death"—had irrupted in many staging areas across the globe. Friendship and kinship became transgressions. Small groups refused to allow anyone else to join for any reason.

Whole masses of survivors overran smaller groups, killing them all, for their food and medicine. The animal man remained the dominant species on the planet, if only until it self-immolated. By the spring of the second year, the population of *Homo sapiens* was well below a hundred million worldwide.

Worse, the small groups that it had fragmented into were themselves fragmenting and disassociating. You learned quickly that your friend had become your enemy. Kill or die killing—these were the only two choices left for humankind. Only the bloodiest survived.

The microphages and virions were loosened upon a virgin planet with much fresh meat to consume. Their human hosts did them justice. The "bugs" spread wide. They multiplied.

And they mutated. Even at the low permutation rates of less than one in a billion, they had hundreds of trillions of specimens reproducing every few hours. Even as they died off from lack of "nutrients"—human flesh—they changed. They evolved on their own macrolevels as species. They also changed at the microlevel, at the nanolevel.

One in a billion altered a genome here, a molecule there. These survived far better than those that made no change. These survivors became the norm very quickly as they scavenged off their common species hosts. Resistance to oxygen—a poison for most small creatures—grew into a template for success. Just as humans developed lactose tolerance with the advent of dairy production, so too did the MII and Ebola develop oxygen tolerance.

The food diseases developed spore-spreading techniques that advanced their feeding area immensely. Pigs and cattle became the first species to move closer to extinction. Those kept in confinement were the first to die, of course. Their field brethren died too, as the diseases changed survival characteristics to adapt to the wild.

Wheat, sorghum, corn, rice, potatoes and maize saw precipitous drops in production—and survival rates. Wild variations became the norm once again as cultivars died beneath the onslaught of disease. Wild grasses and tubers had the endurance, and lack of population intensity, to survive the killing fields.

Against all these challenges, Dr. Blake and her team, along with those survivors from biomedicine they were able to gather together, hoped for a miracle. Their odds were small.

Yet she had CRISPR/Cas9 leads. She had all the facilities of her lab and those around her for exploitation. She had the best remaining minds on the planet.

She also knew that her daughter would survive. Her work had brought it to fruition. What Sally would survive into as she matured was another question, for another time.

Dr. Blake had found the way into the blood cells. She had altered their composition. The survivors had reproduced strong white blood cells. The leukemia was in remission.

How to apply this insight to solve her far greater problem?

"THE MICROBES WILL HAVE THE LAST WORD"

> Hope is an expensive commodity.
> —Thucydides

"Sally, are the titrations for the on-chip pretreatment analyses complete?"

Her daughter had been involved with the work in Geneva since its inception. At sixteen she could perform far more than basic lab work. She took notes for researchers, maintained vessel containments, and actively participated in the laboratory daily. She was also the star witness to their success. She had survived leukemia.

"Batch sequencing is now complete for the final microcentrifugation set. My colleagues remain concerned about plasma skimming and cross flow filtration. I am redoing every vessel sanitation regime this morning."

Each scientist had lavalier mics for communication so that they could continue working while speaking. Sally's was clipped to her uniform collar close to her throat. She was sotto voce.

"Come up to our office please. We have a staff meeting I want you to attend."

"Be right there."

She would take forty-five minutes to complete her work, exit the Level 3 room, and dress for the meeting, Dr. Blake knew. The meeting would begin in less than five minutes. She had time for a final review with the other team members.

"Four new additions here. Welcome. This is our first real meeting since our release two days ago. The rest of the team has been moving forward, thankfully.

"Joel, Becky, Anna, Cyrene, welcome. You each bring amazing insight to our working teams. Joel, your work in nanotoxicology is impressive. Let's hope we can use it here. Becky, you are redefining the field of gene drives. Anna, gene editing and you could have been headed for a Nobel before these crises. Cyrene, DNA counter editing is your specialty. Let's hope we can all work together to destroy our new enemies.

"We are searching for the one in five billion virion or bacteriophage that can survive these plague swarms. We are faced now with at least five human swarms and five fauna swarms. These are decimating human society—and now humanity itself.

"We know how to sequence for CASPR. We think Cas1 and Cas13d are more likely targeting sites for strengthening cellular defenses. But while we are discovering means to defend against one or two of the invaders, we simply cannot defend against all attacks."

Joel was the first to speak. "'When you hear hoofbeats, think horses not zebras.' The old medical adage is no longer true. We must think of every cloven creature."

Becky added, "We are witnessing a trophic cascade across viral, bacterial, and fungal biomes. This must have been planned. Deep pockets only begin to define the enormity of our opponents. This has taken years of research, discovery, planning, and execution."

"Across multidimensional archologies. It is inconceivable that the perpetrators are not part of a governmental organization." Anna continued, "We know better than most of the public the challenges of funding search and implementation."

"That is why I have to disagree." Cyrene was quiet for a moment.

The others waited for her measured response.

"The timeline for these developments and their coalescence into a spherical attack sequence does not speak to the plodding governmental beasts we all know so well. These attacks are coordinated by an intense group of dedicated people—if I can use this word for these creatures. A cowboy leading a herd of cattle. Or a cowgirl.

"The cattle are the plodding, methodical scientists and laboratorians like us who do the work. The cowboy sets the pace."

They all nodded in agreement, just as Sally knocked and then entered the conference room. "Sorry I'm late."

"Allow me to introduce you to our youngest team member, Sally Blake, my daughter. She has been the central focus of our first work on leukemia. Her survival is a testament to the entire group's efforts—and to her resilience."

Anna and Becky immediately got up to greet Sally. Hugs went around the table as she met each scientist.

"I know of your work, Cyrene."

"I am impressed. How do you know of me?"

"The work we did on my leukemia would not have been possible without your level of awareness on counter editing. We built a defense against it into my first DNA samples, and this evolved across several generations for fungibility and stressing. We started with a uTAS, then quickly progressed through dielectrophoretic manipulation of the RNA of the mitochondria in my white blood cells.

"Blood cell lysis, including mechanical, sonication, thermal, electrical lysis, chemical, and optical lysis ultimately discovered the weakest point in the leukemia cycle.

"We employed chip-based microfluidic DNA extraction and purification. The DNA fingerprints are now well known. My polymerase primers are now my strongest suit of armor. The leukemia has evolved into its own destructive tool. And the DNA triggering defenses have been evolved into adapting sequences."

Cyrene looked at the young woman. Her clear eyes gave a warmth that everyone felt. "Thank you. I have never met a survivor."

"Actually, I am more than a survivor. I am a progenitor. My blood has both masking and offensive virion distribution technologies."

Joel jumped in, "Why did you use the word *technologies*?"

"We built the program based upon your research, Dr. Long. We designed AI nanos to strip down and refurbish my platelets. You pointed us in the direction. I was simply the beast of burden for the journey."

Everyone began to speak at once. They were excited by a sixteen-year-old woman who had not only survived leukemia but had participated in the design for its destruction. She had the experience and knowledge to carry the conversation with a room full of geniuses.

The energy was palpable. Each saw in this young woman differing solutions to their problems. Each saw her as a furthering of their own short-missioned lab work.

"One in a billion."

Dr. Drake stilled the group.

"One in a billion."

"Mom, I am that number, aren't I?"

"Yes. You are the kraken that defeats these creatures."

"And the cowgirl?"

"We'll leave him, or her, to others more qualified. Now we have a pathway. Let's get moving. We have lost three years and most of the human race. We have barely begun our own race."

GRAPHENE

> What if our entire world can be remade to meet our needs? Combine programmable materials with graphene's functionality. Carbon might be the most essential of all elements—the basis of all known Earth life forms.
>
> —Les Johnson and Joseph Meany

The team split into two groups—research and development. Sharon was team leader for development, if only because of her commanding presence. She was quickly becoming a lateral leader. That was certainly because of her survival, but there was something else.

Joel led the research group. He set the scientific tone—applied research.

Sharon began. "Anna, how can we edit a gene to destroy itself rather than its host?"

"Cyborg. We build a cyborg. As in *Star Trek*. Only it is not a collective. It is designed to destroy the collective."

"Cyborg production is done with insulin today. Fairly common technology. Recombinant DNA manufactures insulin from bacterium or yeast. Yeast has become the cyborg. The patient is also a cyborg. Just don't tell the patients that!"

"Dr. Lepore at the University of Trento has done interesting work with spiders and nanotubes. Simply by spraying spiders with water and graphene particles, he was able to observe that many of them spun webs of far greater tensile strength than normal. Of course, many did not—and many died. But it's a start.

"If we could encourage our araneid associates to build an anthrax synthetic. Friends in India have built graphene-based transistors. A probe DNA unites with a target DNA to detect harmful genetic material. Can we take this several steps beyond ident? Can we interact with the target DNA to sterilize it? Can we dismember it?"

"Our cyborg can become the spore itself. We use QDs—quantum dots—to trace cellular genesis and stop it when we have reached the desired stage of development. The QDs drive and illuminate simultaneously. We both witness and direct the scene.

"As the microborg responds to electrical or humidity changes, it can attack and destroy. Anthrax depends on a narrow temperature band. We build to its tolerance. Graphene invades the bacteria and destroys it."

Sally asked, "If we create a graphene nanobot cyborg, how do we control it? Carbon is fairly stable. How do we break it down once it has destroyed the beast?"

Cyrene said, "Simple. Reverse DNA editing. We set a timer, a chemical timer. When the timer runs out, it self-destructs. We used shaped material-based timers—Nitinol or Jahn–Teller metal. They are monomolecular computers that respond to binary information—on/off digitals."

"Too complicated. KISS—keep it simple, silly. Use light. Catenanes and rotaxanes are supramolecular—the first nanomachines. They are not self-replicating. They can be used as carriers."

"Of what?"

"Of virion inhibitors. Those we are training with QDs. We have only been discussing bacterial and fungal approaches. Let's consider tRNA. If we can deliver it to the viral wall, it can invade the cellular interstices with graphene oxide."

"We don't need an antidote or cure for Marburg! We can simply disassemble it with one-dimensional carbon tools!"

"And delivery systems. Filtration devices. Purifiers. Graphyne atomic filters to remove the contaminating virions. 'Tensile wires' as Buckminster Fuller described them. Two-dimensional filters. Carbon allotropes."

"Two-dimensional? I don't understand."

"Crystalline materials propagate electrical signals. If the signal is stronger along one axis than another, it is on a two-dimensional material."

"What about the nanocar race of a few years ago. Rice's Dr. Tour won.

Imagine a nanocar delivering graphene ribbon to the Lassa, Marburg, and smallpox viruses.

"I get it. Then if we can alter the signal strength and direction, we can move the material."

"Yes. That is the idea behind the nanocar races."

"Can we also turn the signal on and off to open molecular doors and close molecular prison cells?"

"Let's find out."

Joel finally jumped it. "Shortcuts can make a complex problem-solving expedition easier. Think of Everest. It is climbed in stages, from base camps. We'll do the same. We'll break down the problem into many smaller components.

"As our colleague, Dr. Feynman wrote, 'There is plenty of room at the bottom.' Molecular electronics is our entry point."

Becky added, "We should design to use applied science, right here, right now. We start with graphene. It is toxic to DNA and RNA. When the nuclear membrane breaks away during cellular replication, carbon—or any polycyclic hydrocarbon—can insert itself into genes and cause mutation.

"Can we use this on viral attack vectors? Can we insert nanotubing into the tRNA or mRNA of the virus? Can these be encapsulated chemotherapeutics? Can they be designed to sterilize the virus? How about forcing a replication to our standards? Sterile."

Sally thought for a moment. "Fungal and bacterial attack vectors would of course be somewhat easier, given that we have the entire RNA with which to work. We can build to the enzyme. After apoptosis, the carbon would flow to the surrounding bacteriophages and destroy them."

"A bit simplistic, but yes, that is the idea. And yes, its use would be more functionally designed in a complete RNA sequence." Joel was precise.

"If we have a partial, a tRNA, we know we have a smaller unit to attack. That makes the sequencing easier." For a teenager, Sally was quick on the draw.

"Let's get to work. People are still dying—those who are left alive."

PEOPLE WITH THE TEARS WIPED AWAY

> We can only imagine what this (Soviet) complex really accomplished.
>
> —Sonia Ben Ouagrham-Gormley, *Barriers to Bioweapons*

"We have multiple pandemic cascades without syndromic responses."

"What the hell does that mean?" The president was not impressed with verbiage. He was well beyond the listening mode. He wanted to rip hearts out of flailed breasts over hot coals. Much of the nation was dead or dying. Those who remained were busy killing each other for food.

"The attacks have been coordinated. No one has taken responsibility. You and Joko, God rest his soul, were correct. There was, indeed, the absence of a barking dog." Secretary Haley was as exhausted as the rest. Her voice was hoarse. She—and the others—hoped she was not sickened.

The Indonesian president had died in the second conflagration that hit Jakarta in the fall, two years ago, the MII attack through Makkah. Virtually his entire nation of 240 million had died along with him.

"Tell us something we do not know."

"I just did—as a reminder, sir. There is no barking dog. Never has been. We have only a hint as to why these attacks happened.

"We know who is behind them. We do not know where they came from. We do not know whether they will continue. That speaks volumes. We have only to break these three silences to find the machine."

"What the secretary is saying is an adage from medicine—'people with the tears wiped away.' We must remove the emotions from our responses. We must start from the beginning, again." Jared was always cool. He had to be to survive the storm his father could become.

"The EIS folks in Atlanta still have operational teams—scattered and broken, but still deadly. The EIS group run by Soliz and her friend, Jake, has been particularly successful with finding a perp."

"Get them on the line—if you can find a line to them that works." He was exasperated, not defeated. Twenty-hour days had become weeks, months, two years. There had been no elections in 2020 for fear of contamination. He ruled from will alone. No one else wanted the job.

> Warming fears are the worst scientific scandal in history. When people come to know what the truth is, they will feel deceived by science and scientists.
>
> —Dr. Kiminori Itoh

Volcanism increased around the ring of fire encircling much of the Pacific Ocean. Aerosols of NO_2 and CO_2 and dust particles began to engirdle the planet as two and then eight and then fifteen active volcanoes erupted over the autumn months. The Ring of Fire was engorged with magma.

The driving force of local weather, the oceans, began to cool. The South Atlantic decadal oscillation joined forces with its northern mate to reduce median oceanic water temperatures by four degrees over three years. Hurricanes and typhoons became less frequent and less powerful. Yet rainfall across the tropics increased—as did snowfall across the northern hemisphere.

The first snows came in early September. They blanketed North America as far south as Mexico. The Mediterranean experienced sleet storms with snow buildup across northern Africa and the Middle East. From Marrakech to Jerusalem, from Luxor to Djibouti, the Sahara whitened for the first time in five hundred years.

By December, blizzards were more common than clear skies across the Northern hemisphere. By spring, more than eighty million would be dead, decimating an already reduced population. Mass exodus ran in the opposite direction of the past three decades as ragged remnants of Europe struggled to warmer climes. The rampages of the previous two years had killed most of the inhabitants of the European urban population centers. The lack of transportation, health care, power, and capital forced governments into despair and then collapse.

Local groups quickly took up the challenge.

HPS: HEALTH PASSPORTS

> The goal now is a socialist, redistributionist society, which is nature's proper steward and society's only hope.
>
> —David Brower, Friends of the Earth

When citizens find themselves opposed to one another, opportunity arises for the ruthless. Jim was just such a man. He could see the social order opening, just for him. At last, he was going to enjoy the prosperity that had always eluded him. He would steal from everyone and make himself rich. Why? Because no one else wanted to touch anyone else.

Defection versus cooperation—in endgame scenarios, helping others or deferring gratification can become negative impulses. Specie becomes of less value than hard capital—gold, gems, silver. Social collapse reduces incentives for cooperation. Social elites curry favor and wealth more efficiently than lower castes.

Deaths caused by social collapse can be far higher than from the ab initio disaster itself—which brought exports, travel, and so much else of social structure to a halt.

Fear had become the norm. Crime was the expectation. Those who lived were at the newfound mercy of those who abhorred a vacuum. Power was for the taking, and few turned their backs on such a temptation.

Jim faced the future with his own plan. He was going to take advantage. He would become the new ruler, at least of his neighborhood, his domain. Quarantines became his new fence posts. He worked well within their close confines. As a sheriff, he enforced strict laws of coercion. His first act was to design and create "health passports."

Only those with these papers could traverse the Q zone. He sold these in the currencies of the time—drugs, sex, gold, favors, and expectations. When someone died with an HP in his or her possession, Jim simply washed it in alcohol and reissued it to the next bidder. He rewarded his deputies wisely, and they followed his path eagerly. They each felt he was doing his part to control the outbreak. Each accepted the reward given as confirmation of his bias.

Rich and middle class, each gave of what he or she could to receive what he or she desperately needed. If Jim had been a sadist, he could have established a kingdom of torture. He was not such a man. He just wanted to have what he had been denied all his life. The checkpoints and detention camps were all necessary so that the healthy could survive. Jim was simply acting as the cohort. He made it all happen.

At the barricade, she waited. She and her child were beyond exhausted. They simply stood in line. A hundred had passed through during the night. She was one of a thousand waiting. Short dark hair, long formless skirt, heavy cotton blouse, no makeup—she had been told how to dress.

At last. The gate opened for her and the child holding her hand.

"What do you have?" The guard was firm but tired. Twelve-hour shifts, even for extortionists, can be grueling.

"I'm clean. I have the records of our recent doctor visit," she whispered. Her voice had been defeated by the horrors of the past week.

"What do you have of value? You buy your way in here. Nothing personal, just the rules."

His helmet covered his face, his eyes. She could read nothing from his stance. He was flat-footed, not so much strong as well armed, and had a tired voice.

"I have $600. That's our entire savings. I lost the car and trailer a few miles back to thieves. They killed my husband. We ran and hid in a culvert and ran for miles."

"Go to the table on the right. Next?"

She walked slowly to the small table. A woman sat. She and the child stood. "Let's see your meds report." The voice was quiet, firm. She did not look at either of them.

"We haven't eaten since we were attacked yesterday. They killed my husband—"

"And we shall expel you and the child if you don't shut up. Just do as I say. Respond when I ask you. Where's the money?"

"Here." She handed the clip to her.

A blue-gloved hand took it and dropped it in the large box on the table.

"What is your name? The child's name?" Completing two simple pages and sealing them in a heat sealer plastic cover, the woman handed Shar two warm cards.

"Here are your HPs. One for you, one for Jane. Show these whenever asked. Food is to the left. Bathrooms are to the right. You'll have to negotiate for a room or a bed."

"Thank you." For the first time in days, Shar relaxed, just for a moment.

And then they walked to the bathrooms for a shower.

"Mommy, when is Daddy going to come into the camp?" Looking across the yards to a playground, Jane gasped. "It's fun being here!"

"Let's get something to eat, Jane. Are you as hungry as I am?"

"Do they have hot dogs? I'd like a hot dog with ketchup."

"We can ask at the kitchen, honey."

There were hot dogs and hamburgers. The fellows cooking were friendly enough, but Shar remained wary. She was alone with her seven-year-old daughter, a widow of twenty-five hours. No tears.

Strength and honor.

Jane got her hot dog with ketchup. Shar was content with a large bowl of vegetable soup and bottled water. As they sat at a park bench, she suddenly collapsed, exhausted.

"Is she sick?"

"Can't have any sickies here inside."

"No, I'm simply exhausted." Jane spoke as loudly as she could. The others helped her up.

"We was just trying to protect our own, girl. No worries." A strong tall woman in her forties lifted Jane up like a doll and settled her into the bench. "My name is Surly—because I am, I suppose. Where you two from, honey?"

Always on guard, always prepared for the predator, Shar smiled. "Albuquerque. Got in last night, stood in line all night. Thought there would be food here … Gave the guard my last dollar." She was unused to lying and hoped it didn't show.

"I been there once. Before the troubles. Liked it well enough. Say, you got a place to sleep?"

"No. The guard said I would have to 'negotiate' for a room or a bed."

"Well, today's your lucky day. I got a two-room joint just down the road. Comfortable as long as you don't need no lights at night!" She gurgled. It wasn't a laugh but a gurgle from deep down in her throat.

"We could use a simple bed for a few days. Until we are ready to move on—"

"Where you moving on to, honey? There ain't much out there but creeps and killers. Either way, you both dead soon as you walk out."

Shar sat silent. She finished her soup, wiped Jane's mouth and hands, and then sat back and closed her eyes. *John, why? Why did you stop? You could have just run him over and kept going. They told you don't stop.*

She woke with a start and looked around for Jane.

She was playing with three others in the children's grounds. She seemed oblivious. *Ah, if only I could be so free form, so guiltless and guileless.*

"You must have been run-down, girl. You been sleeping for three hours." Surly sat next to her, a little close. Someone else was looking down at them.

"Name's Jim. John and I run this here little town. How can we help you?" He was trim, tall, had on a rare pair of shades. Boots and old jeans completed the profile. Slim. Tough.

"My daughter and I just arrived. We'd like to stay—for the safety of the town."

"Sure. I can help you. Surly, run off to John and ask him to come here to meet our young new guest."

She stood up, lifted a leg over the bench, and strode off to the large home on the edge of town.

Jane knew what was coming. He was. She just had to relax, let it pass. Her daughter's life depended upon her now.

Survival. All else followed down this path. New rules. Same people.

> The only hope for the world is to make sure there is not another United States. We can't let other countries have the same number of cars, the amount of industrialization, we have in the US. We have to stop these Third World countries right where they are.
>
> —Michael Oppenheimer, Environmental Defense Fund

The viral fellow travelers had finally acquired economies of scale for real death and destruction. Social and cultural bounds broke down. Trade and commercial activity stopped. Food shortages quickly demonstrated the distended underbelly of globalization. Surfeit became subsistence.

When her attacks had finally run their course, they began to fade naturally. Every continent had suffered—again. Five courses of contamination across seven contact groups resulted in the deaths of as much as 80 percent of those infected. More than five billion were dead, just from these plagues.

Another billion or more were dead from the onslaught of chaos and the extreme cold of each winter. Another billion or more were victims of the food terrors. No one knew any longer how many were dying, were dead. No one knew when the killing would stop, if it would ever stop.

Communication was now difficult for anyone reliant upon government and commercial satellites. Her "best estimate" for the agricultural attacks was another six hundred million deaths. And counting. Seven billion or more had fallen to her command, her control. The human population was on its knees now. Survival had become a species-wide problem. Were there enough humans to repopulate the devastated planet? Would even these small packs of wild humans be enough?

Tracker noted the process of disease. More than 90 percent of the human population had now been destroyed. There was yet more to do.

Even the extremes of her pathogenic extinction processes were simply too ineffective, too inefficient. There was so much more work to do. Now it had become very difficult to continue to cull the herd—to eliminate it.

DENOUEMENT

> With advances in gene editing, we can transform benign organisms into vehicles of toxicity or disease without technically inserting recombinant DNA, thus skirting regulatory definitions and the limits of detection.
>
> —J. Kuzma

The first attacks had been dry runs, experiments in infection and transmittal. The major assault on Makkah was an unqualified success, even by Tracker's standards. The kill rate was admirable, particularly for these complex experiments. The world and the CDC were stunned and shocked by the mortality rates. These attacks were facilities of death. Global destruction darkened the horizon now.

The final two releases would complete her mission.

More than seven billion have died over the past twenty-four months. The hajj attack was brilliant in deployment, execution, and coda. The flight and cities experiments were the initial devices of extermination. Whole nations simply ceased to exist. Small bands of survivors struggled against one another and the elements.

The United States was suffering from the chimera attacks, food fears and increasing isolation from the rest of the world; 80 percent of the population of the nation had been wiped out in the previous two years. Sixty million citizens remained. These survivors were barely living. China survived with less than half the US population.

Stage three would have to see an increase in these kill rates to result in the final solution to the human pathogen. Stage two had prepared the human population, the infection, for the endgame. The endgame would be the hardest.

> He that will not apply new remedies must expect new evils, for time is the greatest innovator.
>
> —Sir Francis Bacon, 1601

Tracker had the buildings well designed. The jungle canopy hid much. The exterior walls melded into the greens of the rain forest. Tunnels plied the porous volcanic rock, leading to dozens of interior rooms, assembly halls, isolation chambers, and living quarters. Color-coded tracks ran along the walls and each member knew his color—where to work and eat and sleep. Every comfort had been brought in, according to each professional worker's needs.

The kitchens were below the entertainment assembly. Food and drink were assessed via computer chips for each culture—vegetarian, fish, and meat-based protein sources. Place your chip on the display, and your preferred food for the day arrived in a few minutes behind a well-lit door. Open the door, and the aroma made you happy to enjoy this simply pleasure. You built your menu each day.

No one knew of the additives, the MSP, mind stimulants, muscle-strengthening proteins, and sleep-inducing herbs. Above all, acquiescence to authority was subtly mixed with a need to succeed.

If a man felt he needed a woman's companionship, he had only to press his chip into the pad by his bed. An escort would be at his door in less than thirty minutes, offering to quench his thirst. Their language was not his own, so no talk was possible. No woman ever visited the same man twice. The same applied to the few women researchers, although few acceded to their own desires.

Families were well provided for, and links were open to them each month. Talk was monitored and controlled. If someone omitted or included a forbidden reference, he was reminded of his error and placed on a watch. He was informed of the watch list and encouraged to remove himself from it. Should he fail to do so prior to the next family visit, it was denied. His acquiescence was expected.

A few failed to respond. They disappeared, regardless of their scientific skills. Others noted and learned. It was an orderly society of minds.

PYKLON LAB

> Human hubris and shortsightedness are so profoundly emotionally satisfying.
>
> —Tracker

She spoke to the Amazon forest lab directly. Three of the other labs had been disbanded—destroyed by Tracker at the end of their useful lives, exterminated like all the rest.

"Over the next two hours, we shall review and update our progress. This meeting is not on any record, and your attendance here is not recorded. You are at a field workstation this week, as the record demonstrates.

"Consider the next hour the beginning of the final phase. You have worked for four long years on these projects. You have given everything you have, and more.

"The last part of this review will be ideological. You will be told the purpose of your work, at long last. You will be shocked; believe me.

"Now we shall see how well you have met my expectations.

"These expectations are simple—the extermination of *Homo sapiens.*

"We view humanity as a pestilence, a disease. It must be eradicated for the health of the planet. We must destroy to create. We are the agents of this change.

"This change was accomplished in several stages, over several years. While none of you has complete knowledge of the enormity of the undertaking, I feel safe now going over the strategic details with the group today.

"Of course, from this moment forward, none of you will be allowed to leave the grounds. Your families have been made comfortable for now. You, they, and all of us, will be the first generation of the new species, *Homo environs*. We shall be the vanguard of Gaia, her first defense and last recourse. We are the appointed ones." She lied with such grace, such authority.

"We moved from our primary field of research into bacteriological and viral pathogens to the new fields—nanos. Many of these we can control. Some we shall simply observe. We have yet to determine either perfect access points or secrecy modes.

"We have had tremendous success in the secondary field of psychotropic engineering. Its progress moves in conjunction with our current attack sequencing. We have maintained better control here with tighter secrecy, leading to the successes in KSA and across the northern hemisphere.

As a result, our agents have been nearly flawless in their determination. They have maintained secrecy, withstood tremendous physical and psychological obstacles and have achieved "sainthood" in their valiant efforts. They have all died, of course.

"We shall review the working group's assumptions and derivatives for the final efforts. We have moved beyond war and civil conflict. There are too few humans left.

"Over the past four years, you have had a freer rein in your group discussions than will prevail now. We expected you, prior to this meeting, to devote all of your time, expertise, and energy to your field task.

"Now this expectation is the new threshold—you are required to participate. The final days of humankind demand no less than your perfect participation. Those who survive will welcome the new dawn of the new humankind."

Her voice became authoritarian. "We shall now bring each of you up to speed on our bacteriological and viral work. The computer screens illustrate each of the points being made.

"Punctuated equilibrium designs assume nonlinear disruptions. These have occurred. Each has encouraged institutional breakdown, sociopolitical destruction, and global communications and transportation links destruction—chaos theory in action.

"These disruptions have been coordinated. The first bacteriological pathogens have significantly reduced or eliminated humanity's first layer of defense, the health-care professionals. The very best epistemic professionals have bent and broken under the weight of this disease onslaught. This small class of professionals, those who have the best opportunity to defeat us, was the pathway for all first attack vectors.

"Viral attacks then permeated major urban centers—whole societies. Human greed and fear have initiated civil warfare and self-destruction.

"The third attack was global in scale. Religion was the global testing ground of our previous lab experiments. This destruction has been immediate and thorough. We hoped to see an increase by an order of magnitude in human mortalities. We have succeeded.

"These attacks were preplanned. We have stood backstage awaiting their infection cues. Governance has been disrupted as first responders die, politicians depart, and the wealthiest stronghold themselves behind their 'impenetrable' walls.

"In fact, pulling off these strikes was almost impossible. We know the bacteriological attacks destabilized power centers, socioeconomic coherence, and even the safety of each state. Viral attacks then severely disrupted the societal fabric. Flow-through of natural biome crises, such as the plague, were beneficial, if unexpected. Of course, the longer winters have added to the cemetery population. The suicidal bent of several cultures simply gave glory to the gore.

"Persecution and inequality have allowed further erosion of the social bonds. Fear and anger were encouraged on all fronts—political, economic, religious, and cultural. Fear interrupts rational discourse. Panic ensues. Anger drives. Homicide has resulted, on a massive scaling.

"We have allowed them to consume one another in rage and anger—but most of all, in fear. The dynamics of fear are little understood except by the most tyrannical of leaders. We have learned much from these leaders. In fact, fear may be our most potent weapon. Featureless, immutable, it is like a deadly fog.

"Destabilization and destruction of human capital has resulted from the ensuing violence. We have exploited this chaos with enthusiasm.

"Yet these three events were simply the disruption sequences. They were followed by spontaneous irruptions of ancient biome attacks—the plague and rabies.

"A complete disruption of global food production then closed the circle. Distribution of food stock was terminated, in fear. Cutbacks in international travel and trade are the exact opposite of what humanity needs to survive our onslaught.

"As a result of these efforts, I estimate that more than 90 percent of humanity has been destroyed. We have encouraged such disruption via bacteriological and viral syndetic planetary releases. These releases have been staggered in time and space. Promulgation of these bioagents—effectively developed, sustained, stored, distributed, and aerosolized—has been accomplished. They have reduced the global human population to less than a hundred million.

"Pathogenic infection waves have followed flight-time graphs of dissemination. These differ radically from the usual rhomboidal patterns of linear models. Global scaling has occurred.

"A simple military strike is next. Fear and loathing are paramount here. Exogenous panic will continue to spread. Hatreds are already inflamed. Old tribal antipathies will drive all peoples' final actions.

"The ultimate species destruction will come with the nanos. They will seek out and destroy the remains of humanity.

"This conflagration may be viewed as apocalyptic by remaining religious cultures. Our advantage lies within this illusion, for beliefs have nothing to do with our actions. They are simply the cover story.

"We have maintained perfect 'radio silence' with the world. No one knows or suspects the origins of each of these attacks. No one understands their coordinated efforts. No one has tracked any of our agents to any of our developmental sites." Her lie here was intentional, just in case someone was listening—throw them off once again.

"The resulting disruptions have broken down the secondary barrier to our goal—social cohesion. With the elimination of medical, political, and social capabilities, the final two phases can initiate.

"Utter elimination of the species is the final solution. This is our greatest challenge. Anyone can begin an infectious cycle, but that is the problem, isn't it … the cycle? We want to break through this cycle.

"Yes, I know it is a sigmoid curve. We want to manage the infusion and inflection curve moments to an efficiency unknown in nature. One-to-seven plus is the expectation. We have seen in India, Indonesia, and in the entire Muslim world that the results of your work exceeded a one-to-nine ratio. Population concentrations and poverty rates have contributed to the success of each operation.

"Congratulations on your results.

"We now want to destroy human society's ability to recover. That pernicious, tenacious clinging to life is our real enemy in this fight. The nanos are our final weapon. The ultimate species destruction will come with these nanos. They will seek out and destroy the remains of human culture.

"The dream is in place. We have spent much blood and treasure. We are nearing the summit. There, our task becomes even more challenging. We are trying to destabilize an incredibly complex, self-correcting biosystem on a planetary scale—completely.

"Our recent experiments had some real successes, each in its own manner. We actually expected a kill rate of less than the seven billion seen over the previous sixteen months. This has made a significant dent in the human population of the planet. Thank you.

"Tribalism is now erupting across the globe as smaller and smaller groups try to protect themselves from those who want what they have.

"We cheer just such responses. Xenophobic, scapegoating, and racist behaviors are rapidly becoming the norm. Our role is to encourage all forms of fear, hatred, and violence.

"The beast has begun to destroy itself from within. The scaling of the speedy transmission of death by design along pathogen pathways has resulted from low-cost travel formulas. This afforded us an excellent, almost invisible viaduct to success.

"The entire project rested upon civilization's efforts to expand without limit. Globalization has become the global cancer for humanity as a species.

"Population will be its own harshest critic, at last. Malthus' theory has finally been proven viable and universal.

"Starvation by any other means is now occurring—starvation of health supplies and of food supplies. Poverty will be the reason and the answer to the disease crisis. A full distribution of remaining health resources is encouraged, to allow all to participate in recovery. Of course, this will lead to the useless dispensation of limited supplies.

"Our agricultural attacks have decimated the global food production industry, not by a massive attack but by subtle invasions.

"Low capacity to resist cultures and low-resilience nations were destroyed by the first effective biogens. Hemorrhagics have attacked the less capable nations, while high-capacity, high-resilience nations have been destroyed by chimeric and viral weapons.

"Third strikes via nano attacks of the remaining populations are next. Yet we still lack the means to accomplish these attacks on a global scale. Scaling from laboratory to real environments is in progress.

"CRISPR engineering has brought us the chimeras. Soon it will bring us the power sources for delivery of the nano endgame.

"If we are to achieve our ultimate goal of extinction, the final solution must be just and universal. We are not there yet. Our current ideas have resulted in neither justice nor universality. We have destroyed significant parts of the system in an inhumane fashion. The suffering we have caused was first borne by the less fortunate. The wealthiest have been the last to be affected by our best efforts. This simply won't do. We must be universal in our attack.

"It's a network collapse quandary—just like power grids. Network dynamics research is our final chaos piece. We've yet to discover how to manage that collapse. But from a mathematical point of view, the problem is identical to understanding the nature of a power grid. We're seeking a very rapid collapse of the entire ecosystem once a fail-safe point is reached. It may be as simple as the 1.26 gradient; it may be more.

"We do have time—much time. The cleansing apocalypse is here. It is now. We shall cleanse this planet of the disease of humanity.

"Gradient destruction of health-care workers, social services, and financial loci has led to the disintegration of transportation and virtually all civil services. Systemic collapse has followed as nations, peoples, and regions are ceasing all contact behind senseless quarantine barriers. The nanos will complete the task of eradication."

She paused, for effect. She waited a full minute while staring at each individual in the room. The effect was as she planned. Perfect silence. No one in attendance had ever been told the whole story. Now they knew. Now they each gasped or smiled or cringed. She stepped away from the screen.

"You all have work to do. Let's move forward."

The boardroom doors were unlocked, seats moved, and feet shuffled out. Fifteen leaders of the top echelon rode their scooters and bikes down the long corridors of the lab complex; 874 workers remained in the warren of jungle buildings.

No one spoke to another; the rules were quite clear. You only spoke with your group and your immediate peers across defined interdisciplinary boundaries. Discussion was urged only within these limits.

Contact boundaries were defined by Tracker. Only she knew the others. Even they did not know who she was.

They did know where she fits in the compact. Each knew instinctively to fear her. Each regretted his or her one meeting with her. She had dissembled each and treated each like a petulant child, showing no care, no kindness.

Simply with the glare of her fathomless eyes.

CHANGE IS NO CHANGE

David was one of the jungle camp survivors. He spoke with Muriel, his superior.

"She has a grand vision. Her view is universal in design and in application. She is to be applauded for her extraordinary abilities at heterogeneous engineering."

"You defer to her knowledge and ability."

"As only a true acolyte must."

"You have more to say."

"With all due respect, this will take much time. Many variables are unknown. Many are unknowable. Much remains to be done.

"We do not even know yet were to begin on the 'third wave.' Nanos are the future, but we do not know how to engineer them to our specifications. From whence comes their energy source? How do they move directionally? How are they managed? Will they obey?

"Our views are shared by all here. Why denigrate these views over time, the power over which we have the least control, the least effect?"

"You have other suggestions?"

"Yes. With your guidance, please. I do not have the answers—but I do see the problem.

"It's time—time itself.

"We need more yet have so little to spare. I suggest a more radical approach. Dissolution of society via the release of all pathogens simultaneously. This elegant solution has many merits. Among them are dissipation, violence, and civil war. Irrational behavior will broach all customs. Yet, to what end?

"New customs will become norms. New civilizations will emerge.

Based upon altruisms or torture—who knows? But they will emerge. Humanity will survive.

"Release all agents of change now. The disruption will tear at the remaining fabric of culture and society. Every human will disavow every other human. Chaos will result."

"Surely you of all people know the results of chaos."

"But we are trying to understand chaos as a system. It is anything but systemic. It is self-emergent, self-defining and self-clearing. If death becomes the human normality, then perhaps it will be the end we seek—a self-fulfilling destiny."

"There is no destiny. It evolves or is manufactured by others. Survivors chose how to respond. They do not choose how to participate. Participation is the result of survival, not its cause.

"Your time has been wisely spent. I thank you for your insight. We shall speak again."

An ominous glower from Muriel as the parted told David otherwise. He had overstepped. He was now under suspicion.

COLLAPSE

> Isn't the only hope for the planet that the industrialized civilizations collapse? Isn't it our responsibility to bring that about?
>
> —Maurice Strong, founder, UNEP

Whole economies were devastated. The global interchange of goods and services was not simply interrupted. It was ripped apart. No one could acquire anything from another country, another region, another state, another village. Cash became king. Then barter took its place. Markets rapidly collapsed. New York, London, Singapore, and Shanghai had closed in fall 2019.

Shipping, airlines, trucking—each was crushed. TMT was at the mercy of "just in time" deliveries, which rapidly diminished and then disappeared. New became old—and valuable. If it functioned at all, it had purpose. Recycling was rediscovered with the passion of World War II. Everything could be reused—better than buying something from across the globe or the next town.

Retail consumer discretionary spending crashed. From clothing to cars, sales vaporized. Banks remained open only for client services and by force of government. Investment banking vanished.

Functioning websites and satellites were the saving grace of modern civilization. Communication was taken over by federal governments, too late to reduce deaths but soon enough to communicate essentials. This simple fact reduced rioting in the most advanced economies.

Of course, some were bent on destruction, and they had their way—in spades. Despite the horrors in Europe, more, and worse, occurred in many other locales. Small nations disappeared beneath the anarchy and flames. Tribes became driving forces for humankind—for the worse. Entire groups of people simply disappeared beneath the excuse of rampant infection. Those who didn't die from the diseases were killed by the survivors.

Many governments had control of the media in other nations already. The techniques of information control and distribution so disparaged by the likes of North Korea and Iran became de rigueur for modern democracies. The media was less successful. While people wanted to know, they were afraid to ask. They knew they would be told. The common response was a universal shrug. Oh well … Better to be alive and silent than dead.

As long as electricity flowed down the pylons of power, technology was unaffected. It was, in fact, enhanced as the primary, often sole, source of information. Both hackers and mumblers were prevented from participating. Control lessons were well learned, easily applied on a global scale.

Hopefully benevolent dictatorships temporarily replaced democratic government by unacknowledged fiat. The CDC head became the sun queen. The director and staff tried both to protect and to control entire societies, not just effect disease prevention. Isolation became a national resolve.

The strains upon these societies were tearing the fabric of human culture. All nations saw significant populations saw more than 90% declines within two years. Japan and many European nations were among the hardest hit. These countries with aging populations saw 50 to 75 percent declines in citizenry. The elderly were the first to die. Ineffective disease controls quickly triaged entire cities, quite often by age. The absence of children worsened an already dangerous case for survival.

By the spring of the third year, the remaining humans breathed a collective sigh of relief—or wished they could just join their friends and family burned in the makeshift pyres.

Jake and Sam stood on a knoll overlooking the burning field. It had been a massive dump—of bodies. Their masks held back the stench of death. A pack of dogs approached from their left. Sam fired quickly. The M-16 hit four lead dogs, and the rest converged on their new meal.

Sam shouldered his weapon and said, "News is readily available over the internet. While controlled carefully by the remaining governments, it is factual, if bent to the will of the rulers."

"Yet communication also means an upwelling of hope, swelling with the spring tides. The reduced deaths and pyres acted as any coil would, crafting hope from despair. Perhaps this is finally over." Jake was more hoping than hopeful.

Arrests had been made in dozens of countries. First, perpetrators were taken. Most were led to summary execution, which achieved little, as information died with each sickened prisoner. The few who survived the astonishing brutality of enraged jailers found no solace behind prison walls.

Inmates were a society unto themselves. Quick justice was dispensed. In many cases, the dying spread their infection to a closed population. This rapidly disintegrated into more deaths as guards and doctors died as quickly as inmates.

Survivors ate the dead.

Tracker was frowning on the large screen display. Several leaders were in virtual attendance from the two remaining actualization sites. The private satellite network persisted, unknown to the few remaining government agencies. Her silence condemned many—or so each thought.

"In fact, we have learned much from these primary ventures. We know which pathogens work and which failed. We know which distribution channels are more effective than others. We know that each disease follows its own course, irrespective of tissue supply. We know that the CDCs are effective, despite our attempts to crush them. We also know, as has been amply demonstrated, that disease alone is, ultimately, an ineffective vector for extinction.

"These tiny allies must be conjoined to other higher methods. Societal functions have been permanently disrupted and then destroyed. Communications systems were shattered, utterly. Food sources were destroyed, rather than simply infected. Humanity is now engaged in its own destruction. Our tools are too weak to effect the end we attempt."

She walked away from the lens into the darkened room. Her dark dress helped her nearly disappear. She stopped. Every scanned face was watching, most in fear. She read each of their visages with her own monitor and noted their heartbeats and breathing.

Turning, she walked quickly back to the screen, appearing very close, before stopping a few inches away.

"No one survives!

"Do you understand?

"No one survives!"

Her cold calm voice screamed down their nerve endings, forcing more than a few to look away in abject fear.

"Our next preventive measures will be more explicit. A few will be chosen for the bomb work. We have acquired an EMP device. It will soon be in place. This release will be coordinated over the following six weeks. In three weeks, the refugee camps will have died or been disseminated across the Eurasian continent.

"You who have been working in the nano factory are next for showcasing. Those who I have chosen for this final work will remain. The others are dismissed. Your work is complete.

"You who remain will continue work on the new nanos and their deployment. You have forty-five days to complete your tasks. Deployment will be complete in seventy-two days."

The screen went blank across both remaining sites. Everyone breathed quicker now. Everyone had seen into the vortex. Everyone was frightened. Each knew he or she was marked—for punishing work and then infectious death.

Tracker had instilled the habit of fear. She had brought the crowd down to this level. Now she was going to draw them deeper into her labyrinth. There, they no longer had any choices.

The train had stopped. They had been expelled. Their final resting place was their own desk, their own cubicle, their own vestigial suite of rooms.

They had only to work. Produce the nanos. Perfect them. Infect them. Fly them. Then die.

The simplicity was a comfort to many. Know the path and follow it. Ask no questions. Simply obey. Be among the last to die.

TRACK ONE

Standing on the shoulders of giants, we reach for the stars.

—Bernard of Chartres

Dr. Blake was as pleased as she could be today. "Your teams are assembling their machines far more quickly than had been expected. Most of the molecular work had already been done for you by our associates and their colleagues. Standing on the shoulders of giants, your work has rapidly evolved into applied science. How can you make these nanomachines work?"

Her daughter, now eighteen chimed in, "Synthesis and delivery were simple. Replicate the insulin project. Manufacture the two-dimensional carbon fiber in sufficient amount. Protect the lab workers. Infuse graphene with 'the horror' of Marburg, Lassa, and smallpox.

"Carbon has become the doctor's monster." She knew her mother was no Frankenstein—just the opposite. Nor was she the real doctor imagined so long ago by Mary Shelley.

"Your first release was in a controlled laboratory environment. Six Marburg-infested bodies were delivered by our military hosts to the Level 4 room. The Biops Team fitted them with electrical and chemical readouts.

"Each was injected with 5 cc's of nanodyne, as we have christened our cyborg—a miniscule amount. You have been manufacturing it by the milliliter in our sybaritic testing hosts."

Dr. Blake congratulated the entire team on screen and in the room.

"Within forty-eight hours, the MII viruses were reduced in number. Within six days, the bodies were free of the virions. Well done.

"Your teams repeated their tests on fourteen sets of MII-infected bodies in varying degrees of dissolution—from freshly deceased to dried remnants. Only one body from one sample was unresponsive.

"I couldn't fool any of you. You do very serious work here. Thank you.

"Team Beta quickly recognized the absence of MII virus and, thus, the lack of reduction in its presence. The body was clean. Natural death in such unnatural times."

Jason spoke up. "Our team tried Lassa- and smallpox-infected bodies with similar results. Carbon cyborgs were destroying the viruses faster than they could spread. A few atoms of carbon were all that was necessary.

"These atoms simply entered the viral spaces, disgorged their hosts tRNA, and departed. As in London in the 1890s, no trace, no agent. Jack the Ripper had returned. At the atomic level."

"Great work, Jason. We seem to have demonstrated our concept. We need to test more thoroughly, of course."

Dr. Blake spoke out, "We have no time for thorough testing. We must release these cyborgs now in infected areas. The military can get our guests around the world to hundreds of locales within a month. I have already spoken with the commander. We have no time for research. We must act now."

Her daughter came back. "But we do not know the consequences of a full release. We must be certain that we can control these miniature monsters." A shy smile crept across her face.

"Or what? We will all die at their tiny hands? We are already dead if we do nothing. Choice is no longer a luxury. We have none."

Jason tried to calm the suddenly electrified room. "Some humans will survive these attacks. The population is too large to be entirely exterminated from the planet. We must try to protect these survivors. We have an obligation to them, to the genus *Homo sapiens*."

"An obligation to deny them fruitful friendship? An obligation to ensure that the smallest possible number survives? That the human race is forced back to the forest, to the trees of *Australopithecus*?

"We must release. In fact, I have already done so in the forest outside this building—seven days ago. If you have noticed, the number of reported deaths has declined—for the first time since the initial outbreaks so long ago." Sally had taken the action the others had feared.

"Well, the cat's out of the bag now," said her mother with a tired smile. She hugged her little big girl. "Thank you for taking action. I cannot imagine the consequences. All the more reason we should move ahead with the project."

TAG AND RELEASE

It is a staggeringly small world that is below.
—Richard Feynman, 1959

Naval Commander Davis had spent some time with the Navy's weapons development agency—ten years. He knew enough about aerosol deployment and reactive agents to know the danger.

He spoke directly to Dr. Blake. "What in the hell did you just do? Were we wrong to release you back to your labs? Are you trying to destroy the remainder of the species?"

"No, actually we are trying to save it—to save all of us. We released because it was the right step forward. We have no idea of the consequences. Neither did the Manhattan Project participants in 1945. They did their job. We are doing ours."

"No harm, no foul, I guess. You want me to deliver tens of thousands of these nanocyborgs around the world. You want me to deliver life—or death—to the planet. Do I have the capacity? Yes. Do I have the will? Yes. Do I have the authority? No. The CIC will have to make the decision."

It wasn't long in coming.

"Commander Davis, get those things into the air immediately. I don't care how they work, just that they work. You are certain?" The president was equally direct.

"Yes, sir. I have watched the entire process of development, the laboratory experiments. The bastards crush the viruses. I even tried to fool Dr. Blake with a healthy body. They caught me out immediately—with no results. And I can see no expansion of the cyborg population. Believe me, we have been watching the teams' every action. They are the real deal."

"Deliver to our bases in Germany, Italy, the UK, and Spain. Get sufficient material back to the States for us to deliver in this hemisphere and Asia. Have every enlisted man and woman injected or infected, however it is delivered.

"Make sure more is produced on the journey here. We will need a huge amount. Have at least several of the lab people on these deliveries. They need to monitor and command the dissemination.

"You take care of Europe, the Middle East, and Africa. I will have the JCS issue orders immediately for your actionable support. We have plenty of delivery capability. Fuel is cheap.

"Move your people out. Now. That's an order, sailor!"

"Yes, sir."

"I am a lucky man. I gotta tell you this. No one is luckier than this president. We can beat this bastard yet. Just need enough time for delivery. We can recover. The nation will recover. We will make America great again."

He was speaking to the air.

For once, the air force didn't grumble about civilian interference. Every base commander understood his or her orders. Every person involved in dissemination contributed.

The lab techs accompanying the specimens (species?) had no clear idea how to broadcast the nanodynes. Sleepless days and nights in communication with one another led to a few insights.

Airdrops would take place just after dawn—no wind and little humidity helped. Walking delivery would be the method throughout the cities, the inhabited sections. They would aerosol the jungles and plains where few lived, hoping the creatures would survive until they met their hosts. Small towns were easy—people came out readily and accepted their drops. Anything would be better than the past two years of death.

MII was the fastest to die back, surprisingly. As a new life form, it was evolving rapidly. The rapid onslaught was propelled by urban infection and then declined in the absence of meat. Yet, its evolution was still in a fairly straight line from it originating form. Carbon didn't much care. It simply sliced through the virus and destroyed.

Lassa and plague were easy. Simply leave their carbon degenerators with the rats—billions of rats.

Smallpox was the toughest because it was the smallest of the virions. The fragmented RNA was rudimentary. There wasn't much for the carbon beasties to feast upon. They often simply slipped through the chromosomal interstices without effect.

The fungals would take much longer to design and disseminate. In the complete absence of food supply demand, Dr. Blake had pushed aside their nemesis's development for later. There was plenty of food for the remaining few tens of millions of humanity.

She and her crew had no idea that they were fighting yesterday's battles. Tracker had moved on.

TRACK татTWO:
XENO, EXPANDED VERSIONS OF DNAS

Xeno: nano design of microscopic devices and structures to coax DNA into differing shapes. Nanobots with flexible joints to attach antibodies or drugs for treatment recognize receptors on target cell surfaces, opening the cell wall to delivery. Designer biological parts as a starting point for an entirely new class of therapies.

—Patrick Maxwell, Medical Research Council, molecular and cellular medicine board

Unknown to Dr. Blake's people, Tracker's nanos were nearly ready. Their phase sequencing had begun. Release was due in just a few weeks.

This engineering of functional machines from their molecular components was really a manufacturing process, a molecular manufacturing process, as envisaged by Dr. Richard Feynman in 1959.

The machines were designed to move, change their forms, and perform tasks by control of their physical and chemical properties. Motors, switches, shuttles, and even cars were commonplace today at the molecular level. The nanocars of Dr. Blake's lab discussions were a reality before any of the disease releases had occurred. Applying the concept to disaster propagation was an application of simple manufacturing laws.

Dr. Nay was speaking with his lead processes manager, Estrella. She was also his wife of thirty years. "A change in light or temperature or a chemical reaction allows switches to change the direction of an energy flow. This allows nanos to move as directed, as prescribed or proscribed. We can move them about. But how do we bind them if we wish?"

"The adhesion phenomenon, nanoindentation, is one of the deepest principles of nanotechnology. This adhesion behavior of cells with other nanoparticles is crucial, as these molecules are involved in tethering cells to specific locations. Adhesion molecules are transmembrane molecules that are linked to cytoskeletal actin. Tethering cells is the defining process of nano coupling. We now can proximate virtually any cell to a nanoparticle. Actin is the lock and key."

Nano proliferation is disruptive, cost-effective, and culturally diffusive. Anyone can partake of its features and benefits with a small capital outlay, which outlay will continue to decline with productivity increases. It generates equal amounts of fear, loathing, and unbridled enthusiasm.

For Tracker's fifth element, her nano squad, these changes were rapidly affecting her other laboratory.

"Without guidance, the schemas are developing their own machine tools," said Sally Nella.

"They are building their own machines?"

"Effectively, yes. We have not written these instructions, yet they are evolving. How? Why? Under what guidance?"

"Should we report these activities up the chain?"

"If we do not and they are observed, we are both dead. You know that. Why ask such a petulant question?"

Dom recoiled. Visibly shaken by such harsh comments from his spouse and friend of thirty years, he looked away. Then he returned her gaze. "I'll write it up now. You review it when I'm done in fifteen minutes. Edit as you wish. Then we submit."

"Agreed."

Her finality shocked him. The project had taken them away from everything they loved and deposited them into a hellish nirvana. The steppe of central Asia was a remote locale. They knew they had one-way tickets to paradise. They knew there was no turning back, no escape.

Anything they could want was readily provided—as long as they provided the team with leadership. Neither had ever asked why or how long. They had simply risen to the professional challenge of their careers, happily and with gusto.

Now, they seemed to clash—over their lifelong habit of molecular engineering processes. They had studied under Feynman at Cal State thirty years ago. They had succeeded in many nano start-ups creatively and financially.

Yet the next step was always too distant. Now they had taken the step, had been offered the funding, had arrived at their own plateau of scientific success. And they were arguing, distant, almost fearful of conversation with one another.

Tracker had suspected a "reverse TSM" would stimulate their creative juices. She knew she needed more than functional progress. She needed exponential progress, coupled with timely delivery and a design capability unknown in the world of industrial arts. She enabled Dom and Sally to create via marital dissonance.

They just thought they were sparring over design elements. Perfection of the molecular mills and block assemblers was being augmented up stream to product assembly line miniature factories. Scaling was straightforward once the materials sourcing had been decided upon and automated. Molecular sorting had become automated by chemo-engineering. Crystalline carbon resulted from the hydrogen stripping and bonding of the two carbon atoms. Similarly, silicon, germanium, and neodymium had been crystallized.

The assembly of these concentrated molecular building blocks into chemically designed machines was automated. Based upon the underlying quantum formulas, at the subatomic level, there were almost no choices other than those established by the industrial technology itself.

Machines were built, atomic pair by atomic pair. Precisely arranged molecular components built up the new devices as programmed. Structural, mechanical, and electronic components were strategically built into one another according to their design.

Layering by the billions results in thousands of newly completed nanomachines. Concentrated, internally precise, and functionally perfect, these machines were atomically autonomous.

A Bucky ball formatted structural interface has two hundred times the strength of steel at one-sixth the weight. Add a few hundred of these concentrated carbon filaments, and you had an interior web far stronger and lighter than a spider's web. With electroconductivity, heat resistance, and tensile strength previously unknown in the "real world," these materials were turned to the business at hand.

Now tether these to one another. Then couple the devices to a matrix of structures similarly designed. They could become an entirely new form of life. The had consumption, movement, structural, elimination, and reproductive skills designed into their chemistry. They were alive.

Move them about and them could herd microphages to exact locales within a body and attach and release their bacteria to specific cells, even organs.

For example, vitamin B could be converted into a biohazard information platform, a field-ready indicator, a warning device, by working at the molecular level via MM—molecular manufacturing. E. coli could be detected immediately. Hospital surfaces that had escaped previous detection efforts became superclean as a result.

For her purposes, Tracker's team converted three silicon pairs into a zinc pair. The indicator became a virion enhancer. Each virus it encountered exchanged four carbon atoms for a zinc atom. Its external structure was strengthened tenfold. The zinc allowed for aerosolizing of Marburg II in less than twenty-four days.

This was simply the beginning. The Kyrgyz factory then developed nanobarcodes. The device recorded and displayed the presence of any type of bacteria they wished to observe. These were then subverted to mask the presence of these same bacteriophages and virions. These invisibility cloaks prevented the premature detection by CDC and WHO field scientists of the pathogens Tracker was releasing. It was a nano-cloaking device.

By synthesizing particular strands of RNA and reassembling these, the team designed and built structural RNA shapes that were conducive to genomic nano insertion. These nanosheets were used for replication via repeated motion. The RNA factory was reality. The strengthening of virions became an optical- or thermocouple-generated field tool. A camera taking an image on a cell phone activated the factory. Temperature change could activate a sleeper virion. Heisenberg's uncertainty principle was made real, in real time.

Robust, efficient, low-cost manufacture of hardened, invisible pathogens was their next accomplishment. These factories self-replicated themselves, just as their RNA grandparents had done for billions of years. Tracker's team had enhanced the RNA skills by a factor of a billion.

Her Marburg II was but the first direct consequence of this finding.

Securing shipment and delivery of these lots were the final steps in their initial processes. Delivery had proven the hardest nut to crack. Zines, codified from cornfield waste, were shaped into doughnut-shaped containers. Their adhesive nano-indented, deactivated surface allowed the new pathogens to ride comfortably within the interstices, without interacting with their environment until they were delivered to the exact infection locale—a human mucus membrane. These were the most susceptible areas in the body for viral and bacteriological attack.

The zines simply carried their passengers on their appointed rounds and dropped them off rapidly. Infection was localized and enhanced by this industrialized delivery system.

Once delivered, the nanos could also change the structure and function of certain cells. Of far greater utility than a simple viral attack, yet using the same functional capacity, the reconfiguration of cells initiated a complete redesign program of human tissue.

Smart dust—tiny microelectromechanical systems, or MEMS—are light enough to remain suspended in the air. Initially an industrial application, MEMS had been taken much further thanks to Estrella and Dom. Starting with their use for monitoring traffic lights, potholes, highway, and subway traffic in "smart cities of the future," the Delta team had developed a far-ranging application entirely suited to its use.

The lab seized on the data gathering concept, aligning it with the zine packets for delivery—not of pathogens but of data monitoring systems inside the human body. This data collection then triggered the nanos to redesign cells in line with programmed objectives.

Estrella finally hit upon the idea at dinner. "Why should I eat until I am stuffed? Why not have triggering devices in my saliva that stop me from eating once I have sufficient caloric intake for my current need?"

"We can then program the nanobots, the MEMS, to record enzyme, carbohydrate, vitamin, mineral, and other levels throughout the physical body and demand consumption of what they anticipate as food requirements."

"You would have to know each person's consumption needs at various times throughout their day—"

"Or we could program an ideal range of consumption behaviors and allow the bots to determine how much is required for each body. If you are an athlete, your needs are significantly different from a ten-year-old, a couch potato, or a ninety-year-old."

"What if you are a ninety-year-old athlete?"

"The bots will detect that via its record of your mineral and carb consumption."

"How long would it take for the bots to 'know' your body?"

"We don't know—but we can set the time scale for whatever function we chose."

"So, we can 'design' different people to different uses of their bodies?"

"Yes."

"MEMS can be designed to chemical, temperature, magnetic, light, or vibration sensitivities. We can make you invisible or insensitive to extremes of temperature for short time frames. You can move anywhere without being known. We can even program external computers—security systems, for example, to ignore your presence. We simply alter your temperature or visual signature."

"We can also illuminate you for light, thermal, or magnetic spotters."

"But can we destroy you and your associates?"

"Now comes the best part. Yes, we think we can program the MEMS to enforce starvation."

"How about exposure to extremes of temperature?"

"We can 'urge' you to walk into a burning building or leap into a volcano. We can make your MEMs swim upstream in your blood via magnetism. They find an organ, attach to it, and 'mod' it to the new design."

"Can we urge you to die?"

"Haven't gotten that far—yet. Survival habits are genetically engineered, and we are still at the mechanistic stage."

"We think that programmable self-assembled million MEM swarms are close. We have done smaller swarms for years."

"Nature actually developed the technique—bees, ants, birds, and fish are self-assembled MEMs. Apply chaos theory to their behavior, and you have the answer."

"A self-assembly algorithm has three components—gradient, edge awareness, and a distributed coordinate system. Complex behavior results from the chaotic behavior of many noisy individual MEMs. The swarm becomes the driver. The behavior becomes the tool for design."

NANOSHEETS

Nanosheets were distributed by the tens of millions from drones. Named Taranis after the Celtic god of thunder, the drones flew over the remaining population centers, releasing the nearly invisible sheets. The sheets drifted to the ground, hung in trees, or wrapped around structures. They dissipated in a few minutes, distributing their "designer spores" to the remaining earth-bound citizenry.

Once inhaled, the MEMS began their rapid evolutionary work. Their programs noted the consumption behavior for each individual and monitored these for several weeks. Upon reception of an RFID signal, they began adjusting behavior, focusing upon utilization first.

Those whose eating habits indicated low use of certain minerals, such as iron and silicon, were habituated to eat less and move less. They became habituated to laziness. They grew fat, quickly. They sickened rapidly. Others around them noticed an unpleasant scent, which separated them from the community.

Those whose bodies consumed and used food more efficiently were encouraged to strength enhancement. They were also discouraged from acts of rebellion. They were rapidly becoming the new passive soldiers in the war against humankind.

Reproductive bodies were stigmatized. Women of reproductive age were "taught" to eat less, to thin and emasculate. Their pregnancies were sickly, often leading to death. They became unattractive to male sperm donors. Fertility rates dropped among the young adults remaining on the planet.

Countering the genetic mode of increased reproduction in the face of species reduction was very difficult to pull off, even for the nanos. Species are programmed to repeat sequences that lead to new births. Even bacteria and viruses respond at this elemental level.

THE CLOUD OF WAR

Was she the hunted once again? The streets of the small village in Bessarabia were empty. Yet she knew someone was watching her, tracking her. Who was it?

She faced an unenviable decision. The threat from the Middle East had been subsumed by reality. No need now to infect the camps and watch them spread their virions throughout Europe. There were no camps—only piles of dead. There were few freedom fighters, or military fighters, left to destroy Western defenses. Survivors lived in caravanserai in the desert. Bedouins were better placed to endure than the one billion urban poor Muslims.

What to do with the bomb? Agents were in place. Deliveries were scheduled. The clock was ticking. She had to play her game off the cuff, for the first time. Careful planning and logistics now meant little. She had to move in real time.

Why was the hair on her neck standing up? Who could possibly be following her? She knew it was a male human, certainly. She could smell the difference in biomes. But where was he? The air was dense with fog, which distorted her sensory view. The lack of orientation led her down a dark alley. She was setting a trap.

Jake sensed a change in her step. He paused, waited for several minutes, and then heard a low growl. The dog was close and behind. He had to respond, or it would attack. The silenced shot penetrated the dog and rattled into the gutter. It was enough to give her warning of direction and space. She vanished.

The privacy protocols were deep and wide. She hadn't actually been face-to-face with another human in four years—not since the first of the meetings with the pentacle members. Now she had almost been trapped—by a hunter. She was impressed.

The pursuit now was over, she knew.

The next target?

At the end of her internal soliloquy, she switched her bets. EMP over China. Beijing? Shanghai? Hong Kong? Where would she sink her fangs next? How would she kill? Who would pay the price?

Who would deliver this small envelope of horrific destruction?

An EMP—electromagnetic pulse—bomb is quite different from all other nuclear weapons. It is designed to destroy all electronic equipment, rather than military facilities or cities.

There are different types of pulses. An E1 pulse happens almost instantly after the explosion. An E3 pulse arrives substantially later and does damage to electrical infrastructure-like transformers. There is also an E2 pulse, which is slower than an E1 and essentially acts like lightning—making it less risky, since many electronic systems are capable of handling lightning surges. E2 is a HEMP TREE, a high-altitude electromagnetic pulse with transient radiation effects on electronics.

The bombs had been miniaturized down to a backpack. Her courier list remained strong, with two dozen Mandarin speakers. She simply had to retrain them to their new objectives.

She directed the couriers to their new pickup locales. They responded hesitantly, knowing their task was made nearly impossible by the lack of commercial flights.

MSP helped. Each took the bait of the scented gauze. Each was empowered. Now enervated, they worked with a renewed zeal to their ordered placements.

It took four months to relocate the two bombs. Each courier had five cover personnel, unknown to the courier. Their sole purpose was to protect the courier.

She lost all but one of the couriers in the fighting. Some thought these figures in black had the salvation cure and would die to take it from them. Most died trying. Some actually killed a courier in the process.

Only one was successful. The treatments were repeated as reward. A small stash was released for this courier upon delivery of the system to its ground zero.

Getting in was harder than placement. The yield was too low to make a serious impact unless it was strategically placed near the center of power. Her challenges mounted as time passed. A courier died in her final destination city. One was shot by guards, and one was taken down by a pack of vicious dogs.

The belongings of the one who was shot were taken to police HQ and quickly ID'ed as a serious thermonuclear device—a nuclear bomb.

The central committee was informed. The premier contacted the Russian premier, the prime minister of Great Britain, the president of France—and the US president. Such a feat was quite difficult to accomplish today. The discussion was brief.

"We have a nuclear device. It was found on the body of a man trying to escape arrest. How he got it, where it came from, what he was doing with it—all of these are immaterial now. It was armed."

"Are your people safe?"

"Is anyone safe today?"

"We can trace the source material, just like we did in Atlanta. Can you get a complete scan and send it to us?"

"We are doing the same. It has a Tehran signature."

"But they are dead. Or most of them are."

"Wild card. Deep agent. Triggered chemically to transport and release. He was in ecstasy. Overjoyed. Some drug or chemical stimulant. No amount of convincing could alter his view."

"Was he a lone wolf?"

"Let's hope so."

30° N, 113° E

I don't claim to have any special interest in natural history, but as a boy I was made aware of the annual fluctuations in the number of game animals and the need to adjust the cull to the size of the surplus population.

—Prince Philip, *Down to Earth*

The Dragon Boat Festival was held during the first week of May. On the clear bright morning of May Day, the boats were arranging themselves on Hunghu Lake for the races. Zongzi rice and realgar wine are enjoyed by all.

The races were about to begin. Fresh herbs would be bought at noon. Perfume pouches were hung around children's necks for good health and five-colored string bracelets on their wrists for good fortune.

The EMP was detonated at thirty-eight kilometers above the Yangtze River port of Jinzhou, the ancient Chu state. The launch was from a two-stage rocket from the domed hill overlooking the city. Tracker had purchased the small rocket from her Tbilisi contacts. Price was unimportant to her; delivery in working order was paramount.

A bright flash from directly overhead blinded those looking up. The shock wave knocked the spectators to the ground, but no one was seriously injured. The festival continued.

The blast had little impact at ground zero—no deaths, no radiation, no destruction. It did, however, shut down the entire nation very quickly.

Electricity links our homes, phones, and work. It runs our cars, computers, and classrooms. It cooks our food, powers our TVs, and lights our way at night. It is our invisible servant.

Electronics power almost every component of our lives today, in nearly every corner of the world. Circuit boards, miniaturized factories of information, rule our lives in the electromagnetic background matrix of the twenty-first century—a matrix of which we have little awareness and less understanding.

When a nuclear explosion occurs in the atmosphere, it emits gamma rays. These hit nearby atoms, knocking loose electrons. These electrons give off a radio pulse. The gamma rays and electrons and radio pulses travel toward the ground at the speed of light. Electric circuits in our devices—phones, chips in cars, and computers—act as antennas for the pulse. It deposits high amounts of energy very quickly. It fries the electronics.

This E2 pulse traveled down transmission lines, destroying power distributions and substations across most of the country. The lines themselves remained intact, but the control systems, substations, sensors, and automated controls were ruined.

Draw a radius of 1,200 kilometers around Jinzhou. Every form of communications, transportation, and power distribution was destroyed. No electronic communication was possible for weeks. Virtually all electronic devices either stopped working or were completely destroyed—fried, literally.

Batteries were safe, as was direct current power sourcing. Little of this remained outside of rural China. Battery-powered cell phones and laptops and PCs were destroyed by the pulse. The batteries survived; the mind was absent.

The vast majority of the population of China had simply disappeared—"out from under a cloudless sky." From Beijing to Hainan, from Hong Kong to the eastern edge of the Taklimakan, every city, town, and most villages were thrown back into the seventeenth century. The power grid was shut down. All forms of AC electricity were rendered helpless. Every electronic component in China was instantly cooked if it was working at the time of detonation. A few billion circuit boards designed for a fraction of a volt of power melted under five thousand-volt surges. DC circuits such as old radios and some cars and boats were still functioning. Nothing that was electronically powered worked.

Very little communication came out. Much went in but was not received. Banned DC-powered SSB radios were at a premium. The Chinese military had the best options, at least for those vessels off shore at the blast moment. They were quickly organized under Admiral Hue and steamed for ports along the littoral.

When they arrived, their worst nightmares were swamped by reality. Bodies had begun to float down the Yangtze and Yellow Rivers by the hundreds. In a month the rivers would be engulfed with millions upon millions of human, cattle, pig, and domestic animal bodies. As the fleet separated for Hong Kong, Shanghai, and Rizhao, they knew they were depleting an already small force.

Beneath the invisible halo of destruction, city people were the first to die. Food, power, and water were quickly disabled or unavailable. Those who were from the country—most of New China—tried to return by foot or horse cart or bicycle. Millions lined the roads out of the city centers. Most died before they arrived home. Starvation gave way to anarchy. Cannibalism followed. When the dogs were gone and the fish all taken from the streams and the fields cleared of food staples, survivors ate rats and made "stone soup." The weakest became the stone for the survivors' soup kettles. No one was spared the atrocity of survival, yet again.

Xixi was hungry. She was a vibrant four-year-old. Her mother had run to her school and taken her home for safety. Now she too was dying at her child's side. The trail of survivors simply stumbled past, seeking their own death or shelter. Xixi died before the rats came for her mother. A few soldiers killed the rats and began a fight over the meat of the dying child.

Fires burned. People died. The rats ate their fill. Yet again…

How could Tracker be certain she had not made an error? There could be no follow-through because there was no communication. Few, other than the militaries of the world, knew about the bomb because no one could or would comment. Other than some DC lines and the battery-powered devices, the entire nation was blacked out.

Was this a saving grace? She had wanted to start an internecine war. Instead she got a cloud of unknowing.

The US military had ultra-low frequency communication lines, and they had "shared" these with the Chinese five years ago. Now the president and the premier were able to speak directly with one another, even as they could not speak with their military commanders or urban leaders.

"Premier Hu, understand that the US government had nothing to do with the recent attack on your cities. We have our hands full with our own deaths. We do not seek retribution or retaliation. Today I simply want to speak together with you. There is little we can offer except an open channel of communication."

"Mr. President, we have suffered greatly today. We do not even know how much. I cannot even speak with my wife and children, much less my field commanders. If you have the means to extend your secret lo-frequency channels, we welcome the chance to exploit them to aid the suffering cities.

"As for your people, we too suffer from the Marburg disease, but in lesser degree and confined to the far west in Xinjiang province. We know there is no cure other than time.

"We, that is, I, feel that these events are coordinated in some fashion. But the level of sophistication goes far beyond the skills of the rabid beasts of Islam. The reliance upon disease vectors, the quiet delivery methods, and the complete absence of claim for responsibility stand out as signals in this dark world.

"Who could be trying to destroy all civilization? Only the Russians, you, and our great nation have the means to such ends. Yet even we are not so foolish. Or so I have always believed until this year."

"I am reminded of your ninja warriors in the past—stealthy, well trained, crafty beyond measure. We have SEALs and secret agents, but they act as individuals within a tightly structured team facility. This work is different."

"Ninja. Interesting. Hashisheem in the Muslim literary world … Who would have such capabilities? Who would undertake these ghoulish experiments of such a catastrophic and dangerous focus? What devilish agenda could drive someone to these depths of depravity?"

"You just said it, Premier. Agenda. Experiments. Capabilities. I do know of some who have the means and the device to carry out this intrigue."

"Please inform me."

"In due time, my friend, in due time. We must tighten the noose before we alert the hunted of the trap.

"Who do you have close to you that is of the utmost trust and of the utmost cruelty? Someone you would trust not with your life but would with your nation, your people?"

"If I could contact her—"

"I will not keep you any longer. We shall give you access to our low-frequency transmitters immediately. I shall instruct my Pacific Group commander to train your designated commander in their use.

"I will pursue my thoughts here and make you aware as soon as I have certainty that my fears are justified. We will act together to crush these monsters. Then perhaps we can rebuild our worlds."

"Yes, perhaps we will still be able to do so. Thank you, Mr. President."

COUNTERATTACK:

The Common Enemy of Humanity Is Man

The line went dead.

"Get me Admiral Gaines from CINCPAC. Then call Mr. Gates of Microsoft. I want him here in Washington for dinner tonight."

The president spoke as soon as the connection was established. "Admiral, please open a line with Admiral Hue of the PRC Pacific Fleet. I want you to offer them our VLF communications access immediately."

"Sir, we have them on our ship-to-ship already. He is asking for food and water aid immediately. I can have the Vinson Carrier Group and the Bush Carrier Group in the South China Sea in three days. They have the ability to produce nearly infinite water supplies and have food for a year for their fleet crews on the support ships."

"Let him know these will be at their disposal. Ask him to arrange land and sea guard details ... Excuse me. I don't need to tell you how to do your job."

"No, sir. We have done this before. We supplied a quarter million refugees with food and water after the Andaman Sea tsunami."

"Now you will be faced with millions refugees, I fear."

"I'd like the Third Carrier Group to continue steaming for San Francisco Bay. These people will need all you can muster. Please keep me posted."

"Third will be in the Bay Area by tomorrow evening. They are making all good speed—new records actually."

"Contact the governor, HSA, and DOT. I want the facilities ready for disgorgement before the group arrives."

"Sir, Mr. Gates will land at Dulles at 1800. Shall we escort him here for dinner tomorrow?"

"We don't have the luxury of such a delay. I want him here in the White House by 1900. Have a chopper pick him up as soon as he lands. Now on to congressional issues. Are Nancy and crew outside?"

"Yes, sir."

He opened the door himself and greeted the four with a hearty handshake and hug. He'd never hugged before or did so only in response; now he had taken up the habit and enjoyed it.

"Friends, we have to work through this Section 7 order."

I Want the Names of Your Cohorts!

At a few minutes before 7:00 p.m., the door to the dining room opened. "Bill, I need to have a very long, very private conversation with you. No one else will be here. We shall serve ourselves from the buffet. Let's get started."

"Mr. President, while we have rarely seen eye to eye on any subject of mutual interest—"

"We do see eye to eye on one issue, I believe—the survival of these United States. Please correct me if I am wrong. Do so now." His stance was secure. He had no time for politics or pleasantries. He was used to being the biggest, loudest, and most directed man in the room. He had to establish this now.

"I am in support of our national security."

"That's not enough, Mr. Gates. I need to know your unqualified support for the survival of this nation."

"You have my support on this issue."

"Sorry. That's not enough."

"What do you want, Mr. President? Control of my firm, of the industry, of the web?"

"I already have these things or can grab them with a signature. You know this."

The contest had begun. Neither man was used to being second in any room, but the president did have home court advantage.

"What do you want?"

"The names of your cohorts."

"Excuse me?" He stood face-to-face, inches away from his opponent. He was unused to such jungle behavior. He had no idea what was coming.

"I have a personal suspicion, call it a hunch. My hunches are never wrong by the way. I've made billions with them. I've destroyed bigger men than you."

The guest stepped back from the buffet, shaken. He had not had such a confrontation in decades. Suddenly, he just wanted to get on the line to Melinda, tell her what was going on; she would know what to do.

"Sit down." The president pressed his fists on the table, leaned over

Gates's plate, and knocked it across the room. The door immediately opened.

"Get out!

"Do you want to know my hunch? Do you want to know why I told you to be here tonight? Do you want to live another five minutes?"

Now he was frightened. Had this megalomaniac finally crossed over? Was his life in real danger? Would the guards or servers outside help?

"What do you want from me?" he asked for the third time. He could not look into the other man's eyes; fear was driving him. He was cornered, trapped. He cast furtive glances at the window and the doors.

"Yes, you are trapped." Still inches from his face, the president peered into his opponent's eyes for what seemed a minute and then demanded loudly, "I want the names of your cohorts!"

He backed away and turned to the buffet, breathing deeply. He poured a glass of cold water and drank it—as if it was nectar. He always loved a good glass of cold water.

Silence engulfed the room.

The president turned silently and examined his prey from the left side, just beyond the shoulder.

The sweat was pouring down Gates's face. His hands trembled. He alternately stared at them and then looked around the room as if to find a weapon.

"Would this suit you?" The president walked over to the bust of Churchill, bronze heavy, and felted on the bottom. "The weight would do. You'd have to turn it, so the felted bottom was at the contact point—unless of course you were simply scared; then you would just toss it as a distraction.

"No, I don't think you have the physical strength to raise this over your head to bring it down with enough force to kill. I know you do not have the moral fortitude to execute another human."

"What, what are you talking about?"

"You'd like to get out of here just now. You've thought, *If I strike him, he will fall, and I can run to the door.* Haven't you thought just these words?"

"Yes."

He had him. He was broken. "I want the names of your cohorts. You want to hear my hunch? Give me a name and that will tell me if I am right."

"Tom Steyer."

"See. That wasn't so hard, was it?" He came up behind him and whispered gently into his ear, almost like a lover, "Who else? Who else?"

"You, you must know. Why do you ask?"

"I want to hear your voice. Say these words to me."

The intimacy strangled his reaction. He couldn't breathe. His throat was tight. He felt nauseous. Fear rippled through the room. Gates had ventured a name, more as an offering than an answer. He was holding back, even in his desperation.

"Go ahead. Tell me what I want to know." His breath was now caustic on Gates's neck. The breath was burning him. This intimacy with another man was tearing him apart. No one had ever negotiated with him in such a passion. If he could just walk away.

"If I tell you, will you grant me immunity?"

"No. You will die with the others. Perhaps I will hang you. If you are full and complete with me, perhaps I will shoot you. Shooting is so much quicker, less painful.

"I will do so before the assembled crowds of the world as broadcast over your computers. No Super Bowl will have had the audience you will have during your execution."

"Will you protect my wife?"

"Do you know what Kim Jong Un does in North Korea? He fed his favorite uncle to a pack of starving dogs just to watch what happened.

"If she knew of the conspiracy, no. I'd like to throw her to the dogs myself.

"If you are responsible for the deaths of hundreds of millions or billions of people, you deserve no less."

"Why are you doing this to me?" Gates had collapsed to the floor, trembling. He had wet his pants. The president walked over, leaned down, and helped him to a chair.

"Now. Names!"

"Soros. Steyer. The others are not American."

"Neither are those monsters. Give me the names!" he roared.

Again, the door opened. This time he simply looked over, and the door closed.

"Mello. Khosla. Stordalen, I think. Wobbin yes, him. Gore. Two Chinese, Shei Wu and Hon Shu."

"Now, don't you feel better?" the president said calmly. "None of this is recorded. Only you and I know what words worked their way around the table tonight." He paused. "Would you like a glass of water?"

"Yes, thank you." He was utterly defeated.

"You will remain with us for your own safety. Drink."

He opened the door. "I want a national security briefing in ten minutes. No. Make that five. Get on it. Now!

"Get me Premier Hu before the NSA call."

It less than two minutes, the call came in from China. "Mr. President, what do you have for me?"

"My hunch was correct. A gang of six or eight has conspired to destroy your country, my country, and perhaps the entire human population. I am sending you their names now. I think you will see the relationship.

"There are a few in China who may be involved as well. You can determine who and what should happen. For now, I need your help in tracking a beast. I asked you—"

"Yes, I have extended contact to this individual. When she contacts me, I shall set her up for the track. I understand perfectly."

"You have much to do for your people. I'll let you get back to it. Goodbye."

The NSA group came in. More than one is thinking, *Should we invoke the Twenty-Fifth? Has he finally gone mad?*

They were shaken by what they had heard, by the violence just across the door frame. Each looked at the man slumped in the chair. He was sobbing. He had lost everything. His desperation may have saved humanity.

"Gentlemen, we have targets, very easy targets, I suspect. Here is the list. I want them apprehended and brought to Guantanamo. This should be a coordinated effort—a global thrust against each of these men simultaneously.

"Not one of these monsters should know what is about to happen. If one escapes our net, we are all doomed. Get on it. McMaster, let me know when the apprehension initiates."

As they each looked at the names, they quickly understood. These men had a common purpose. These men had a common thread. They had a common ancestor—Maurice Strong. Lights went on. Each responded with alarm and functional action simultaneously. They were trained to assume leadership during a crisis. This was the most dangerous crisis any had faced—ever.

Thoughts of the Twenty-Fifth receded, never disappearing completely.

The operation took three days to organize. It involved eight teams in six countries, twelve men to a team—four Navy SEAL teams and four Army Special Forces teams. The takings were coordinated to the minute. Norway. Hungary. Italy. India. Canada. United States. The Chinese premier did his own work.

No other national leaders were consulted. No media or legal outlets were notified

Only one offered resistance. He was shot in the right thigh by a sniper covering the operation. Recovery was slow and painful.

All were now residents of Guantanamo Bay Naval Base. Each was sequestered from the others and from the few remaining Muslim detainees. Each demanded his lawyer. No one was spoken to or given eye contact. Food was military rations. There were no toilet seats and no visitors, only silence broken by their occasional sobs and screams.

One died, the oldest. His body was kept in storage.

One was an alcoholic. A bottle of his favorite bourbon was placed on a table with a full glass wafting its scent through the bars. Detox was horrible for this guy. He crawled with imaginary—and real—insects. He slept in his own excrement. Once, a hooded individual poured the glass onto the floor and watched it roll towards the prisoner. Rat desperate, he licked from the floor.

And spat it out. Laced with hydrochloric acid, it burned his gums, the inner lining of his mouth. He screamed in real agony. No one came.

After four days of suffering, the lights went out. The cell door opened. He was hooded and dragged along a corridor stinking with the smell and noise of the others.

Each cell had a monitor. Each prisoner watched the waterboarding. Each reacted in horror.

No one was present in the room during these interrogations.

His head was wrapped tightly in a wet towel via robot.

Breathing was intermittent at best. Water was poured over the towel. He gagged. They stopped. He struggled for breath. He was forced on to the wooden board and strapped down.

"You have exactly one chance to speak. Do it now."

"I want my attorney!"

The board tilted head down, nearly upside down now. His matted hair dangled into the deep bucket. The plunge was slow at first, until his lips were underwater. Then he dropped deep under, to his shoulders. His scream forced him to inhale—water. As he tried to choke, more water was taken in.

The board lifted out slowly. As he tried to breathe through the towel and water, the board dropped again. He passed out.

When he awoke, he was watching another under the same torture. He heard the screams from other cells—begging, pleading, demanding, mostly crying uncontrollably.

The third man was the strongest. He had prepared as he watched the event, breathing deeply, slowing his heart rate, and calming himself for the passion to come. He was fifty, fit and infallible.

He was the first to break. The towel undid him. Wrapped in the scent of fear, he couldn't breathe. He gasped for air that was not there. He shook uncontrollably when they tied him to the board.

"You have exactly once chance to speak. Do it now."

He answered quickly. "I'll tell you anything! Just let me breath—please!"

He went under quickly. He tried not to struggle. His autonomous response system refused his order. He inhaled water, again and again. He was pulled from the bucket and then dropped down again.

"Now you can speak. Tell us where you sent US$2 billion in September 2014. Tell us all you know about your group. You have three minutes to avoid the board again." The voice was distant, a computer sound mimicking a human female voice.

He told them everything he knew. He told them things he didn't know. He cried and begged and stammered.

In less than an hour, the bank account for the stiftung was traced. The CEO of UBS received a direct call from the president.

"I need you to freeze this account and any activity for it immediately.

We need a complete record of its actions since inception in September 2014. This account holder is directly responsible for the hundreds of millions of deaths across the globe."

"We have very clear restrictions upon—"

"If you do not comply immediately, the bank and all of its US assets will be seized. The orders are here on my desk now. It will take less than three seconds."

"I shall have to speak to—"

"You will speak only to me and only now. Your board will be arrested by Swiss Army officers who right now are in front of their homes. Look."

A quick series of sixteen-second videos appeared on his television monitor above his desk.

"How did you—"

"You now have thirty seconds. Freeze the account and give us access immediately. Time is critical."

The president's screen suddenly went fuzzy.

"What happened?"

"We have surveillance on the ground. Seems the entire top floor of the UBS building in Zurich has exploded in a ball of fire."

"Ask the Swiss authorities to move in and arrest the board members. Now! Damn."

"Get the others to talk. We need more information."

The other prisoners had been talking for the hour it took for the bank operation. Each spoke of the group, implicating one another. Each knew little of the operation, only the reason for the funds. Each acknowledged their US$2 billion "contribution to world peace."

Tracker was aware. She knew the banker would crack eventually. She had the office watched via robot. The robot was programmed to respond to certain worlds only. Certain voices. When it signaled her that it recognized the voice, she simply implemented the control device in the suite's floor joists. Seventy kilos of plastic explosive lifted the entire top floor into the air and down upon the Bahnhofstrasse.

She continued with her work. The next phase was about to begin. Then the final mop-up. She had to get on track. This was a serious disruption to her efforts, but she had no time or inclination for revenge. Time would be her ally now for once.

ENDGAME: AN OPEN WINDOW

> Working on mysteries without any clues.
> —Tom Seeger

Jake's calm methodical demeanor was suddenly disturbed. He was a professional, the kind of person you wanted around during a crisis.

But the open window was unusual. No one opened windows any longer. The air was presumed pestilential. Someone had committed a small transgression. She had wanted to hear birdsong—a small price to pay for her isolation.

He noticed the open window via satellite feed. The program had been run to seek unusual features of the remaining inhabited locales of humanity. No reason other than a search protocol. His first actual lead was to—an open window.

In Istanbul, of all places.

The city was in flames or had been recently. Black smoke hung in the still air. The strait was empty, except for the stranded ships left at a dock or simply drifting on the strong current.

And the bodies.

They covered the surface of the water, so thick you could have walked across them had they not been bloated and stinking and blackening. Smashing against the piers of the bridges, they piled deep, rolling and breaking in the current.

The open window was in the northwest of the city, in Sisli by the American Hospital in Nisantasi. Back from the Bosporus, the suburb had been a center of arts and the middle class for a century. Next to Okmeydani that had been the archery range for the Ottomans for many centuries. In 1597, the Sultan ordered three weeks of prayers during the Black Plague here. Killing fields and healing fields.

She had heard the nightingale early in the morning, a pleasant relief from the morning chants of the mullahs—all dead now. A first reddish dawn colored her wall, and then came a softer skein of mauve as light rose across the east. She did not look out the window; she simply enjoyed the mating call of the small bird.

She had accomplished her mission—the elimination of all humanity from around the Bosporus. Her true home, she wanted it to become her new Garden of Eden. She departed as she had come.

He had an address. He had a satellite view of the street as the morning sun exposed the vaporous city to its daily nightmares. The screams and wailings of the dying were slowly being replaced by dogs and cats become feral—the survivors.

Suddenly a helo came into view, a very small one. He thought it a drone and then realized it was piloted. Landing quickly on the rooftop, it ferreted a strong, muscular body away in a quick blur. He had never seen such an aircraft. He had a good image of it and a facial shot of the pilot.

His second lead. Now he was feeling better, but not much. He had tangible leads—a locale, a face, a vehicle. His impression of immense strength was entirely psychological. He only sensed a blackness, a turmoil of darkness, a hidden face.

He followed the helo as it crossed the Balkans. By the time he lost it as it dropped into the hidden valleys of Thrace, most of the day had passed. The heat signature disappeared, as a wisp of smoke on the breeze. But he knew where to maintain vigilance. He brought in the next lower satellite and waited. Only an hour would pass before its transit took it beyond the peninsula, and then he would have eight hours of darkness. He would, for a few minutes, have much better imaging potential.

Nothing. No movement. No engine heat. Nothing below. He had to go in by truck and GPS. He had a final lat-lon for the small aircraft. Getting there would take a few days of struggling past the dead and their vehicles.

She walked nearly 140 kilometers to Kiyikoy. She was in her own world here, suspecting her follower and purposefully leading him into the deep mountains.

Avoiding all human contact with local Turkish survivors, she called for the sub nineteen days after opening her window to the world. Without knowing who or where or how, she had circled her hunter and escaped the trap.

Commandeering a small fishing vessel, she headed out into the slick gray Black Sea, setting her ULF indicator for one-second intervals every few minutes. A fast zodiac circled the vessel. She signaled and jumped onto the camouflaged hull. On the submarine deck, she decontaminated alone, suited up, and stepped below. She immediately entered a "safe cabin" and remained there for the three days of deep-sea travel. Stepping up to the conning tower each morning, she emerged cloaked in a dark cloak of her own making, unwilling to be seen.

He turned the strange reddish metal in his hands—components of the aircraft.

He had found the helo with its dead pilot a few days after her departure. There were no prints, no hair, and no physical remains—other than a dead man. There was no scent of a human—nothing but a destroyed hulk. All that remained were the components to a unique aircraft he'd never seen before. These components had serial numbers and manufacturers names—more leads.

A cold winter air warned him: *Move on, move on*. He climbed a hill for cell reception—and was nearly knocked off the cliff face by the explosion. Whether it was timed or timely, he had barely escaped. His newly found helo was destroyed. His lead was blackened. The pilot's body was in flames, as was the hulk.

Yet still, he had a skull. He opened his Walter blade and removed the skull with a few deep cuts to the black throat. With a skull, he could get teeth—a dental print. He could get a set of teeth imprints if not fingerprints.

Now he had to get it back to civilization.

The wait was cold. The night was bitter. Wolves called his name. Only his fire kept him alive, shivering through a late winter snow. The dark morning brought snow. Drifts of dry wet powder piled before him, prevented his escape. Three days of this, and he was near death. His only source of food—the skull, cooked well done—blackened him with rage.

He shot a calf in a barn on the fourth day; the skull remains were wrapped in his backpack. Her blood and flesh maintained him for the four days of tough terrain. Eight more days of drifting through the Danube marshes brought him to within a few kilometers of her departure spot, unknown to him. He too borrowed a fishing vessel and refueled for the slow coastal slog back to the city.

Greeted a day out by his commander, he too was detoxed and quarantined. The head was "printed" and discarded.

James Slater was ID'd as the pilot, an American from Arkansas. He was on the work roles of an aircraft leasing firm in Bermuda, nothing more. The Bermuda firm was owned by three different holding companies in the Indian Ocean, the South China Sea, and the western Caribbean.

The trail disappeared. Slater was of no help. He had been an Afghan pilot for three tours and had then flown for United before going private. His family had died during the California crisis of last year. His vehicle and his license were valueless. Only the locale, the open window, was left.

On the street below, smaller rats were dead. Larger ones were consuming them as prey. The human remains must have finally turned foul even for the rodents.

He stepped across a threshold of white mortar, an ancient wooden door hanging open on its monkish frame. Each room was clean and orderly. His "team" of one tried for prints, hair, skin—nothing. This hunter was good, very good. He left no trace. Only the open window.

The sun reflected across the room, window ajar, slowly swinging in the afternoon breeze. The reflection was wrong. He held the window in place and then moved it back and forth slowly. He saw her face, the faintest of dust glow from her long-exhaled breath against the moist windowpane.

The image was clear. A face stared back at him, faint, only brought to light by the dark dust motes. Someone had breathed here, had looked out without being seen. He had a glimpse of his victim, his nemesis.

She had been here. He dusted the walls for prints and, to his delight, picked up three faint but detectable ghosts—thumb, forefinger, and middle. For now, he had a trail, a meager trail of an ineluctable phantom.

His database was cloud stored, so he was able to access it from Istanbul.

The matches came up quickly. More than three thousand with common features, thirty-four with close matches. Of these, twenty-seven had died in the holocausts. Of the seven remaining, five were male, two females.

With that ghost on the mirror, he had found her match and her doppelganger. The prints were an odd match. A Navy SEALs member of twenty years ago; she was their first female member. Now he had her.

Now he had real running room. No longer was he clawing off a lee shore.

The women had similar genetic backgrounds—Caucasian, central European, with significant Cossack history. Either could be his target, or both. He knew he was close.

He had no idea how close. Tracker was in the Bosporus running for ancient Trebizond. She was actually ninety feet below the surface, running at fourteen knots through a tangle of wreckage. Had the passage been clear, the sub captain could have made the turn to starboard in three hours. As it happened, the sub's props snagged on fishing gear. They surfaced and dragged it all behind them. Slowed to a stop, the sub drifted in the current northwards at more than six knots on the tidal flow.

In the distance, he though he saw turbulence on the water but ignored it for a minute. He leaned across the window ledge to peer at the water just across the roadway, the Bosporus just by Galata Bridge.

It didn't go away. The conning tower emerged as he reached into his pack for the binoculars. Why would a sub be trying to run the strait? As he peered through the lenses, he could see a dozen burly men in dark fatigues cutting away at a massive tangle of wires and lines wrapped around the prop guards. They were not seamen of any navy he knew.

They were clandestine personnel, not sailors. Their steps twisted with the gentle sea swell, unsure of their footing. On this information, and his knack for the correct hunch, he contacted his friend at the Gölcük Naval Shipyard. In an hour, he was on one of their corvettes racing toward the disabled vessel "to offer aid and assistance."

Their approach to the sub, just two hundred meters away now, was guarded, bow on to the stricken vessel. At less than fifty feet, the sub crew's response was hard to believe. They were preparing to fire at their rescuers despite their difficulties. They had no chance against the small ship, in weaponry or armaments. The Bozcaada was 250 feet long with a complement of 104 crew on board. Her Exocet missiles and 100mm cannon were combined with six machine guns and half a dozen L-5 torpedoes.

The sub's torpedo hatches opened and immediately fired twice at the corvette. They hit the corvette, but the proximity fuses had yet to go off, and they bounced along the hull, sinking quickly. Below, 140 feet down, they hit the bottom mud and exploded, sending skyward two columns of dirty water.

With the ships' motion, these cascaded upon the sub and drenched the sub's tail workers, sending several over the side. Suddenly, she began to descend, with crew and the tangled mesh of gear trailing behind. Clearly, she was desperate to escape. The corvette fired both cannons at the coning tower, which erupted in flames with the explosions. She was now dead in the water.

Still the mariners fought on against the corvette, firing rifles and handguns even as the corvette came alongside. Not until every crew member was dead or disabled did the fighting on deck stop.

As the Turkish sailors descended, the forward and after hatches opened with more firing from below. The corvette commander could not sink the vessel, secured as it was alongside. He ordered the cannon to fire at first one hatch until it was quieted and then the other.

Smoke billowed from the hatches and conning tower. No one emerged, but suddenly the corvette began to list to port. The sub was sinking, whether of its own death or some devise of its commander no one knew. It was fully the size of the Turkish vessel in length, if not size.

The Turks began cutting away the guy-lines holding the two ships together, each one springing out over the water as the tension was released, fiercely whipping the sea and the corvette with violent blows.

The sub sank quickly. She was on the radar screen and clearly was still trying to escape, despite the water that had partially drowned her. With no depth charges, the Turkish skipper ordered a torpedo launch. It flew from the deck, dropped to the sea, and engaged in a long arch as it turned to its prey. The corvette sped forward at twenty knots for ninety seconds to avoid the explosion.

Nothing happened. The echo began to disappear from their radar. The torpedo tracked back and forth for its now invisible target.

"We can wait here on patrol for at most six hours. Then we must return to port," said the captain.

"I understand. Let's keep watch until you have to leave."

Dusk on the Bosporus comes slowly. An inky dissolve spreads across the sea and sky as both blend into the pitch of night. As they were about to depart station, the radar operator caught a ping. The sub was still down there, settled into the bottom. Their motion had revealed her as the pings devolved with their Doppler effect once again. She was directly below.

"I'll call for a sub chaser. That will bring her up or crush her."

By 10:00 p.m., the sub was on the surface—or what was left of her was. When the remaining crew blew ballast, she rose nose first and then bobbed on the surface. The conning tower was just submerged, but they had somehow sealed it from further leaks. They sub crew was trapped inside with no escape, other than the one blasted forward hatch.

One by one, they emerged, bloodied and dying. As the final members struggled up the gangway to the corvette, the rear torpedo hatch opened and fired. One final explosion erupted below. The sub sank.

"Why would they be so desperate? Are they infected? You there—allow no one below decks until the physician has completed inspection of each survivor for the viruses."

"Evet."

She didn't fit into the torpedo casing. She greased her skin after stripping down. They packed a small raft, her clothing, and food behind her in the narrow tube, an oxygen bottle at her feet with its line running to her mouth. When it rose to the surface four kilometers away, explosive bolts allowed the sea to rush in and her to escape—in five seconds. The raft opened behind her. She rolled into it just as she had in her Navy SEAL days, closing the flaps, dressing, and opening a channel to her tender.

She was bruised, had a shoulder wound from a 20 mm round, and was bleeding internally. They hauled her onboard, covered her, and took her below. She walked ashore in Trabzon four days later.

She had escaped yet again from her predators. While not drinking of their blood this time, she was satisfied with her preparations.

Now, on to the next phase of the mission.

BLACK MANTIS

Women in Asia were rarely treated as she was treated. Most men didn't even look at her. A comment about "the Black Mantis" was enough to shackle the fiercest man to his innermost fear. She was rumored to be Chinese or Korean or Tibetan or Javanese.

All knew she was to be avoided. Should she have requested your participation, you responded with gleeful dread, for you knew you would die upon her simple movement.

She was as similar to Tracker as a man is to a woman. They shared common human ancestry and femininity. They also shared their common hunting instincts. And they shared a deeply embedded thirst for blood—pure, simple hunting rage. For those who know of what I speak, the danger always lies deep within. Each human remains a hunting animal. Most of us have had the bloodlust bred out of us—or ripped out by societal norms. The few remaining true hunters were to be respected. And shunned.

During the previous three years of horror, she had been approached by several Asian governments. She had simply ignored their calls. It was none of her concern. She was far more interested in her opera. Composing had become an addiction, one she found fascinating because it was so foreign—to a trained killer.

On the island of Bali, hundreds of years of cultural empathy had engrained the story of their ruler family into each heart. Families told the tale to young children, who then watched the puppeteers playing it out on stage. The puppets were intricately designed and cut paperwork—word craft with scissors. The ultimate theatre was the one acted out on a full stage, in every village and town in Bali during a full moon. The story was always the same:

Grantang finally has the chance to fight Cupak in a duel. Mustikaning, his betrothed, promises that his request will be granted.

Having arrived at the palace, she tells her father that she only wants to marry the strongest person in the kingdom of Daha. Many young noblemen try their luck to beat the strong and powerful Cupak, but they are all beaten.

Grantang succeeds, defeating his brother and marrying the king's daughter.

The clowns are the commentators, while the crow is the symbol of death. She struggles with the romance between Grantang and Mustikaning. The fierce fights and battles are exquisite pleasure. The four-hour epic requires an entire gamelan orchestra and a stage full of beautifully costumed dancers, men and women.

On the day of her own work's performance three years ago, the entire city of Tegalalang was shuttered in reaction to the viral attack. She was urged on once again to rewrite the story. She responded, less in vengeance than in retribution for this interference in her village life.

She had no idea how close she was to her future prey. Her prey had no idea how close this ultimate protagonist was to her home, her nest. Both were fierce warriors, trained in tracking and combat. Both expected to die in the arena. Neither cared how they died. Both simply wished to die with honor, whether against a large cat or a virus, a mantis or a scorpion.

Two months later, the opera was as finished as she could make it. No one was left to perform for, as the entire island had died in the aftermath of the Saudi attack—Muslim, Hindu, Christian. Marburg was agnostic.

The aged servant entered the meditation room silently. She waited for a signal as the cool morning breeze moved through the open room. A bird of paradise couple was singing softly to one another. An hour passed in gentle harmony of breeze and birdsong.

"You have a call from Hu. You asked me to tell you if he called you. Please."

The last word was a plea for mercy. She was to be left alone until she emerged from her "state of restfulness."

Mantis remembered her mother, Heiren Wanghou. She had been ageless to her fierce young daughter. Neither woman had ever felt a moment of compassion or joy. Both had survived despite of, because of, humanity's cruelest impulse.

Today, no one asked her a question, ever. She was to be responded to, never prompted. The rule was simple, precise—to be followed. Yet this time she allowed the transgression to pass.

She had been in contemplation of the desperation in 1937 when her mother's family was starving. The Japanese had come into the village. They were monsters, killing her own mother and forcing the neighbors to drink the soup they made of her remains from her small skull. She had watched from below, buried beneath the floor by her brother. He had told her to be very quiet. She wept in silence—and remembered the faces of every soldier in her home.

When they had left, she'd squirmed free from the bloodied filth. She'd survived. She was seven years old. Her future had just been defined for her, her pathway described in blood. She had no choice but to follow.

When the war was over, she had volunteered for Japanese translation services. Her time in their devastated homeland was fruitful. She discovered eight of the fourteen soldiers who had been in her family's home. She learned from two that the others had died.

For each of those eight she prepared tea. Each was presented with a simple bowl of tea in a close estimation of the formal Chanoyu, the tea ceremony. The ceremony was followed exactly. Each recipient drank gently from the tiny porcelain cup.

Each had been drugged. When he awoke, he was bound and gagged. No one was present except the young mother of Black Mantis. She told each prisoner what she had seen, in quiet detail. Each sat in a large cauldron of water, a bath. Each was secured and could not move. As the temperature increased, each tried to scream or drown himself or cry. She simply looked into their eyes.

Some died more quickly than others. The commander took the longest to die. He just returned her gaze, forever hateful of the foreign devil she was in his mind—until he could take no more. He tried to chew through the bindings across his mouth. He tried to chew his own tongue, to drown in his own blood. She simply crushed his jaw with her own hands, always watching his eyes. Blood flowed from his eye sockets. She watched. As he died, she drank from his blood. The last thing he would see was her smile.

Her daughter was trained in her own ways of death. She was designed from birth to continue the tradition of torture. She was taught how to kill in a hundred ways—always to stop evil, always to turn away those who were monsters.

Once she became a mother, she named her child Mantis. Still. An illusion. Formless, like a twig. Homunculus. Useless to everyone around her. Yet filled with the deepest threat to the Crow. And his minion.

When her mother died, the young woman took her skull, washed it, cooked it to remove the flesh, and then placed it on the temple shelf—not as a reminder of the horror, but as a guide to attack the remaining Crow. She never lost a battle. She killed many.

Whenever a black bird flew near her, it suddenly veered away. She never looked at the bird, yet it died in the air. Others saw her power and fell away from her presence. They knew she was not of humanity, not of the animal world. She was to be avoided in fear.

No one ever disturbed her.

But this call was allowed. She did not punish the small woman who shook her gently with a silk-covered gloved hand. She rose, cleansed herself, and answered the call.

"You have taken my call quickly. We thank you."

"Who thanks me?"

"The people of China."

"What do they want with me? They sent me here many years ago."

"To honor your wisdom during Guangfu. And to recognize your culinary skills in Hefeng."

"You should consider *qiqing* as a state of *youji*. A lingering—"

"We have become vexed by a very serious animal. She is destroying the Han people."

"Why should I care about your devils?"

He had to speak firmly but correctly. He knew he had but one chance to capture this viper. Perhaps the Mantis could do so. He was both desperate and fearful. Even he, the most powerful Han, with the clearest Maoist mind, was wary of her renown.

"The Uighurs were the first to die under her claws. Very few remain outside of the desert. She killed from the farthest deserts of Arabia. She has killed nearly all Uighurs in the west."

He paused. Set the trap or die in it, one way or the other. He had little time. He was a patient man, but time was killing his nation—by the millions each day.

The silence was painful. She stretched it out as she sensed his youji. The lingering was like the final notes of a gamelan voice.

"Tell me."

Hu shared with her what he and the American president knew—how these foreign devils had broken their own code to help the Han people, how the madman in the White House had found the *heibang* leaders and now held them in captivity.

He told her how the Chinese people were now dying and how the viper's only solution was complete extermination.

And he told her that Tracker was still unfound. Inspired for just a moment, he referred to her as Crow.

"She will be dead in one month."

"Xixi."

ACT 3

The enemy of my enemy is my friend.
—Arabic expression

FINAL SEQUENCING BEGINS

The greatest mosque in Istanbul was once the Santa Sophia cathedral, dedicated to the wisdom of God, the second member of the Holy Trinity. Sophos, wisdom.

Unlike its neighbor, the Blue Mosque, built in 1620, its origins descended far deeper into history's caverns, tunnels, and cisterns.

The site has been a holy quarter since the fourth century. The largest church in the world for more than a thousand years, Hagia Sophia was a center of learning and devotion for the Roman Empire, for both the Orthodox Church and for the Latin Church. It was converted into the principal mosque for his new caliphate by Mehmed the Conqueror after the capture of the city in 1453.

In ultimate preparation for the attack, the young Sultan had surrounded the capital with tens of thousands of fighters, war siege engines, and cannons. He had cut it off from the northern and southern seas. But he could not take the urban fortress. He shelled the city for the summer, but it held fast. The Venetians, Genovese, and Spanish were able to provide support.

A sly maneuver allowed a few of his horsemen access through a little-used gate. The city fell into three days of slaughter and death. The cathedral had sheltered thousands of children and women, the elderly and wounded. These were divided into groups of value—for slaves and for torture; the others were slaughtered.

The entire populace was destroyed. The fall of the empire brought down the wrath of Islam upon Europe's back door. Only a century more of battle would determine her fate.

Half a thousand years later, it had become an earthly temple to wisdom.

The newly secular Turkish rulers opened the caliphate to the world. Santa Sophia was its center.

Santa Sophia—Hagia Sophia—cathedral is renowned for its construction. It is one of those incredible buildings in which you can whisper in a corner of the edifice and be heard five hundred meters away near the top of the dome, along a narrow passageway known only to a few.

Returning to Istanbul, Tracker had arrived at the Hagia several days ago. She knew it well and had planned to her advantage. She expected an attack. Indeed, she welcomed the diversion from her pursuer. The hunt was on. Her game. Her rules. Her arena. Victor!

She laid the grounds for her response. The large central space that had been the nave had been cleared by Mehmed seven hundred years ago.

It had been a wide-open arena, large enough for a chariot race. "Nika" would have been shouted at the finish line, victor! When Justinian planned the first church on the site in 532, his one word was, "Victor!"

She would be that victor, certainly. She planned on it.

Tracker knew of the seraphim pendentives above, foreshadowing the coming battle. These four elements of a spherical triangle bore the weight of the massive dome away from itself, throwing it down the supporting piers. The seraphim were God's protection squad, each with six wings. Gravity gave weight to the beauty of the design.

Tracker was imagining the ensuing attack, her strategy, her escape whether triumphant or in disguise. Whether she was God's agent or His nemesis, she was the current seraph in command. She had studied the Hagia as a student. Now she would be the professor of death by design.

Nine gates led into the nave. Beneath the nave, at the very center of the nave, one narrow warren opened with a constricted entrance and vertical drop. Seven tunnels led away, three to the city cisterns (large enough for a galley), two to Topkapi Palace, one to Anemas Prison, and the longest one to the Princes Islands, more than twenty-five kilometers distant. The walls of these tunnels were either stone laid or lathe and plaster—from seven centuries ago.

Here she would stage the attack and prepare her possible defense. She had no idea who her tracker was. Nor did she care. It was just another hunting—just another horror.

She picked the setting. Her tracker would pursue her. How little he knew of the forthcoming battle.

Jake had ID'd her just a few kilometers away exactly one month ago in small hotel with an open window. He had lost her a few tens of kilometers away, in the Bosporus just a few hours after finding her. It had taken several days, but he now knew who she was; he knew her background, her training, and her superb skills. Wary as a cat, he sweated through the vacant streets.

The vast open space surrounding the Hagia would undo him, certainly. He had to be more vigilant than her, more brutal, more bloodthirsty, just to try to keep up. She'd had years of experience as a killing beast. He'd had years of survival too—without the menace of bloodlust. That may be his only weakness.

Mantis had Jake's track, just behind and to the left. She was invisible to anyone who might have been on the streets—had there been any survivors. She had tagged his shoes a few days ago, while he slept. A slight crease in the left shoe hid her tiny electronic device, a tracking tool.

She moved on to the Hagia, fore-tracking her kill. The enemy of my enemy is my friend. She dropped out of sight, knowing where he was going in the morning.

The remains of the US Sixth Fleet were watching him and the two killers from just over the horizon at the southern entrance to the Bosporus at the Sea of Marmara. It also watched from well above the sphere of the earth. Three "warm zones" appeared in three-dimensional forms on the command cruiser's navigation screen. Actually, thousands of heat lamps were active. The skipper had directed his best plotters to wash out the rats and dogs. All of them disappeared.

They could have simply destroyed the Hagia Sophia, the center for the study of God's wisdom, with a Hellfire missile—or six. But the president demurred.

His instructions were clear. "I want the bitch secured and brought to trial. No one should simply die after what she has done."

Tracker had planted "devices" along the underground labyrinth to block passage for anyone else should she have to depart through this maze. She would close off every exit except her own. She had left a few dozen light sticks as guidance, of a sort.

She knew three of the routes perfectly well. She had discovered them as a teenager. Her family had been posted to Istanbul just prior to Berlin. Her new BFF was the daughter of the imam. They had spoken Turkish together, as friends. Gimza had shown her the first maze one afternoon after mezes.

They had trailed through the easy walkways at first. Slowly, Gimza had opened up deeper doors beneath the galleries. Passages ran off in seven directions, down into the bowels of the city, and beneath even these warrens.

Three passages ran long and deep. The Topkapi trail was clear and accessible for the entire four kilometers, if partially submerged at intervals.

The route to the outer wall and Anemas Prison was partially collapsed under the rumble of trucks and hoofs of camels over half a millennium.

The route to the Princes' Islands was the longest and darkest. No one had been down the course for at least two centuries—according to Gimza's father. Even he had not traversed its entire length.

This route was Tracker's choice for her kill zone. She had walked its length several times, twice in complete darkness. Fourteen turns along a passage dropped steeply below the shallow Sea of Marmara and then rose again steeply to bring her to the ancient copper mining tunnels brachiating out from the islands. These stretched unevenly for the last two kilometers. Better lighting was in place for the final half kilometer—she turned a knob and ceramic switch to illuminate the narrow way.

At the end was a small massive wooden door. Once unlocked, you had to crawl through on your hands and knees. This final passage itself was nearly twenty meters long. The scent of mimosa trickled down through the partially exposed roots that tangled her tight head scarf.

Tiny Kinaliada Island was home to a small surviving Armenian community. Its remoteness allayed the onslaught of the diseases. Very few travelers knew of the island, even in the good days of summer tourism. No one had visited it since the first days of the Makkah attack.

On the island's main street, the Sirin Sarkuteri delicatessen sold homemade eggplant salad and stuffed peppers. Behind the counter, Zafer, a mustachioed man in a short-sleeved white shirt, opened the door in the floor to her coded knock. She greeted him in fluid Armenian. As he offered her a small plate of mez, she nodded in respect.

Her local estate rested on the hill above the deli, two hundred meters away. She walked serenely, as if on a return from the village market. The pool was warm in the late fall sunshine. A quick swim and a short nap prepared her for the trials to begin. Then she returned to Santa Sophia.

When she closed the thick wooden door, she attached a small parcel to the interior rock pintel. She left light sticks at intervals along two darkened concourses that broke away from the main line, luring the unwary to be broken.

At the low point of the long return passageway, she secured another larger parcel to the overhanging carved granite blocks with jambs into the crevices. The porous rock leaked from the nearby sea floor.

She returned via the Anemas dungeons. Here she expected to trap her prey—here or at the wooden door, or in a wrong turn, or in the depths of the tunnel.

She emerged, crosses Derviszade Street, and entered the eponymous café. Goksel offered her a coffee as she liked it, strong and sweet.

She asked him in Turkish, "How is it that you are still alive and serving me coffee today?"

"I have been expecting you for many weeks. Your drop-off note told me to be here. A friend always stands by a friend."

"Sag olun." (Stay healthy. Be strong.)

She walked away, her headscarf completely covering her face and hair, in respect.

At the end of her last joyful summer on the islands of Istanbul with Gimza her youthful friend, she had been sent home to Tel Aviv as a simple precaution by her wise father. "Better that one of the family survives than all are exterminated." He was always kind with his words.

She had survived. Would she survive again?

FINAL ACT: MULTIVERSE I

Mantis had already entered the underground passageway. She had noted the small moist streak across the floor of the nave two days previously. The moisture led her to the very center of the nave and the loosened tile. Just a hint of disturbed dust had given it away. A long wait answered her question.

The tile moved and then rose and scraped across its neighbor softly. A darkened body climbed up and out. The tile was replaced and the dirt removed to a small bag. The figure disappeared.

Why not take her now? Vulnerable for a brief moment, Tracker was disappearing into the darkened recesses of Sophia. She had no idea that Mantis was so close or that she was even being tracked by her. Mantis gambled that there was more to come, so she waited.

A few moments later, she was down the hole, exploring the warren of tunnels, caves, hallways, and cisterns, guided by her headlamp.

Inadvertently, she discovered footsteps leading further down, away from the higher mazes. She ignored the normal attraction of the cisterns to pursue the unusual. The earth-laden steps dropped below and curved off to the left, toward the sea.

Mantis's trek to the wooden door took six hours of painful passage making. She had never been in such a darkened tunnel. She considered its use for the penultimate act of her opera. Her hero would escape in a similar manner. She left the door untouched, wisely, and then returned along the wet tunnel beneath the sea. At the low point of the journey, she put her hand up to steady herself and felt the jambs. Mantis slowly removed the parcel, emptied its contents into a small black satchel, and replaced it.

Returning the length of the tunnel again to the copper mine, she reattached the satchel to the wooden door on the inside, conspicuous to someone who had been here before.

Finally returning to the basement beneath the nave after eighteen hours, she quietly lifted the tile and listened—for another hour—and then exited and replaced the tile.

Now, a dozen hours later, she was in the tunnel again, off to the right on a ramp down to the cisterns. She had eaten a rice cake and swallowed a few sips of water. She had shared a few crumbs with some rats, befriending each one. She granted each a gift of a scarlet ribbon scented with lavender—to quiet them. Attached was a package. Eventually the rats would eat through it and die. She had other plans.

Mantis has meditated in perfect silence for three hours before she heard the tile's movement and saw the light reflection on the wet stone. She stilled her heartbeat, as her mother had taught her.

She had the advantage. Her small friends disappeared into the darkness, their well-known home.

Jake had run across the open palisade, the immense grounds surrounding the church. He was begging for a track. He thought he had her. Did he?

Tracker watched him. She knew this scent, recalled it from a track of a few weeks ago—in Bessarabia—and a time far in the distant past, as a SEAL. He would be a formidable prey. She grinned in bloodlust. This was why she existed—the hunt.

The door was open, and he slid in sideways, as if hiding. Jake stepped inside the enormous cavern of Sophia. He was actually looking back as he moved forward, seeking a trail, a form, a ghost. Nothing.

The morning light opened the interior to him—the vast vaulted ceiling, the nine entrances, the incredible mosaic of life covering the walls. No living thing was depicted. Yet these walls danced with the lives of their ancient artists. Hundreds of workers over dozens of years had each added his artisanal skill to the basalt masterpiece.

Listening, looking up, he sensed a runner in the catwalk above. A door was open to his left, and he stalked into it, knowing he was being drawn in—to the battlefield.

Rising to the interior surrounding carapace just below the dome, he stepped out into the dewy light and heard a scraping below. Looking over the edge, he saw a hole in the center of the floor. Why?

Cat and mouse. He was the bait. He knew it and hated that he was already trapped. But he had to move forward into the maze. He ran down the stairwell and over to the gaping wound in the flooring. The giant alabaster sarcophagi lay just to the north, as if in tipping range.

Slipping a light stick down the hole, he could see a slight drop-off of two meters to a dirt floor.

"Do you have me?" he whispered to the com onboard the tracking vessel.

They had moved up the strait, just above the deep passageway and a few hundred meters out from the Hagia hill. "Roger that. Another image to your left about three meters and below. A third image quite distant. Must be a rat."

"Confirm."

He slid down the opening, landing on his flexed feet, and rolled right. No sound. Darkness. He stared left.

"You've come for me. Again. Will you die today?" Her voice echoed as if from above.

He knew not to turn away toward the sound. Peering at the darkness, he saw two thin slits—her eyes—and then darkness.

"Your breathing is controlled, but still fearful. Or is it vivacious? Are you enjoying this as much as I am? I still wonder about your escape—but not too much. You are good at what you do."

He fired a dart from his shoulder harness, hoping for a lucky hit. The dart was a horse tranquilizer. It would still any body it entered but fell silently to the stone floor.

She had moved, he knew. He adjusted his headlamp, turned it on, and looked left. The red light traced her running down the tunnel, and he fired again. Another miss. Damn these shoulder harnesses. He knew he was jerking right when he fired.

He walked. Running was her game, so he walked. *No need to rush to your death*, he told himself. *You have no chance against this animal. She has set the stage, so follow her lead and wait for the opening.* There was always an opening.

As he turned toward the cisterns on the obvious pathway, he heard, "Jake, take the unknown path."

He had no idea who said this. He waited, listened for a sound of a third tracker. Qi.

A rat ran over his feet. Off to his left, it ran, but it has a pretty bow around its neck. He followed it deeper into the tunnel. The headroom was dropping, so he walked bent kneed. This couldn't keep up, or his legs would give out eventually.

"Jake, we are losing contact. You are somewhere just below us, but we are losing signal. Repeat, we are losing signal."

He came to a turning—stairs leading down; mossy wet walls; no sound, only his steady breathing. He stopped. Listened. Heard her just a few meters away. "Jake, are you following me? Are you coming this way?"

She taunted him forward. Down. The steps were dark, wet, and rank with moisture. And rats. Rats covered the steps as he moved forward—hundreds of rats.

After four more turns, he followed further steps down. Finally, he came to a level passage. A few more steps, and then he stopped. Downward again. Her voice was more distant now, perhaps an echo.

Moving forward down the dank downward sloping steps, he found level ground, wet but level. The light pulled him forward—toward the unknown, toward her voice, toward his own death.

Mantis followed, at a distance. She knew the track of a tracker. She knew the lead. She understood the draw, the dynamic of death. She waited at a distance—a pace just beyond hearing. She waited for her own kill.

Jake has been walking, trekking, hiking, slipping, and falling for four hours now. The way was difficult, at best. He had not been down here. He had not been in a cave since childhood. Then he was terrified.

Now he was just consumed with rage. She had drawn him in to her web. She had all the cards, all the answers. She dominated the deal. How could he win?

Then came a slight error, a mistake. She slipped, edged against the small wooden door, and slid forward, just missing her step. It wasn't like her, certainly.

It was just enough for Jake to hear the fall, to know where she was, to sense the distance between himself and her.

Now he felt a slight tipping of the scales. Perhaps he could win this fight. Perhaps she was just vincible enough—to die.

He fired again and then moved forward at an even pace, just enough to keep track of her footsteps in the mud. He must have missed with the dart. She would've been down now.

She was just ahead. He knew he must keep a distance until she made another error.

Now he knew how far away she walked. Now he knew how she stepped—he could hear her footfalls. He could almost see her. He knew she had stopped, heard a slight scraping sound as she opened the door and crawled through. He saw her now as a smaller version of herself as she stooped to a crawl, moving slowly through the last tunnel.

The sudden quiet was disturbing. Had she stopped? She had only one direction to move—forward. Or did she? Was there another way out? Could she double back on him? Did she know these tunnels too well?

A sudden muffled explosion shook the air. One of Mantis's rats has tripped the explosive device on its ribbon and covered the tunnel with viscera. But neither Jake nor Tracker knew the source.

They both stopped and listened.

And he heard her breathing. With the wisp of a wand, he has become the tracker, she the prey. She was close. He breathed quietly, exhaling in silent emotion, inhaling in silent exhilaration. He was on to her.

Death By Design

She paused. Waited. She knew how to listen, to breath, to heartbeat, to sweat, to fear. What was that? Just a whiff of sweat, of greed—of attack!

He lunged toward her. She pushed off his attack with a knife thrust that slashed his arm deeply, blood flowing freely. He pounced again.

The narrow corridor filled with dust and blood and their heavy breathing. He was on top of her and then purposefully sinking to her left and below her. His arms encased her neck and head as she writhed against him, smashing their bodies repeatedly against the walls.

Now he had hold of her neck. He grappled, whipping her arm away as he locked her windpipe in his arms. If he could just hold on long enough to throttle her into exhaustion. She fought, struggled, feints collapse—only to lift both bodies and crush his against the dirt roof. It partially collapsed on them.

He still had the advantage—the weather gage. He grabbed her arm and tossed her against the tunnel wall. They both heard the crack of bone. Her left arm was gashed open and broken. She tried to stand but he pulled her down into his body hold, stifling her breath, tightening his grip. She fought; grabbed the knife in her ankle sleeve; and stabbed at his leg, opening yet another wound.

He was weakening from loss of blood. He had to finish this now. She was beginning to win. He had to finish the fight. Or lose.

Broken arm. Bloodied left leg and right arm. Here were two gladiators seeking no respite.

They tumbled out of the last meters of tunnel into the small basement beneath the delicatessen. No one opened the hatchway door despite their noisesome battle. He lost his hold as she broke away and stumbled to her feet. He rose on his good leg in blood and filth and exhaustion. He had to finish this now.

She looked him in the eyes. "Do you think I will die in your arms? In your bloodied arms? Don't confuse romance with valor!"

She whipped out at him with an angled foot and swayed him with a blow to the ribcage, another to his crotch, a third to his windpipe. He staggered but regained his stance. She pulled the last knife from her ankle pocket and slashed him a glancing blow. She licked her blade of his blood. "Drink from this chalice, the blood of life everlasting!"

Her lunge was to the left as Jake moved right, grabbed her good arm and broke her wrist against his chest. The knife fell out of her helpless grasp. She had only her feet but remained a wounded killer. Jumping back, she leaped high and crashed both feet into his chest. He fell back, pulling her down with him. Her legs scissored around his abdomen from behind. He was losing his breath, and she still tightened. Grabbing the knife from the dirt, he stabbed her legs again and again and again.

They relaxed their hold and then loosened completely. He was covered in her blood, running from several gashes in her legs and torso. She breathed heavier, as if gasping and then not at all. Her heart still beat, but for how long?

He ripped his shirt into four shreds and tied off each of her extremities to reduce the blood loss. Setting her arm and daubing earth and mud on her wounds, he realized they were all superficial. She would survive. He took the tightly wound scarf from around her head and she growled subconsciously, feral. Her teeth snapped, ripping flesh from the back of his hand, exposing tendrils and bone.

He wrapped the scarf around his bloodied leg and rubbed his hand in muddy water. The cold water numbed the pain and eased the blood flow. He rested.

He needed to think, to pray, to recover his energy and insight.

He had to drag her back the entire tunnel length and up the many levels of stairs. But how?

If she awakened and loosens her bonds, she would disappear, certainly. She had set this trap; she knew the territory.

He tried his contact with the ship but got no response. He had no idea that she lay just overhead, less than a hundred meters above. They know to wait for twenty-four hours before destroying the Hagia, so he had time.

He would think, pray, and recover his energy and insight. If she remained still, he can get out of the tunnel in a few hours and signal for corpsmen to return for her.

He felt another small explosion. What the hell was that? *There is someone else down here ... They haven't attacked me. They have either disappeared, died, or are waiting.*

He chose the latter. If this person was waiting, he or she could help. He just had to get whoever it was to work with him. If this person was down here, he or she was seeking her too. They knew her wrath.

"Listen! I know you are near. I know you want her. I have her, and help is on the way. Do you want to help me or simply to kill her and leave? You know who she is. You know we want her under control. We want to put her on trial. What about you?"

"Youji."

He listened, quietly.

"Youji," again, closer yet quieter.

"You have Youji. You can be still."

"What does … Never mind. I am asking you to stay here with her, keep her alive but bound. When I return, we'll take her to the naval vessel. There she will be under control. We must close this with justice."

"We'll wait. She must be tried and executed before the world."

"I have to get back to Hagia to get medics down here. Will you wait with her?"

"Xixi."

"Okay. I am going back up the tunnel. You know I will be gone for several hours. Do you need any food or water?"

"Go."

"Will she be here? Will she be alive when I return?"

"Go."

He had no choice.

When the medics arrived four hours later, only Tracker was found, alive. Her wounds had been tended to professionally. She was asleep, under the strong narcotic of the horse tranq.

They bound her to the carrier and moved up to Hagia where a dozen men took charge. She was awakened and then bound in chain, with two tires around her upper body. They smelled of gasoline. If she ran, they would ignite—a Johannesburg necktie. Four men held each of four chain ends, and they had four men behind them. They took no chances with this caged beast.

Exhausted, Jake whispered, "'I have her. Here is the impression of her teeth."

"We need to know for certain, without question."

"Dental records. Look for her dental records with Mossad and USMC. She is here."

The records revealed Tracker as Ms. Ruth Ishmael. Right upper molar missing.

The call was routed directly to the president. The battle group was en route to the Caribbean. He listened quietly to the Chinese premier.

"Mr. President, we have confirmation of her death. You can see the records now."

"Yes, I do see.

"I am disappointed in you, Premier. I thought we were friends. I thought we had an understanding. I risked much in giving your navy our military access. You disappoint me.

"You see, I have her at Gitmo now. She arrived yesterday from Istanbul. She was hobbled and quiet but remains quite dangerous. We will begin her trial very soon, very quickly now. Then she will be executed.

"Why did you lie to me just now? Why do you disappoint me?"

"Are we to be Cain and Abel? Shall we repeat the cycle?"

"Or shall I simply destroy you now?"

He dropped the line, tossing the phone across the HQ floor.

Youji. The power of silence in a hurricane.

To be continued.

MULTIVERSE II

Mantis Wins

She licked her blade of his blood. "Drink from this chalice, the blood of life everlasting!"

Her knife sliced his carotid artery cleanly. He died as she fell to his side.

She took time to catch her breath. She knew she had won. Yet again. She was Tracker.

"I am the storm!"

Another small explosion startled her. Could there be another? She ripped his shirt off, cut his arm free from his body, and quickly cleaned the bones of flesh. She uses the humerus as a splint for her broken arm and tied it tightly to her arm with his torn shirt. She returned to the wooden door, perhaps fifteen meters away.

As she closed on the door, she felt exhilaration at fending off her newest rival. She was still Tracker. She was the alpha queen of her surroundings.

Yet another explosion sounded. What was that? She came to the wooden door, feeling for the latch. But what was this? No package was attached to the door. She had left it here—she'd left it on the interior.

What was happening? Had she forgotten something? Had the blood loss enfeebled her?

She had the presence of mind to turn away from the door. The blast forced her into a crouched position and heaved her into the ceiling. It collapsed around her. She was buried in dirt and her own sweat and blood.

She had to move back down the tunnel not to the Hagia, to Anemas

Prison. As she crawled out from beneath the rubble, she lifted herself out through the blown door frame.

Yet she saw light now—down tunnel.

What was this?

No one knew of her design. No one had been down here. She must be hallucinating. She must be suffering from loss of blood.

Then came another explosion. Closer now. Much closer. Who was hunting her? Why the tiny explosions?

She stepped aside into one of the "false" tunnels and grabbed a light stick. Once illuminated, it would last forty-five minutes—enough time to make it back to the first flight of steps. She moved further into the tunnel and grabbed two more. She had enough now to escape to the prison.

These explosions were too small to worry her about damage to the walls. Her reasoning was returning. They were a diversion. Something more was coming toward her. Someone more.

Out of the darkness, Mantis attacked—from below. She had been lying in the mud of the dirt floor, just her nose exposed. She could feel the footsteps.

She reached up through the slime. She grabbed Tracker's legs to bring her down and then cut deep.

Once begun, the struggle was quick. Tracker was caught unaware. Mantis had the advantage.

She killed with one thrust. She ripped out the heart. Then quickly, she beheaded Tracker and carried the head down and out the corridors back to Sophia.

"I have her."

Premier Hu gasped. "We need to know for certain, without question."

"Dental records. Look for her dental records with Mossad and USMC. She is dead."

"Xi xi."

The head was found on the Chinese Premier's private doorstep in four days. The records revealed Tracker as Ms. Ruth Ishmael. Right upper molar missing.

"Mr. President, we have confirmation of her death. You can see the records now." Hu was soft spoken. The challenge ahead was impossible.

"It's over. Thank God, it's over. Thank you for finding her and killing her. Now we must regroup. We must find the living and struggle forward to a new world."

"With help, humanity will survive."

"Let's hope you're right."

"Godspeed to us all."

Small groups of humanity existed across the planet, none larger than a few thousand. Most of them, if not all, were starving or ill or dying. Even the wealthiest had a difficult time with subsistence living. No one had much.

They say you need a group of at least 150 for survival, for mating and next generation living. How many groups of 150 people were left on the planet? How could they communicate across broken lines, across deadly battlefields? How could enough groups survive the biomes infecting the skies, the waters, the earth itself?

The remains of the militaries were functioning units. The Chinese and the US navies operated on a very limited scale. A few dozen vessels remained that were unaffected by the diseases. A few hundred other ships and boats around the world could function.

Fishing would prosper. The most healthful of foods, fish would replenish the human race over the next several generations. Workboats that were out to sea, perhaps 15 percent of the worldwide fishing fleet during the worst of the disease attacks, survived. They return home with food for the remainder. They would go out again and again. Their work pulled humanity back from the edge of extinction.

For that edge was perilously close to reality. With small pockets of a dozen to a few hundred people, with very limited communication as batteries ran down or electricity was impaired, few know the rudiments of wilderness survival. Perhaps one in a hundred such groups had the wherewithal to survive the winters to come.

Those groups in the wilds, the hinterlands, by lakes and rivers, in the mountains, on the seas and oceans, these groups would survive. Some had real wilderness skills; many had known survival if only for a few days or weeks. Few survivors were city folk; few were feeble urban monkeys unable to deal with the real world.

Much time would pass before humanity reached 10 percent of its previous population of 7.7 billion. Society, culture, nations, economies, careers, and work itself would be redefined, reinvented.

Communication is the species' strong suit. Virtually all of the technology, media, and telecommunication was in place and functional globally. As long as electricity flowed, humanity would survive.

Natural gas and crude oil extraction, delivery, storage, and use become the new backbone of the world. With sufficient supplies of methane, communications would continue unabated. With sufficient supplies of crude oil for transportation liquids, commerce and economies would reappear quickly. The workers who manned these outfits were the new heroes. Their professional efforts brought humankind back from the precipice.

Security would be maintained, at least on the water. Fuel was not a problem; it lay in tankers and bunkers across the globe. Education and training of energy staff up and down the pipeline would become an international priority. For three generations, most graduates of any training were in the energy field.

Hunters would do well—once they killed the feral dogs and rapid rats. With more than three billion rounds of ammunition stored privately across the country, the former were slowly rounded up and destroyed—or occasionally retrained.

The rats were more difficult.

In many cities, they commanded every aspect of life. They had become the dominant urban species. They were prolific. Food was readily available, at least until the rotting carcasses were eaten or destroyed. Then they turned on each other and the human urban survivors. Very few humans survived in these enraptured cities.

Most rats killed in packs. When the packs exceeded a thousand, there were no defenses. You could kill ten thousand and die from the bites of four hundred more. You could kill every one of a herd, and the next group was larger and more ferocious. They ate their dead, and then they ate you. They would consume anything on their path to your flesh—wood, plaster, concrete. They would climb or dig or run anywhere you could hide. Suicide was far better than death by a thousand bites.

To be continued.

MULTIVERSE III

Among the Fields of Chaos

This is the way the world ends, not with a bang but with a whisper.

Tracker ignored the Hagia Sophia trap. She smelled the cunning in the air and moved on to her central Asian HQ. Jake had no choice but to retreat to the small fleet in the Black Sea.

A year passed and then another. The dying had quieted down to a soft rumble of death—like the waves on a broken shoreline. Survivors clung to their lives in fear and anguish. No one knew.

Each person now felt savaged, hunted. "I had no choice but to run." Each tread that littoral shift between night and day, when dishonor and shame become the aproned flurry of the new day.

Small groups of humanity remained—mostly tribal and increasingly more primitive. These were peoples who had never actually participated in the global crush. Most had little contact with the twenty-first century, few with any modern men. They survived because they had no enemy—yet.

Some of the urban elite also survived, by dint of wealth and the ability to disappear. These were the easiest to find and destroy, given their enormous social footprints.

Yet others were agile. These were the modern hunters and fishermen of yesterday's world who had "put something away" for just these days. Survivalists were Tracker's deadliest enemies. They knew what to expect and were prepared for combat at any level. They were canny and suspicious.

No drone approached their camps without attack. Most were destroyed immediately.

A few urban cowboys managed to work within the confines of the new metropolitan jungle of cats and rats and rapid dogs. Younger, more aggressive, and easier to kill, these youth were the new "gamekeeper's trophies."

Tracker herself had aged. The past decade had brought her physical suffering from her many survivals in the wild. She no longer hunted for her psychotic meals. She survived upon the skills of her slaves. "Low overhead, low tech, and self-financing," she muttered to herself.

Few humans were left; she had no idea the actual figure. True to her word, she had contracted for extinction, and she would not rest until her side of the deal had been fulfilled. She never thought of the actual consequences of her actions—the death, the horrors, the abjuration of humanity.

Small and mid-sized drones were her weapons of choice. The few remaining technicians she had not destroyed were their distant pilots—taken from the ranks of the old military training schools. They spent hours tracking communities and communes. One technician could run a hundred drones. One drone could launch a hundred strikes.

These pitiless automatons were becoming self-aware and independent of human control. They only needed attention if they were attacked in significant numbers by other drones or ground-based fire.

Heat signatures were easy. A fire, a few bodies in the snow, a running dog would invariably lead a tracker to a hunting pack—a pack of humans. Smaller and more agile, each seemed to learn from previous skyborne attacks. Humankind was proving quite difficult to kill—to exterminate.

"I have a sig just coming over the hill at two o'clock. Deploy."

He was talking to his drone as if it was a coworker. It had no weaponry, only virals. He could aim the trajectory as it dropped, often just touching the hand or leg of the human victim. Once in contact, death was assured. Ideally, the beast would return to its haunt and infect its minions.

The deskbound trackers had food and drink. They could roam the enclosed walls of their worksite for an hour every four hours. They could "visit" with others via local cell phone. The range was less than two kilometers. No voice, just texting. That was fine for these grown children, as they disliked "adulting" as a rule. They slept as they wished. They bathed as they wished. They died when she wished.

Compensation was another day of survival. They each knew they had to kill to survive. You ate when you killed. It was the only rule. They shared kill rates and bragged about hits, playing the deadliest game left on the planet. Four hundred were assigned to each continent. Antarctica was ignored. All who had once lived in Antarctica had died long ago. Without supplies flown in, humans were no match for the ice, the raging storms, the blanketing white nothing.

She had 2,400 pilots and four sets of ground crew, two each for fueling, repairs and resupply of virals. There was no shortage of either fuel or virals. The world's deserted airports had hundreds of thousands of liters of avgas and the bugs were a penny a billion from the corpses. The crews would be the last to go and so were the best protected and fed. She always maintained a one-to-three man to woman ratio as well. Too few women brought the juices flowing for the males. Here was yet another animal to be played—so easy, so pitiful. So soon to die.

The urban jungles—for that is exactly what the former urban metropolises of the world had become—were ideal for aerosol releases. Just the sign of one inhabitant would bring a "sprayer" down, circling the fetid blocks. Anthrax was always the first choice because it also contained its chimeric partners Ebola and Marburg II.

A few brave hunters shot at the drones. The pilots quickly dropped to the level of the barbs and sprayed before rising just as quickly again. No one had yet been shot down, but one poor fellow brought back an arrow in the rudder of his larger drone. The poison killed two service crew. Tracker killed the pilot. She did so with a scorpion on closed-circuit monitor for all to watch—and learn.

She used to join in the hunt on the ground each month, to keep her hand in the game. All drones were grounded for the duration, so they couldn't accidentally attack her. She wore a bottle suit of flex armor and enough oxygen conversion nano for three days.

She would miss a kill occasionally, to her regret. Her hand was not as steady; her will was quieter. Perhaps it was the weight of billions on her shriveled soul. She reduced the number of her forays each year until they became an annual event. At least this still thrilled her. She used the time to build her strength back, work on her accuracy, recall her blood instinct. Eventually, she never missed a kill again. Only then was she "satisfied."

Eight years after the first nano attacks, the supply of "game" began to dry up. She doubted that the actual number of humans was zero on any continent, so she devised new methodology.

Radio and the internet were still functioning in the presence of electricity. She began broadcasts as SOS, alerting listeners to "survival screens." Slow at first, more people came out into the open for help as the broadcasts continued. Realizing she had a Fibonacci sequencing opportunity, she let them grow for a few days.

Then the attacks began. Drones dropped viral panes, expanded into the form of leaflets. Some ran away. A few drones followed the runners from a distance, hovering overhead waiting for a camp or cave to appear. If none did, the leaflets were dropped across the valley floor or plain, scattering with the wind their deadly diseases. She had perfected the chimeras to three stage events, each deadlier. The most interesting combinations were anthrax, Marburg, and Ebola. Survival rates were zero.

Yet they persisted in surviving. Fewer did so, certainly. The count was well below the minimal figures required for genetic coupling to achieve biological variation. A generation or two, and these would die too. Once a species' population was reduced to a limited number, diversity also declined. Each new generation added more DNA-based diseases to the stock. Rather than outbreeding with external groups that may possess healthier traits, inbreeding concentrated the propensity for death—the final death by design.

Aging meant that Tracker wasn't about to wait. Time remained her greatest enemy. She had no cure for maturity.

Coupling two teams together on two continents, she focused attacks. Pilots had more time to reconnoiter and had more fuel, nanos, and virals. Blanketing a geographic area seemed to dispel the larger bands. Caves and shelters were attacked frequently. Then the crews would move on, moving south—always south.

She saved Africa for last—because it was the hardest. The smaller bands of prey were increasingly more adept at surviving—especially the primitives and the survivalists. They simply wouldn't die. Urbans were all dead, as were the islanders and most Central Asian tribes. Easy kills.

The climate worked to her advantage, as winters became longer and summers disappeared. Until the solar minimum passed, the planet was at the mercy of the galaxy. Gamma rays penetrated deep in the Earth's atmosphere, urging hydrogen to couple with two oxygen in a chemical ménage à trois. Their offspring were cloud cover and cooler temperatures across the surface of the planet.

The Thames and the Hudson, the Ob and the Dnieper froze over in the winter and never thawed completely in the summer. Snow became the norm all year. The increased albedo further lowered planetary temperature. More snow accumulated in lower latitudes. The seas began to retreat from the continental shores, just as they had a dozen times before. They were feeding the skies with moisture. The Atlantic and Pacific decadal oscillations broke down early, further reducing oceanic temperatures.

The northern tribes—Eskimo, Aleut, and their northern Asian fellows—retreated to the south at the edges of the ice world. Game was plentiful. Storms preempted drone strikes for weeks at a time. Survivalists began to join with the northern peoples as each group learned and respected the other's survival skills.

The snow became shelter and home for more humans. Slowly, babies were born and survived the weather and the intermittent attacks. The smallest of humans became the spark of hope for the diminished tribes.

> Unto us a child is born.
> —New Testament, et al.

Women and children were the new goddesses, survivors against all odds. Each child became a center of protection and care. Each was the gift of life for a dying species. Hope springs eternal in the devastated breast.

Each new birth forced a tribe to protect its only hope. Clans were ascribed the task of protection, education, and sustenance. Warriors made sure that survival was the primary goal for each newborn. The mother was equally protected during initial sustenance, and a young brother or sister was dedicated to the weaned small hope of the clan. As each child grew, he or she learned how to hide, how to be silent, how to run. The art of warfare came later, in adolescence.

Health care was primitive, but many clans remembered important nutrition and feeding processes. Cleanliness was primary, as was education. Nurses who survived had high tribal status. Everyone knew that survival was primary. Everyone had some remembrance of the past, of civilized society.

"Keep her warm with your bodies. If she vomits or has diarrhea, get me. Many childhood illnesses are important for survival. Some are deadly. If she has the latter, we will destroy her. We have no choice." The male nurse was clear and kind, but firm. They had no time for kindness.

"She slept well during the night. No runs, no tears."

"Good news. She has a cold, nothing more. We have antibiotics for her. Keep her drinking water."

The child was two. She had been born in the spring. Mother had been fertile, giving birth every year for six years now. She was a hallowed member of the group.

"Aleah is doing well today, mother Alta."

"I shall visit with her when the hunt is complete. Watch the skies."

Mother Alta was dark-haired, wholesome, blissful. Fair-skinned and strong of will, she survived because she willed it so. She had been a young medical student in Santiago, Chile. Her country had survived far longer than most—perhaps because of the native background coupled with modern knowledge. She would have become a doctor.

Thus, she had her status as a mother, a proto physician, and an intelligent leader. She chose her mating partners for their physique, not because they were "guapo." Handsome had little value. Strength, agility, and survival prowess were the new "handsome." Rather than act as a leader, she taught by example. Leaders were important, survivors far more so.

"Watch the skies."

No order, no comment, held more power.

ENDGAME

> The far more serious problem is that modern AI systems routinely reinforce the human biases baked into the data from which they learn.
>
> —Steven Poole, WSJ, 2017

Yet the killing continued. The drones added their deadly brood to the cooling atmosphere. More people died than survived. Entire continents were now "human free"—Asia, South America, Antarctica, Europe, Australia.

Tracker had "retained" Dr. Blake and her teams in the fall of '22. Once the military escort was reduced to a friendly guard, her shock troops simply attacked, killing everyone who resisted—everyone except the scientists in their laboratories. These were exposed to MSP in the air. They slept for a few days and then were awoken by their escorts.

Tracker's guise worked well.

"We have a severe task ahead. We must develop a shield against these mutant killers. You can help us. We are the last remnants of intelligent life on the planet.

"Will you work with me?"

They all readily agreed. They simply continued their work on the CRISPR and nanos as before. Their guards changed names and uniforms. Nothing else was different—except their newly positive attitudes.

WELCOME

"I'm uncertain as to how to explain it. We seem to have the properties of a gas, a liquid, and a solid appearing simultaneously and ubiquitously across the entire nanosphere."

Sally Blake was in her early twenties now. She was thin, gaunt, underfed, and overworked.

"Impossible." Dr. Blake was exhausted. She carried on out of harried effort, out of rote behavior now.

"Yes. Yet you can watch the transmutations here on the screen."

The containment sphere was deep, seven miles deep, at the bottom of the Marianas Trench. The sphere was sixty meters in diameter. It was like a fusion bottle gone mad.

Within the sphere, another universe had arisen. They thought they were acting responsibly in holding the nanos here. They could not escape. The weight of the massive globe held it in the depths. The structure prevented access from within or without. Data was recorded via four ports, actually degenerated nanoglass fiber.

Within, a "community of creatures" was constantly forming, reshaping, and redesigning its individuals every few hours. The human observers cold detect no distinction between the matter states. They weren't even sure what they were observing was even matter as they knew it. The attempt to communicate between species took the form of letters—in English. As if they had been listening.

"We" suddenly formed from the creatures. There was no mistaking the letters, the word.

Everyone watched in silence. Tracker watched from her observation point, silently, invisibly.

As suddenly as the word appeared, it dissolved.

"We" reappeared followed by "I."

"Is this communication?"

"Is it intimidation?"

"What do you mean?"

"Are they trying to talk to us or trap us?"

"Come."

"Now we are going *Twilight Zone* folks. This just can't be happening, yet it is. Right here. Right in front of us."

"Actually, the sphere isn't exactly right in front of us."

"But the words are here, in our eyes, in our minds! They are trying to take over our minds!"

A voice came from over their left ear. "Shoot him. Shoot him now."

A single shot echoed around the conference room. The agitated speaker fell dead, his blood staining the cashmere carpet. The door opened. Two guards picked the body up and walked out. A moment later, a cleaning bot entered through its passageway and covered the stain with a gel, cleaned up the mess, and left again.

"No one speaks like that again." She was using her own voice.

Only one other in the room of twenty had ever heard it. He was visibly shaken, eyes darting around the room, sweat beads on his forehead and hands.

"I want each of you to grasp the significance of this event. We have been contacted by a new species. It is both alien and earthbound. It has something to communicate. You will listen and learn."

The silence was painful.

Dr. Blake spoke. "'We' and 'I' are indicative of self-awareness. The verb is obvious. This species comes as one and as a group, simultaneously."

"'Come' could have it or us as the subject. It/they may want us to join, or vice versa."

"How could we ... Look!"

"Welcome."

To be continued.

MULTIVERSE N

I put down the pen. I leave the keyboard. I push it over to you.

Dear reader, now is your chance to finish the story—to add another ending, to embellish where you wish something else had happened.

Many thanks to Blake Crouch for the concept of the multiverse from his book, *Dark Matter*. Also to Robert Preston for the concept of 'silver panes'.

I am suggesting we all apply it here—to this story. Build you own storyline.

Send it to this email: jgraves@west.net.

These offerings from each of you will appear on the book's website. As a continuation of the story of Black Mantis, of Jake, and of Tracker.

With whom do you identify? Who do you despise? Why? Develop your thoughts. Send them to the website.

The story has yet to be told. There is so much more to tell.

Here's a storyline. Run with it.

The borgs and nanos communicate not only with humans but also with one another. They discover how to connect the three multiverses via quantum computing. A new multiverse is created. Jake, Tracker, and Mantis live again.

THE JOURNEY OF THE MAGI

T. S. Eliot, 1927
A cold coming we had of it,
Just the worst time of the year
…
A hard time we had of it.
All this was a long time ago, I remember
…
We returned to our places, these Kingdoms,
But no longer at ease here, in the old dispensation,
With an alien people clutching their gods.
I should be glad of another death.

AUTHOR'S NOTES

> I should dearly love that the world should be ever so slightly better for my presence. Even on this small stage something might be done by throwing all one's weight of breadth, tolerance, charity, temperance, peace, and kindliness to man and beast. We can't all strike very big blows, but even the little ones count.
>
> —Arthur Conan Doyle, 1877

This book began as an intellectual exploration into the "extreme green" idea of willful, forcible human extinction.

While many dystopian novels and movies have been developed on this theme, I am unaware of any that delve deeply into the actual process of humanity's enforced extinction.

How would an entire species be "done in" exactly? How would someone terminate the genus *Homo sapiens*?

More than a few environmental websites, papers, and individuals have raised the question of humanity as a disease on our planet Earth. Regardless of the validity or insanity of this premise, I became curious as to the possibility of a designed extinction process.

Was it actually possible?

How would it transpire?

And the unintended consequences?

It is nearly impossible to purposefully wipe out an entire species. While less than 1 percent of all species have left any physical records, 99 percent of all species that have ever existed on Earth are extinct.

Yet none were purposefully "done in." as far as we know (https://www.theatlantic.com/science/archive/2017/06/the-ends-of-the-world/529545/).

Mass extinctions are the closest we can get to species extinction, and these have occurred rarely—five times over four billion years.

External causes are always the culprits.

We have no idea why many of these extinctions happened. Actually, that's not completely true. We do know how several happened—volcanoes, sunspots, an excess of gamma rays, meteors, methane burbles, CO_2 reduction, massive ice sheets, and so on.

And life always survives—in some form.

But what would be the process of purposefully eradicating an entire species?

The diseases of humanity (of the past five hundred years or so) have "put down" 10 percent to 40 percent of our forebears, depending upon the circumstances.

Three elements seem to meet the initial requirement—proximity, propagation and an external driver.

Proximity is always the dealmaker—and the deal breaker. Diseases need bodies to infect, whether bacterial, viral, or fungal. While some can survive for decades or centuries in stasis and while viruses are the longest surviving "creatures" on Earth, none can propagate without fresh meat.

Propagation is the next requirement. The mass migration each year to Makkah is an example of an external driver that allows for rapid propagation. Air travel allows for density propagation in short time intervals. EMP attacks provide a cover for death and starvation. Food supply attacks are the simplest forms of death events. Relatively easy to apply, they are long lasting and difficult to trace or even discover.

Yet, an external intervention is still required. Hence, CRISPR/Cas9 and the nanos.

The "facts" of this story are purposefully distorted. No one is going to be able to repeat any of these sequences and kill millions. The names have been changed to protect the innocent—the names of the molecular and chemical strategies here mentioned.

The heroine of the tale, Dr. Blake, is a real person, again with a new nomenclature. She will remain nameless, distorted beyond recognition by the author's slippery pen.

The "protectors of the realm," the Star Chamber, is the CDC, the Centers for Disease Control and Prevention. Their weapons of choice are the EIS teams. These teams are the real ninja warriors of today's biological warfare marketplace. They intervene in near real time, often upon the discovery of but a single infected person. While they succeed in two of the endings, in the third, they are done in by Tracker.

Their defenses are deep and significant. I do not describe them too deeply for fear of tipping the scale in favor of a real Tracker or group thereof. Most of what is described here is quite literally a figment of my own imagination. It is meant to tell a tale both fascinating in its macabre nature and precautionary in its potential endgame.

There are Trackers and Kurtzes in our real world, have no doubt. Whether an individual or demented group, they can wreak havoc on our global society today. And there are far more of those than we want to realize—those who delight in dipping their hand into a chest and ripping out a beating heart. Aztlan indeed.

Perhaps that is one of the objectives of this tale. Globalization brings with its success its own potential for destruction. The seed of death lies within the seed of life. Cancer spreads within healthy cells.

Another is the clear warning. Madmen willfully seek to destroy because they love to watch the flames. Whether arsonists or weathermen, Stalinists or climate fearmongers, they use a front to dissemble. Their hustle is neither a workers' proletariat nor an excess of atmospheric molecular diffusion. It is destruction via control—or destruction for the sake of itself. Nero is doing quite well in today's world. We are the new Christians, offered in bloodlust to the heartless gods of modernity.

We have been taught that money and power are the greatest evils. These are not our enemies. They are simply tools. As a tool, each can leverage skills in nearly infinite ways. Ask any wealthy, powerful person. The joy of the hunt, the thrill of the kill—each of these is the real draw. The game is in the candle's making, not its selling. This was Adam Smith's brazen truth.

Each tool in its own way may encourage slaughter. Kurtz and Tracker both are driven by one lust—bloodlust. All else is fabrication.

The third, most important tale here is of praise for those who give of time and blood and treasure. These members of the EIS, the doctors and the directors at CDC and the WHO are the first and often last line of defense against such things as have been here imagined. While they may be defeated here by an excess of death, in our world, they rarely fail. They are true civil servants. They serve society.

And they run through scenarios such as we have here every few years at John Hopkins University. Each time they build a scene and spend days working through it, they learn more—about coordination, the unknown, and the facts and fissile of epidemics. And the bugs always win.

Fifteen years ago, and again three years ago, US contingency planners developed simpler scenarios than those here described. In both cases the "story runs" had to be suspended after a few days of real-time development with real-time players from real government agencies. The outbreaks broke the game. Millions of imaginary citizens were dying as the diseases outran every effort of control. The participants described their genuine fears resulting from the experience. The second run was in direct response to the prior decadal event. The outcome was worse … And these are the frontline professionals playing the game

So, take me to task for plot, scene, or storyline certainly. But do not worry yourselves over frivolous facts herein described. They are willfully falsified.

As for some of the background information on techniques herein described, apps for private communication between cells (terrorist and the like) are readily available. Threema, Zello, Telegram, Tutanota, and ProtonMail are but a few examples of fully encrypted platforms.

Websites abound with information on CRISPR/Cas9, all of the diseases herein, each of the methods of development and profusion, and the reactive abilities of the CDCs of our world.

As a postscript, please find attended here a rather complete list of quotes from those who advise climate fear, climate control, or human extinction. These men, and more than a few women, advise for a global government, "life by design," or the eradication of *Homo sapiens*.

They know best what is best for the rest of us. As you read these, know that these people hold enormous power. They do so irrespective of who is in government at any moment, regardless of which political party rules, despite the opinions of others and in spite of the effect upon the poor, particularly the poorest in every country on the planet.

These quotes are purposefully undated. You can google them yourself for the exact date. My point is that these sentiments are timeless. Whether from 1972 or 2018, they reflect a continuum of thought. Some are clearly more equal than others.

DD Notes

These phrases stand out particularly sharply:

> 'The deliberate quest for poverty.'
> 'Too many people doing too well'.
> 'Destroy the industrial complex'.
> 'Mankind is the most dangerous animal on Earth.'
> 'The Earth has a cancer and that cancer is Man.'
> 'I wish...to lower human population levels.'
> 'The eradication of the human species may be a good thing.'
> 'Child bearing should be a punishable crime.'
> 'Cheap fusion energy is the worst that could happen.'
> 'The goal is a socialist, redistributionist society.'

The last words are reminiscent of Dr. Frankenstein's creature. He simply cannot be killed. Concerns expressed about saving the earth, being good stewards or apprehension for other species safety and survival are simply cover for the actual goal: power and wealth through redistribution.

As Adam Smith, Julian Simon, Jagdish Bhagwati, Hernando De Soto and dozens of others have demonstrated, wealth, freedom, access to education and rights of ownership and, most importantly, health for women and children are the driving forces of humanity's success. Nothing else compares to a healthy family that owns a home and land, can vote and has access to education.

"My three main goals would be to reduce human population to about 100 million worldwide, destroy the industrial infrastructure and see wilderness, with its full complement of species, returning throughout the world."
-Dave Foreman,
co-founder of Earth First!

"Current lifestyles and consumption patterns of the affluent middle class - involving high meat intake, use of fossil fuels, appliances, air-conditioning, and suburban housing - are not sustainable."
- **Maurice Strong**,
Rio Earth Summit

"A total population of 250-300 million people, a 95% decline from present levels, would be ideal."
- **Ted Turner**,
founder of CNN and major UN donor

"One America burdens the earth much more than twenty Bangladeshis

"The spirit of our planet is stirring!
The Consciousness of Goddess Earth
is now rising against all odds,
in spite of millennia of suppression,
repression and oppression inflicted on Her
by a hubristic and misguided humanity.

The Earth is a living entity, a biological organism
with psychic and spiritual dimensions.

With the expansion of the patriarchal religions that focused on a male God majestically stationed in Heaven ruling over the Earth and the Universe, the memory of our planet's innate Divinity was repressed and banished into the collective unconscious of humanity."
- **Envision Earth**

"The Earth has cancer and the cancer is Man."
- **Club of Rome**, Mankind at the Turning Point

"The prospect of cheap fusion energy is the worst thing that could happen to the planet."
- **Jeremy Rifkin**, Greenhouse Crisis Foundation

"Effective execution of Agenda 21 will require a profound reorientation of all human society, unlike anything the world has ever experienced a major shift in the priorities of both governments and individuals and an unprecedented redeployment of human and financial resources. This shift will demand that a concern for the environmental consequences of every human action be integrated into individual and collective decision-making at every level."
- **UN Agenda 21**

"The current course of development is thus clearly unsustainable. Current problems cannot be solved by piecemeal measures. More of the same is not enough. Radical change from the current trajectory is not an option, but an absolute necessity. Fundamental economic, social and cultural changes that address the root causes of poverty and environmental

degradation are required and they are required now."
– from the **Earth Charter website**

"We must make this an insecure and inhospitable place for capitalists and their projects. We must reclaim the roads and plowed land, halt dam construction, tear down existing dams, free shackled rivers and return to wilderness millions of acres of presently settled land."
- **David Foreman**,
co-founder of Earth First!

If we don't overthrow capitalism, we don't have a chance of saving the world ecologically. I think it is possible to have an ecologically sound society under socialism. I don't think it is possible under capitalism.

- Judi Bari,
Earth First!

"*In searching for a new enemy to unite us, we came up with the idea that the threat of global warming would fit the bill, the real enemy, then, is humanity itself. we believe humanity requires a common motivation, namely a common adversary in order to realize world government. It does not matter if this common enemy is a real one or….one invented for the purpose."* — Club of Rome

If we don't change, our species will not survive… Frankly, we may get to the point where the only way of saving the world will be for industrial civilization to collapse.
- o   Maurice Strong, September 1, 1997 National Review; founder of the UN Environment Program (UNEP)

'Human hubris and shortsightedness are so profoundly emotionally satisfying…

"Bacteria have a memory. They're carrying about pieces of their evolutionary history in unexpected forms, waiting to be expressed".

Joshua Lederberg
<u>Emerging Epidemics</u>

CPSIA information can be obtained
at www.ICGtesting.com
Printed in the USA
LVHW052129150321
681605LV00016B/618